### By Deborah Crombie

# DEBORAH CROMBIE

## WHERE MEMORIES LIE

AVON

*An Imprint of HarperCollinsPublishers*

This book was originally published in hardcover July 2008 by William Morrow, an Imprint of HarperCollins Publishers.

AVON BOOKS
*An Imprint of* HarperCollins*Publishers*
10 East 53rd Street
New York, New York 10022-5299

Copyright © 2008 by Deborah Crombie
Map drawn by Laura Hartman Maestro
Excerpt from *Necessary as Blood* copyright © 2009 by Deborah Crombie
ISBN 978-0-06-128752-7
**www.avonmystery.com**

First Avon Books paperback printing: July 2009
First William Morrow hardcover printing: July 2008

Avon Trademark Reg. U.S. Pat. Off. and in Other Countries, Marca Registrada, Hecho en U.S.A.
HarperCollins® is a registered trademark of HarperCollins Publishers.

Printed in the U.S.A.

10 9 8 7 6 5 4 3 2 1

*FOR DIANE*

# *Acknowledgments*

Many thanks to the team at HarperCollins who have made this book possible, especially my editor, Carrie Feron, as well as Tessa Woodward, Lisa Gallagher, Danielle Barlett, and copy editor Victoria Mathews, who has once again crossed my *i*'s and dotted my *t*'s.

The members of the Every Other Tuesday Night Writers' Group are stalwart and much appreciated: Steve Copling, Dale Denton, Jim Evans, Diane Sullivan Hale, Viqui Litman, Gigi Norwood, and Steve Russell.

My brainstorming buddies Kate Charles and Marcia Talley helped with the genesis of the plot, as did Arabella Stein and Kate Walker at Abner Stein, U.K.

My ever-patient agent, Nancy Yost, deserves medals, as she very well knows.

Diane Hale, Gigi Norwood, and Steve Ullathorne deserve very special thanks for support and encouragement when much needed.

Illustrator Laura Maestro has brought the characters and settings of *Where Memories Lie* to life with her charming map.

And last but not least, thanks to Rick and Kayti for once again putting up with a writer in the family.

THE FRENCH HOUSE

The French House

City Road

St. Paul's

CLERKEN-
WELL
EC1

British
Museum &
Library

St. Bart's
Hospital

BLOOMSBURY
WC1

Charterhouse St.

HOLBORN
WC2

Holborn Viaduct

Gemma
gets sight
of St. Paul's

New Cavendish Street

Harry Pevensey's
Flat,
Hanway Place

Tottenham Ct. Road

Great Russell

Oxford Street

Drury Lane

Fleet Street

St. Paul's
Cathedral

SOHO
W1

The
French
House

Embankment

Waterloo
Bridge

River
Thames

Blackfriars
Bridge

Mo

Southwark St.

SOUTHWARK
SE1

The Mall

Victoria

St. James's Park

Whitehall

Westminster Bridge

The Cut

Southwark Bridge

Constitution Hill
Buckingham
Palace

Birdcage Walk

Parliament

Lambeth Palace Rd.

Westminster Bridge Rd.

Gavin's house
(Jedworth Sq.)

Lambeth Bridge

Lambeth Road

WESTMINSTER
SW1

LAMBETH
SE11

N

POLICE

S

Millbank

Vauxhall
Bridge

Kennington Lane

Albert Bridge

Grosvenor Road

Chelsea
Royal
Hospital

Thames

VAUXHALL
SW8

KENNINGTON
SE11

Lambeth Rd.

Sid &
Geordie

Illustrated map by Laura Hartman Maestro ©2008

# Prologue

*And then the passion of my life, that is, the City of London—to see London all blasted, that too raked my heart.*
*—Virginia Woolf, from a letter to Ethel Smyth, September 1940*

*October 1945*

Erika Rosenthal woke, her body jerking to the whump of the bomb, the flash of light from the incendiary flickering against her closed eyelids. She threw back the scratchy wool blanket and had half reached for David to shake him awake when she realized the night was silent. No sirens, no rumble and thump of guns. Rubbing at her sleep-fogged eyes, she saw that light from the streetlamp was shining through the gap in the bedroom curtains, etching a pattern lucid as moonlight across the counterpane. It must have been that gleam that had insinuated itself into her subconscious—or perhaps a reflection from the moving lights of a passing car. She had yet to become accustomed to the unshuttered headlamps. Even in her waking hours, the brightness caused her to flinch.

She lay back against the pillows, heart pounding painfully in her chest, cursing herself for a fool. It was over, the war—had been over for months now, London preternaturally quiet. Her mind knew it, but not her body, nor her dreams.

David lay on his back, still as marble, the rise and fall of his chest invisible even in the light that spilled through the curtains. Again she felt the irrational spike of fear. Reaching out, she laid her fingers ever so lightly against the thin skin on the inside of his wrist, feeling for the reassuring steady beat of his pulse. This was a habit she'd developed during the Blitz, when she'd worked for the rescue crew in their part of Notting Hill, a compelling and irresistible need to assure herself that life was not so easily snuffed out.

The rhythm of David's breathing became suddenly audible, and beneath her fingertips she felt the tension of awareness flood through her husband's body.

"I'm sorry, darling," she said. "I didn't mean to wake you." She heard the tremble of longing in her voice, barely controlled, but David's only response was to slip his hand from hers and turn away.

# 1

*The vast stucco palaces of Kensington Park Road and the adjoining streets had long ago been converted into self-contained flats where an ever-increasing stream of refugees from every part of the once civilized world had found improvised homes, like the dark-age troglodytes who sheltered in the galleries and boxes of the Colosseum.*
— Sir Osbert Lancaster,
All Done from Memory, *1963*

THE DAY WAS UTTERLY miserable for early May, even considering the expected vagaries of English weather. At a few minutes to four in the afternoon, it was dark as twilight, and the rain came down in relentless, pounding sheets. The gusts of wind had repeatedly turned Henri Durrell's umbrella wrong side out, so he had given up, and trudged down the Old Brompton Road with his head down and his shoulders hunched against the torrent, trying to avoid losing an eye to carelessly wielded umbrellas that had proved stronger than his own, and dodging the waves thrown up by passing automobiles.

Pain shot through his hip and he slowed, wincing. He was nearing eighty, and the damp did quite unpleasant things to his joints, even without the stress of an unaccustomed jog.

What had he been thinking? He should have stayed at the V&A until closing, then perhaps the worst of the storm would have blown through. He'd met a friend at the museum's café for Saturday-afternoon tea, always a pleasant treat, but his haste in leaving had been inspired by his desire to get home to his flat in Roland Gardens and its seductive comforts—his book; a stiff whisky; the gas fire; and his cat, Matilde.

Jostled by a hurrying passerby, Henri stopped to recover his balance and found himself gazing into the windows of Harrowby's, the auction house. A poster advertised an upcoming sale of Art Deco jewelry. An avid collector, Henri usually kept up with such things, but he had been away for a spring holiday in his native Burgundy—where the sun had shone, thank God—and missed notice of this one.

The auction was to take place the following Wednesday, he saw with relief. He could still buy a catalog and peruse it thoroughly—if he hadn't missed the four o'clock closing time, that is. A quick glance at his watch showed one minute to the hour. Henri shook his wet umbrella, showering himself in the process, and dashed through Harrowby's still-open doors.

A few minutes later, he emerged, cheered by his acquisition and a friendly chat with the woman at reception. The rest of his walk home seemed less laborious, even though the rain had not abated. He toweled himself off and changed into dry socks and slippers, with Matilde impeding the process by purring and butting against his ankles. He decided on tea rather than whisky, the better to ward off a chill, and when the pot had steeped he lit the gas fire and settled himself in his favorite chair, the catalog resting carefully on his knees. It was beautifully produced, as Harrowby's catalogs always were—the house had never been known to lack style—and Henri opened it with a sigh of pleasure. Making room for the insistent cat, he thumbed through the pages, his breath catching at the beauty of the pieces. He had taught art history before his recent retirement, and something about the clean, innovative shapes of this period appealed to him above all others.

Here, the master artists were well represented; a diamond and sapphire pendant by Georges Fouquet, a diamond cocktail ring by Rene Boivin—

Then his hand froze. An entry caught his eye, and his heart gave an uncomfortable flutter. Surely that couldn't be possible?

He studied the photo more closely. Henri appreciated color, so diamonds alone had never thrilled him as much as pieces that set platinum against the red, blue, or green of rubies, sapphires, or emeralds, but this—

The brooch was made of diamonds set in platinum, a double drop that reminded him of a waterfall or the swoop of a peacock's tail. The curving style was unusual for Art Deco, where the emphasis had been highly geometric. But the date of the piece was late, 1938, and the name—the name he recognized with a jolt that sent the blood pounding through his veins.

Shaking his head, he stood, dumping Matilde unceremoniously from his lap. Then he hesitated. Should he ask to view the piece before taking any action? But no, the auction house would be closed now until Monday, and he doubted a mistake in the attribution, or in his memory.

He slipped the catalog carefully back into its bag and carried it into the hall, where he donned his wet boots and coat once again, and reluctantly left the shelter of his flat.

"Why the bloody hell did it have to rain?" Gemma James dropped supermarket carrier bags on her kitchen table and pushed a sodden strand of hair from her face. Rivulets from the bags pooled on the scrubbed pine table. Grabbing a tea towel, Gemma blotted up the water as Duncan Kincaid set down his own load of dripping plastic.

"Because it's May in London?" he asked, grinning. "Or because the patron saint of dinner parties has it in for you?"

She swatted at him with the damp towel, but smiled in spite of herself. "Okay, point taken. But seriously, I meant to do the flowers from our garden, and now that's out. Not to mention that between boys and dogs, the house will be a sea of mud."

"The boys are with Wesley, probably making themselves sick on Wesley's mother's sweets and watching God knows what on the telly. As for the dogs, I will personally wipe every trace of muck from errant paws, and I can run down and get flowers from one of the stalls on Portobello." He slipped his arm round her shoulders. "Don't worry, love. You'll be brilliant."

For a moment, she allowed herself to rest her head against his shoulder. His shirt was damp from the rain, and through the fabric she could feel the comforting warmth of his skin. She leaned a little closer, then forced herself to quash the thought that there were better ways to spend a rainy Saturday afternoon with the children out of the house.

They had begun as partners at Scotland Yard, then against her better judgment they had become clandestine lovers until her promotion to inspector and transfer to Notting Hill Police Station had separated them professionally. With no barrier to their relationship, they had moved in together, each bringing a son from a previous marriage and complications that at times had seemed insurmountable. But they had got through these challenges, including the midterm loss of the child they had conceived together, and since their visit to Duncan's family in Cheshire this last Christmas, the dynamics of their cobbled-together family seemed to have meshed more smoothly.

It was a stroke of luck that had landed them in a house in an upmarket area of Notting Hill they would not normally have been able to afford, even with Kincaid's higher superintendent's salary. The house belonged to Duncan's chief superintendent's sister, whose family had gone abroad on a five-year contract, and Duncan and Gemma had been recommended to her as the ideal tenants.

Gemma had never thought she would adjust to life in Notting Hill, so different was it from the working-class area of London where she had grown up, but now she found that she loved the house and neighborhood so passionately that she couldn't imagine leaving, and the end of their lease hovered in her mind like a distant specter.

What she hadn't learned to love was the art of formal

entertaining, and tonight she'd agreed to host a dinner party, the anticipation of which had sent her into a paroxysm of nerves. The guest list included Chief Superintendent Denis Childs—Duncan's guv'nor and their landlady's brother—along with his wife, whom Gemma had never met; Superintendent Mark Lamb, Gemma's boss, and his wife; Doug Cullen, who was now Kincaid's sergeant; and PC Melody Talbot, who worked with Gemma at Notting Hill.

Doug Cullen and Melody Talbot didn't know each other well, and Gemma was indulging an impulse to play at matchmaker, although Kincaid had teasingly warned her that she'd better be prepared to deal with the consequences of meddling.

She sighed and straightened up, gazing at the abundance spilling from the carrier bags onto the kitchen table. There were fillets of fresh salmon, lemons, frilly bunches of fennel, and tiny jewel-like grape tomatoes, as well as bread from her favorite bakery on Portobello Road, several bottles of crisp white wine, and the makings for enough salad to feed an army. The dessert she had bought ready-made—to her shame, baker's daughter that she was—a beautiful fruit tart from Mr. Christian's Deli on Elgin Crescent. Attempting to bake would definitely have sent her over the edge into blithering idiocy.

"It all looked so easy in the cookery book," she said. "What if the chief super doesn't like it? Or what if he tells his sister we've made a wreck of her house?"

"You can't call him *guv'nor* at dinner, you know. You'll have to practice saying *Denis*." Kincaid gave her shoulder a squeeze and began pulling groceries from the bags. "And as for the house, it looks better than it did when we moved in. The food will be fabulous, the table stunning, and if all else fails," he added, grinning, "you can play the piano. What could possibly go wrong?"

Gemma stuck out her tongue. "Something," she said darkly, "always does."

The rain fell in relentless torrents, streaming down the garden window in a solid sheet of silver gilt, drumming against the glass roof of the conservatory like machine-gun fire.

Erika Rosenthal had always liked rain, liked the secretive sense it engendered, the opportunity it offered to shut out the world, but today, as the deluge darkened the May afternoon to evening, she was finding it uncomfortably oppressive.

She sat in her favorite chair in her sitting room, book open on her lap, cooling cup of coffee—decaffeinated, by her doctor's orders—on the side table, feeling as if the ceaseless pounding of the rain might penetrate roof and walls until it pierced the frail barrier of her skin.

She, who had never been able to find enough hours in the day to read, to write, to listen to music, to arrange her beloved flowers, had lately found herself unable to settle to anything. Her concentration had scattered like thrown pennies, and her mind seemed to wander of its own accord, in and out of recollections as vivid as waking dreams.

That morning, as she had been dressing, she'd suddenly found herself thinking that she must hurry or she'd be late for work at Whiteleys. Then with a start she'd realized that those days were long gone, and David with them, and the stab of grief she'd felt for the past had been as fresh as if it were yesterday.

She'd sat back on the edge of the bed, her breath rasping painfully in her throat, and forced herself to think of the discipline she had so carefully practiced over the years, the balancing of each day's small, luminous joys against the ever-threatening beast of despair.

Had she lost that struggle? Could it be that life coalesced, at the end, and that one had no choice but to shuttle back and forth in time, repeating the traumas one had thought long put to bed?

No, she thought now, chiding herself for allowing such self-pity to take hold. She stood up from her chair with a grimace. When one was her age, one was allowed an occasional bad day, and that was all this was. Tomorrow the sun would be shining, she would sit outside with the Sunday papers, watching children playing in the communal garden and discussing compost and birds' nests with her neighbor, and the world would right itself. Until then, she would pour herself a well-deserved sherry and abandon the meandering literary novel on her table for something pleasurably familiar—Jane Austen, perhaps.

She had reached her kitchen and was pouring the sludge that passed itself for coffee down the sink when the door buzzer sounded. Startled, she glanced out the garden window at the still-pouring rain, wondering who could be calling in such ungodly weather. A neighbor, perhaps, taken ill?

But when she pressed the intercom, a familiar voice said, "Erika? It's Henri. Henri Durrell. Can I come in?" He sounded agitated.

She hurried to unlock the door, shaking her head and tut-tutting when she saw the state of his coat and hat. "Henri! What on earth are you doing out in this?" she asked as she ushered him in. "It's wet enough to drown an otter."

He kissed her on the cheek as she took his things and hung them, dripping, on the pegs by the door.

"Lovely as ever, I see," he said in lieu of a reply, smoothing his damp but abundant white hair. He was still a good-looking man, with a fine chin and direct blue eyes, and he carried himself with a military erectness in spite of the problems she knew he had with his hips.

It amused her that he had lost almost all trace of his native Burgundian accent, just as it amused her to remember that he had once been her student, and that she had contemplated an affair with him. In the end, she'd rejected his advances, afraid the difference in their ages would make her a fool; now she thought herself foolish to have forsaken pleasure for the sake of dignity.

The memory of another lost opportunity flashed through her mind, but this one was too painful to contemplate even now. Pushing the recollection aside, she squeezed Henri's hand and urged, "Come in, come in." She felt inordinately pleased to see him.

"We'll light the fire, even though it's considered a sin so late in the year, and I'll pour us a sherry."

"You know I can't abide the stuff," Henri said as he followed her into the sitting room, brushing carefully at his trousers as he sat in the chair nearest hers, then wiping the plastic carrier bag he held with a handkerchief fished from his jacket.

"A whisky, then. You know I keep a bottle just for you."

Hesitating, he said, "No, really, Erika, I won't impose on your hospitality." He cleared his throat. "This is not actually a social call."

Alarmed, she said, "What is it, Henri? Are you ill?"

"Oh, no, it's nothing like that. Only the arthritis playing up in this infernal damp. It's just—" He stopped, running his hand over the carrier bag, and she noticed that it was embossed with the label of Harrowby's, the auction house. "It's just that I ran across something very odd today, and I may be interfering where I've no business, but I thought you should see it."

"Henri, whatever are you talking about?"

He pulled a thin soft-cover book from the bag, and it, too, carried the Harrowby's label. Looking more closely, she saw that it was a catalog of items in an upcoming sale of Art Deco jewelry, and her breath seemed to stop in her throat.

Opening it, Henri thumbed quickly to a page near the end and handed the book to her. "There. I recognized it from the name, of course, and from your description."

Erika's hands trembled as she picked up her reading glasses from on top of the attempted novel. As she put them on, the picture jumped sharply into focus. There was no need for her to read the description. The room seemed to recede, and with an effort she fought back the tide of memory.

She looked up at Henri, uncomprehending. "But this is not possible. I never thought to see this again."

Henri reached out and set the catalog aside, and it was only when he gathered her hands between his that she realized hers were icy cold. "I don't see how this can be a mistake, Erika." Very gently, he added, "Perhaps the time has come for the past to give back."

The party had reached the pudding and coffee stage, and Gemma had, at last, begun to relax. She'd been glad to see Chief Superintendent Childs again—*Denis,* she reminded herself—and his wife, Diane, had proved charming, as talk-ative as he was self-contained. Her own boss, Mark Lamb, was an old police college friend of Duncan's, and Gemma had met his wife, Christine, often at departmental functions.

Everyone exclaimed over the house, the roasted salmon and fennel had proved a great success, and the only thing marring Gemma's warm glow of accomplishment was the fact that Doug Cullen and Melody Talbot didn't seem to have hit it off particularly well.

She had just stood to refill coffee cups when the kitchen phone rang. From the other end of the table, Kincaid met her eyes and lifted a brow in question.

Shaking her head, she mouthed, "I'll get it." It was the home line, not her mobile, so it was not likely to be work. Her heart gave an anxious little jerk, as it always did when the boys were out, even though she knew they were with Wesley Howard, who often looked after them and was very responsible.

Excusing herself, she made her way to the kitchen, cof-feepot in hand, and snatched the phone from its cradle on the worktop.

"Gemma?" The voice was female, and so tremulous that at first Gemma didn't recognize it. "Gemma, it's Erika. I'm so sorry to disturb you, and on a Saturday evening. I can hear that you have guests. I can ring back tomorrow if—"

"No, no, Erika, it's all right," Gemma assured her, al-though surprised. She had met Erika when she was first posted to Notting Hill, and although they'd developed a friendship that Gemma valued, she'd never known Erika to call except to issue an invitation to tea or lunch, or to re-ply to an invitation from Gemma. Dr. Erika Rosenthal was a retired academic, a German Jew who had immigrated at the beginning of the war and made a noted career as a his-torian, and although Gemma had felt flattered by the older woman's interest and support, Erika had always guarded her independence fiercely.

"Is there something wrong?" Gemma asked now, putting down the coffeepot and listening intently.

"I don't quite know," answered Erika, some of the usual crispness returning to her voice, although her accent was still more pronounced than usual. "But something very strange has happened, and I think—I'm very much afraid I need your help."

# 2

## ♣

*First they came for the Jews.*
*—Attributed to German anti-Nazi activist and*
*former U-boat captain Pastor Martin Niemöller*

*May 1952, Chelsea*

*He knew the peculiarities of the latch so well that even with
his coordination slightly impaired, he could ease the key
round and swing the door open without a whisper of sound.
Not that his delicate entry did him any good, because there
was no way he could prevent the click as the lock snicked
closed behind him.*

*"Gavin? Is that you?" called Linda from the kitchen.
His wife had ears like a bat.*

*Of course it bloody was, he thought, unless it was a bur-
glar with a key, but he merely sighed and said, "Sorry I'm
late. Had some things to wind up."*

*"You and the rest of the station." Linda came into the
hall, wiping her hands on her pink-flowered pinny, her nose
wrinkling in the way that meant she could pick up the scent
of beer or tobacco from twenty feet. Bloodhound, maybe,
not bat, he mused, and his mouth must have twitched involuntarily because she said, "What's so funny? You've been
down the pub with your mates, and your dinner's burned
again."*

*He caught the sickly sweet smell of charred shepherd's*

*pie, and felt his stomach give an uneasy flip-flop.* "I ate something at the station—" *he began, and saw her lips compress into the thin line that meant she was going to tell him he'd wasted his ration of mince.*

"I know," *he interrupted,* "the children could have had it." *He noticed, then, that the flat was quiet except for the faint mutter of the wireless that Linda kept in the kitchen for company. The children must be out. His instant's relief was followed by a flush of shame.*

*In the course of his job, he visited homes where children clustered round their parents, hugging their legs and clamoring for attention, but he couldn't remember his ever behaving that way, and the older they got, the less he seemed to have to say to them, or they to him.*

*Stuart was twelve, conceived in the first flush of his courtship with Linda, when the threat of war lent an urgency to lovemaking that had long since vanished. Susan was a product of a brief leave from the front two years later, procreation fueled this time by a desperate need to leave something of himself behind if he did not come back.*

*But he had survived, and if the truth be told, he found his children a disappointment. The son he had imagined as his companion, the boy he would teach to play football and take for long afternoons of idling along the Thames, was thin and serious, his nose always in a book, and didn't seem to know the difference between rugger and cricket.*

*And Susan, the princess he had longed to hold and tickle, was a solid, stodgy girl who giggled like a hyena with her girlfriends but only gave him a blank stare from her mother's opaque brown eyes.*

*He felt the weight of it all then, so suddenly that his body sagged and he touched his shoulder to the wall for support. It had been a bad day—they'd followed up on a report of an unpleasant smell from a neighboring flat, and on forcing entry had found a man sitting in a chair in the dingy bed-sitter, looking quite relaxed except for the fact that his brains were splattered in an arc on the wall behind him, and his service revolver lay where it had fallen in his lap.*

*The neighbors, now thronging round with interest, told*

*Gavin the man had been a decorated war hero, but had re-turned to find his family gone and no jobs available for a man partially crippled at D-Day. Since then the man, one Terence Billings, had kept himself to himself, getting by, they supposed, on his pension.*

*"What was it?" Gavin had asked his team when they'd finished their report and retired to the pub nearest the sta-tion, squeezing into the corner table with foaming pints. "What do you suppose was the final straw?"*

*"Probably couldn't get fags at the corner shop," said PC Will Collins, shaking his head.*

*"Maybe his cat died," offered Gavin's sergeant, John Rogers, only half in jest. All of them had seen the most triv-ial things push people over the edge into despair. And all of them had served on the front—all knew the man in the chair could just as easily have been them, and it was this bond, shared but unspoken, that kept them there, smoking and drinking too much beer, until long after they should have been home.*

*"What is it, Gav? Are you all right?" Linda's voice hov-ered between censure and concern.*

*He thought of her as he'd first met her, how he'd loved her for her piss-and-vinegar pluck. He'd thought she could take on anything, but she hadn't signed on to be a police-man's wife, and it had brought her to this—a sharp-faced shadow of that long-ago girl.*

*And the children—was he the one at fault? Had he failed them all? And if so, what had he accomplished by it? He'd certainly done nothing to make life better for the man in the chair today, or others like him.*

*"Gav? You look like you've seen a ghost." His wife came to him and lifted her hand, brushing the backs of her fingers against his cheek.*

*The gesture was so unexpected, the gentleness of it so long forgotten, that he felt tears spring to his eyes. He closed his hand over hers. The pressure of his grip brought her body lightly against his, her weight delicate and warm. Swallowing, he whispered, "I'm sorry—I've made a mess of things—I—"*

The clang of the phone made them jerk apart, like guilty teenagers. Their eyes met for a moment, then, unable to resist, he glanced towards the telephone. It sat like a black beast on the table at the end of the hall, pulsing with insistent sound.

"I suppose I should get that," he said.

"You always do," answered his wife, slipping her hand from his.

Gavin walked down Tite Street towards the river from the flat in Tedworth Square, angling into Royal Hospital Road, stopping for a moment as he reached the Embankment to glance west at the sparkling outline of the Albert Bridge framed against an orange-and-purple-streaked sky. A year ago the bridge had been draped with electric lights for the Festival of Britain, and the sight still made his breath catch in his throat. Airy and insubstantial, it added to the odd sense of disconnectedness he'd felt since leaving the flat.

He'd protested, of course, but the duty sergeant at Chelsea Station had insisted he was the nearest ranking CID officer available, and Gavin had sighed and acquiesced.

Now he wondered if he had left a part of himself behind, the self that might have stayed and caressed his wife. Had he seen a glimmer of understanding in her eyes as she watched him go? Or had he taken the wrong turning at an irrevocable fork?

Nonsense, that was; utter rubbish. He had a job to do. He shook himself and, turning away, headed east into the gathering darkness.

The constable, a dark-uniformed silhouette, was waiting near the gate that led into a heavily wooded garden at the end of Cheyne Walk. "Inspector Hoxley."

Gavin recognized him as he spoke, a young constable named Simms, and the tightness in the man's voice made the hair rise on Gavin's neck. This was more than a wino sleeping it off in the park. "Anyone else here yet?" he asked.

"No, sir. I didn't like to leave it—him—sir, but I was afraid you wouldn't see me if I didn't wait near the gates."

"All right, then, Simms, let's see what you've found."

He followed the flickering light of Simms's torch as the constable picked his way through the gate and along a gravel path that shone faintly. Around a curve, the outline of a bench loomed out of the dimness, and beneath that, another form, dark with a glint of white.

There was no mistaking the shape of a human body, or the awkwardness of death. "Hold the light, man," said Gavin as the torch wavered. As he glanced back, the light bobbed upwards, and he saw that the constable looked dangerously corpselike himself.

Too young to have been in the war, Gavin reminded himself—this might even be the man's first body. "If you're going to be sick, get right away," he cautioned, but his tone was gentle.

"No, sir, I'll be all right." Simms straightened and steadied the torch.

Pushing back his hat, Gavin thought that if this were the young man's first death, he'd got off easy. More than likely one of the pensioners had sat on the bench for a smoke and a view of the river, and his heart had clapped out.

But as he looked more closely, he saw that the figure was not clothed in the traditional navy uniform of the Chelsea pensioner, but in a black suit. Frowning, he knelt, and the smell of blood hit him in a foul wave.

"Christ," he muttered, swallowing, then barked at Simms, "Give me the torch." He held it closer, the light illuminating a slender man, his body twisted so that his chest and face were turned upwards. One arm was flung out, as if he had reached for something—the bench, perhaps, to stop himself falling. His thick, wavy hair was streaked with gray, but his clean-shaven face took a few years from his age—he might, Gavin thought, have been in his late forties or early fifties. Where his dark coat fell open, great gouts of blood stained the white of his shirt.

"Any identification?" Gavin asked, glancing at Simms.

"No, sir. I just had a quick look in his pockets for a wallet, but there was nothing, not even coins."

"You didn't move him?"

"No, sir." Simms sounded affronted. "I did find an old

briefcase, a soft one, like a satchel, by the side of the bench, but there was nothing in that, either."

"Odd," Gavin said aloud, turning back to the corpse. An odd place for a robbery, and although the man's clothes were of good quality, they were worn. The edges of his shirt collar had been darned with careful stitches.

What could this man of obviously reduced means have been carrying that was worth this sort of violence? And why would a common thief remove all traces of identification from his victim?

Then a glint at the man's throat caught his eye and he held the torch nearer. It was a thin gold chain, half hidden by the neck of the white shirt. Taking his handkerchief from his pocket, Gavin carefully turned back the shirt collar. A small pendant, no bigger than his fingernail, lay against the white skin of the man's exposed clavicle. He lifted it as delicately as he could with his handkerchief-shrouded fingers and the chain came free, broken near the clasp.

Gavin sat back on his heels, frowning as he studied the pendant.

"What is it, sir?" asked Simms, breathing heavily over Gavin's shoulder. "Looks like a miniature dumbbell."

"No." Gavin's thoughts went back to his childhood neighbors, the Kaplans, and the games of tag he and the Kaplan boys had played on fine days, racing in and out of the front door. He held the object up, so that it spun and glittered in the torchlight.

"If I'm not mistaken, it's a mezuzah, a Jewish symbol of protection."

Even over the hum of conversation at the table, Kincaid heard the slight rise of alarm in Gemma's voice. Excusing himself with a smile at the other guests and a quick look at Cullen, who gave him a small nod, he slipped from his chair and threaded his way round the table and into the kitchen.

"We're in the midst of a dinner party, but I could come in the morning," he overheard as he came in. When he raised a brow in question, she covered the phone with her hand. "It's Erika. She says there's something she needs to talk to me about. But I—" She looked back at the dining room and shrugged.

Kincaid was surprised. He couldn't imagine the independent and elegantly mannered Erika Rosenthal calling so late with such a request unless something was wrong.

"Go," he said. "You've pulled the party off with flying colors, and things are winding down." He gestured towards the guests assembled in the dining room. "We'll tell them your friend's ill. And you'll get out of the washing-up."

"Lucky you." Gemma shot him a quick smile, then uncovered the phone. "Erika, I'll be there in a quarter of an hour."

The rain had stopped sometime during dinner, leaving the air fresh and cool. Realizing her head was a bit fuzzy from the wine she'd drunk, Gemma decided to walk the short distance to Arundel Gardens. It would give her a chance to clear out the high-energy chatter of the dinner party.

Just as a precaution, she took a brolly from the stand in the hall, and as she walked she swung it, tapping the end on the pavement. The leafy avenue of Lansdowne Road soon gave way to the terraces of Arundel Gardens, and light shone like a beacon from the lower windows of Erika's house.

It occurred to Gemma that she had never been to Erika's house in the evening, always for lunch or tea. She had always assumed Erika was early to bed and early to rise. She glanced at her watch as she rang the bell; it was half eleven.

Erika came quickly, however, and grasped Gemma's hands in an unexpectedly physical gesture. As she led Gemma into the sitting room, she said, "I shouldn't have got you out so late. You'll think I'm taking advantage of our friendship."

Gemma looked round with the pleasure she always felt. She had loved this room since the first time she had seen it, when, as a newly promoted inspector posted to Notting Hill, she had personally taken a burglary call, just to get the feel of the streets again. She had found Dr. Erika Rosenthal, a delicate white-haired woman with a fierce sparkle to her dark eyes, fuming over the theft of her television and some trinkets. It had been the invasion that had upset her more than the loss, and Gemma, worried about the older woman's vulnerability on her own, had suggested she improve her security. She had known that the recovery of the woman's possessions was highly unlikely.

She had stayed to chat a bit, she remembered, admiring the room with its deep red walls, expensive but comfortably worn furniture, shelves of books, and glowing landscape paintings. And then there had been Erika's grand piano, an object much envied by Gemma before Duncan had given her one of her own.

A few weeks later, embroiled in an odd case involving Duncan's family in Glastonbury, Gemma had been researching goddess worship and had pulled up a monograph by Dr. Erika Rosenthal. Recognizing the name from their previous meeting, she had called on Erika for advice, and so had begun a rather unusual friendship.

They differed widely in age, education, and background, and yet Erika had given Gemma support and advice, and had taken a keen interest in the boys, particularly Kit, encouraging him to pursue his dream of becoming a biologist.

Now, Gemma wondered if she had given half as much to the relationship as she had taken. "Of course you're not taking advantage of me," she said crisply, glancing at the open book by Erika's chair, and a half-empty tumbler of what looked like whisky. She felt a frisson of unease—she'd never seen her friend drink anything stronger than the occasional sherry or glass of wine.

"Do let me get you something," Erika was saying, "for coming out at this hour. I've sherry or whisky, or I could make you tea."

"No, I'm fine, really." Gemma sat in her usual spot, the chair nearest Erika's, and studied her friend. "Just tell me what's wrong."

Erika subsided into her own seat and, after her burst of welcoming energy, seemed to shrink into herself. She looked frail and tired, and unnatural spots of color bloomed in her cheeks. Fingering the open book on her reading table, she said, "I feel foolish now, ringing you, when there's nothing . . . But it was such a shock, and I couldn't—"

The book slipped from her hands and landed, open, crumpled pages down, on the floor near Gemma's foot. Lifting it, she saw that it was not a book but an elegantly produced soft-cover catalog from the auction house Harrowby's. "'Art Deco Jewelry'?" she said aloud, reading the cover. "I don't understand."

"No, of course not." Erika shook her head, but made no attempt to retrieve the book. "And I hardly know where to begin."

Gemma sat quietly, making of her listening an almost physical thing, as she had learned to do in interviews.

After a few moments, Erika sighed and met her eyes briefly. "I don't often speak of these things. There are a few friends who know a little, because we share some experiences . . . but even so, after all these years, it is not easy." Her language began to slip into a more formal cadence, as if her native German were closer to the surface of her mind.

"You know I came here to London from Berlin, at the beginning of the war?"

"With your husband. Yes, you've told me that," agreed Gemma, realizing that she knew very little more.

"It sounds so simple, yes?" Erika's smile didn't reach her eyes, and her hands seemed to twist together of their own accord. "My father came to Germany from Russia," she continued, "after the Great War, thinking to make a new future for himself and his bride. So we are, you see, refugees by tradition, as are almost all Jews. His name was Jakob Goldshtein, and he was a tradesman with some skill in metalwork. He apprenticed himself to a jewelry maker, and by the beginning of the 1930s he had surpassed his late master and made a reputation for himself.

"He loved the new Art Deco styles, the influence of Egyptian and African art—he said it made him think of all the places he would never see. He loved the contrast of silver and platinum against the brightly colored stones, but above all, he loved diamonds. He was a jolly man, my father, who liked to make jokes about his name. It amused him that he only worked in silver metals.

"By the time the Nazis began their rise to power, my mother had died, and my father had acquired wealth as well as reputation. He took commissions from the new German elite, even if it meant adding hooks to his beautiful necklaces and brooches so that they could attach their swastikas." Erika's face had softened as she talked about her father, and there was no censure in her voice.

"He thought, of course, that it would pass, the new regime, as such things usually did. And so it was that he sent his spoiled only daughter to university, and there she fell in love with her tutor, and married."

Erika stopped, her hands still now, and silence descended upon the room. There were no muffled voices from the houses on either side, no footsteps from the street, and Gemma hesitated on the precipice of speech, not sure whether she might extend the spell or break it. At last she said, very softly, "This was your husband?" and as she spoke she realized how seldom she had heard Erika speak of her marriage.

"David, yes. He was fifteen years older than I, a philosopher, and a pacifist, quite well known in intellectual circles. There was even talk that he might be nominated for the Nobel Prize. But in 1938, Carl von Ossietzky died in police custody, and my father knew what David refused to see, that neither David nor his ideas would be tolerated.

"We had little money, but my father had funds and connections. He arranged for us to leave the country, quietly, anonymously, and David was forced to agree."

The tension in the air grew palpable, and Gemma saw the movement of Erika's throat as she swallowed. She found herself holding her breath, this time not daring to interrupt.

"My father gave me a parting gift, the most beautiful of all the things he had created. It was to be my inheritance, and my bulwark against the future, if things did not go as we planned."

Just as Gemma began to guess the import of the book she held, Erika reached for it. Slowly, deliberately, she smoothed the pages, then let it fall open of its own accord. As Erika gazed down, transfixed, Gemma got up and looked over her shoulder.

She gave a gasp of surprise and pleasure. The photo was full page, the background black, and against the velvety darkness the diamonds fell in a double cascade. The caption on the right-hand page read, *Jakob Goldshtein, a diamond cascade double-clip brooch, 1938*. "It's lovely," breathed Gemma.

"Yes. My father's masterpiece." Erika looked up and met her eyes. "I last saw it in Germany, more than fifty years ago. I want you to help me find out how it came to be in an English auction."

"So how did you get on with Melody?" Kincaid handed Doug Cullen a dripping saucepan, glancing over as his friend was applying a tea towel industriously.

He and Doug had seen off the rest of the well-fed and well-lubricated guests, and now, with Kit and Toby home and the dogs having given up any hope of scraps, they'd loaded the dishwasher and begun on the pots and pans.

Doug Cullen's blond schoolboy good looks and expressive face made him usually easy to read, but for once the glance he gave Kincaid was inscrutable. "No joy, there, I think," he said, reaching for another pan.

"She doesn't fancy you, or vice versa?" asked Kincaid, thinking that Gemma would be disappointed by the failure of her matchmaking scheme.

Shrugging, Cullen pushed his glasses up on his nose with the damp edge of the tea towel. "It might just be my bruised ego, but I don't think PC Talbot fancies blokes much, full stop."

Kincaid glanced at him in surprise. "Seriously?"

"There's definitely a *Let's all be blokes together* vibe."

"Might be armor. That's common enough." Melody Talbot was attractive, dark haired, dark eyed, and cheerfully efficient, and Gemma had come to depend on her a good deal at work. If Melody was gay and had chosen not to make her sexual orientation public, then that was her business. It was tough enough for women officers as it was—his thought stopped suddenly short as he remembered Melody's solicitousness towards Gemma, all the little thoughtful gestures that Gemma often repeated to him at day's end.

"What about the prickly Maura Bell, then?" Kincaid asked.

They had worked a case in Southwark with the Scottish Inspector Bell, and although she and Cullen seemed as mismatched as chalk and cheese, there had been an attraction between them. Doug had even broken it off with his longtime girlfriend, Stella Fairchild-Priestly, but then gradually any mentions of Maura had disappeared.

This time Cullen's feelings were all too apparent, as he flushed to the roots of his fair hair. "I couldn't say," he answered tersely, and Kincaid knew he'd overstepped the mark. It occurred to him that he was as clueless about Cullen's personal life as Gemma apparently was about Melody Talbot's.

It was not something he was going to be given a chance to remedy that night, however, as Cullen quickly finished his drying and took himself off with a muttered excuse.

"You bloody sad wanker!" Cullen said aloud as he settled into a seat on the night bus that trundled its way down Bishop's Bridge Road, earning him a look from an old lady bundled in too many coats for the May night. He'd contemplated the tube, certainly a quicker alternative, but had found himself unable to cope with the thought of sharing a carriage with drunken Saturday-night revelers and snogging couples.

But the brisk walk and the wait at the bus stop hadn't made it any easier to put Maura Bell out of his mind, and his face burned with shame again as he remembered his reaction to Kincaid's question. Why couldn't he have just shrugged and offered some manly and macho platitude. *Easy come, easy go. You know women.*

But no, he had to make an utter fool of himself in front of his boss.

The truth was that he'd taken Maura Bell out a number of times, for drinks, for dinner, to the cinema. He had thought she liked him, but a public school education combined with a deep and fundamental shyness had handicapped his nerve severely. When he finally got up the courage to make a serious advance, she'd drawn away from him as if stung.

He'd stammered out apologies; she'd made excuses and left him standing in the middle of the Millennium Bridge, so humiliated that for a moment he'd contemplated jumping in. But good sense had prevailed. Perhaps even that was sad—that he was incapable of making a grand romantic gesture.

He'd gone home to his gray flat in the Euston Road, and when Maura had rung him repeatedly over the next few days, he'd refused to take her calls. After a bit the calls stopped, and in the months since, he'd devoted himself to work with excessive zeal, becoming the best researcher in the department, and limited his social life to an occasional after-work drink with Kincaid, and a monthly visit home to his parents in Saint Albans, during which he told them exaggerated stories of his importance at work.

The bus slowed for Great Portland Street, and for an instant Cullen had a wild thought. He could still take the Circle Line. Then the Docklands Light Railway to the Isle of Dogs. He could stand outside Maura Bell's flat, waiting for a glimpse of her, just to see if she was still as he remembered.

Then he snorted in disgust. *Stalking,* that's what he was contemplating, and he wasn't that far gone—at least not yet. But the woman in the multiple coats seemed to disagree. She glared at him, chins quivering, making it clear she thought he was a nutter, then got up and waddled her way to the very back of the bus.

After Cullen had left, Kincaid gave the worktops one last wipe, turned out all but the small lamp in the kitchen, then stood and listened. Wesley had brought the boys home wired on pizza and lemonade, but now the giggles had faded upstairs. Even the dogs had disappeared; Tess, thirteen-year-old Kit's little terrier, would be with him, while Geordie, Gemma's cocker spaniel, would be curled on the foot of their bed, accompanied like sticking plaster by their black cat,

Sid, who had developed a perversely unfeline passion for the little dog.

The house seemed to exhale, settling into the profound silence of night inching towards morning, and Kincaid gave a worried glance at the clock above the cooker. It was half-past twelve—surely Gemma would be home soon.

He felt a niggle of worry about Erika's phone call. It seemed so out of character, but then he found Gemma's relationship with Erika rather odd as well. It wasn't that he didn't like the older woman, but when she studied him with her keen glance he felt like a suitor sized up and found wanting, an uncomfortable sensation for a man unused to feeling intimidated.

Did she disapprove of the fact that they weren't married? he wondered. But surely she knew Gemma well enough to know that was her choice, rather than his.

Kincaid shrugged, irritated with himself for letting his thoughts go down that path, but he found he couldn't contemplate going to bed or settling down with a book while Gemma was still out. He'd decided he might turn on the telly when the doorbell rang. The sound was shockingly loud in the quiet house, and upstairs one of the dogs gave a single yip of surprise.

Hurrying towards the front door, he was spurred by an instant, clutching panic. Gemma was out—had something happened to her?

He was telling himself not to be daft, that one of the guests had forgotten something, when he swung open the door and found Gemma's father standing on the doorstep.

The restaurant and club on All Saints Road was one of the latest ventures meant to upgrade the still dubious nether regions of Notting Hill. But on this Saturday night, the veterinary clinic across the street and the barred shop fronts seemed only to add to the ambience, and inside the restaurant, the aura of cool could have cut glass. No patron was much over thirty; all were rich, or pretending to be rich.

Kristin Cahill was one of those pretending to a status as yet unachieved. She stood at the bar in a little black dress, a designer copy that made up in élan what it lacked in label, and that set off her milky-white skin. Her dark hair was feather cut, flattering her gamine features and long neck, and her full lips were carefully outlined in deep pink.

She checked her lipstick for the hundredth time, then snapped her compact closed, satisfied. She could pass for French—a Leslie Caron, even an Edith Piaf—but there was no one to appreciate her efforts except the bartender, and she was tired of fielding his too-interested glances.

Lifting her martini, she turned her back and sipped, gazing with growing irritation at the door. Where the hell was Dominic? The DJ had started in the club downstairs; she could hear a blare of sound when the stairway door swung open, feel the vibration through the soles of her feet. Dom always had an excuse, more often than not having to do with his mother, the controlling bitch from hell. But then what had she expected when she started going out with an almost thirty-year-old man who lived with his mum?

Of course, she'd thought that both Dom *and* his mum had money, then, and the house, bloody hell, the house had reduced her to openmouthed goggling. That had been a mistake. Dom's mum had given her a knowing little smile that had put her in her place quickly enough.

*Grasping middle class,* the look had said. Grasping middle class with a comprehensive education, an art history degree from a middlebrow university, and aspirations that would never amount to anything her son would fancy. And maybe, Kristin thought as she looked at her watch, Mummy had been right.

A girl waiting alone at the bar for half an hour might have a date who was unavoidably detained; a girl waiting alone for more than half an hour shouted *stood up*. Some of the other customers were beginning to eye her, too, and she could imagine the whispers, more malicious than sympathetic. She knocked back what was left of her drink with an unladylike gulp, set her glass on the bar, and flashed the bartender a dazzling smile as she stalked towards the stairs.

She hadn't come out—not to mention spending half her pay on the dress—to stand about like a stupid cow. If Dom didn't have the decency to show up, she was going to have a good time without him.

Still, as she negotiated the steep stairs to the club rather gingerly in her four-inch heels, she felt an unwelcome jab of worry. Dominic, for all his faults, had always been kind, and she'd seen some things lately that made her suspect he was in real trouble. There had been whispered conversations in the corners of pubs with men whose reputations frightened her, and there were other signs: even his rich-boy good looks were becoming a little worn around the edges, and yesterday she had noticed his hands shaking, although he'd tried to hide it by lighting cigarette after cigarette.

And then there was the business with Harry, which made her profoundly uneasy. She didn't want to get involved with anything dodgy, but on the other hand, it just might give her the step-up she needed, and then she could tell Dominic Scott to go to hell.

There were other men who would appreciate what she had to offer. Men who were going someplace with their lives—men who were free of Dominic's baggage, and whose families wouldn't sneer at her background.

Before her, a sea of people moved in the eerie blue light, swaying like sea anemones in an underwater current. The beat of the house music was mesmerizing, vibrating nerve and bone, and she wanted to dance. A tall man with skin the color of espresso smiled at her across the floor. Before she lost her resolution, she eased into the flow of bodies and met him halfway.

# 3

*Notting Hill Gate is a superstitious place because it seems to exceed rational prescriptions and explanations. On the Portobello Road, one feels oneself growing more insubstantial, less and less able to keep a sense of personal proportion in the crowd of people who all look so much poorer, or richer, or wilder, or more conventional than one is oneself.*
—Jonathan Raban, Soft Cities

**"MR. WALTERS?" KINCAID CAUGHT** his slip as soon as the words left his mouth. "Ern?" he corrected himself. "Is everything all right?" He'd never got comfortable with calling Gemma's dad by his first name.

"Gemma here?" Ern Walters asked it so tersely that it might have been a statement. A small, wiry man, he was dressed in his usual outfit of tweed jacket and tie, with a weathered flat wool cap covering what remained of his thinning hair.

"No, no, actually she's not. But come in, please." His sense of apprehension growing, Kincaid held the door wide and gestured him in. Gemma's parents had visited them only once since they'd moved into the Notting Hill house, for Toby's birthday party.

Walters followed, but once in the hall, he planted his feet and, taking off his cap, crumpled it in his hands as he spoke. "Work, is it?" From the disapproval in his tone, Gemma might have been soliciting.

Kincaid frowned but said merely, "No. She's gone to see a friend who rang up. Some sort of problem."

"Always has time for her friends, does she?"

Bewildered by the other man's belligerent tone, Kincaid wondered if he had been drinking. But there was no smell of alcohol on Walters's breath or any wavering in his stance, and Kincaid felt a greater prickling of alarm. "Come into the kitchen and sit down, Mr. Walters," he said, reverting instinctively to the more formal address. "Let me fix you a drink or a cup of tea, and you can tell me what's wrong."

"I'll not be stopping." Ern Walters set his chin in a stubborn line that suddenly reminded Kincaid of Gemma. "It's just I thought she should know. Gemma. It's her mum. She's been taken ill. Collapsed."

"What?" Kincaid stared at him in shock. Whatever he'd expected, it hadn't been this. Vi Walters was one of the toughest women he'd ever met, an indomitable life force. "When? Where? Is she all right? Why didn't you ring us?" The questions tumbled out, too fast, he knew, for coherent answers. He stopped himself, giving Ern Walters time to speak.

"Right in the middle of Saturday-afternoon rush. Said she didn't feel well. Then she went down like a felled tree. I couldn't get her up."

Now Kincaid heard the terror beneath Ern Walters's gruff manner. He clamped down his impatience, made himself wait until Walters went on.

"The ambulance took her to Whipps Cross. They say she's resting comfortably, whatever that means."

"You didn't know she was ill?"

Walters glared at him. "She'd complained of feeling a bit tired lately. Wanting to put her feet up and have a cuppa. I never thought—"

"No, of course not." Knowing Vi, Kincaid guessed she wouldn't have taken kindly to a suggestion that she see a doctor. "What will they do now?"

"Tests, they said. And more tests in the morning."

Kincaid pulled out his phone. "I'll ring Gemma. She'll want to go—"

"No." Ern Walters cut him off before his finger touched the first key. "There's no need for her. Cyn's there."

Harry Pevensey rubbed the crust from the rim of his cold cream jar, flicked it from his fingers, then took a very long swallow of his Bombay Sapphire on ice before switching his glass to his left hand and methodically working the greasy cream into his face with his right. Round strokes from the chin up, around the eyes and the forehead, so as not to cause wrinkles, then the wiping with tissues tossed carelessly in the direction of the waste bin. Carefully, he examined the face that emerged from beneath the white mask, and took another swig of gin.

That was one of the few perks still accorded him, the drink sent down from the bar to his dressing room after a performance, even in this miserable pub in Kennington.

His dressing room, indeed. The thought made him laugh. Once it *would* have been his dressing room, when he'd played leads, or even second leads. But now he'd been relegated to the Stranger in a profit-share production of Chekhov's *The Cherry Orchard,* with an appearance only in act two, and insult added to injury, sharing a room with a half-dozen amateurs with even smaller parts. There was perhaps no greater sign of an actor's career in decline.

He'd waited for the others to swipe off their makeup and go giggling into the night so that he could have his gin and contemplation in peace. That much dignity, at least, he had left.

The face that regarded him in the mirror was still handsome enough, the complexion a pale olive, the hair thick and dark except for the smattering of gray at the temples that he covered carefully with dye on a toothbrush. A closer inspection, however, revealed the faint web of broken veins in the nose and cheeks, the slight sagging of jowls, all signs and portents of worse things to come.

Yes, there was no denying that his career was in decline, but the truth was that his whole life had been a decline, except for one brief spark, and that had turned to ashes quickly enough.

He was born Hari Pevensey, the given name a sop from his Anglo father to his Indian mother. His father, the youngest son of declining Dorset gentry, had gone out to "Indya" to try his hand at engineering. At that he had failed dismally, but he had managed to bring home the youngest, dowryless daughter of a minor Indian prince whose fortune had not survived India's independence.

Nor had the couple's return to England been a success. What remained of the family had been horrified by the foreign bride who *gave herself airs*. His father had been found work managing a box factory, his parents and their newborn son installed in a two-up, two-down Victorian semidetached, and Harry suspected that shortly thereafter marital relations cooled to an arctic level that had precluded more children. He could certainly not remember any sign of affection between his parents, both of whom must have felt royally cheated by fate.

Then, when he was five, Harry's parents had performed the most dramatic feat of their lives by orphaning him spectacularly, having drunk to excess and crashed their car into a Dorset hedge. Spending the remainder of his formative years passed among aunts and his English grandmother, Harry buried Hari as thoroughly as he could; it was his skill in protective coloration as well as his slightly exotic good looks that had got him into a London art school.

Those had been the days, he thought with a nostalgic sigh as he wiped the last dabs of white from his chin. In the early seventies, heady with his first flush of success, he'd hobnobbed with rock stars in Chelsea clubs, drunk too much, slept with anyone who took his fancy, and gradually discovered that his looks concealed a talent that was facile at best.

And now here he was, examining the pouches under his eyes, cultivating a taste for gin he couldn't afford, and contemplating with great reluctance his return to his once-trendy flat in Fitzrovia.

There was one small ray of hope in his dismal outlook, however. There might be a payoff from the recent little financial gamble he had let himself be talked into, against his better judgment. But then, what good had his judgment ever done him, and what had he to lose? Besides, there had been the satisfaction of spiting Ellen. Even now that thought was enough to make the Sapphire burn more warmly in his stomach.

But in fact, he'd since realized, there might be more to gain than that. If the deal came off, his percentage might keep the creditors at bay a bit longer. Optimism inspired an attempt at a jaunty smile in the mirror. There might still be life in the old devil yet. He ran a brush through his hair, collected his raincoat, and flipped off the lights, and when the doorman tipped his cap to him, Harry saluted in return and set off home whistling.

Like Doug Cullen, Melody Talbot left Duncan and Gemma's house on foot. She, however, had not far to go, and had been glad to walk in the rain-freshened air. Pulling her coat a bit tighter, she'd detoured around St. John's Gardens, taking Lansdowne Walk instead. Although she'd never admit it to anyone else, since the Arrowood murders she hadn't liked walking down St. John's alone at night.

At Ladbroke Grove she'd cut over a street and entered the station, ostensibly to collect some of her things, but in truth she'd just needed a dose of familiarity. But the building echoed emptily, and few of the faces on the Saturday-night rota were familiar. She rummaged in her desk, to save face, then went out again into Ladbroke Road, the clack of her footsteps loud on the pavement.

The dressy shoes felt artificial, just as she had felt all evening. What had she been thinking, to put herself in such a situation, with superior officers and that nosey parker Doug Cullen to boot?

She'd been flattered to be asked. But it had been much too dangerous, the temptation too great, the revelatory stakes much too high.

Her footsteps finally slowed as she neared her flat. She had never invited anyone there, not even Gemma. It was one of her hard-and-fast rules, and although her address was available in her personnel file, so far no one had had the temerity, or possibly the interest, to show up on her doorstep.

The second thought saddened her, and as she entered her building and took the lift to her top-floor flat, she felt more regret than her usual relief.

What had she got herself into, leading this double life? It had been the rebellion, the gamble of it, in the beginning, the pleasure of flaunting her father's disapproval, but she hadn't realized how much she would come to love the job, or just how lonely and isolated her secrecy would make her.

Was she overly paranoid, refusing to invite anyone to her home? The flat, in an updated 1930s mansion block, had been her bargain with her father, his concern for her safety set against her desire for anonymity. But she'd made sure the place was small enough, and sparsely furnished enough, that she could get by with saying it was only a let, and that she'd got a good deal. Admitting that she owned the place was a different matter entirely.

Lowly police constables did not *buy* flats in Notting Hill. Not unless they had money and influence, both things she'd worked hard at denying since childhood.

But things would never be the same if she were found out. Oh, they couldn't fire her outright, that would cause a scandal greater than her presence. But she would be quietly pulled from the more sensitive jobs, and there would be no possibility of promotion, not even to some isolated hamlet in Outer Mongolia. There would be jeers and whispers in the canteen, conversations that would stop when she entered the room, and she would never again be one of the mates.

The lift stopped and Melody stood for a moment, blinking in the light of the corridor, before taking the last few steps to her door.

The flat looked just as neat and tidy as she had left it, radio on, Classic FM playing quietly in the background for company. Not neat and tidy, she corrected herself. Sterile.

For once, she kicked off her shoes haphazardly and tossed her coat over the arm of the sofa. Barefoot, she padded to the corner bay window that overlooked Portobello Road. No sound rose from the street. It was past closing and even the pubs were quiet.

It was too bad, Melody thought, that she hadn't fancied Doug Cullen, the little swot, because she suspected that she just might have encountered someone as lonely as she was.

Gemma made the drive to Leyton on autopilot. It was a good deal farther than it had been when she'd lived in her friend Hazel's garage flat in Islington, and there was no easy route. She wound her way through the quiet streets, north, then west, skirting Willesden, Hampstead, then Camden Town, all the while her mind revolving in tight little circles of denial. Not her mother, dear God, not her mother. It just wasn't possible.

Kincaid had argued with her about going to hospital, of course, told her there was nothing she could do tonight, that her father hadn't wanted her to go.

How like her dad, to have trekked halfway across London rather than to have rung her. He'd wanted to confront her, she suspected, to let her know that he felt what had happened to her mother was somehow her fault.

That had stung, but it wasn't her brief flare of temper at her dad's pigheadedness that had sent her flying across London, but panic, and a wash of guilt. How could her mother have been ill and she not known?

She had seen her just a few weeks ago—or had it been longer? Time flew, work and the children kept her busy, and then when she did visit, it was to contend with her father's silent pall of disapproval. But these were all excuses that seemed flimsy and selfish now.

Leyton slid by, the streets of her childhood suddenly painfully familiar, and then she was entering the grounds of Whipps Cross University Hospital. The silhouettes of the late-Victorian buildings loomed fittingly massive against the pink glow cast by the ever-present city lights.

She had been born here, as had Toby, as had her sister and her sister's children, not to mention much more noteworthy personages such as David Beckham and Jonathan Ross. But even they were minor footnotes to all the births and deaths this place had seen in the last century.

Familiarity with the complex allowed Gemma to park

and find her mother's ward easily enough, and there she found her sister as well. Cyn was sound asleep, sprawled across three chairs in the waiting area, her red-gold hair tumbled back like a drowning Ophelia's, her tanned midriff showing, tropical-pink toenails peeking coyly from beneath the hem of her jeans. Trust Cyn to look fetching in even the worst of circumstances, Gemma thought with a burst of irritation, but then her sister emitted a faint snore and Gemma sighed. Cyn was Cyn, after all, but *she* could at least have rung. She had probably been enjoying her role as the good sister too much—or perhaps, Gemma thought more charitably, she'd just been too worried.

She'd meant to wake her sister, but decided to let Sleeping Beauty lie and speak to the charge nurse instead.

Her heart quickened as she entered the ward itself. The bright lights of the corridor couldn't combat the dead-of-night silence, the sense she always felt at such times in such places of life hanging by a thread.

But the charge nurse, a slightly tubby Pakistani man, was cheerful enough, and was willing to bend the rules and allow her into her mother's room. "Anything for London's finest," he said, with an assessing stare that meant she probably didn't measure up to her sister.

"About my mum, do you know anything at all?" she asked, hesitantly, not sure she was ready for an answer.

"Waiting for blood tests, love," was all he would say. "It's just down on the right. You can sit with her as long as you're quiet."

The cubicle was dark except for the bluish fluorescent light burning above the bed. Her mum looked oddly small and withered against the starched white sheets, and Gemma noticed for the first time that her mother's red curls were fading to gray. An IV line snaked from a shunt in her hand to the standing pole at the head of the bed, but otherwise there were no wires or tubes, no indication that Vi Walters's universe had been turned on its head.

Her eyes were closed, her forehead creased in a slight frown, as if sleeping were an effort. When, Gemma wondered, had she last seen her mother in repose? Her mum was always busy, always doing, the only respite she allowed herself the occasional cup of tea in the small kitchen of the flat above the bakery. Sometimes, after a particularly hard day, she would prop her feet on one of the other chairs and sigh, but if Gemma's dad came in, she would right herself briskly, as if she didn't want to be seen slacking.

Gemma pulled the stiffly upright visitor's chair as close to the bed as she could and took her mother's hand a little awkwardly, unsure if the touch would wake her, but her mum's eyelids merely fluttered, then the line on her forehead relaxed, as if she'd found some subconscious comfort.

Dawn found Gemma still there, her cheek now pillowed on the bed beside her mother's hand, when the consultant making early rounds came in with his diagnosis.

# 4

*As the years go by the truth becomes more and more agitated; the energies that go into the maintenance of the fortress are Herculean; they must be manned night and day . . .*
    —Diana Petre, The Secret
                Orchard of Roger Ackerley

"He was circumcised, if that helps." Dr. Rainey peered over his half-glasses at Gavin Hoxley, then back down at the body on his mortuary table. "He could very well have been Jewish."

Hoxley averted his eyes. Circumcised or not, the sight of naked male genitalia, blue tinged and limp, made him feel acutely vulnerable. Nor did he like seeing his unidentified victim stripped of all dignity. The man's hands and nails had been clean, his hair and face barbered and shaved. He had been someone, this thin man with the salt-and-pepper hair, and now he was nothing but a specimen to be poked and prodded on Dr. Rainey's table.

The fact that the man might have been a Jew made Hoxley still more uncomfortable. If it was true, it meant that the autopsy itself would be considered a desecration of the remains.

Not that Hoxley put much stock in autopsies himself, or cared much for pathologists under the best of circumstances. Most of them treated wrongful-death investigations as a nuisance, but Rainey, a small, agile man with a long, mobile face and curly brown hair, had a policeman's curiosity. Hoxley had requested him specifically, even though it had meant trekking across London Bridge to Guy's Hospital.

Looking up, he found Rainey regarding him with the same intense gaze he leveled at his corpses. "You look a bit worse for wear yourself," Rainey commented.

"Thanks, Doc. We try to impress." With a grimace, Hoxley brushed his hat at the front of his suit, a futile gesture. Arriving home in the early hours of the morning, he had flung jacket, shirt, and trousers across a chair without a thought for wrinkles.

Then, when he climbed into bed, he'd discovered that the small détente he'd established with Linda earlier in the evening had vanished—she'd turned away from him, balancing on her edge of the bed like a tightrope walker, and the inches between them seemed as cold and dangerous as no-man's-land.

When he'd roused himself from a fitful sleep a few hours later, she hadn't spoken, even though he'd known from her breathing that she was awake. Not wanting to disturb the children, he'd settled for a quick wash and shave instead of a bath, and it was only when he'd looked in his car's driving mirror that he'd seen the patches he'd missed on his chin. It was fitting, he thought, that he looked like the walking wounded.

"Late night, early start," he went on with a shrug, "and I don't have a thing on the victim. What else can you tell me, Doc?" A fingertip search of the garden started at first light had turned up no trace of a murder weapon or any of the victim's possessions, nor had nearby neighbors admitted to knowing the man or to seeing anything unusual.

Rainey turned up the victim's palms. "No defense wounds, so I'd say he knew his killer, or was approached in some way that enabled the killer to take him completely by surprise." With a gloved finger, he traced the wound on the left side of the chest, just beneath the breast. "I'd say this was the first blow, and the killing blow. It was an upward thrust to the heart, and more than likely made by someone *who knew what he was doing. These others"*—his finger skimmed four more dark slashes in the white skin—*"might have been done to mask the deliberateness of the first blow, or perhaps rage got the better of our killer."*

*"You said 'someone who knew what he was doing.' You're assuming the killer was male?"*

*"Merely being grammatical,"* Rainey answered, shaking his head. *"A woman could have wielded that knife, if she had knowledge and upper-body strength. That might account for the element of surprise. Still . . ."* Rainey studied the wounds. *"I'd put my money on a man, probably ex-service. That would account for the knowledge, and the knife."*

Hoxley waited, eyebrow raised, knowing Rainey liked the drama of his revelations.

*"I assume you'll want to know what sort of weapon was used?"*

*"So tell me about the knife,"* said Hoxley, giving in.

Rainey smiled, showing even white teeth. *"A wide, double-edged blade, with a definitive hilt. If you look carefully, you can see the faint indentation it left on the skin."*

Following the pathologist's pointing finger, Hoxley saw nothing, and decided Rainey's eyes must be better than his. He nodded agreement, however, not wanting to stop the flow of information.

*"My guess would be a hunting knife, or more likely, considering the location of the crime, a combat knife."*

*"Ah. Near the Royal Hospital. That's why you think the killer might have been ex-service."* Hoxley frowned. *"Very neat, but then, I don't trust neat."*

*"A wager?"*

*"I'll buy you a pint if you're right,"* replied Hoxley. *"That's about all my salary will cover. Anything else you can tell me from the external exam?"* He wouldn't stay for the dissection—Rainey could send him a report on the state of his victim's internal organs.

*"The hands are soft, but he has a callus on the side of his right index finger, probably from holding a pen. And his*

*teeth. The dental work's not English. Maybe Eastern European."*

"So I have a middle-aged, moderately well-nourished, literate, possibly European, possibly Jewish, white male. Thanks, Doc."

"Do I detect a note of sarcasm, Inspector?" Rainey looked hurt. "What did you expect, the poor man's name tattooed on his privates?"

"More to the point," said Hoxley, "there's no tattoo on his forearm. This man was never in the camps."

The morning dawned clear and fine, but brought Erika no peace. She had slept fitfully—shivering beneath the duvet and an extra woolen blanket, even though the night was mild—and had slipped in and out of vague dreams that left her with only an ache under her breastbone.

She lay in bed, thinking, until the sun coming in the garden window crept across the counterpane, then she rose and forced herself to bathe and dress as if it were any ordinary Sunday. Sweeping up the white hair she still wore long and fastening it with pins, she gazed at her shadowed eyes in the dressing table mirror. Already she regretted speaking to Gemma. The confidence had left her feeling violated, and she had a sudden desire to undo it, to forget the whole matter, push it back into the recesses of her life like a wayward jack-in-the-box.

After a meager breakfast, she made coffee—the real thing, to combat her weariness, doctor's orders be damned—and took it out into the garden. Setting the newspaper carefully on the white iron table, she sat, but when she raised the delicate china cup to her lips, her hand trembled. She set the cup down and pulled her cardigan more closely about her shoulders, but not even the brilliant sun seemed able to warm her.

Closing her eyes, she tried to recapture the anticipation of her morning's idyll, but to one side the neighbor's children were as raucous as jackdaws, drowning out the birdsong with their shrieks, and on the other the middle-aged husband was industriously spreading organic fertilizer and whistling through his teeth.

It was a good thing, she knew, the communal garden healthy and well tended, the children happy and well fed, but she found herself remembering the shabby comradeship of the war years, when she had been a mere tenant in the garden flat and the neighbors had come down in the raids, sharing mattresses spread on the floor and endless cups of weak tea. Back then they had been bonded by more than self-interest and the desire to discuss their property values.

She and David had ended up in Notting Hill by a combination of necessity and happenstance, and assessing the future value of their property had been the farthest thing from their minds. All Jewish refugees had been placed by the Jewish relief organizations—a guarantee to the government by established English Jews that the incomers would not be a burden on the state. David had been found a job as secretary to an organization official, while she had been taken on that first year at Whiteleys in Bayswater, in the millinery department. Lodging had been found for them near David's employer.

Those connections had made their transition easier, although her German accent had caused neighbors and coworkers to regard her with suspicion at first. And even then, she'd had to learn to keep quiet when her English friends gloated over the RAF's retaliation bombings in Germany. She took no pleasure in an eye for an eye, seeing only suffering piled upon suffering, but her efforts to explain that the average German family had no more control over circumstances than the English were met with glassy-eyed hostility.

Later, after the war, when Erika had secured a university teaching position, she bought the garden flat and then the entire house, putting tenants in the upper three floors, never dreaming that she'd end up with a gold mine—a gold mine that meant nothing, as there was no one to benefit when she was gone.

Suddenly the breeze shifted and the earthy farmyard smell of her neighbor's fertilizer hit her in a wave, bringing an unexpected rush of memory that made the bile rise in her throat. Pushing away from the table, she left her coffee untouched and hurried back into the house, swallowing and wiping at her stinging eyes.

When she reached the sitting room she stopped, panting, and clutched a chair back for support. How had her father's brooch got from a German barn to an auction house in South Kensington? And why did it matter so much, after all this time? That had been another life, and she had been a different person, a phantom of a girl held to her now by the most tenuous of threads.

Erika looked round the sitting room, at the beautiful cocoon she had made for herself, and saw it for a hollow shell, a facade created to hold the past at bay.

But yesterday her life had cracked open and there could be no putting it back. She owed the truth to that long-ago girl, and that meant she would have to accept the help she had enlisted, no matter how difficult either of them found it.

"Drink up." Kincaid set a cup of hot tea on the kitchen table. Gemma seemed to hesitate for a moment, then sank into a chair and wrapped her hands round the mug. Bringing his own mug to the table, Kincaid sat down opposite and studied her.

She still wore her clothes from the night before, a filmy spring skirt in a soft green print, with a matching green-and-cream beaded cardigan over a lacy camisole. But her makeup had long since rubbed off, the smattering of freckles across her nose and cheeks standing out starkly against skin translucently pale, while the combination of exhaustion and last night's mascara had left dark smudges beneath her eyes.

Absently, she reached up to pull her thick copper hair, recently cut, into the plait she could no longer make. Frowning, she settled for tucking disheveled strands behind one ear and returned her hands to her cup.

Geordie settled himself against her feet with a gusty, doggy sigh, and her face relaxed a bit. "Are the boys up?" she asked, sipping her tea.

"No, but they will be soon. So talk." It was unlike her not to have rung him from hospital, and when he'd tried her mobile it had been switched off. He'd finally drifted off to sleep at the presage of dawn, awaking to find it full light and Gemma still gone, still not answering her mobile.

He'd showered and dressed and was pacing the kitchen by the time she came in. She'd given him a quick hug, her face turned away, murmuring, "Sorry, sorry. I should have rung. But it was hospital regs, and then when I left, I wasn't sure you'd be up." It was a fragile excuse, merely confirming that she hadn't wanted to talk on the phone, and that meant the news was bad.

Reaching across to free one of her hands from the cup, Kincaid squeezed it encouragingly. "Gemma, what's happened? Your mum—"

"Leukemia." She met his eyes for the first time. "The consultant says they think she has leukemia."

He sat back, his grip loosening. "What? But—how could she—"

"She'd been complaining about being tired. For my mum, that meant exhausted. All the symptoms were there, the bruising, the breathlessness, if anyone had noticed." Her voice was bitter.

"Surely you're not blaming yourself, Gem? There's no way you could have known."

"If I'd seen her more often, I might have— And Dad, he should have seen— If he'd told me—" Her eyes glazed with unshed tears.

"You'd have been a bit worried, maybe. You'd have tried to convince her to see a doctor. She'd have refused. So don't go there. The important thing is what happens now."

After a moment, she nodded. "They're moving her this morning to St. Barts, to the cancer specialty ward. The consultant said they would do more tests. And then . . . He said they'd see."

"He doesn't know your mum," Kincaid said briskly, covering his own dismay. In his experience, doctors were usually encouraging past all reasonable hope. He grasped Gemma's hand again. "What will we tell the boys?"

"I hate to worry Kit, but he'll have to know the truth. And Toby . . . for now, let's just say Gran's not feeling well. I don't think they'll be able to see her. Her immune system is vulnerable." She looked at him, stricken. "That means . . . She could . . . Anything could—"

"You need to get some sleep," Kincaid interrupted gently. "Things won't seem so insurmountable when you've had some rest. I'll talk to the boys, if you want—"

"No." She was already shaking her head. "I should do it. And this afternoon, when she's settled, I'll go to St. Barts—"

"What about Cynthia?"

"Oh, Cyn will be there, with bells on." One corner of Gemma's mouth quirked into a reluctant smile. "If she can rope Gerry into minding the kids." She made no secret of the fact that she thought her sister's husband was a lout.

"And your dad?"

Gemma's face went still. "I don't know. I tried to ring him this morning, but he didn't answer. Cyn said she'd talk to him. Better her than me, anyway."

Kincaid thought back to her father's abrupt visit the night before. "I never realized your dad disliked me quite so much."

"Oh, it's not you, specifically. It's everything. This"— her gesture encompassed the house—"my job. He thinks I've got above my station."

"And he's not comfortable with things being out of order on his patch?" Kincaid could see that, he supposed. "But your mum—why didn't he stay with her, last night?"

"Because he wouldn't have known what to do."

In the end, Kristin hadn't gone home with the bloke from the dance floor. Partly caution had kicked in through the haze of music and alcohol, partly guilt, and very largely embarrassment. She hadn't wanted to admit that she still lived at home, that her parents were expecting her. Silly, really, as no one young with an ordinary job could afford to live on her own in central London these days, and it wasn't as if she had a curfew or anything. It was just that she knew her mum would wake in the night, and if Kristin hadn't come in, her mum wouldn't be able to get back to sleep. Hardwired, the worrying, her mum told her apologetically. Just because your kids were grown didn't mean you automatically stopped.

She'd been tempted, though. He—she'd never learned his name—had nuzzled and stroked her while they danced, until she was breathless and wobbly kneed. But when the lights came up for last call, she'd excused herself to the loo and fled up the stairs into the cool night air. Then, her feet pinching in her impossibly high heels, shivering in her flimsy dress, she'd cursed Dominic Scott all the way up the hill to her bus stop.

There were no messages on her phone—voice or text— nor were there any when she woke late that morning, her head throbbing. She groaned, shielding her eyes from the sun spilling in through her bedroom window. Then she rolled over and lobbed her mobile at the far wall in a fit of pique. Damn Dominic. If he thought she was going to take being treated like this, he was bloody well wrong.

She threw on jeans and hoodie and laced up trainers, then, staggering to the bathroom, splashed cold water on her face and swallowed a couple of paracetamol. For a moment, she contemplated makeup, then decided she didn't care and settled for running a brush through her short hair.

Her parents had gone out to Sunday lunch, saving her having to explain her intentions. She let herself out of the flat and started east on the King's Road. Walking made her feel better, gave her a chance to sort out her thoughts. At Edith Grove she turned towards the river, only absently aware of the Sunday walkers and the pewter glint of sun on the Thames. This way she avoided passing the World's End, the pub where she had met Dom Scott, a junction point between her world and his. It had seemed bridgeable, then, the gap between her parents' council flat and his mum's great house on Cheyne Walk.

Of course, she hadn't met Ellen Miller-Scott. Nor had she known that Dom didn't actually *work,* only put on expensive suits and made the occasional command appearance at his mother's board meetings. *The family business,* referred to with the hushed reverence accorded a religious institution. It was not, she had learned, Dom's father's business, but his grandfather's, Ellen's father's. And although he was expected to take it over, Ellen seemed little inclined to let Dom do anything. It was only lately that Kristin had begun to wonder if Dom was actually capable of holding down a real job.

How hard could it be, investment banking? As far as she could figure, they took people's money, and when it didn't look like things were going to work out, they dumped the poor sods in the shit. Dom could do that in a heartbeat.

Her steps slowed as she neared the end of Cheyne Walk. What exactly would she say to him? That she'd had it? That she should have gone home with the lovely guy from the club last night? That she should go out with Giles, the anorak from work who fancied her like mad? (She tried to ignore the little voice that said she didn't fancy Giles at all, no matter how hard she'd tried.) That Dominic Scott was going to ruin her life, and her career, if she didn't put a stop to it?

Kristin rang the bell at Dominic's house, heard it chime musically. Suddenly she felt queasy and almost turned away, but the door swung open.

It wasn't Dom. Ellen Miller-Scott stared at her, one perfect eyebrow raised quizzically. She wore designer yoga gear in pale gray, and Kristin felt sure the outfit had never seen a particle of sweat. Her blond hair was flawless, her makeup understatedly glowing.

"I want to talk to Dom," Kristin blurted out, sounding to her own ears like a petulant child.

"I'm sorry, darling, he's not here." Ellen smiled. "I rather fancied he was with you. Can I give him a message?"

Kristin felt a painful flush of color rise to the roots of her hair. "I'll ring him. Or I'll tell him when he rings me." Bitch. She could feel the woman laughing at her humiliation, was sure she would have snickered at Kristin's attack of middle-class morals last night. "Thanks," she forced out, turning on her heel.

"You're welcome," Ellen called after her, silvery sweet.

Kristin started back the way she had come, eyes on her

feet, face still burning. It was only when someone knocked into her shoulder, hard, that she looked up and saw Dom coming towards her along Cheyne Walk. Her heart did its usual flip-flop, regardless of her wishes. He hadn't seen her.

She had an instant to take in the too-long hair, unwashed, brushed back from his face, the suit jacket and dress shirt over jeans and trainers, worn with a disregard that spoke not of style but of his having thrown on the first things within reach on the floor. Where the hell *had* he spent the night?

Then he looked up and saw her. "Kristin!" He paled, a hard feat for someone whose skin already looked like putty. Reaching her, he touched her shoulder, then her face, gazing at her with a painful intensity. "What are you doing here? I tried to ring you—"

"You did not." She stepped back. "I checked my messages. You left me stranded at that fucking club—"

"I can explain—"

"No, you can't." The words seemed to come from an unexpected place within her. "There's no excuse, Dom. I deserve better than that."

He stared at her. Passersby parted around them, as if they were the Rock of Gibraltar in a moving sea. "No, you're right," he said slowly, and a fear she couldn't explain shot through her.

Her resolution failed. "Look, I didn't mean—"

"No. You're right. There's no excuse." He was still looking at her with that gobsmacked expression, his gray eyes wide. "No excuse for expecting you to deal with me being fucked up. I'm not worth it." He touched her cheek again, and she shuddered with a sinking dread. "I think maybe we shouldn't see each other for a bit, while I try to straighten things out," he went on. "If there's anything, you know, with the job, Harry can let me know. That's for the best, don't you think, love?" He waited, head slightly bowed, as if expecting absolution.

"You bastard." Planting her feet a little more firmly, Kristin pulled back her arm and smacked him across the face as hard as she could.

\* \* \*

It wasn't until Kincaid had gone up to check on Gemma after her bath that he thought to ask her about Erika.

Gemma lay curled under the duvet, Geordie snuggled beside her. "Sometimes I think this dog is out to replace me," he said, sitting on the bed and fondling one of Geordie's dark gray ears.

"He can't do the washing-up, so I think you're safe," Gemma answered drowsily as he pulled the duvet up around her shoulders a bit more firmly.

"You never told me what Erika wanted last night."

"Oh." Gemma blinked and pulled herself up a little. "She lost a valuable brooch during the war, and it's turned up for auction at Harrowby's. She wants me to look into it."

Frowning, Kincaid said, "How are you going to manage that, with your mum ill? Can't you tell her it's too much?"

"I can't *not* help Erika. I'll manage somehow. I could stop at Harrowby's in the morning, once I've been to check on Mum."

"You can't ask questions officially unless Erika's filed a complaint," he protested.

"I'm sure I'll think of something," Gemma said firmly. "Official or not."

# 5

*. . . auctioneering was for centuries regarded as a rather raffish—even dishonourable—activity.*
    —*Peter Watson*, Sotheby's: Inside Story

GEMMA TOOK THE Central Line straight to St. Paul's tube station, glad that it was Sunday and the crowds were light, and grateful that for once the weekend tube closures hadn't affected her travel. Emerging into the sunlight, she walked west up Newgate Street, worry over her mum running like a treadmill in her head.

That afternoon, she had got on the Internet and looked up types of leukemia, treatments, and prognoses. The prospects had terrified her.

But as she passed an opening leading to St. Paul's Churchyard, she glanced up and stopped, transfixed. A slice of the cathedral appeared in the narrow gap, the great dome dead center, like a jewel in the eye of the needle, glowing in the setting sun.

A man bumped into her and she murmured, "Sorry," but still she hesitated, then on an impulse turned and walked down into the churchyard itself. The weekday City bankers were absent, and she guessed it was mostly tourists who sat on the cathedral steps, faces turned to catch the last of the afternoon warmth. The days were lengthening. It would be summer before she knew it, and for just an instant the passage of time seemed inexorably fast.

A sudden hollow feeling possessed her, and for a moment she considered going in, then chided herself. She hadn't any idea how to pray, and would feel silly trying.

And besides, she thought St. Paul's, glorious as it was, was more a commemoration of Christopher Wren than an offering to God. She turned back, and as she threaded her way towards Newgate Street, she wondered if Wren would have liked the pristine and sterile place his City had become. In his day it would have been teeming with refuse and smells and colors, and the cathedral would have risen out of the muck, a monument to higher things. What awe must have filled people as they looked at it, and what was there now to take its place?

Giving herself a mental shake, she lengthened her stride and left St. Paul's behind. But as she reached the hospital, its ancient walls looked grim as battlements, and she had to steel herself to walk in through the main gate.

The courtyard, with its gentle fountain, came as a relief, and shrill childish voices echoed through the open space— familiar voices, Gemma realized, as she saw a flash of red curls bob up on the far side of the fountain. It was her niece and nephew, playing hide-and-seek, her brother-in-law watching.

Spotting her, the children ran over, wrapping themselves around her legs with welcoming shrieks of "Auntie Gemma!" Gemma knelt to hug them, and in the process little Tiffani somehow managed to transfer chewing gum to Gemma's hair, while, with a shout of glee, Brendan clouted her in the side of the head with a plastic lorry.

"Well," she addressed her brother-in-law, Gerry, as she disentangled herself and tried to pick the pink sticky gobs from her hair, "they're in good form, don't you think, Ger?"

Gerry nodded agreeably from his bench. "Expect so. Can't do a thing with them, myself." He folded his hands over his paunch with an air of satisfaction. Gemma could have sworn he'd put on a stone since she'd seen him at the New Year.

"For heaven's sake, Gerry, there are ill people here," she retorted, giving in to exasperation.

"And your point is?" The look he gave her was not half

so friendly, and left her wondering if he was really as dim as he seemed. It occurred to her that it was quite possible he thought her a self-righteous cow, and went out of his way to let the children misbehave just to irritate her.

The children, the girl just older than Toby and the boy just younger, began to tussle over the lorry, their voices rising towards full-blown conflict. "Cyn's in with Mum?" Gemma asked, resisting the impulse to correct them.

"And your dad."

"Oh, lord," she breathed. "Look, I'll see you."

"Good luck," Gerry called after her, and she couldn't be sure whether his tone was mocking or sympathetic.

She followed the rabbit warren of tunnels that led to the King George V ward with a sinking heart and an incipient sense of panic. The hospital was undergoing renovation, the tunnels makeshift, grim affairs connecting disparate wings, and as one turn led to another, her mouth went dry.

God, she hated hospitals in the best of circumstances, and she'd never thought to find herself visiting a loved one in this old pile. It was, Duncan had informed her, the oldest hospital in London, and when she reached the wing itself she could well believe it. It had been modernized many times over the centuries, of course, but there was an air of age and illness that no amount of refurbishment could quite erase.

Checking the directions to her mother's ward, she took the stairs, not trusting her sudden attack of claustrophobia to the lift. A sister buzzed her into the ward, where she found her father and sister sitting sentinel on either side of her mother's bed. Her mother lay propped up against the pillows, her hair arranged in tight curls and her lips and cheeks rouged an unnaturally bright red—Cyn's doing, no doubt. Her mum was making an obvious effort to seem brisk and cheerful and, when Gemma came in, to play her usual role as mediator.

When she kissed Gemma on the cheek, her lips felt dry as paper. "I'm so glad you've come, love. The boys—did you bring them?"

"No, since they couldn't come in to see you." Gemma resisted the urge to elaborate, realizing that the fact that Cyn's kids were there, even in the courtyard, made her look as if she'd let her mum down. Instead, she asked, "How are you feeling, Mummy?"

"Your dad brought me a filled roll from the bakery," her mother answered, deflecting. "Wasn't that nice? The food here's dreadful, but what can you expect?"

Gemma took in the remains of the roll on the bedside tray, barely nibbled, and felt her own stomach clench with anxiety. Her mother was eating like a bird, and she'd lost more weight than Gemma had realized. "Have the doctors been in? What have they said?"

"Oh, more tests. You know doc—"

"We don't really need to be talking about that, do we now?" her dad cut in, speaking for the first time. "We're here to cheer your mother up."

"Surely Mummy is the one to decide whether she wants to—"

"It's all right, love." Her mother forced a smile. "I'm sure they know what they're doing."

Gemma bit her lip. The last thing her mum needed to hear were the statistics Gemma had read on the shockingly bad quality of hospital care or the chance of secondary infection.

Her sister, who had been remarkably quiet, looked up from examining her long pink nails and gave her a very slight shake of the head. In spite of the fact that she didn't often see Cyn these days, and that they had fought like demons growing up, they shared an ingrained understanding of the family dynamic. That one gesture spoke volumes—things were bad, and their mother meant to keep it from their father, with his full cooperation. Vi Walters had spent her life protecting her husband from upsets, and she wasn't about to let a little thing like illness change matters.

"Right, then." Gemma stood and kissed her mother again, more gently this time. "I'll come in the morning, Mum, see how you're getting on." With her father manning the bakery, she might have a chance of learning the truth.

* * *

Melody Talbot's mobile rang on Monday morning one minute before her alarm was due to ring. Muzzily, she groaned as the horrible buzzing noise went on.

"What?" she mumbled when she managed to get the phone right side up and pressed to her ear.

"Melody? Are you okay?" Gemma's voice.

Melody came fully awake, ignoring the pain that shot through her head as she sat fully upright. "Boss. Yeah. Yeah, I'm all right. What's up?" Her father had called a command performance yesterday at the Kensington town house, as a result of which, Melody, normally a moderate drinker at most, had come home and polished off the better part of a bottle of red wine.

"Could you handle the incoming for me this morning? Just for a bit. I've some personal business. Shouldn't take long."

Frowning, Melody answered, "Okay. No problem. I'll be in as soon as I can." Delegating wasn't one of Gemma's strong points, nor was it like her to skive off work, especially on a Monday morning. Tentatively, Melody said, "Is there anything else I can—"

"No. I'll ring you as soon as I'm on my way back to the station. And thanks."

The mobile went dead. Slowly, Melody disconnected and sat up, throwing back the duvet. Pain shot through her head and she winced. But it was nothing that a cocktail of aspirin and paracetamol and a hot shower wouldn't fix, and it was a minor distraction compared to the warm glow she felt knowing Gemma depended on her.

Kincaid had volunteered to get the children off to school, giving Gemma an early start. It was a duty they rotated, depending on whose workload was most demanding, but as Notting Hill Police Station was a short walk for Gemma, and Toby's infant school just next door, the morning routine fell to Gemma more often than not.

In truth, Kincaid enjoyed the extra hour with Toby and Kit. Although he tried to spend some time on his own with the boys on the weekends, he'd found there was a special closeness about mornings in the kitchen.

He'd made soft-boiled eggs and toast, with juice for Toby and hot milk with a splash of coffee for Kit. It was a house rule that the boys sat at the table, even if only for five minutes, and he wasn't sure if the restriction made them eat at light speed or if they would inhale their food under any circumstances.

This morning, however, Toby had dawdled, picking pieces from his eggshell, then dipping them in the yolk and drawing on the plate. Kincaid suspected he'd picked up on Gemma's worry, even though he'd been told only that Gran wasn't feeling well. "Enough," Kincaid said to him. "Go wash and get your lessons." These morning boys, freshly scrubbed and brushed and in their school uniforms, looked slightly alien to him, like someone else's children. By afternoon their hair would be tousled, their shirttails half out, their ties askew, and they would look comfortably themselves again.

When Toby had slipped from the table and gone pounding up the stairs, Kincaid scooped out the remainder of his egg, mixed it with the toast crusts, and set it on the floor for the dogs.

"Gemma would throw a wobbly," said Kit, taking his cornflakes bowl to the sink.

"I'll bet she does the same thing when I'm not here."

Kit gave him a half smile. "I'm not supposed to tell you." He lingered while Kincaid rinsed his own plate, and when Kincaid looked up he said tentatively, "About Gran. Is she going to be all right?"

The fear of loss always hovered very near the surface for Kit, and although Kincaid would have preferred not to worry him, they'd had to tell him all that they knew.

Kincaid knew he couldn't sugarcoat it. "We'll know more after this morning. But the disease is treatable, and Gran's a fighter." He tried to block out Gemma's description of her mum on yesterday afternoon's visit.

"I've been looking it up," said Kit. "Leukemia. It's cancer of the blood and bone marrow, and it can spread all over the body, even into the brain. She'll need radiation and chemotherapy, and if those don't work—"

"Kit, stop. You're jumping the gun here." Kincaid turned and grasped his son's shoulders. "We don't know how far advanced the cancer is. And Gran's never been ill. That must give her a better chance."

"But if the treatments don't work, the best option for bone marrow replacement is from a sibling, and Gran doesn't have brothers or sisters."

Kincaid saw the unvoiced echo in his son's eyes. *And neither do I.*

Damn and blast the Internet. Sometimes it was a bigger curse than a blessing, especially with a bright and vulnerable child. Did Kit feel they had failed him by not providing him with a half brother or sister? Kincaid tried to shrug off the thought. That was a subject that had been dropped the last few months, and it had eased a tension in his relationship with Gemma.

He heard Toby singing to himself as he thumped back down the stairs, dragging his backpack behind him. To Kit, he said, "Listen, sport, we're all going to be late. We'll talk more tonight." Then, as a distraction, he added, "Did Gemma tell you about Erika's long-lost brooch turning up for auction?"

"Yeah." Kit's expression lightened. "Cool. Except Gemma said she seemed upset. Maybe I could stop by and see her after school?"

*"I think we've got a live one, guv," the desk sergeant at Chelsea Station told Hoxley when he walked into reception.*

*"Live what?" asked Hoxley, amused. Nearing retirement, Ben Watson was bald as a billiard ball, heavyset, and little inclined to stir himself except for the walk from desk to pub, but he kept an avuncular finger on the pulse of everything that went on in the station. He was also inordinately fond of fishing analogies, although Hoxley doubted he'd ever held a fishing rod in his life.*

*"Your unidentified corpus. Notting Hill rang. They've*

*a woman reported her husband missing. Fits the description."*

*Hoxley gave him his full attention. "Address?"*

*"They've kept her at the station. Told them you'd be there soonest."*

*Wincing, Hoxley muttered, "Damn." Delivering bad news was difficult enough in the familiar environment of the home, and he didn't look forward to questioning a bereaved widow in a sterile interview room. But if indeed this was his victim's wife, she would be prepared for the worst, and he would be able to put a name, and a life, to the man he had left on the postmortem table.*

Once more outside St. Paul's tube station, Gemma hesitated. She could go straight on to work, or she could change at Notting Hill for South Kensington and make the inquiry at Harrowby's auction house she'd promised Erika. She felt frustrated and restless, this morning's visit to hospital having proved as fruitless as the previous evening's. Her mum had been out of the ward, having a bone marrow biopsy, the charge nurse had revealed reluctantly, as if imparting state secrets. *And no, she didn't know how long it would take, and there was a good possibility the patient would go to X-ray and sonography as well.*

"The *patient* is my mother," Gemma had snapped. The impersonalization of bureaucracy-speak irritated her just as much in the hospital as it did in the police station. But her little outburst did her no good, and after an hour's wait she gave up the vigil. Cyn would be in later in the morning, and she would have to depend on her sister for news.

Now, however, her patience frayed, she found herself particularly unwilling to sit in her cramped office, dealing with an onslaught of petty complaints from both sides of the police/public divide.

On an impulse, she pulled her mobile from her bag and dialed Melody Talbot. "So what sort of Monday is it?" she asked.

"A fairly placid one." Melody sounded her usual brisk self, and Gemma supposed she'd just been sleepy earlier.

"I've left a few reports for you to look over, and consigned most of the rest to the dustbin."

"Good riddance, I'm sure." Cheered by Melody's voice, Gemma found herself saying, "I'm in the City, but I've got to make a stop in South Ken. Do you want to come along?"

"Business?"

"Um, I'm actually not certain."

"Sounds intriguing," said Melody. "Where should I meet you?"

"Harrowby's. I'll wait for you outside." Gemma rang off, pleased with herself for having piqued Melody's curiosity.

Half an hour later, she found Melody gazing in the windows of the venerable auction house on the Old Brompton Road. While that day Gemma had opted for trousers and a long aubergine cardigan over a soft-collared shirt, Melody wore a tailored navy suit, pressed to the nines, hemmed tastefully at the knee. Gemma thought, not for the first time, that either PC Talbot was aiming for assistant commissioner or she was trying to show up all her female colleagues. Now Gemma wasn't sure if inviting Melody along had been such a good idea.

Melody turned from inspecting an Art Deco pottery display that made Gemma's heart skip. "What's up, boss? Have we been seconded to the Fraud squad?"

Hesitating, Gemma said, "Actually, I'm doing a favor for a friend. Unofficially."

"Ah." Melody ruffled her hair, slipped off her jacket and tossed it over her arm, and unbuttoned another button on her blouse. "Unofficial it is."

Gemma grinned. "Got it in one."

"So what's the story?"

Gemma explained briefly, then added, with an uncertain glance at the window, "Have you ever been to an auction?"

"Once or twice. Just curiosity," Melody added quickly. "It's not as intimidating as it looks. They want you to feel comfortable."

"Right." Gemma led the way into the foyer. Opposite a friendly looking gray-haired woman at a reception desk, a long table held copies of catalogs for all upcoming sales.

The Art Deco jewelry was easy enough to spot: brilliant red, green, and blue gems in a geometric-patterned bracelet blazed from the cover. Finding the entry for the brooch that she'd seen at Erika's, Gemma reread the text. It was as she remembered—there was no provenance.

Holding her place, she took the book to the desk. "I'm inquiring for a friend," she explained, tapping the picture of the waterfall brooch with her fingertip, "who thinks this brooch belonged to her family. It was lost during the war."

For the first time, the woman looked uneasy. "Mr. Khan's our jewelry expert, but he's out doing a valuation—"

Gemma wasn't going to be put off so easily. "Is there someone else?"

"Well, there's Miss Cahill, but—" She flicked a glance at Melody, and Gemma guessed she took her for a lawyer.

"I'm sure Miss Cahill will be able to help." Gemma smiled brightly.

The woman hesitated. Then, frowning, she used an internal phone. "Kristin, could you come to the front, please?"

Gemma took advantage of the wait to inspect her surroundings. The reception area led into a much larger room. Modern paintings tagged with lot numbers lined the walls. A dozen people sat in the comfortably padded chairs filling the room's center, some occasionally languidly raising numbered paddles. The auctioneer stood on a podium, above which appeared the featured item on a large-screen television. His delivery was as relaxed as the bids, and Gemma thought it all rather disappointingly low key. She wondered where the jewelry was.

"No big items in this lot," whispered Melody. A snore escaped from a large lady in the back row.

"So I was gathering."

A side door opened and a young woman came towards the front desk, her expression anxious. She was waif slender, with short dark hair shaped to her head, and wore a crisp white blouse and narrow dark skirt as if they'd just come off the catwalk. "Mrs. March?" she said, glancing from the receptionist to Gemma and Melody.

"These ladies have some questions regarding an item in

the jewelry catalog. I told them Mr. Khan was out." Mrs. March, as Gemma supposed, made her disapproval clear, and turned back to sorting brochures.

The young woman looked round as if expecting rescue, glanced at the auction in progress, then motioned them towards the door through which she had come. "I'm Kristin Cahill," she said over her shoulder. "I'm not sure I can help you, but you'd better come into the office." She looked as though she couldn't be long out of university.

"We won't take much of your time," said Gemma, hoping to put her at ease.

Kristin Cahill led them through another display room, where furniture was being arranged and labeled by a crew in jeans and trainers, then into a small office. Paper, brochures, and catalogs spilled off two inelegant desks. Kristin shrugged at the absence of seating. "Mr. Khan usually talks to clients in the showroom—"

"We're not clients. Look, it's just this." Gemma held up the catalog, page folded back. "I have a friend. Jakob Goldshtein, who made this piece, was her father. Her name is Erika Rosenthal. She says it was lost during her escape from Germany before the war, and she had no idea of its whereabouts until she saw your catalog. There's no provenance listed. Can you tell us where—"

Kristin was already shaking her head. "Oh, no. Mr. Khan said provenance wasn't required. The piece is stamped with Jakob Goldshtein's mark, and his work has become quite collectible in the last twenty years—"

"But surely you must have provenance," interrupted Gemma, although out of the corner of her eye she saw Melody give a slight shake of her head.

"It's never that simple," said Kristin. "With antiquities, we never have complete provenance, and even with more recent pieces we seldom have a complete record."

"But perhaps the seller—"

"We can't divulge the seller's details. Look, I took that brooch in myself, but Mr. Khan would kill me—"

The office door swung open. A tall, slender man in an impeccably bespoke suit came in, quirking his eyebrow at

Kristin. "And what have you done to deserve that, Miss Cahill?"

Kristin looked down at the nearest desk and shuffled some papers. "Nothing, Mr. Khan. These ladies had some questions about the Goldshtein brooch, but I was just saying—"

"A lovely piece, isn't it? The curved lines are unusual for Art Deco, but Goldshtein did move in that direction towards the end of his career. All I can tell you is that the seller was very fortunate to have come across such a find. It does happen, you know. Cash in the attic." He gave a sardonic smile.

Melody spoke for the first time. "Mr. Khan, I take it?"

He held out a perfectly manicured hand with the long fingers of a pianist. "Amir Khan. May I—"

"Gemma James." Gemma handed him a card. "Inspector. Metropolitan Police. And this is PC Talbot. But this is a personal matter, Mr. Khan, for the moment."

Khan looked unfazed. "How very interesting, Inspector"—he glanced at her card—"James. But—"

"What if the piece was looted?" broke in Melody.

Khan's lips turned down in an expression of distaste. Gemma thought she saw a flicker in his dark eyes—was it alarm? But he sounded as unperturbed as ever when he spoke. "Now *that* happens much less than the media would have you believe. But if that was the case, I'd suggest that your friend get a solicitor."

# 6

❦

*1935*
*Bad Saarow, April 21 (Easter)*

> *The hotel is mainly filled with Jews and we are a little surprised to see so many of them still prospering and apparently unafraid. I think they are unduly optimistic.*
> —*William L. Shirer,* Berlin Diary: The Journal of a Foreign Correspondent, 1934–1941

**THE FLOWERS CAME JUST** after the two police officers left, two dozen perfect pink roses, left at the front desk by a courier. Mrs. March carried them back to the office, saying, "Oh, Kristin, aren't they lovely?"

Mr. Khan raised one arched brow but made no comment. Giles, who had come in with some paperwork, flushed a blotchy red and retreated, head tucked in like a tortoise. Kristin would have fallen through the floor if she could.

But Mrs. March oohed and aahed and fussed over the card until Kristin was forced to slip it from its envelope. "Anonymous admirer," Kristin said, knowing it was likely to make poor Giles suspect but not about to tell the truth. The signature read simply "D," but that was enough.

As soon as the door closed behind Mrs. March, Khan turned to her, all the civilized veneer stripped from his handsome face.

"You may have an admirer, Miss Cahill," he said, his voice level and articulate, and all the more venomous for it. "But I promise you it isn't me. If I find you've done anything to jeopardize the reputation of this salesroom, I'll personally see you out the door. You'd better watch—"

Giles had interrupted then, looking even more miserable than before, to tell Khan that a prospective seller wished to see him.

"Why does he hate you so much?" whispered Giles when Khan had stepped into the display room.

"God, I wish I knew." Kristin's legs were shaking and it was all she could do not to cry. It had been Khan who'd assessed the piece, after all. She hadn't done anything wrong—or at least nothing that a thousand other salesroom clerks hadn't done before her. But she knew now that she would be the one to catch it if any impropriety came to light.

Her mobile began to vibrate and she knew who it was without looking. She gave Giles a pointed glance, then waited until he'd left to answer.

"I told you not to call me at work," she hissed into the phone, wondering if he'd been watching from the street, timing his call to the flower delivery.

"No one will know who it—"

"I don't care. *He* doesn't like me talking on my mobile, and I'm in enough trouble already. And I told you I didn't want—"

"Look, love." He dropped his voice, Dom at his most persuasive, and she fought the warmth that began to spread through her. "I didn't mean what I said yesterday," he went on. "I was a little—I'd had a bad night, you know? But I've been thinking—" *Bad night, bollocks.* Strung out was more like it, and now he sounded too hyped.

She could see Khan through the half-open door, talking to a client, a chubby, balding man in an expensive-looking jacket. "Don't think, Dom," she whispered, hanging on to the anger. "It's not your strong suit. And don't send me bloody flowers."

"Kris, please. I was screwed up. Meet me tonight. We need to talk. Something's happened—"

"You'd better believe something's happened. The freaking cops were here."

"What?"

Khan had looked her way. "You heard me," she whispered, moving farther from the door. "They wanted to know about the brooch—"

"You didn't mention me?"

"Of course I didn't mention you. What sort of idiot do you take me for?"

"I'm sorry, Kris. I'm sorry. Look, you have to meet me. We have to talk." Dom's voice was urgent. "The Gate. After ten. Please."

"No," Kristin repeated, but the phone went dead in her ear. She was staring at it, biting her lip, when it gave the soft bleep that meant she had a text message. After another furtive glance into the gallery, she opened the message and read the words as they scrolled down the screen.

*You said you hated red.*

*"Is she . . . upset?" Gavin asked the officer who met him at the Notting Hill nick. He'd always liked this station, with its graceful lines and leafy surroundings. Like Lucan Place, it had survived the war intact. But God, he hated dealing with grieving widows. Sometimes it made him wonder if he was cut out for the job.*

*"No, not exactly," the constable replied, looking back as he led Gavin towards the interview rooms. "I wouldn't describe her as upset. I've put her in the best room. She's not the sort belongs in the—well, never mind. You'd best see for yourself." He shrugged and left Gavin at an unmarked door.*

*Squaring his shoulders, Gavin entered the room.*

*She was young, much younger than he'd imagined, given the age of the victim, and instantly he wondered if the possible identification was a mistake.*

*Glancing down at the few notes he'd made, he said, "Mrs. Rosenthal? I'm Gavin Hoxley, from Chelsea Police Station." He'd deliberately not looked at the written report,*

*wanting to evaluate this woman's story without any precon-
ceptions.*

*She sat on the opposite side of the scarred table, but had
pushed her chair back so that she could clasp her hands in
her lap. Her clothes were simple—a pale blue shirtwaist
dress, probably reworked from an earlier style, and a white
cardigan. But the wide belt emphasized her slender waist,
and the dress's color set off her fine, pale skin. Her dark
hair was cut short and waved loosely, as if she hadn't bothered much with styling, but the effect was the more appealing for its casualness.*

*"Yes, I'm Erika Rosenthal," she said in faintly accented
English, and looked up into his eyes. "What can you tell me
about my husband?"*

It had seemed like a good idea that morning, asking if he
could visit Erika, but as Kit walked slowly up Ladbroke
Grove after school, he began to have reservations. He'd
never been to Erika's house on his own, nor without an invitation, and Erika didn't seem the sort of person you just
dropped in on.

But he was curious about the missing brooch, and he
didn't want to go home and think about Gran. Adjusting
his backpack, he picked up his pace, and soon turned into
Arundel Gardens. He was glad Erika lived on the north side,
where the houses were stuccoed and painted in colors—the
plain, cream brick houses on the south side of the street never
seemed as inviting. Sometimes he imagined that the more
exotic houses in Lansdowne Road, with their bright colors
and almost Moroccan feel, had bled a bit into the north side
of Arundel Gardens, like paint running.

The afternoon was warm, and by the time he reached
Erika's door he was sweating, the wool of his school blazer
scratching his shoulders beneath the straps of his bag. Slipping off the heavy pack, he let it sag from one hand as he
rang the bell. He always brought home more books than he
needed, but somehow he didn't like to leave things behind.

The buzzer echoed inside the otherwise quiet flat, but

there was no reply on the intercom. Kit shuffled his feet and swung his pack, suddenly aware of the distant sound of a dog barking, and nearer by, a car door slamming and the wail of a child. The spring pansies in Erika's basement window box were looking faded and leggy, and the small yard was unswept.

He'd almost made up his mind to go when the door swung open. Erika looked out expectantly, and Kit could have sworn he saw a flicker of disappointment before she smiled and said, "Kit! What a nice surprise."

"You shouldn't answer the door without checking to see who it is, you know." The words came out involuntarily and he flushed, hearing the rudeness.

But Erika merely nodded. "You're right, of course. It's just that I was expecting—I thought it might be Gemma. Do come in. I'll make you something cold to drink."

As Kit followed her into the flat, he realized for the first time that he was looking down at her. He suddenly felt large and gawky, and deliberately pulled in his elbows, afraid he might knock a book or an ornament off the hall shelves.

In the sitting room, there were books and newspapers scattered about, and three empty cups on the table beside Erika's chair. Having been taught early on by his mum to pick up, Kit stacked the cups and saucers and carried them into the kitchen. "I could help with the washing-up," he offered when he saw the worktop and the tiny sink.

"Oh." Erika stood still, as if she'd lost her bearings. "I can't seem to settle to anything." She frowned. "But I'm certain I have ginger beer in the fridge, and some ice cubes in the freezer. The glasses—"

"I'll get the glasses." Kit knew where they were kept. When Erika didn't protest, he very quickly put the drinks together, even adding a sprig of mint from a pot on the kitchen table. The window overlooking the garden was open and the soft, warm air blew in like a caress. Thinking of the unexpected disorder of Erika's sitting room, he said, "Can we sit outside?"

"Oh, of course." She wore a heavy blue cardigan, the buttons misaligned, and hugged it to herself as if she were cold.

Kit led the way through the French doors onto the small terrace that overlooked the communal garden. Pulling out one of the white wrought-iron chairs so that it faced the sun, he said, "Sit here. It will warm you."

Erika complied, then looked up at him with a glimmer of a smile. "You're quite bossy, you know."

"That's what my mum used to say," answered Kit, taking the chair opposite.

"You never talk about your mum."

"No," he said, and found to his surprise that he could. "She quite liked it. Me managing her. She used to call me *bossy-boots*."

"I can see why." Erika cradled her drink, then sipped. "I like the mint."

"My mum grew it in the garden. We always put it in our summer drinks." He pushed away the thought of long summer evenings in the Cambridgeshire garden that ran down to the river. "Was your father really a jeweler?"

"Oh, a jeweler, yes, but so much more. He was an artist. And a bit of a magpie." Erika gave a surprisingly throaty laugh. "He loved bright things." Sobering, she added slowly, "I sometimes think it was a good thing he didn't survive the first years of the war. He would have hated what Berlin became, what Germany became in those years. He liked his creature comforts, my father."

"He—" Kit hesitated, not sure how to go on.

"Oh, he died in a camp. In 1942, as far as I was able to learn."

"And there wasn't anyone else?"

When she shook her head, wisps of white hair came loose from her smooth knot and danced round her face. "No. Just the two of us. My mother had died when I was younger."

Kit nodded and they sat quietly, sipping their drinks, shared knowledge lying easily between them.

After a bit, Kit said, "What was it like, Berlin before the war?"

Erika smiled. "I always think of flowers. Our garden was full of flowers in summer. Red and pink geraniums, petunias, roses. My father was a very social man, and entertaining was good for his business. Summer seemed one long round of garden parties, shimmering dresses, laughter, the scent of cigarette smoke on the night air. But—" She gave a small sigh, then added more briskly, "But I was a child. And I'm sure if I had been older, I would have realized that even then it mattered that we were Jewish.

"My father was tolerated because he made beautiful things for the wealthy, and even after Hitler came to power in 1933, the elite were reluctant to give up their luxuries. And my father was an optimist. He always wanted to believe the best of people."

"But how could he? When such terrible things were happening?" asked Kit.

Erika gazed out into the communal garden, her eyes focused on a young woman playing with her child. "After Kristallnacht not even my father and David could ignore the danger, although in David's case, it had been stubbornness, not optimism, that kept us in Berlin."

Crystal Night. Kit had read about it in school, first with interest, because the name had intrigued him, then with growing horror as he realized what it meant. But somehow he had failed to connect Erika with that terrible tale of violence and destruction.

"The Night of the Broken Glass," Erika said softly. "November tenth, 1938. The windows of thousands of Jewish shops and homes throughout Germany and Austria were smashed, Jews were beaten and killed, and over thirty thousand Jewish men were taken to concentration camps. It was called, literally, crystal-glass night, because most shopkeepers' windows were made of more expensive crystal, rather than ordinary glass.

"It's considered politically incorrect to use that term now in Germany—it's felt it romanticizes what happened." She shook her head. "But for those who lived through it, we never forgot the sound of hammers smashing crystal. To this day I can't bear to break a glass." Pulling her cardigan a little closer, she sipped her drink. The few ice cubes had melted, diluting the liquid to a gold as pale as the afternoon sunlight. "But that's enough of such talk for this beautiful day. We should—"

"No," broke in Kit. "I want to hear. What happened after that? Did they break into your father's shop? Who was David? Why didn't he want to leave?"

Erika gazed at her drink, turning the glass in her fingers, and for a moment Kit thought she wouldn't answer. Then she glanced up at him, her dark eyes crinkled with affection. "That's a hard task you've set me. Are you sure you want to be a biologist and not a journalist?"

"Don't prevaricate," said Kit, trying out a new word. The last time he'd come for tea with Gemma, Erika had challenged him to learn a new word every day, and to teach Toby a simpler one. He hadn't done so well with Toby, but was rather proud of his own progress.

"You've been swotting."

The slang sounded funny coming from Erika, who usually spoke quite formal English. "All right," she said after a moment. "Yes. My father's shop was smashed. But he had heard rumors a few hours before and had managed to hide the most valuable pieces in our house. Because we lived in one of the more elegant parts of town, our home was spared, although we hid for hours in the cellar with the maids. I didn't know where David was and I was more terrified for him than for myself." At Kit's questioning look, she added, "David was my husband. He had been my teacher at university. The Nazis had forbidden the universities to hire Jews as lecturers, so David worked as a private tutor. Most of his students were children of the wealthy whose parents could afford to give them an extra edge, and some of them rose in the Nazi elite. It made David feel he had failed. Failed them, failed himself."

The sun had moved and Erika's face was now in shadow. When she didn't go on, Kit said uncertainly, "What did he teach?"

This time Erika's smile held no humor. "Philosophy. He believed in a rational, peaceful state."

Kit suddenly felt as if he'd got in over his head, but didn't know how to backpedal gracefully. Instead, he plunged ahead. "But you got out, didn't you? You and your husband. Why did you leave your father behind?"

As soon as the words left his lips, he'd have given anything to call them back.

*Finding he didn't want to loom over this woman, Gavin pulled out a chair, and the legs scraping across the lino seemed unnaturally loud.*

*"Mrs. Rosenthal, first I need you to tell me about your husband."*

*"But I've already—"*

*"Please."*

*"But I—" Her protest subsided, but he thought she clasped her hands a little more tightly. Her nails were short and neat, her only jewelry a simple gold band.*

*"My husband," she said on an exhaled breath, as if marshaling patience, "is named David Rosenthal. He is a lecturer at a small college in North Hampstead, a school for Jewish boys. On Saturdays it is his habit to write in the Reading Room at the British Museum."*

*"On the Sabbath?" asked Gavin.*

*The glance she gave him was sharp. "My husband is not an observant Jew, Mr. Hoxley."*

*"All right." He nodded. "Go on."*

*"When he didn't come home for his supper, I thought perhaps he had gone to a meeting, and that he had forgotten to tell me. But he never came home. Not that night. Not yesterday. And this morning he did not show up for work at his college. They rang me at my work, and I came here."*

*It could still be a case of a wandering husband, Gavin told himself, although he couldn't imagine a man straying from this woman. "Can you describe your husband for me?"*

*She closed her eyes, as if building a picture in her mind. "David . . . is . . . a good deal older than I. Forty-eight last January. He is slender—too thin—and not as tall as you, Mr. Hoxley. He has blue eyes and dark hair that is becoming gray. Salt and pepper, I think is the English term."*

*Gavin felt a twist in his gut, half excitement, half dread. There was no avoiding it now.* "Mrs. Rosenthal, did your husband wear any jewelry?"

*Her eyes flew open.* "Jewelry? A trinket only, a gift from one of his students. A little Jewish symbol on a chain, a mezuzah."

*She must have seen the truth in his face, because she went quite still, so still he thought for a moment she had ceased to breathe, and that stillness was more devastating than all the tears he had witnessed in his years on the force.*

*Then she took a breath, like a drowning swimmer coming up for air, and said, very clearly,* "Mr. Hoxley. I know my husband is dead. Did he—did he . . . harm himself?"

The afternoon dragged. Gemma's office grew stuffy from the heat, and opening the window brought only a current of warm air mixed with exhaust fumes. The mountain of paperwork on her desk seemed unshrinking, and she slogged through it with increasing irritation.

When Melody popped her head in to say she was going home, Gemma snapped, "Fine," then called her back.

"Sorry," she said. "Headache."

Melody, still looking as fresh and crisp as she had that morning, leaned against the doorjamb. "You're not looking forward to talking to your friend."

"No." Gemma sighed. "And I—" On the verge of telling Melody about her mum, she hesitated. She knew no more than she had that morning. Having traded text messages with Cyn, all she'd learned was that the consultants were still waiting on test results. Shaking her head, she finished lamely, "I'll have to do it in person. I suppose there's no point postponing."

Melody studied her, tilting her head in a gesture Gemma had learned meant she was assessing the truthfulness of a statement. But she merely said, "Call it a day, boss. Policy implementations can wait." Grinning, she added, "Forever, as far as I'm concerned."

"Right. See you tomorrow, then," answered Gemma, cheered.

When Melody had gone, she pushed her unfinished papers into a stack and smacked her pen on top for emphasis, then rang home. No answer.

Kincaid had told her that Kit wanted to go to Erika's after school, but surely he should be home by now. She didn't like it when Kit was out of touch—she supposed that eventually they were going to have to give in and get him a mobile, although she dreaded the thought of a teenager permanently wired to the world by his thumbs.

Except that Kit hadn't asked for a phone, and that made her wonder if he had enough friends. Since Christmas he had been getting on better, at least with his studies, but he still seemed to spend most of his time at home on his own or with Wesley.

Wesley—there was a thought. She rang Wesley, asking if he could pick Toby up from his after-school care. That would leave her free to go straight to Erika's, and possibly track down Kit in the process.

It was cooler outside than in, and the brisk walk down Ladbroke Grove cleared her aching head. The fruit trees were in bloom, and a rainbow of late tulips brightened front gardens and window boxes. It seemed to her that this time of year London was bursting at its seams, life pushing through the cracked cocoon of winter, and her spirits always lifted along with the city's pulse.

The wind had picked up by the time she reached Erika's house in Arundel Gardens, cooling the back of her neck where it had gone damp from the heat, swirling bits of debris about her ankles.

She rang the bell, and after a long wait, it was Kit rather than Erika who opened the door.

"Hi," he said, looking unusually pleased to see her, and her desire to scold him over not checking in vanished. "We were in the garden. I thought I heard the bell. I'll make you something to drink if you want to go out."

There was more to his offer than manners. "Is everything all right?" Gemma asked, touching his shoulder briefly as they walked towards the kitchen.

"Yes. But she's waiting for you."

Taking the hint, she left him and went out through the French doors into the garden. Erika rose, a little slowly, from her seat at the garden table and came to meet her.

"I thought it must be you," she said, her expression anxious. "Did you find out—"

But Gemma was already shaking her head. "I'm sorry, no. They won't release any information about the seller. Their jewelry expert believes the piece is authentic, and they're not required to give provenance. The expert is a man named Amir Khan." Gemma pulled out a chair for herself as Erika sank back into hers. Kit had come out and set down a drink for her, then stepped back, listening quietly. "The girl who took the piece in—Kristin—might have told me more, but Khan came in and shut her up."

"Is there any point in you going back, having another word with her on her own?" asked Erika.

Gemma shook her head. "I don't think so. She'll have been well warned. He—Mr. Khan—said that you'd have to get a lawyer. And that if it were a matter of proving that an item was looted by the Nazis, the case could drag on forever. I'm afraid he's right," she added gently. "You may have to let it—"

"Oh, no," broke in Erika, and the fire was back in her eyes. "I've let it go long enough. And it wasn't the Nazis who stole the brooch from me."

Kristin fidgeted through dinner, earning a concerned glance from her mother and an irritated "Will you sit still, for heaven's sake?" from her dad.

When she did little more than push her food round her plate, her mum shook her head. "Kristin, you need to eat."

"I had lunch out." It was an easy lie, so she embroidered. "With some mates from work. At Carluccio's." Right, she thought. Who exactly would she have gone to Carluccio's with, even if she could afford it? Giles?

Before her mother's look of interest turned into questions about what she'd eaten, she said, "And I'm going out tonight.

Just for a bit." She glared at her dad, daring him to criticize. That was one of the worst things about being forced to live at home—her parents still treated her like a teenager, even though she was more than a year out of university.

She'd never introduced them to Dom, nor told them anything about him. She could just imagine what her dad, a supervisor at Abbey Mills Pumping Station who had worked hard to put his only daughter through university, would have to say about a man who lived on inherited money. That was grief she didn't need.

Her mobile rang. When she saw that it was Giles, she quickly pressed Ignore. Her father looked up from his pork chop, frowning. "I've told you not to bring that thing to the table."

But before Kristin could defend herself, the home phone rang. Her mum was closest and answered it, receiving a second scowl from her dad. "I thought we'd agreed. No phone calls during—"

"It's your friend Giles, darling," her mother interrupted, smiling as she handed Kristin the phone.

"Bugger," Kristin muttered under her breath. Giles was already waffling on in her ear. ". . . wasn't fair what Khan did to you today. Don't know what gets into him, but I'm sure you didn't deserve it."

"Thanks, Giles. That's nice of you." She tried to keep the sarcasm out of her voice. "But I have to—"

"Thought you might want to go out for a coffee, talk about it. Or—or you could come to the flat. We could listen to—"

"Thanks, but I can't, really." There was no way she was going to his flat. The thought of being alone with Giles was bad enough—although she couldn't imagine he'd get up the nerve to make a move—but she certainly wasn't spending the evening with that dog he was always going on about. She knew what effort it must have taken him to invite her, however, and tried to be kind. Excusing herself, she left the dining room and retreated to her bedroom. "I'm going out already, Giles," she said when she was out of her parents' hearing. "Meeting someone at the Gate, in Notting Hill."

"You're meeting *him,* aren't you? The bloke who sent you the roses."

"You're starting to sound like my father, Giles," she said, all inclination to be gentle vanishing. "And besides, it's none of your business. Look, I'll see you at work tomorrow." She started to hang up, then put the phone back to her ear. "And by the way, don't call me at home—

"—And sod you," she added, tossing the phone on the bed. Now she had to get out quickly, before her mum started asking questions about her *friend.* Leaving her work clothes in a heap on the floor, she changed into jeans and a slightly tatty rose-colored cardigan. This was one night she didn't intend to tart herself up for Dominic Scott. Nor did she intend to wait if he wasn't there.

She'd told herself a hundred times that she was only going to finish what she'd tried to say that afternoon, but there was a small, traitorous part of her that knew it wasn't true— a part that imagined the roses were real, that she would see him and he would look into her eyes and everything would be all right.

Serve her bloody well right if he didn't turn up, she thought as she walked up the road towards Earl's Court tube station, head down against the wind.

When she emerged at Notting Hill Gate a few minutes later, it was well past ten, but the streets were still busy with late shoppers and patrons coming and going from the restaurants and pubs. Waiting to cross at the light, she saw the woman beside her start to step out into the path of a 52 bus barreling round the corner into Pembridge Road. Kristin grabbed the shoulder of her jacket and yanked her back, feeling the draft rock her as the bus passed.

"Christ!" she said, loosing her hold, her heart pounding. "Can't you watch where you're going?"

"Sorry," the woman mumbled, without looking at her, and when the light changed she walked on, head still down.

*Some people,* Kristin thought, shaking her head, but then she was crossing Notting Hill Gate, and the door to one side of the Gate Cinema yawned before her.

There was no bouncer, as Monday was a light crowd, but

it was only as she started down the stairs into the club that she remembered it was salsa night. The driving beat of Latin music rose up to meet her, and as she reached the basement she saw that instead of the usual milling bodies, couples were dancing in sync, touching. Her heart sank. That temptation was a complication she didn't need, and she wondered if Dom had remembered and had chosen the club because of it.

She pushed her way through the knot of people blocking the bottom of the stairs, into the purple-blue glow of the light from the bar. One of the bartenders, a pretty blond girl, waved at her, but she shook her head and kept looking.

Then she saw him, sitting alone, in the corner farthest from the bar and the dance floor. He'd washed his hair and dressed with obvious care, and she wondered if the pallor of his face was simply a reflection of the lights from the bar.

When he saw her, he smiled and stood, beckoning her over, and when she reached him he kissed her, brushing his lips against her cheek.

Kristin shivered and pulled away. "I came to talk, Dom." She sat on the banquette, putting a good foot of space between them.

"Let me get you a drink."

"No, I don't want—"

But the barmaid came by and Dom signaled her, ordering her a mojito. He was drinking, Kristin saw, neat whisky, never a good sign.

"You look gorgeous." He ran a hand down her arm.

"You think?" she retorted. "You should have seen me on Saturday."

"Look, love, things just got a bit out of control. I—"

"They're only as out of control as you want them to be, Dom, and I'm—"

The barmaid brought her drink and Kristin took it, giving the girl an absent smile. She took a drink, tasting mint and lime and feeling the kick of the rum as it went down. *Dutch courage.* She needed Dutch courage.

"Drink up," Dom said quietly, and she saw then that in

spite of the whisky he was sober, and there was no affection in his gray eyes. "And tell me about the cops."

Kristin swallowed. The fear she'd damped down since that morning came back in a rush. "She said it was personal, the inspector, that she was doing a favor for a friend, a woman named Erika Rosenthal. She said the brooch had belonged to her friend and it was lost during the war. She wanted to know who was selling it."

"You're sure you didn't tell her?" Dom's voice rose.

"No. Of course not," she said, thinking how perilously close she had come to spilling everything. There had been something sympathetic about the inspector, with her open face and coppery hair. "And Khan read them the lawyer act. But I don't—"

"You have to take it out of the sale." Dom was sweating now, the calm of a moment before gone, and when he raised his glass, his hand shook.

"Take it out of the sale?" Kristin stared at him. "Are you mad? You know I can't take it out of the sale. Only Harry can do that."

"Harry's convinced himself his twenty percent will keep the wolves from the door. He—"

"Twenty percent?" Kristin's voice shot up. "You offered Harry twenty percent, against me risking the wrath of Khan for my four percent bringing-in fee?"

"I'd have made it up to you, Kris. But now—"

"Now, nothing. You and Harry work it out between you." She set down her glass, miraculously empty. "As far as I'm concerned, I don't know you—or Harry—from Adam, and I took in that brooch in good faith. And if it sells, you can keep my bloody four percent."

She stood, the room spinning as the alcohol hit her system. The rhythm of the samba playing on the DJ's turntable seemed almost tangible in the air. Steadying herself with a hand on the back of the banquette, she leaned over and kissed Dom, very lightly, on the cheek. " 'Bye, Dom. Have a nice life."

When she reached the street, she looked back, but he

hadn't followed, and she didn't know if she felt relief or despair.

Quickly, she walked round the corner into Kensington Church Street and started south, and when a 49 bus came along she got on. It would take her through South Ken, and she had a sudden desire to see the familiar museums and to pass by the showroom. It was, she told herself, all she had left.

But when the bus trundled past the Old Brompton Road, she stayed on, resisting the impulse to stop and look in the showroom windows. After all, if Khan found out she'd known there was something dodgy about that brooch, he would fire her in a heartbeat, and then there would be nothing at all.

It was only as the bus neared the King's Road that she realized Dom had changed his mind about the sale even before she'd told him about the cops. She got off, still thinking, walking slowly towards World's End. The road was empty, the pub dark—somehow it had got to be past closing time.

She waited to cross at the light, pulling her cardigan up around her throat, wondering just what she would say to Khan if Harry Pevensey *did* pull the brooch from the sale. Khan would hold her responsible, and there would be hell to pay. She felt suddenly exhausted and a bit dizzy, as if the alcohol had taken an unexpected toll on her empty stomach.

The light changed. As Kristin stepped off the curb, she heard the high-pitched squeal of tires on tarmac. Turning towards the sound, she saw a blur of motion, oncoming, and had the odd impression of lights reflecting off a smooth expanse of metal.

Her brain sent flight signals to her body, too late. And at the moment of impact, she felt nothing at all.

# 7

*1940*
*Aboard the Excambian, December 13, midnight*

> *It had been a long time, but they had been happy
> years, personally, and for all people in Europe they
> had had meaning and borne hope until the war
> came and the Nazi blight and the hatred and the
> fraud and the political gangsterism and the murder
> and the massacre and the incredible intolerance
> and all the suffering and the starving and cold and
> the thud of a bomb blowing the people in a house
> to pieces, the thud of all the bombs blasting man's
> hope and decency.*
> —*William L. Shirer,* Berlin Diary: The Journal
> of a Foreign Correspondent, 1934–1941

KIT LAY AWAKE, watching the numerals on his bedside
clock change. One minute before his alarm was set to go off,
he reached out and tapped the button. Tess was lying on the
floor by the door, gazing at him balefully. He'd tossed and
turned so much during the night that he'd pushed her off the
bed, and her feelings were hurt.

"Here, girl." He patted the bed. She stood, giving her
customary wiggly stretch, then padded over to the bed and
leapt up, but without much enthusiasm. It appeared he was
not quite forgiven. He rolled over, lifting her wiry little body

onto his chest, and she obliged by licking him on the chin. "There, that's better," he said, and scratched her behind the ears.

Even though he hadn't slept well, he was reluctant to get up. He'd gone to bed angry, and not even listening to "London Calling" over and over on his earphones had made him feel better.

He hated it when grown-ups treated him like a child, and his dad and Gemma had brushed him off when he'd asked them how serious Gemma's mum's diagnosis was.

Of course, Vi wasn't his real grandmother, but he found that didn't matter. She had always been kind to him, had fed him and brusquely jollied him and welcomed him into her family when he'd felt the most lost and alone.

And then there was Gemma. It wasn't so bad for Toby, he was too young to mind much, but Gemma . . . He wished he knew what to say to her. He felt stupid and tongue-tied and frozen. What did you say to someone whose mum might die?

It had been the same with Erika, yesterday. He hadn't known what to say when she had told him about leaving Germany, about her father dying in the camps. When he got home he had looked up the camp where Jewish men from Berlin had been sent—Sachsenhausen—and wished he hadn't. But still, curiosity nagged at him like an itch, and he wished he'd heard the rest of Erika's story. What had she meant when she'd said the Nazis hadn't stolen her brooch? She'd changed the subject after that, refusing to say more, and Gemma hadn't pushed her.

"Kit! Rise and shine!" His dad's voice came from the second floor. Kit imagined him standing at the top of the stairs, buttoning his shirt, fresh from the shower and smelling of soap, his hair still damp and combed with a neatness that would last only until it was dry.

Gemma would be down soon, helping Toby dress—or at least arguing with him over his choices—and then there would be breakfast, and a kitchen full of chatter and barking dogs. Suddenly the day seemed a good deal brighter.

Dumping Tess unceremoniously onto the floor, Kit threw back the covers. "I'm up," he shouted back.

* * *

When Gemma came into the kitchen, Kincaid already had coffee on and was putting out cereal boxes for the boys. But when he held out a mug, she shook her head.

"No time. Toby was determined to wear his Spider-Man T-shirt with holes in it rather than his uniform this morning. And I want to get in early, see what's up, then dash to hosp—"

Kincaid was shaking his head.

"What?" asked Gemma, stopping a quick grab for juice.

"You can't keep on delegating to Melody and ducking out of the job. You're going to have to tell your super and Melody about your mum, request some time—"

"But I don't want—I don't like to—" She ran a hand through her shorter hair and the bareness of her neck made her feel vulnerable. She still missed the weight of her long plait on her back. "I don't like airing my personal business at work. In five minutes it will be all over the station and everyone will be giving me sympathetic looks."

"Would you rather they thought you were slipping out for trysts with the milkman?"

Gemma couldn't help smiling. "*Trysts?* Who on earth says *trysts*? And no, I don't suppose I want anyone thinking I'm having them—whatever they are—with the milkman." She sighed. "I'll have a word with Mark first thing. And then Melody."

He came round the table and pulled her into a hug, and she let herself relax against him, taking momentary comfort from the warm solidity of his body. "A wise choice," he whispered in her ear. "And besides, I'm better than the milkman."

"And how do you know that?" she whispered back.

*He'd put her off, telling her he wanted her to make a positive identification of the body before he discussed details. But instead of sending Erika Rosenthal to the mortuary with a WPC, as would have been his usual custom, Gavin ordered a car and took her himself. If anyone had questioned his* reasoning, he would have said it was because he thought he might learn more, and that he wanted no delay in confirming the identity of his victim, and both rationalizations were, in part, true.

But the core of it was that he felt protective, that he didn't want her to face the body on the mortuary slab alone. And then there were the barely admitted thoughts—that he could sit next to her in the back of the car, that her arm might touch his, that the day was warm and her dark hair might blow round her face in the draft from the open window.

She didn't speak as they drove along the Embankment, but sat beside him with her pale blue skirt draped demurely over her knees and her hands clasped once more in her lap. And when they crossed the river at Waterloo, she stared out at the sunlight flickering on the water as if she were any young woman on an outing on a beautiful spring day. Except there was a tension in her he could sense, as if every cell in her body were holding itself in check.

The desire to place his hand over hers became so intense that in order to distract himself he leaned forward and spoke to the driver, suggesting where the officer might wait while they were inside Guy's, and he must have spoken more sharply than he intended because she glanced at him, startled, then looked away.

The car left them at the main gate, and as they crossed the courtyard and entered the corridors that led to the morgue, Gavin allowed himself to guide her by touching her elbow lightly. If she were aware of his touch, she did not object. Nor did she comment on the elusively sweet smell of decay, never quite masked by the antiseptics.

Then they had reached the morgue, and having made sure the body was ready for viewing, Gavin took her in.

The gurney had been moved near the door, and Dr. Rainey's assistant carefully folded back the sheet to reveal the face. The flesh had sunk since the postmortem, making forehead, cheekbones, and chin more prominent, but the features were still recognizable to Gavin, and to Erika Rosenthal as well.

She put a hand to her mouth, the first involuntary gesture

he had seen her make. Then she nodded once and dropped her hand to her side. "That's David," she whispered, then she spoke again, more loudly, "Yes, that's my husband," as if Gavin might not have heard her. Or as if, Gavin thought, she needed to lay claim to him.

"Do you . . . would you like some time—"

"No. No. Tell me how he died."

"Your husband was found in Chelsea, in a garden across from the Embankment. Someone stabbed him, Mrs. Rosenthal. Repeatedly, in the chest. He didn't try to protect himself. And then it looks as though your husband's killer emptied his pockets and his satchel."

She turned away from the gurney, and he saw that her eyes were dry. "Can we go, please?"

"Of course." He led her out, and her footsteps beside his were unfaltering. But when they reached the courtyard, she stopped suddenly and looked round, as if she had lost her bearings.

"Here." Gavin led her to a bench. "Just sit for a bit."

She sank down beside him and closed her eyes. After a moment, she said, "I'll have to make arrangements straightaway. He can't be embalmed, you know. Or cremated. Even though David was not an observant Jew, these are things that would have mattered to him. So burial must take place as soon as possible."

"Yes, I know. But it will be several days before the authorities will release his . . . body."

Turning, she met his eyes. "How do you know these things, Mr. Hoxley?"

"When I was a child in Chelsea, our neighbors were Jewish. We were close, and I was a curious boy. I wanted to know why they did things differently."

"A curious boy grown into a curious man. And one without prejudice, I think." Her gaze probed him. "Will you find out who did this to my husband? And why?"

"If I can." He didn't know whether to be flattered or frightened by her approbation. "But you'll have to help me. Tell me why you were afraid your husband had committed suicide."

The breeze stirred her skirt, then feathered a tendril of hair across her cheek. "My husband . . . my husband felt his obligations deeply, Inspector. There were . . . debts . . . in his life he could never fulfill—at least not in his eyes." She sighed. "And David was a deeply disillusioned man. Before the war he was a firebrand. He spoke out against the Nazis, putting himself at risk. He couldn't believe that so barbaric a philosophy would be taken seriously by Germans, by the world, and he certainly did not believe that they could prevail."

"He was right, in the end," said Gavin, his mind skittering away from the bloody fields of France.

"Yes. But victory came too late for David, and at too great a cost. He couldn't forgive. Or find anything worthwhile in the present." Had that included his wife? Gavin wondered, then felt a rush of guilt as he realized just how often he had looked at his own wife, and his children, and thought the same. Had Linda and the children known they were being measured and found wanting?

Too quickly, he said, "You mentioned your husband went to the British Museum to work. Do you know what he was writing?"

"A book. But I never saw it. David was always secretive, even before the war. I suppose it was part of his character, the hoarding of emotions, both good and bad."

Gavin thought of the empty satchel found by David Rosenthal's body. "You must have had some idea what it was about, this book."

"Oh, yes. There were only certain things that occupied his mind, other than the necessities of everyday living. I think he was writing about the war, a personal indictment of all those who perpetrated, or allowed, such violence."

Gavin considered. "Do you mean you think he was naming names?"

"It's possible. I know he thought there were many who had escaped censure after the war. And he hated collaborators most. Somehow it was easier for him to understand those driven by hatred than those who allowed suffering because they were afraid or greedy. Or perhaps, Inspector . . ." *She met his eyes once more. "Perhaps he despised himself most of all. For surviving."*

Erika had thanked Gemma and Kit as graciously as possible, but she had been fretting to have them gone. She needed to think about what Gemma had told her, and she was already regretting her outburst about the brooch. It had been the shock. She'd never meant to reveal so much.

Gemma had been kind to undertake the task, but Erika realized that it had been cowardice that had led her to ask Gemma to do something she should have done herself. She'd always prided herself on her ability to face things—now she saw that her pride had been merely hubris. Why, when she had faced so much, had she failed at this one thing?

By the time she woke on Tuesday morning, she knew what she must do. She dressed carefully in her best suit, even though she knew it was slightly out of fashion—it seemed she wore suits only to funerals these days—and did her hair and makeup with concentration and hands that trembled only slightly.

When she left the flat, she found the air damp and fresh, but the sky clear. It had rained in the night, washing the city clean, and she tried to find an omen in that.

She flagged a taxi, and as the cab inched its way through the busy morning traffic, Erika felt suspended in time, knowing that the end of the journey would mark an irrevocable change in her life.

The cabbie, an older West Indian with a cheerful patter, went out of his way to set her down right at Harrowby's door. Erika overtipped him, one last delaying tactic, then she was left standing on the pavement, on her own.

She was familiar with the place, partly from Henri's descriptions of his finds at auction over the years, but she had never actually attended an auction or set foot in the salesrooms.

Examining the windows, she saw that the displays were beautifully done but held only Art Deco pottery and furniture, not jewelry. If she was going to see her brooch, her father's gift, at last, there was nothing for it but to go inside.

# 8

❦

*In those days all auction houses maintained the fiction that every artwork that came on the block was sold. Nowadays, if a painting or other object is "bought in"—that is to say, if it fails to reach its reserve, the minimum price the seller will accept— the auctioneer calls out, "Pass."*
— *Peter Watson,* Sotheby's: Inside Story

SUPERINTENDENT MARK LAMB HAD been both understanding and sympathetic. Not that Gemma had expected less—he was a personal friend as well as her boss, and a generous and diplomatic administrator. He'd told her to take what time she needed, but to let him know if she were going to be out of the station for more than a day. As she turned to go, he added, "Lovely party, by the way," and she flushed at the unexpected compliment.

After that, confiding in Melody was easier, and Melody took the news in her usual matter-of-fact fashion. "I'm sure she'll be fine, boss. Now, you go and have a nice visit, and I'll—"

Whatever practical help Melody had meant to offer was cut off by the chirping of Gemma's mobile. "Sorry," said Gemma, surprised to see Erika's name come up on the caller ID.

As she answered, Erika's voice came over the line. "Gemma? I couldn't find a phone box." She sounded breathy, near panic. "I tried, but it's all mobiles these days, and I thought if I came home— But I should have rung right away—"

"Erika, what is it?" Gemma asked, dropping her bag on her desk and sinking back into her chair.

"Harrowby's. The salesrooms. I went to see the brooch— I—" Erika took a ragged breath, then began more calmly. "I wanted to see it for myself. But everything was in an uproar. The girl—the one you said you thought might know something—Kristin. I remembered the name."

Gemma felt cold. "Kristin Cahill."

"That's right. They said she was killed last night. An accident. A hit-and-run, near where she lived, in World's End. Gemma, if this had anything to do with me, with the brooch—I should never have—"

"Erika, no. Listen, I'm sure it's just coincidence, just an awful coincidence." But Gemma was mouthing words automatically, fighting nausea as she remembered Kristin Cahill's pale gamine face, and the young woman's frightened look when her boss had come into the room.

"But, Gemma—"

"I'm sure it's nothing," said Gemma firmly. "But I'll look into it. Straightaway. I promise."

Coincidence. Gemma didn't bloody believe in coincidence. Not like this—talking to a girl one day about something that seemed very slightly dodgy, having the same girl turn up dead the next.

She sat at her desk, tapping her phone on the blotter, straightening pencils and pens into neat regiments. Melody had gone to take a call, leaving Gemma to contemplate the ugly implications of Erika's story, and the more she thought, the less she liked it.

But was it possible there was more than one Kristin at Harrowby's? Erika hadn't heard a last name. Before she talked to anyone at the salesroom, Gemma had better make absolutely sure of her facts. Erika had said the accident happened in World's End, the westernmost edge of Chelsea, so the obvious place to start would be the Chelsea nick.

\* \* \*

Harry Pevensey had never believed that the early bird got the worm. Late to bed and late to rise, that was an actor's life, and it had always suited him. He had his routines, everything just so, drapes drawn to keep out the morning's harsh intrusiveness, eye mask ditto, dressing gown to hand and kettle ready to boil, so that he could slip into the day as painlessly as his usual hangover would allow. And no less than eight hours' sleep—otherwise he'd look like hell, and no amount of makeup would make amends.

So Harry was affronted on Tuesday morning when, just as he was opening one eye and then the other, testing the intensity of the light compared to the sharpness of the knife tip between his eyes and contemplating the operation of verticality, someone began a bloody pounding on his door.

"What the hell," he muttered, sitting up with more force than necessary and wincing at the consequences. Whoever it was had bypassed the downstairs buzzer—had his wannabe rock-god neighbor, Andy Monahan, left the building's main door off the latch again? Or— Harry froze with his feet halfway into his worn slippers.

There was the wine merchant's bill he hadn't paid, and the shirtmaker's—couldn't go to auditions looking like something the cat dragged in, after all. And if they got a bit impatient, they were likely to employ less-than-civilized means of collecting their filthy lucre.

For a moment he considered putting his head back under the covers, but if they broke his door down, there would be hell to pay, and he'd have lost any chance of presenting a dignified front.

He'd got back into his slippers and donned his dressing gown when the pounding grew even louder and someone shouted, "Harry! I know you're in there. Open the fucking door!"

Recognizing the voice, Harry said, "Dom?" What was Dominic Scott doing here, and making such a racket? "Just shut up, would you?" he called out as he shuffled to the door, his head pounding like a jackhammer.

"Harry, let me—" Dom staggered in, fist raised, as Harry opened the door. He looked worse than Harry felt—

unwashed hair, pasty faced, and his breath reeked of stale alcohol and cigarettes, which Harry despised.

Harry closed the door, then grimaced, backing off a step. "You smell like a pub ashtray. And what do you think you're doing knocking me up at this hour? Not to mention giving the neighbors something to gossip about for weeks."

"Since when have you ever minded giving anyone cause for gossip," retorted Dom, sinking into Harry's brocaded slipper chair, a bequest from his paternal grandmother.

"And you look like shit," Harry continued, undeterred. It was a shame the boy let himself go, Harry thought, as he had looks Harry would have envied in his day. He considered booting Dom out of his favorite chair, but couldn't decide where he'd rather have him sit. He settled for taking the other armchair himself, after he'd straightened the covers on the bed. "What do you want, Dom?"

Dom leaned forward, and Harry saw that his hands were shaking. "Have you got anything, Harry? Offer a mate a drink? I'm not feeling too well."

"No. Bar's closed," said Harry, thinking longingly of the bottle of gin tucked away in his kitchen cupboard. The hair of the dog would ease his headache, but he wanted Dom Scott out of his flat as soon as possible, and he certainly wasn't inclined to share his medicinal stash.

"Coffee, then? Or even tea?"

Harry glanced at his filled kettle, his favorite cup set out beside it, along with the tea caddy, and sighed. "All right. One cup. But then you'd better make it quick." Not that he had anywhere to go, but the young man's behavior was making him anxious. Dom Scott was used to demanding, not pleading, which made Harry suspect there was a serious spanner in the works.

He made the tea while Dom fidgeted in the chair like a fretful child, pulling at his shirt cuffs, tugging at his already disarrayed dark hair. Harry had seen the signs before, and they weren't good, nor did they bode well for their joint scheme.

While the tea brewed, he excused himself to the loo, running a brush through his hair and examining his face—

definitely the worse for wear—in the fly-specked mirror. Visions floated through his mind. Unsuccessful auditions. Bad parts in unheated village theaters. Mothers' unions, God forbid. Bill collectors who wouldn't, couldn't, be put off.

No, he was not going to let go of the merry-go-round. Not now, boyo. He could deal with Dominic Scott, a spoiled little tosser who didn't have half his mother's bollocks.

Harry went back into the sitting room with a smile and a new and steely resolve. He poured Dom's tea into a china cup that he hated to trust to the boy's twitchy fingers, then poured his own and sat on the arm of a chair, ankles crossed, as if he hadn't a care in the world.

"All right, Dom. What seems to be the problem?"

Dom gulped his tea until his cup was empty, then stared at him as if he'd suddenly lost the power of speech. Then he swallowed visibly and said, "Harry, we have to take the brooch out of the sale."

"What? Take it *out* of the sale?" Harry had expected him to try cutting his percentage, but not this. "Are you mad?"

"No. Look, I'm telling you. It has to come out."

"Why on earth would you want to do that? We're talking about a more-than-six-figure profit, and you're the one needed—"

Dom was shaking his head. "The police have been round. They talked to Kristin. They're asking questions about the brooch. Some woman says it was stolen from her during the war."

"Stolen?" Harry thought swiftly. "What did Kristin tell them?"

"Nothing. But she could lose her job. I asked her to take the brooch out, but she says she can't. She says you're the only one who can withdraw it."

"I bought it at a car boot sale," Harry said with an off-hand shrug. "So why should it matter to me what some woman says?"

Dom twisted the teacup until it fell from his fingers and bounced on the threadbare Axminster carpet. "Harry, you don't underst—"

"No. *You* don't understand." For the first time in his life, Harry Pevensey knew he had the advantage. "The brooch stays in the sale. And maybe, if you're a really good boy, I'll give *you* a percentage of the profit."

Gemma had always liked the Lucan Place Police Station. Like Notting Hill, it was one of the few prewar buildings still functioning as an active station, and like Notting Hill, it had a warmth and grace most of the newer stations lacked.

It was also just a few streets from the South Kensington tube station, not far from Harrowby's, another rather uncomfortable coincidence, it seemed to Gemma.

She identified herself at reception and asked to see the officer in charge of the hit-and-run accident investigation. While the duty officer gave her a curious look, she was told she could see Inspector Boatman, and was soon shown into an office not unlike her own.

The officer who stood to greet her was female, short, stocky, dark haired, and somewhere in her indeterminate thirties, Gemma guessed. She wore a serviceable suit and no makeup, but when she smiled and held out her hand to Gemma, any notion of her as unattractive vanished.

"You're Inspector James?" she asked. "I'm Kerry Boatman. Have a seat." Like Gemma's, her desk was cluttered with paperwork, but the visitors' chairs were clear and looked as though they had seen much use. Spaced among the files on Boatman's desk, however, were a half-dozen photos, showing, from the sideways angle Gemma could see, various poses of a balding man, two toothy little girls, and a large tabby cat. Gemma, on the other hand, displayed nothing personal in her office, feeling it was inappropriate to cross those professional boundaries, but she suddenly felt a little ache of envy under her breastbone.

"I see you're here about last night's hit-and-run," said Boatman, glancing down at a scribbled note by her phone. "That's a bit odd, as it's not on your patch." There was no hint of hostility in her voice, just interest.

"The victim— It *was* Kristin Cahill? The girl who worked at Harrowby's?" asked Gemma.

"Yes." Boatman consulted her notes again. "Twenty-three years old, a junior sales assistant for the last year at Harrowby's. She lived with her parents in a flat at World's End."

Since Erika's phone call, Gemma had been sure of the victim's identity, but she felt a stab of regret at the confirmation. "I met her yesterday," she told Boatman. "I was making an inquiry, unofficially, for a friend." She went on to explain about Erika and the brooch, and that she had felt Kristin was slightly uncomfortable with her questions. "Then this morning my friend went to Harrowby's. She wanted to see the brooch for herself, and to talk to someone more senior. When she heard about Kristin, she rang me. And I just felt it was . . . odd."

Kerry Boatman studied her for a moment. "It seems your instincts may have been right. I've just had the preliminary from the accident scene investigation. Nothing concrete, of course, but from the tire marks, it looks as though the car that hit Kristin Cahill accelerated, rather than braked. And that, before it accelerated, it was parked at the curb near Kristin's building."

"Someone was waiting for her?"

"It seems possible, yes."

"Any witnesses?"

"No one saw anything. The pub had cleared out, the street was empty. But someone who lived opposite the scene said they heard the squeal of tires. A Mr. Madha. It was he who went out to investigate, and called 999."

"Did she—was she—"

"The ambulance service transported her, but she was pronounced dead on admittance. Internal bleeding, a smashed pelvis, and severe head injuries."

Gemma shut her eyes, as if she might shut out the vision of the graceful girl's broken body. When she looked up again, she found the other officer watching her with evident compassion. "It's difficult," said Boatman, "when you've met someone, however briefly."

"If I could be sure that it wasn't something I said or did, some question I asked . . ."

"Well." Boatman sighed. "That won't be for us to determine. It's out of our remit now. I'll be turning it over to a Murder Investigation Team from the Yard."

# 9

*The United Kingdom was the first refuge for perhaps half the 2,200 refugee scholars who had emigrated from Germany by 1938.*
—*Louise London,* Whitehall
and the Jews, 1933–1948

**GEMMA HAD HER MOBILE** in hand as she walked out the door of Lucan Place. She'd thanked Inspector Boatman and taken her leave as quickly as was polite. "If there's anything you can tell the team, once an SIO is assigned," Boatman had added. "We still can't be sure at this point that it wasn't drink-driving-related manslaughter, or that she wasn't a random victim, if it *was* homicide. But if it should have some connection with your inquiry . . ."

Gemma had responded with no small irony that she would certainly be in touch.

MIT. The Metropolitan Police's Murder Investigation Teams, sometimes called Major Investigation Teams. But no matter the nomenclature, this was Kincaid's job, his territory—why not his team?

He answered on the first ring. "Hullo, love. What's up? Are you at hosp—"

"No. No, I haven't made it yet. Something's come up. The girl I met yesterday at Harrowby's, Kristin Cahill—she's been killed in a hit-and-run. Manslaughter at the least, homicide at the worst. Chelsea is calling in the Yard. I want you to request the case."

There was silence on the line. She could almost see him thinking, his brow creased in a slight frown. "Look," she said. "I know it's slightly irregular, but—"

"Slightly? Gemma, I've a personal involvement—"

"No, what you have is a bit of background information that would give you an advantage. You never met Kristin Cahill. And who else," she added, "would take what I have to say as seriously?"

"But that's just it, isn't it?" he argued. "You're too close—"

"I met this girl. I asked questions that might have got her into trouble. I want to know, one way or the other. And I want justice for her, even if her death had nothing to do with my questions about the Goldshtein brooch. She was twenty-three years old, for heaven's sake, just starting out in her life," Gemma added vehemently. "And I liked her."

She was still standing on the pavement outside Lucan Place, and a shopping-laden woman passing by gave her a curious glance. Gemma started back toward the Fulham Road, and dropped her voice. "Duncan—"

"I don't like it," Kincaid broke in. "But I'm never going to hear the end of it, otherwise, am I? And what exactly do you suggest I tell Chief Superintendent Childs?"

*Although Gavin now had some idea of what had been in David Rosenthal's satchel, he was no closer to knowing why it had been taken, or what Rosenthal had been doing in Cheyne Walk.*

*He had been to the school in North Hampstead where David had taught. Rosenthal "kept himself to himself," his fellow teachers had said, with a wariness that made Gavin wonder what they might have said had he not been an outsider, a gentile, as well as a policeman.*

*He met the head last, who invited him into his office. Saul Bernstein was younger than Gavin had expected, perhaps only in his thirties, a chubby man who seemed to be compensating for his lack of years with an air of gravitas and a billowing pipe.*

*The day had turned unseasonably hot for May, and the*

small room was stuffy but nonetheless pleasant, with its odor of books and pipe tobacco. The sound of boys playing at some game drifted in through the open window.

"Did no one like David Rosenthal?" asked Gavin, when he'd taken the proffered seat on the far side of Bernstein's desk.

"Like?" Bernstein sounded slightly puzzled. "I wouldn't say that David's colleagues didn't like him. Everyone is still quite shocked, you know—David's death is not the sort of thing one expects—"

"Murder," Gavin interrupted, suddenly wanting to shake this man's complacency. "David Rosenthal was murdered. Violently. I'd say someone disliked him intensely."

"Quite." Bernstein paled a little, and set the pipe in an ashtray. "But I assure you it wasn't anyone here. As I said, it wasn't a question of David's colleagues disliking him. David was civil, considerate, uninterested in petty staff squabbles, and did his job with dedication. And that was all. I don't think I've ever met anyone who seemed less interested in the approval of his peers."

"What about the approval of his students?"

"David was a good teacher, as I've said. Very thorough, and well prepared. But I doubt he would have noticed whether or not his students liked him."

"David Rosenthal wore a tiny gold mezuzah on a chain round his neck. It was the only thing not taken when he was killed. His wife said that one of his students gave it to him."

Bernstein frowned. "We don't allow the boys to give gifts to the teachers, or vice versa. It too easily creates a climate of favoritism. And misunderstandings."

"And did David have any misunderstandings with anyone? Any arguments?"

"No." Bernstein hesitated, then shrugged. "Not here, at least. But there was something. The Jewish community has dispersed somewhat since the war, but it is still fairly close knit. There is a network of sorts, so that one picks up information—not necessarily true, of course—about people that one doesn't know personally."

Gavin waited, and after a moment, Bernstein went on. "I don't like to tell tales, Inspector. But I saw David once, in the East End, talking to a man who is reputed to be involved with a . . . vengeance group." He pinched his lips together as if the words themselves were distasteful.

"Vengeance?"

Bernstein settled himself more solidly in his chair. "It's my opinion that we must move forward, put the past behind us. But there are those who . . . feel differently. Those who believe that not all who committed atrocities against the Jews during the war received justice. This man . . . he was pointed out to me once, as someone who espoused those . . . philosophies."

Tired of the circumlocution, Gavin said, "What was the man's name?"

"I don't know. I only recognized his face."

"And did you ever ask David about this man, or this meeting?"

"No." Bernstein looked uncomfortable. "He didn't see me, and I thought it best . . . left alone." He didn't meet Gavin's eyes. "There was something about him that repelled any attempt at confidence . . . You may think this fanciful, Inspector, but a bitterness hung about David Rosenthal . . . It made me think of the odor of charred ashes."

Kincaid had always found the truth to be the most effective measure in dealing with Chief Superintendent Denis Childs. After a brief wait in the anteroom, during which he chatted with Childs's secretary, he was called into the inner sanctum.

He found his boss looking less sanguine than usual. His doctor had put him on a fitness and slimming regime, and while Childs might have dropped a few pounds, it had not improved his temper. It seemed to Kincaid that Childs was simply one of those men who were meant to be fat. It suited his personality, and attempting to change his essential physiology was more than likely an exercise in futility.

Still, he asked, "How are you, sir?" as Childs invited him to sit, and got a grimace and a mutter in reply.

"A treadmill," Childs said. "They have me walking on a treadmill! As if one doesn't walk enough in London."

Kincaid hid a grin. "You look well."

"Ha." Childs glared at him. "I'll have to get a new wardrobe soon, and I hate shopping. But"—he leaned back in his chair and steepled his fingers in his familiar pose—"you didn't come to see me to discuss my suits."

"No. There's been a suspicious death in Chelsea, and Lucan Place is going to be calling for a team. I'd like to take it."

Childs raised a brow. "Have you acquired telepathy, then?"

"No, sir," Kincaid said. "Although there are days when it might prove helpful."

He proceeded to explain how Gemma had met Kristin Cahill, had thought something seemed a little dodgy, and how Kristin had subsequently died.

"I take it Gemma wants you on the case?"

"Yes. But I have to admit I'm curious, too. Gemma's instincts are seldom wrong, and if this has to do with the auction house, we could be looking at something big."

"And what about Gemma? I can't see her being content to take a backseat, and I don't imagine Mark Lamb would be too happy to have her haring off after a Homicide division inquiry."

"As it happens, Gemma's taking a bit of personal time at the moment. Her mum's ill."

"Sorry to hear that," said Childs, but there was an unmistakable glint of humor in his eyes. "Ring Lucan Place, then, and get the record transfer started. And keep me informed."

Doug Cullen was less than pleased to be assigned a case on some whim of Gemma James's. Although he'd worked with Kincaid long enough now to have got over the first rash of professional jealousy, and he'd come to know Gemma well enough to like her personally, he didn't fancy being dictated to by his guv'nor's former sergeant, much less his girlfriend.

He was skeptical about the investigation's validity, as

well. That was a notoriously bad stretch of road—there had been a fatality there just recently, when some idiot in a fast car had blown through World's End at three in the morning and wrapped himself round a light pole. Odds were that this girl had stepped out in front of someone equally careless—wrong place, wrong time.

But as the material began to come through from Chelsea, his certainty wavered. It had been fairly early, for one thing, not long after pub closing time, and before the staggeringly pissed emptied out of the nightclubs. And although a lack of braking wouldn't have convinced him, the preliminary accident investigation reports showed clear signs that the car had accelerated away from the curb west of Edith Grove and into the intersection.

And then there was the photo of the girl herself, a copy of a recent snapshot contributed by her parents. Kristin Cahill had been undeniably pretty, but it was more than that. There was a slightly wistful appeal in her eyes, and in the little half smile she had thrown at the camera. Finding himself wishing that he had met her, Doug began to see why Gemma might have got her knickers in a twist over the girl's death.

Still, when he and Kincaid arrived at Harrowby's an hour later to begin questioning the staff, he wasn't best pleased to find Gemma James waiting on the pavement.

"I thought I might be able to help," said Gemma, taking in Cullen's glare and the slight twitch of Kincaid's lips.

"And I thought you were going to hospital," Kincaid replied.

Gemma tamped down a twinge of guilt. "Cyn rang. She said they've taken Mum down for more tests, so there was nothing I could do until later. And since I'd met some of the staff here . . ." Seeing Cullen's blank look, she realized Kincaid hadn't told him about her mother. "My mum's in St. Barts," she explained to Cullen. "Having some tests."

"Oh, sorry."

Unwilling to say more, Gemma nodded her thanks and let Kincaid lead the way towards the salesroom door.

Kincaid was, after all, the senior investigating officer,

and while she might tag along, she had better not charge into things like Boadicea come to conquer. What she'd have done if another team had shown up, she didn't like to think.

"I'm glad you took the case," she murmured to him.

"You were persuasive." He paused, studying her. "And as long as you're here, it might not be a bad idea for you to introduce us. Up the ante a bit if they think that something they said to you, or that Kristin said to you, brought you back."

Harrowby's seemed eerily quiet, the auctioneer's podium empty, the large television dark, the rows of chairs that had held yesterday's bidders unfilled. And gone was the composed Mrs. March who had greeted them at reception the previous day. Although neatly dressed in what appeared to be a cashmere twinset, her nose was red, her makeup smudged, and she held a ragged wad of tissues in her hand.

For a moment she looked blankly at Gemma, then recognition dawned. "You didn't say you were with the police. Yesterday." Mrs. March gave a slow, baffled shake of her head. "She's dead. Kristin's dead."

"It *was* a personal visit yesterday, Mrs. March," said Gemma gently, glancing at Kincaid, who seemed content to stay in the background. "But yes, we know Kristin's dead. That's why we're here. Can you tell me a bit about what happened?"

"Kristin didn't come in for work this morning. That's very unlike her. She's a good girl." The look she gave them was beseeching. "You do have favorites, you know. And Kristin, for all her cheekiness . . . She wanted to please. And she was . . . kind to me."

Suddenly Gemma saw, beneath the starchily prim exterior, a lonely woman who had taken any crumbs Kristin had, however unwittingly, thrown in her wake, and turned them into gems.

"So you were worried about her this morning," she prompted as Mrs. March's eyes filled and she pressed the ball of tissue to her nose.

Mrs. March sniffed and lowered her hand, tears temporarily staved off. "I rang her at home. Just to see if she was all right. She seemed a bit . . . unsettled . . . yesterday. I wasn't sure if it was your visit or the flowers, or if it was because Mr. Khan . . ." Glancing round, Mrs. March lowered her voice. "Well, he was a bit rough on her, to tell you the truth."

Gemma sensed a quickening of attention from Kincaid and Cullen, but she didn't want either of them to interrupt her rapport with Mrs. March. "Was this before or after our visit, Kristin's little . . . um, disagreement with Mr. Khan?"

"After." For the first time, Mrs. March seemed to take in the two men with Gemma, both wearing suits and carrying themselves with the indefinable but unmistakable bearing that marked them as police officers. "I—I don't want to speak out of turn. You're all police, aren't you?"

Kincaid stepped in. "Mrs. March, we only want to help. I'm Detective Superintendent Kincaid, and this is Detective Sergeant Cullen. Can you tell us what happened when you rang Kristin's home this morning?"

It was a good deflection, Gemma thought. They would save Mr. Khan for later.

"A police officer answered the phone. She said she was a family liaison officer, and that there had been an accident." The tears began to flow, this time unchecked. "She said that Kristin was dead. That she had been hit by a car as she was crossing the road last night. I still can't believe it."

"And after the call?" asked Gemma. "You told the rest of the staff? It seems very quiet round here today." She gestured towards the empty auction area. "Is it on account of Kristin?"

"No. There's no sale on today. Everyone is working on the displays and cataloging things that are upcoming. Although some of the girls were very upset." Mrs. March blew her nose, with signs of returning to her usual briskness. "And then there was Giles, of course. He was completely shattered. Even Mr. Khan insisted that he should go home."

"Giles?"

"Another one of our sales assistants. He and Kristin were . . . special friends."

Gemma vaguely remembered a pudgy-faced young man watching them as Kristin had led her back to the office. "Were they going out?"

"No . . . At least I don't think so. But Giles was . . . fond of her. Very cut up." Mrs. March glanced up, and her expression grew suddenly wary. "Oh, there's Mr. Khan now."

Turning, Gemma saw Amir Khan striding towards them from the corridor that led to his—and Kristin's—office.

"Mrs. March, you should have rung me," he said as he reached them, and Gemma knew they would get nothing more from the receptionist for the moment. "Inspector James." Khan's gaze flicked from Gemma to Kincaid and Cullen. "If you are here about the brooch, I'm afraid that what I said yesterday still stands."

"It's a bit more complicated than that, Mr. Khan. We're here about Kristin Cahill's death, and I should think that might have changed things considerably. Oh, and this is Superintendent Kincaid and Sergeant Cullen. From Scotland Yard."

Khan stared at her with what she could have sworn was genuine astonishment, and Gemma felt a moment's pleasure in seeing this slickly urbane man discomfited.

But he seemed to recover quickly enough, giving her a smile that showed a flash of even white teeth. "Certainly, Kristin's accident was unfortunate, but I don't see—"

"Unfortunate!" Mrs. March rose from her chair. "Mr. Khan, how can you possibly say such a thing?" She was trembling. "The poor girl is dead! I'd call that more than unfortunate!"

"Nonetheless, Mrs. March," Khan sounded more annoyed than placating. "That has nothing to—"

"Actually, we're not here about the Goldshtein brooch," Kincaid interrupted. "At least not directly. We're here because we have reason to believe that Kristin Cahill's death was no accident."

Amir Khan hustled them into his office before Mrs. March had a chance to do anything but sink back into her chair, looking stunned.

Cullen, who had been occupying himself by examining an intricate wooden model of a steamship that was apparently going on the block, followed, unease now added to his aggravation. He hadn't cared for feeling like a piece of furniture while Gemma led the questioning, although he had to admit she had probably got more from the receptionist than he would have if it had been his call. But by rights it should have been his guv'nor in the lead, not Gemma, who had no business here.

And now he was faced with Amir Khan, the sort of man who as a boy would have been his nemesis at school—Anglo-Indian, yes, but the product of money and breeding, with the perfect accent, the perfect clothes, an undoubtedly sharp and sarcastic tongue, and who had probably captained his cricket team. Doug hated him on sight.

"Now you've set the cat among the pigeons," said Khan as soon as he had them sequestered in his office. The space was cramped, and he didn't ask them to sit. A bouquet of long-stemmed pink roses sat on the far desk, some of its buds already drooping. "I don't know what sort of nonsense this is," Khan continued, "but Mrs. March will have it spread round the salesroom in five minutes." He glanced at his watch, which Doug suspected was a real Cartier and not a copy. "Or sooner. I don't appre—"

"Mr. Khan." This time Kincaid took the lead. "This is not nonsense. Someone ran Kristin Cahill down last night, brutally and deliberately. I don't care if it upsets your staff. And as we will be talking to each of them in turn, there's no way you could keep the news from them."

"But surely that's not possible." Khan glanced from Kincaid to Gemma, his certainty wavering. "Why would anyone want to hurt Kristin?"

"We were hoping you might tell us," Kincaid said. "It seems you gave her a bit of a bollocking yesterday, after Inspector James left."

"Bollocking?" Khan gave a grimace of distaste. "I'd hardly say that, even if I were to use such a word."

"Then what would you call it? A row?"

"Certainly not. I merely reminded Kristin that our first

priority is our clients' confidentiality, and asked her to be discreet."

"You mean discreet about the Goldshtein brooch?" asked Gemma.

"Discreet as regards giving out information pertaining to any of our buyers *or* sellers, and that included the seller of the Goldshtein brooch."

"Kristin had been working for you a year, I think? Why would you suddenly feel a need to remind her of something she surely knew quite well?"

Khan leaned against his desk and picked at his perfectly starched shirt cuff, looking less than comfortable for the first time. "Of course, Kristin was well aware of our policy. But this was the first time she was to receive an introductory commission. And to my knowledge, this was the first time she'd ever had someone make a prior claim on an object taken in for auction."

"An introductory commission?" asked Gemma. "I remember you saying Kristin had brought the piece in. What does that mean, exactly?"

"Kristin had an acquaintance with the seller. When one of our staff brings in someone with a piece to auction, the staff member receives a small commission."

"How small?" Kincaid asked sharply.

"Four percent."

"Four percent of how much?"

"The reserve price on the brooch is one hundred twenty thousand pounds. But with the reputation of the designer, and the size of the diamonds, it could go considerably higher."

Cullen heard Gemma give a small whistle under her breath. "So Kristin could have made as much as five or six thousand pounds?" she asked. "Or more?"

"Or nothing," replied Khan. "The brooch might not meet its reserve. That's always the danger when setting a limit."

"When you say Kristin brought in the seller, does that mean she knew him or her personally?" asked Cullen.

"I've no idea. She didn't explain the connection to me, and I didn't ask."

"You keep talking as if the sale of the brooch is still on," said Gemma. "With Kristin's death—"

"Kristin's death doesn't change anything, Inspector. Of course, it's regrettable, but there is certainly no reason we should consider removing an item from the sale because of it."

"But if Kristin had a connection with the seller—"

"It doesn't matter," Khan said with finality. "That association is now meaningless."

"And Kristin's commission?"

Khan shrugged. "A moot point, obviously."

"And that means more profit to the salesroom," put in Cullen, wanting to ruffle this man's smooth exterior.

But Khan merely gave him an amused look down his aquiline nose. "And more for the seller, Sergeant— I'm sorry, I don't remem—"

"Cullen," Doug said sharply.

"Sergeant Cullen, then. You can't seriously think that the seller would have murdered Kristin for the paltry few thousand pounds' difference her commission would have made in his profit?" While Doug was considering the difference that paltry sum would make in his life, Gemma stepped up to Khan and looked him in the eye.

"Possibly not, Mr. Khan. But under the circumstances, you can see that we must interview the seller."

"Then I'd suggest you have a word with Kristin's friends and associates. But as a representative of Harrowby's, I can't give you that information. Our client confidentiality cannot be breached."

Kincaid, who had been leaning against a filing cabinet, hands in pockets, straightened up and gave a deceptively courteous smile. "Then I suspect a warrant will make a fairly good battering ram."

# 10

❧

*About half the estimated total of 5.1 million murders of Jews by the Nazis were committed in the year 1942.*

—*Louise London,* Whitehall
and the Jews, 1933–1948

**"WE'LL HAVE TO START** with the parents," Kincaid said as they pushed through the salesroom doors back out into the ordinary hustle of the Old Brompton Road, where passersby untouched by this particular tragedy bumbled past on their own urgent errands, and the lunchtime scent of pizza and kebabs wafted from the open doors of restaurants and cafés.

Gemma knew he hated such interviews as much as she did, but he was better at concealing it. She stopped him with a touch on his arm, having remembered a fragment of conversation. "Wait just a sec."

She ducked back into Harrowby's and emerged a moment later. "I've got Kristin's friend Giles's address from Mrs. March. If he was cut up enough to go home, we should have a word. Especially if Giles might have sent the flowers."

"Where does he live?" Kincaid asked.

"Fulham."

"We'll see the parents on the way, then." He turned to Cullen. "Doug, can you go back to the Yard and get a start on that warrant? I want to know who put that brooch up for sale, whether Mr. Khan likes it or not. And, Gemma, about those flowers—"

"Already on it," Gemma said as she pulled Melody up on her mobile. She'd got the name of the florist from Mrs. March along with Giles's address, and when Melody answered, she asked her if she could use her powers of persuasion to get the name of the sender *without* a warrant.

"That's asking a lot, boss," Melody said, but she sounded more amused than aggrieved. It might save them valuable time, and she knew it.

"I've no doubt you can do it." Gemma gave her the information and rang off, her smile cut short as she saw the play of emotions on Doug Cullen's face as he watched her.

There was resentment—she guessed as much at her involvement in general as at being given the tedious job of getting a warrant—combined with what might have been a flicker of relief. He was probably glad not to have to cope with Kristin Cahill's parents, she thought, but then again, she'd never seen Cullen display much empathy in interviews.

But he merely nodded at Kincaid and said, "I'll find a sympathetic judge," before handing Kincaid the car keys and heading off towards the tube station.

While Gemma had come via tube, Kincaid and Cullen had come in a Yard Rover, and now Kincaid took over the wheel as he and Gemma made the short drive to World's End. The car was silver and anonymously discreet—nothing obvious to set the neighbors gossiping, Gemma thought as they pulled up to the block of flats just to the west of Edith Grove.

The address they had been given was not in the monolithic seventies-era block of flats that dominated the skyline between the King's Road and the Thames, but rather a more modest council estate that Gemma guessed had been built not long after the war. It looked well tended and comfortable, an image marred by the orange stripes of paint on the street and the Sokkia team working the accident site.

When Kincaid had found a spot to park the Rover, they walked over to speak to the lead investigating officer.

"Don't often get the Yard in an accident reconstruction," the officer said when Kincaid had introduced them.

"Anything interesting yet?" Kincaid asked.

"The laser's faster, not miraculous. I'm Bill Davis, by the way." Davis was a stocky man with a bristle of gray hair and lines round his eyes that suggested he liked a joke. "And there's not much to work with here. Still might have been a drink driver who didn't even see the poor kid. Except that from what we can see of the tire marks, it looks like the driver might have swerved *towards* the pedestrian." He nodded at the camera mounted over the traffic light. "Maybe you'll get something off the CCTV."

"I've got the Yard on it now," Kincaid told him.

"Going to interview the family?" Davis shook his head, said, "Don't envy you," and went back to his laser.

They found the flat easily. Gemma rang the bell with a slight tightening of the throat and a sympathetic smile at the ready, but the woman who answered almost immediately gave them a quick assessing glance before saying quietly, "Homicide team, then?" and motioning them in.

"Yolanda Fish." She extended a firm, dark-skinned hand to each of them as they introduced themselves. "Detective constable. Family liaison officer." She had a competent sort of compassion about her, just the right balance for family liaison.

It was not a job Gemma envied. The liaison officer was there to provide support and information about an ongoing investigation for the families of victims, but they were also police officers, and bound to report anything they learned in confidence that might have an impact on an investigation.

"Mr. Cahill is taking a bit of a . . . rest. Not feeling too well." DC Fish glanced towards what Gemma assumed were the bedrooms and lifted a hand to her mouth in a quick but unmistakable mime of drinking. "But Mrs. Cahill— Wanda—is in the kitchen. I'll just tell her you're here before I take you back."

Gemma stopped her. "Is she—"

"Holding up as well as you'd expect. Kristin was an only child, and there aren't any close relatives nearby. Nor a priest, although I know someone who might come in for a bit."

Yolanda's momentary absence gave Gemma a chance to look round the flat, and although the block may have originally been owned by the council, it looked as though this flat had been bought by the owners and refurbished. The sitting room was beautifully proportioned, fitted with expensive hardwood flooring, and arranged with a pleasing assortment of antiques and contemporary furnishings. The walls had been hand finished in a pale buff that set off the artwork and furniture.

The kitchen, when Yolanda beckoned them in, confirmed Gemma's opinion. Pale blue walls set off the collection of antique china on a Welsh dresser and the warm woods of contemporary cupboards and a refectory table.

But then her attention was taken by the woman who sat at the table's end. Gemma put her age in the mid to late forties, and with her chin-length dark hair and her daughter's slight build, she might have passed for a good deal younger on a different day. But on this morning her face was ravaged by grief. The eyes she raised to Gemma's were swollen, her stare blankly uncomprehending. A mug filled with untouched tea sat before her.

Yolanda went to her and put a hand on her shoulder. "Wanda, these are the police officers I told you about. They need to ask you a few questions." She glanced up at Gemma and Kincaid, adding, "I can make you a cuppa—"

Shaking his head, Kincaid pulled out a chair and sat facing Wanda Cahill. "We won't trouble you long." Yolanda nodded and, moving back to the sink, began drying cups with a tea towel.

Gemma felt a stab of relief at Kincaid's declaration, then was ashamed of her reaction. But the pain in the room was palpable, a miasma in the air that made it seem hard to breathe. She slid into a chair at the opposite end of the table, as if the physical distance might provide some barrier.

As Gemma watched, Wanda Cahill made a visible effort to focus on Kincaid. "I don't understand," she whispered, and her voice sounded rusty, as if sobbing had rasped her throat. "They rang the bell. At first I thought it was a dream, the same dream I'd had since Kristin was a child, whenever she was away from home. And always I would wake up and know it was a dream, and then I could go back to sleep. But it didn't stop, the sound, and I couldn't—I couldn't—I knew—" She looked from Kincaid to Gemma, her brow creased, her fingers pinching at the edge of her unevenly buttoned cardigan.

Gemma knew the dream, had had it herself, waking with a jolt and thumping heart in the darkest hour of the night to the imagined sound of a knock or the bell. She would sit up in bed, listening, and when she realized the dogs were quiet, she'd know that she had imagined it, that the children were safe. But for this woman, the nightmare had become real.

She stood and went to Wanda Cahill, kneeling and taking the woman's unresisting hand in her own. "Mrs. Cahill, tell me about last night. Was Kristin at home?"

Wanda Cahill looked at Gemma with the same baffled expression she had turned on Kincaid, but after a moment a spark flared in her eyes, and she spoke, her voice stronger. "She came home after work, for dinner. It's hard for her sometimes, living at home. Her father still treats her like a child, and I try to buffer things as much as I can." Her face came alive as the recollection moved her into the past.

"Did she talk to you about anything in particular, at dinner?"

"No. But her mobile rang while we were eating, and Bob made a fuss over no phones at the table—you mustn't think he doesn't love her," she added, suddenly entreating. "He just wants things to stay the way they were when she was younger. Maybe he loves her too much—"

As Wanda's face began to crumple again, Gemma said quickly, "Do you know who rang her on her mobile?"

"No. She didn't answer. But I assumed it was the young man who called just afterwards on our phone. It was her friend from work, Giles. He was very polite, but she didn't seem particularly happy to talk to him."

"What did she say?"

"Well, he must have been asking her to do something, because she said thanks, but she couldn't, really. But Bob was grumbling at her by that time, so she left the room . . ."

"She didn't say anything about work? Or tell you where she was going?"

Wanda shook her head slowly, and Gemma could see the grief swamping her again, a rising tide. "No. She kissed me, the way she always does when she goes out, and said she loved me. But she was that aggravated with her dad. If he hadn't—if she hadn't— When he asked where she was going, she said out with friends, and that she wouldn't be late . . ."

Kincaid, who had been listening intently, spoke for the first time. "Mrs. Cahill, I'm sure that your daughter's little tiff with her father meant nothing at all. These things happen in families all the time."

"They do, don't they?" said Wanda Cahill, latching on to the offered crumb of comfort. "And she never ordinarily said, you know, who she was meeting, or where she was going. It was . . . she was defending her independence, I think."

"Did she ever talk about work?" asked Gemma.

"To me, sometimes. I run a small antiques shop, just across the way, so I know a bit about the business."

"Did she mention a brooch, an Art Deco diamond brooch that she'd taken in for sale?"

"Kristin? A diamond brooch?" Mrs. Cahill looked at Gemma so blankly that the answer was obvious.

"Never mind," Gemma said gently. "I'm sure it wasn't important." She started to rise. "We'll leave you to—"

"There was one thing." Wanda Cahill squeezed her hand, hanging on. "That phone call she took. She was friendly enough, at first. But when she went to her bedroom, before she closed the door, she said again, 'No, I don't want to come over,' but this time she sounded angry." Frowning, she seemed to search for a word. "Not just angry. Final."

"She won't forgive him." Kincaid slammed the car door harder than he'd intended.

"Who?" asked Gemma. "Who won't forgive who— I mean whom?"

"The mother. She won't forgive the father. And the poor bastard will probably spend the rest of his life blaming himself as well. I'll give you odds that marriage won't last a year."

"It was bad. It will be bad." Gemma touched his cheek. "I'm sorry."

"No." He covered her hand with his for a moment. "I'm sorry. I shouldn't be taking it out on you. And you were brilliant with Mrs. Cahill, by the way. It made me miss you, miss doing this together, every day."

Reaching for the ignition, he glanced at her. "You hungry?"

"After that?" Gemma shook her head. "Can't bear the thought."

"All right. We'll give it a bit. No word from Doug, or from the Yard on the CCTV or Kristin's phone records, so let's pay a call on Kristin's mate Giles. Do we have a last name for him?"

Gemma checked the notes she'd made at Harrowby's. "Oliver." She gave him the address.

It was a fairly well-heeled area in Fulham, near enough to Stamford Bridge that you'd not be able to get through the streets before or after a football match, nor get a foot in the door of the local pub on a match day. Kincaid thought the young man must be doing quite well for himself as a sales assistant at the auction house, unless he, like Kristin, still lived with his parents.

But when they reached the address Gemma had written down, they found a terraced house in bad repair, obviously a rental property. Paint flaked off the cream stucco and peeled from window and door trim; dead plants drooped from a first-floor window box, and the small yard attached to the garden flat was littered with empty crisp packets and beer bottles, and smelled of rotting food and cat pee.

"Lovely," Gemma muttered under her breath as Kincaid rang the bell for the top flat. A release buzzer sounded for the main door—there was apparently no intercom system. Kincaid opened the door for Gemma with a flourish. "Oh, you're going to make me go in first?" she said, teasing. "Very gallant of you." But as they entered the communal hall, she wrinkled her nose in real distaste. The ambience was on a par with the yard in front, but there was less fresh air to dilute it.

They climbed, Kincaid leading the way, passing scarred doors and treading on ever more threadbare carpet. A small, smudgy window on the landing let in much-needed light and air.

They reached the top floor, but before Kincaid could raise a hand to the door, a great woofing roar shook the corridor. Gemma started visibly and even Kincaid took a step back. "What the hell does he have in there, a bloody lion?"

"Get back, Mo, you great oaf!" came a shout from inside the flat, but the voice lacked a reassuring element of command.

Then the door swung open and a young man faced them, panting, hanging on to the collar of the largest dog Kincaid had ever seen. "Don't worry," the young man said. "He won't do anything worse than drool on you."

From the size of the dog's drooping jowls, Kincaid didn't doubt the drooling, and as the beast's tail was whipping back and forth in a frantically friendly wag, he decided to take the owner's word for the rest. "Mr. Oliver? We're from the police. We'd like to talk to you about Kristin—"

"Mo, sit." Giles Oliver dragged the dog into a sitting position away from the door, giving them room to step inside, although Kincaid noticed Gemma stayed a pace behind him. "You want to talk to me about Kris—Kristin?" Oliver's voice broke on the name. The dog stopped straining towards the visitors and leaned against his master's leg, looking up at him with a furrowed canine brow.

"If you don't mind. I'm Duncan Kincaid and this is Gemma James." The young man's face, Kincaid saw, was almost as puffy with weeping as Wanda Cahill's, and he suspected that, for the moment, sympathy would be more persuasive than rank.

Oliver gestured towards a small sofa. "Here, sit down. I'll just give it a brush—"

"We'll be fine," Kincaid said, preferring the risk of dog hair on trousers to the possibility of being bowled over if Oliver let go of the dog.

"He's a mastiff, isn't he?" asked Gemma, apparently unfazed by the dog's size. "He's lovely." While Kincaid gingerly took a seat, she dropped into a crouch and added, "Can I stroke him?"

Giles Oliver's rather weak-chinned face lit in a smile. "You don't mind? Most people would rather not. Just let me bring him to you so he won't knock you down."

Kincaid imagined Gemma saying a prayer for her newest Per Una skirt and layered cardigan, but she weathered the onslaught heroically, even to the slurp across her cheek with the longest pink tongue Kincaid had ever seen. Then she gave the dog a last scratch behind his floppy ears and joined Kincaid on the sofa, arranging her skirt demurely over her knees and obviously making an effort not to brush at the wet streaks.

Her exercise in canine bonding had given Kincaid a chance to examine the flat. Although small—the back of the sofa served as a divider between the living and sleeping areas—it didn't share the dilapidated state of the rest of the building. The place was clean and freshly painted—although there was a definite odor of dog—and the few pieces of furniture were of good quality, as was the rich-hued oriental carpet. But the studio's outstanding feature was a solid wall of shelving filled with vinyl LPs. To one side stood a double turntable and mixing station. It was apparent that Giles Oliver had at least one passion other than his dog, and he wondered where Kristin Cahill had figured in the equation.

"I know you," Giles said to Gemma as he settled into a squat, using an arm over the dog's shoulders as a prop. "You came into the salesroom, to talk to Kris. That's why she got a bollocking from Mr. Khan," he added, his tone becoming less friendly.

"I didn't mean to get her into trouble," answered Gemma. "Was he very cross?"

"More than usual. Although he's always harder on Kris than on anyone else. Was." His chin wobbled, giving him a fleeting resemblance to his dog. "*Was* harder on her."

"Have you any idea why?"

"No. I asked her, as a matter of fact, and she said she'd no idea. I wondered, though, if he, you know . . . fancied her. And if she'd turned him down . . ."

"Does Mr. Khan have a reputation for chatting up the female assistants?" asked Kincaid, interested.

"Well, no. But Kristin—I mean how could he *not* want . . ." His arm went a bit tighter round the dog, who groaned and slid down into a fawn-and-black mound on the carpet. The poor kid really had been besotted with Kristin Cahill, Kincaid thought with a flash of sympathy, and would not have had a snowball's chance in hell. But that made him all the more viable as a suspect.

Oliver righted himself, left the dog, and perched on the edge of a chair with smooth, curving, burnished wooden arms. Furniture design was not Kincaid's forte, but he guessed the chair was expensive, and original. "He'll be all right now," Oliver said, with a look at the dog. "Once he's out, he's out." As if in answer, Mo began to snore, and his owner looked at Gemma and frowned. "I don't understand. What were you doing at the salesroom yesterday, and why do you want to talk to me about Kristin?"

"Giles," said Gemma, "are you sure it was after I was there that Mr. Khan was upset with her?"

His face darkened. "Well, before . . . all this . . . I thought it might have been because of the roses. They came just after you left."

"Mrs. March said someone sent her roses. It wasn't you?"

"Are you kidding?" His laugh was bitter. "I just barely manage to pay the rent on this dump. There's no way I could afford flowers like that."

Priorities, Kincaid thought—Oliver apparently managed fine furniture and collector's vinyl on his pittance quite well.

"Do you know who did send the flowers?" asked Gemma.

Giles shook his head, tight lipped. "No."

Kincaid picked up the questioning, changing tack. "Did Kristin talk to you about the brooch?"

"What brooch?" Giles looked from Kincaid to Gemma.

"The Jakob Goldshtein diamond brooch," Gemma answered.

"Oh, that. She helped Mr. Khan catalog it. That's her job." Giles merely looked puzzled.

"She didn't tell you she was getting a bringing-in fee?"

"Kristin? Where would Kristin come across something like that?"

"We thought you might be able to tell us. That Kristin might have talked to you about it." Gemma leaned forward, inviting him to confide in her.

He colored, an ugly flush that brought out splotches on his neck. "No. She never said anything."

"What about when you called her last night?" asked Kincaid, taking the opportunity to play bad cop. At the sharpness in his voice, the dog raised his head and gave a low rumble, and Kincaid suddenly remembered reading that mastiffs were very protective of their owners.

But Giles Oliver seemed unaware of his dog's distress. "What?" he said, staring at them, but the blotches deepened in color.

"We talked to her mum," said Gemma. "What was it that you wanted Kristin to do?"

"I—I just wanted—I thought she might want someone to talk to about Khan giving her such a hard time."

"You asked her out?"

"No, not out, exactly. I thought she might want to come over. Listen to some records. You know, chill a bit. But—" He looked round the flat, as if seeing it through their eyes. "I should have known, shouldn't I?"

"That she'd say no?"

"She said she was going out," he retorted, as if trying to recover a shred of pride. "Meeting someone. At the Gate. That's why she couldn't come over."

"The Gate in Notting Hill?" Kincaid asked, frowning. The Gate was the nightclub in the basement of the cinema of the same name, a Notting Hill landmark.

"Yeah. I guess. I don't go places like that. Can't afford

the drinks, and I'd rather make my own music." He gestured at the records and turntable.

"Did she say who she was meeting?"

"No. Maybe the same guy who sent her the roses. She was on her mobile with someone, after she argued with Mr. Khan."

"Or maybe you're making it all up," Kincaid said slowly. "Maybe when she turned you down, let you know you were a stupid git to even think she would consider going out with you, you decided to get even. You drove over and waited for her to come home, then gunned the car at her. Maybe you just thought you'd teach her a lesson."

"What?" Giles stood, and the dog rose onto his massive haunches, growling. "Are you saying someone ran Kristin down on purpose?"

"You had good reason."

"Me? Why would I do that? I loved her!" He began to laugh, with a hint of hysteria. "And I don't have a bloody fucking car."

# 11

❧

*It was after Germany had occupied Austria in March 1938, and the dreadful events of Kristall-nacht on 9 November 1938, when 269 synagogues, 1,000 Jewish shops and dwellings were burned and 30,000 arrests made, that emigration escalated. Thousands of Jews were thrown into concentration camps, and there were desperate attempts to flee. By the end of 1938 there were 38,000 German and Austrian Jewish refugees in Britain, and by 1940 about 73,000...*

> —Dr. Gerry Black, *Jewish London:*
> *An Illustrated History*

"**WELL, THAT WAS A** great success," Kincaid said as he eased the Rover back into traffic. He'd rung Cullen as soon as they were back in the car, learning that Giles Oliver not only had no car registered in his name, he had no driving license.

"Sarcasm doesn't become you," Gemma replied mildly. "And it wasn't a waste of time. We know where Kristin went—"

"Or at least where she told Giles she was going."

She glanced at him—his lips were set in a straight line. He didn't like feeling a fool. "You're determined to be diffi-cult," she told him. "We at least have a place to start. And we know that there was a bloke in her life who probably sent her roses. Was that what made Khan angry, or was it me asking her about the brooch? And is Giles right? Did she meet the rose sender when she went out?"

"Or maybe Giles borrowed a neighbor's car, license or not."

"Do you really see Giles Oliver running someone down?"

"Vehicular homicide doesn't require getting up close and personal. Although I have to admit I can't see him asking for someone's keys, much less hot-wiring the neighbor's Volvo." His mouth relaxed, quirking into a smile. "Now if it had been accidental assault by dog . . ."

"I can't blame Kristin for resisting the dog and DJ combo," Gemma said, but the thought made Kristin seem very real. Sobering, Gemma wondered what would have happened if Kristin had accepted Giles's invitation. Would Giles and Mo have seen her home and kept her safe, at least for that night? "We'll have to check with his neighbors. Someone might have seen something, however unlikely."

"Where do you want to go, love?" Kincaid asked as they reached the King's Road again. "We seem to be at a momentary standstill. I can drop you at the Yard, if you want to get the tube to the hospital."

Gemma realized that for the last hour she'd hardly given her mum a thought, and with the prick of guilt all her worries came rushing back, both for her mum and for Erika. Glancing at her watch, she saw that Kit would just be getting home from school. An idea struck her and she said, "Let me make a quick call."

She caught Kit just as he was coming into the house, spoke to him, and was ringing off when Melody beeped in, her voice filled with cat-in-the-cream satisfaction.

"You'll never guess what I found out, boss."

Kit felt rather pleased. He liked Gemma's thinking that he could be helpful, and he wanted to talk to Erika again. He was curious about what had happened to her family, but felt he had put his foot in it a bit yesterday. He would have to bring it up more tactfully. Nor was he quite sure how to talk to Erika about the girl Gemma said had been killed, but he supposed he would think of something.

And, unlike yesterday, this time he had the opportunity to get out of his school clothes. Today was even warmer, so he swapped blazer and tie for jeans and T-shirt, let the dogs out into the garden for a quick pee and gave them biscuits, then set off down Lansdowne Road. When a gaggle of uniformed schoolgirls passed him and gave him the eye, giggling, he grinned at them with an unaccustomed sense of power and quickened his step.

When he rang the bell in Arundel Gardens, Erika answered immediately, and she didn't seem at all surprised to see him.

"I've made lemonade," she said. "Real lemonade, the way we used to make it in the summers in Germany when I was a child, not the fizzy stuff from a bottle."

"Did Gemma ring you?" he asked, following her into the flat.

"She's fussing over me. And sending you to fuss by proxy," Erika answered, but she didn't sound displeased. "Anyone would think I was an old biddy, although I've never been sure just what a biddy is. It sounds rather unpleasant.

"It's cooler inside today than out," she added as they reached the kitchen.

She had put two tall glasses on a tray, along with a clear glass jug in which floated a few ice cubes and slices of lemon. When she poured Kit a glass he drank it down thirstily, finding he liked the tartness. He slid into a seat at the small table, and at Erika's nod, poured himself another glass.

Erika sat across from him, but barely touched her own drink. He saw now that in spite of her chatter, she looked tired, and bright spots of color burned in her cheeks.

"I'm sorry about the girl who was killed," he said, finding it suddenly easy. "And I'm sorry for what I said about your father yesterday. It wasn't fair of me."

"No." She shrugged aside his apology. "It was what happened that wasn't fair. Nothing was fair then, but you were right, you know. We should never have let my father talk us into letting him stay behind. But he was a stubborn man, and he convinced himself that if he carried on as usual and pretended we had gone to visit relatives in Tilsit, then there was less likely to be an alert for us.

"Not that the Nazis were averse to letting Jews out of the country at that point, mind you, but David was a troublemaker, and they might have thought he would stir up antagonism against the regime if he reached a country where he could speak freely."

"But once you got out—couldn't your dad—"

Shaking her head, Erika said, "It was 1939. By the time we were settled in London, Germany invaded Poland. After that, we lost all communication, although we tried, everyone tried. But even the news broadcasts were censored by the Nazis, and we could only guess, and listen to the tales told by those who came after us. It was only after the war, when records began to become available, that I learned my father lost his business not long after we left, and then our home. He was taken to a work camp—that was what they called them, then."

"Sachsenhausen?"

"Yes. As far as I was able to discover, he died in Camp Z."

Kit couldn't imagine the not knowing, the imagining that could not have comprehended the horrors her father must have endured. At least he knew what had happened to his mum, what she had suffered, and that her death had been quick.

And what had it been like for Erika, a stranger in London, marked out by her accent as an alien, and worse, as a German? But at least she hadn't been alone.

"Your husband. When you came to London, did he do what the Nazis thought he would do? Did he tell people what had happened?"

Erika looked out into the garden. The fig tree outside the kitchen window made moving green shapes of the sunlight, like liquid puzzle pieces, and Kit caught the scent of hyacinths through the open window. He was sweating, and drops of condensation trickled down the outside of the lemonade jug. She was quiet for so long that, once again, he had begun to wish he hadn't asked, when she turned back to him.

She studied him for a moment, her dark eyes intent, until he felt he was being measured, or tested.

Then she said, "Let's go for a walk, shall we? In the sun. And I'll tell you about my husband."

*The CID room stank. There were too many bodies in a small space, wearing clothes rancid with sweat from the heat. Too many fag ends put out in desktop ashtrays, too many grease-stained chip wrappers, all mixed with the pervasive odor of burnt coffee.*

*Gavin put down the phone for what seemed the hundredth time and rubbed at his ear, damp from contact with the heavy earpiece. His head ached and his stomach burned from too much of the same coffee whose smell permeated the air. He wondered why he had ever wished for it to be spring, and why he refused to give up on a case that was going nowhere.*

*Last night he had stayed late at the station, compiling every report on David Rosenthal—the detailed postmortem, the house-to-house reports from the area near the murder, his own carefully typed interviews with Erika Rosenthal and David Rosenthal's colleagues—and he had come up with nothing.*

*When he had gone home at last, Linda had been awake, her hair in papers, reading a magazine in bed. She had studied him, her nose wrinkled in distaste, and he'd wondered if he still smelled of death from the mortuary, or if he somehow carried the mark of his desire for another woman. Guilt had made him brusque, and he had been careful not to touch her as he climbed into bed. He suddenly found the thought of intimacy with his own wife unimaginable, and he drifted into sleep facing away from her, clutching his pillow like a drowning man clinging to a spar.*

*He had awakened early and had spent the morning making phone calls to contacts at newspapers and to the few underlings in government offices he could count as reliable sources, but no one would admit to knowing anything concrete.*

*Yes, there were rumors—one assistant to an undersec-*

*retary at the Home Office had even said he'd heard whispers that the Haganah, the Jewish terrorist organization, had offshoots in London. But these figures seemed mythical, shadowy, as hard to pin down as wolves flitting in and out of the edge of a forest.*

*Nor could he see any reason why, if David Rosenthal had supported such people, they would have had reason to kill him. Unless . . . Unless David had fallen out with their ideals, and had threatened to expose them.*

*Frustrated with the endless loop of questions, Gavin pushed back from his desk. David Rosenthal had kept more than one part of his life hidden from his wife and his colleagues. It was past time he paid a visit to the British Museum.*

Having appropriated Gemma's desk, Melody leaned back in the chair and prepared to enjoy her disclosures. Although Kristin Cahill had apparently thrown away the card that came with the flowers, Mrs. March had remembered the name on the florist's delivery van.

It was indeed an upmarket floral design shop in Knightsbridge, and Melody had put on her best posh voice when she made the phone call, the accent she tried her best to rub out of her daily existence. When she explained her mission, the salesclerk, sounding decidedly frosty, informed her that they were not in the habit of giving out their customers' private information.

Melody explained, very politely, that they could of course get a warrant, but that would entail disrupting the business considerably, and that the presence of the police would certainly be of interest to the shop's clientele. And besides, she added, who was to say that the recipient of the bouquet in question hadn't told a friend or coworker who had sent them?

Having been assured of discretion, the florist hesitated. "How do I know you are who you say you are?" she asked. "You could be some journalist prying into our clients' private lives."

The thought made Melody smile, but she schooled her

expression back into earnest sincerity and asked the woman to ring her back at the station number. That done, the florist reluctantly gave her the name.

Melody stared at the name she had scribbled, her eyes wide, then began checking references on the Internet. When she was satisfied and had printed a photo, she rang Gemma.

"His name," she said, "is Dominic Scott. His grandfather was Joss Miller, a financier who made his fortune rebuilding London after the Blitz, often using less than respectable methods.

"Kristin Cahill was definitely dabbling outside of her sphere—or stratosphere might be more accurate. Dominic Scott's mother, Ellen, who goes by the awkward hyphenate of Miller-Scott, has devoted herself to turning her father into a saint through philanthropy and arts patronage, especially now that she no longer has to reckon with the old man himself. He died two years ago from liver cancer."

"So what about the grandson?" asked Gemma.

"Dominic, on the other hand, has a bit of a rep as a bad boy. A few run-ins on minor charges—public intoxication, creating a disturbance, that sort of thing. But it doesn't seem to amount to more than spoiled rich-boy antics."

"And this was Kristin's mysterious boyfriend?" asked Gemma, sounding suitably impressed.

"Unless Dominic Scott was sending flowers to a stranger."

*Gavin took the bus to Bloomsbury, not being able to bear the thought of sweltering on the tube. He sat on the top deck by an open window, watching the spring green of Hyde Park, then the bustle of Oxford Street, and by the time he alighted at Tottenham Court Road, his head had cleared. A breeze picked up as he walked the last few streets to the museum, drying his damp hair and collar.*

*The Reading Room itself was dark and cool, an oasis from the unrelenting glare of the sun. This was an unfamiliar world to Gavin, and as he looked round the curving vault, its walls lined with a bulwark of books, the lamps in*

*the cubicles illuminating heads bent over books and papers,
a wave of inadequacy swept over him. David Rosenthal had
been like these men, educated, a scholar. How could he,
Gavin, have entertained, even for a moment, the fantasy
that Erika Rosenthal could fancy him, a plodding policeman?*

*But plod he was, and he had a job to do. Although the li-
brarian agreed to show him the cubicle that David Rosenthal
had used, he assured him that he would find nothing personal of interest.*

*"The cubicles are used by more than one reader," the
librarian explained, "and David was always careful to take
his materials with him."*

*"Nevertheless, I'd like to see it," Gavin had insisted.*

*But the librarian had been right. Having been led half-
way round the room, then left on his own, Gavin contemplated the empty chair, the scarred but clean surface of the
desk, the darkened lamp. There was nothing here, no hiding
places, no secret messages, no trace of the man who had
spent his precious free time here instead of with his wife.*

*Gavin turned his attention to the man working in the
next cubicle, his dark head bent over a rat's nest of papers
illuminated by his green-shaded lamp.*

*"Excuse me," said Gavin, stepping nearer. The man
pulled his attention from his work with obvious reluctance,
then his gaze sharpened as he looked Gavin over. He was
younger than Gavin had realized. With his curly dark hair
and rather delicate, pointed face, he made Gavin think of
a faun.*

*"Can I help you?" he asked in perfect, unaccented Eng-
lish, and Gavin realized he had unconsciously assumed the
man was foreign.*

*Introducing himself, Gavin asked, "I was wondering if
you knew David Rosenthal? Do you work often in this particular cubicle?"*

*"Abraham Krumholtz." The man half stood and shook
Gavin's hand. "Yes, I knew David. At least as well as anyone could say they knew David, I suspect." Krumholtz kept*

*his voice just above a whisper, so as not to disturb the other readers.*

Gavin pulled up the empty chair and sat near enough that the pool of light from Krumholtz's lamp spilled onto his knees.

Krumholtz, however, seemed not to mind the invasion of his space, and went on quietly. "A constable came round yesterday, asking about his things. That was the first we knew. I still can't quite believe he's gone. I've worked beside him, on and off, since the end of the war. I'm a Yiddish scholar," he added, seeing Gavin's curious look at his papers. "That's what comes of being a second-generation immigrant—I'm fascinated by things my parents and grandparents took for granted."

"And David," asked Gavin, "what was David working on?"

"A memoir of his last years in Germany, and I think perhaps his escape from Germany as well. He never actually said, you understand. This I deduced over the years from bits of conversation."

"He never showed you the manuscript?"

"Oh, no. David was very . . . possessive . . . about his work."

"Do you think that David might have been naming names in his book? Some of his colleagues at work believed he had connections with some sort of vengeance organization."

It was difficult to be certain in the green-tinged light, but Gavin thought Krumholtz paled. "Look, I'm not political," he said, sounding wary. "I stay well out of these things. But David did hint, more than once, that there were many Germans who were guilty but were never implicated as collaborators. But he couldn't have intended to publish such things . . ."

"Why not? Surely if that were the case, the truth should be told."

Krumholtz leaned forward until their heads almost touched, and Gavin smelled peppermint on his breath. "Our *government would never allow it, for one. No one wants to disturb the status quo with Germany." For the first time his voice held a bitter note. "Nor do they want anything to call into question the Home Office's record of rescuing Jews. Things are touchy enough these days with Palestine."*

Gavin considered this and didn't like the implications. "Last Saturday, did David say or do anything unusual?"

Krumholtz started to shake his head, then stopped, putting a finger to the tip of his nose. "Now that you mention it, there was one thing. David had a newspaper with him, as he usually did. But as we were both tidying up, at closing time, I heard a ripping sound. When I looked over, I saw that David had torn out part of a page. When he saw me, he folded the fragment and put it into his satchel, along with the rest of the paper."

"And you didn't ask him what it was?"

"Of course not." Krumholtz smiled. "You didn't know David. One didn't ask questions. And besides, there was something a bit furtive about it. I said good night and left."

"And you didn't notice which paper he had that day?"

"No. Sorry." Krumholtz glanced back at his desk, as if his attention had been drawn too long from his work. "And there was no real pattern to what he bought—David read them all, highbrow and low."

"Thank you." Gavin stood. "If you think of anything else . . ." He handed a card with the station phone number to Krumholtz, who set it among his papers with a casual disregard that didn't augur well for further communication.

But as Gavin turned to go, Krumholtz stopped him, his brow creased in an expression of concern. "Look," he said, dropping his voice all the way to a whisper. "These people you mentioned. I'd leave it alone. Rumor has it that the government looks the other way. You could get into real trouble."

The address Melody had given them was in Cheyne Walk, and made Kincaid give a low whistle. "At least it's convenient," he said, "although I'd say little Kristin was out of her element."

"Not far as the crow flies, though," mused Gemma. "I wonder how she met Dominic Scott." As they curved round into Cheyne Walk, Gemma gazed out at the houseboats moored beyond Cremorne Gardens. The boats made her think of the garage flat, tiny as one of these floating homes, that she had once occupied behind her friend Hazel Cavendish's house. She felt saddened by how quickly parts of life that had seemed terribly important faded from memory, pushed out like falling dominoes by new experience. "There's not room for it all," she said aloud, and Kincaid gave her a quizzical look but went back to address hunting.

They had almost reached the Chelsea Embankment when he said, "There," and pulled the car up on the double yellows. He popped a POLICE notice in the windscreen and they got out, surveying Dominic Scott's house. It was red-bricked and gabled, almost Dutch in feel, four stories with basement, and with its own small front garden surrounded by a delicate wrought-iron railing.

"I take it," Kincaid said with great understatement, "that he lives with his mum."

Gemma realized that Melody hadn't said anything about Dominic Scott's father. "Nice," she agreed, sudden nerves making her sarcastic. "Upstairs, downstairs. Maybe we should consider the servants' entrance."

He grinned back at her as he opened the gate smartly and strode to the topiary-flanked door. "Not on your bloody life."

But the woman who answered on the first ring of the bell was no starched, uniformed maid. Small enough to make Gemma feel awkward, slender, and blond, she wore jeans Gemma recognized as expensive designer label and a silky pale blue sweater. If the color of her chin-length hair owed more to art than nature, it was expensively done, and her skin was flawless. A slightly prominent nose saved her from banal prettiness, but still, the overall effect was stunning, and Gemma suspected Kincaid must be gaping.

"Can I help you?" the woman asked, gazing at them with a slightly bemused smile.

"Mrs. Miller-Scott?" asked Gemma, wishing she dared dig Kincaid in the ribs. "I'm Inspector James, and this is Superintendent Kincaid, from Scotland Yard."

"Please, I prefer Ms., irritating as it is. I haven't been anyone's Mrs. for a good many years. And knowing who you are doesn't tell me what you want." She was still polite, but there was a slight edge to her voice.

"It's actually your son we'd like a word with, Ms. Miller-Scott." Kincaid had apparently recovered his powers of speech. "Dominic. He does live at this address?"

This time a definite flash of emotion disturbed the woman's composed face, but Gemma couldn't be sure if it had been worry or annoyance. "Yes, Dom has an apartment here. But he's not in right now, although I expect he'll be back soon. Is he in some sort of trouble?"

"We'd just like to have a chat with him," Kincaid said easily. "Could we come in and wait?"

Ellen Miller-Scott shrugged, and this time the annoyance was unmistakable. "Please yourself." As she led them into the house, it was Gemma's turn to gape.

The exterior of the house had led her to expect the traditional, a chocolate box of color and gilt. But while the floors of the entry hall and sitting room were a dark glossy wood, the walls were a crisp white, a backdrop for the paintings that filled much of the space, gallery style. Gemma thought she recognized a Hockney, and a Lowry, but there were too many to take in, and all were stunning.

Splashes of colorful contemporary rugs anchored sleek leather furniture, tables held flower arrangements that must have cost a month of Gemma's wages—probably done by the florist responsible for Kristin's roses, which now seemed paltry in comparison—and in what seemed a perfect, if rather eccentric, counterpoint, a huge crystal chandelier hung from the Adam rose in the center of the ceiling.

"It was my father's." Miller-Scott had followed Gemma's gaze. She sounded amused. "A bit incongruous, I admit, but I like it. Do sit."

Gemma managed a strangled "Lovely," and sank as

gracefully as she could manage onto the sofa near the marble fireplace. On the backs of her bare calves the leather felt as sensuous as skin.

Not looking the least bit gobsmacked, Kincaid sat down beside her, adjusted the crease in his trousers, and smiled at their hostess. "You have quite a collection, Ms. Miller-Scott."

She perched on the arm of the opposite sofa, a position that indicated limited tolerance of their presence, and did not offer them refreshment. "My father had a knack for knowing what would become valuable—a trait that is apparently not inheritable, if my son is any indication. Now, what is Dominic supposed to have done? I don't suppose you send out superintendents for parking tickets."

In spite of the bored voice, there was something in the line of the woman's body, in the angle of her head, in the way her manicured fingers grasped her crossed knee a little too tightly, that made Gemma think she was more worried about her son than she admitted.

"We don't *know* that your son has done anything," Kincaid answered, with careful emphasis. "It's merely a matter of help—"

The front door slammed. Gemma saw the ripple of shock in Ellen Miller-Scott's body, the instinct to rise quickly controlled. Instead, she called out, "Dom! In here."

Dominic Scott's voice preceded him into the room. "Mum, I'm really not in the mood for a family discussion at the mo—" He stopped on the threshold, frozen, as he took in the tableau.

Unlike his mother, he was dark, and he was older than Gemma had imagined, nearer thirty than twenty. His hair was slightly too long, and brushed carelessly away from his face. He wore a suit that had *not* come from Marks and Sparks, with a white dress shirt open at the neck. And in spite of the pallor of his skin and the dark circles under his eyes, he had grace, and that indefinable combination of features that makes for striking physical beauty, male or female.

Gemma felt an instant's stab of pity for Kristin Cahill, who must have been as vulnerable as a moth flying too near a candle, and for poor Giles Oliver, who had had as much chance as a pug set against a greyhound.

Then Kincaid stood and, before Dominic's mother could get in an explanation, said, "Hullo, Dominic. My name's Duncan Kincaid, and this is Gemma James. We're from the Metropolitan Police, and we'd like to talk to you about Kristin Cahill."

"What?" Dom Scott looked from one to the other, and Gemma wondered if she had imagined the flicker of relief. What had he been expecting? "Look, I know she's a bit pissed off with me at the moment, but this is beyond funny." He came a few steps into the room, but stayed an uncommitted halfway between the sitting area and the door.

Oh, Christ, thought Gemma. If it was an act, he was very cool. But if not . . . "Dominic," she said quietly, "tell us when you saw Kristin last."

"Monday. Monday night. Look, what's this about? She's not returning my calls."

Kristin's phone had been found in her jeans pocket, crushed beyond recovery.

Kincaid took up Gemma's lead. "Tell us what happened on Monday night, Dominic. Where did you see Kristin?"

Ellen Miller-Scott glanced from Kincaid to Gemma, and the knuckles of the hand on her knee whitened. Dom took another hesitant half step forward, then ran a hand through his already disheveled hair. "At the Gate. It was only a row. I can't believe she's complained about it. She was still on at me about Saturday night."

"What happened on Saturday?" Kincaid asked, as relaxed as if they were discussing what they'd had for tea.

Dom shifted and rubbed at his nose. "I—I stood her up. I was supposed to meet her at this club, and I—I never got there."

"And that's why you sent her the roses at work on Monday?" said Gemma.

"What? How do you— The roses were to say, 'Sorry.'" He glanced at his mother, as if gauging her reaction, then went on. "And she—Kristin—agreed to come out that night, but she was still being a bit of a cow about the whole business, if you want the truth. If she's gone and done something stupid—"

He stopped, perhaps reading something in their faces. "What aren't you telling me?" he said, his voice rising.

"And that's the last you saw of her? At the Gate?"

"I've just said—"

"You didn't see her home?"

"See her home? No. She left me sitting in the Gate like a stupid git, and I thought if she was going to be bloody minded, she could—" He stopped, and Gemma saw his chest rise with a sharp, frightened intake of breath as he seemed to realize something was very, very wrong.

Gemma rose, and out of the corner of her eye saw Kincaid give her a slight nod. She said, "Dominic, someone ran Kristin down on Monday night, in the King's Road. She's dead."

Dominic Scott stared at them, his dark eyes dilating to black. He lifted a hand, as if reaching for an invisible support, then crumpled to the floor as if someone had removed the bones from his body.

# 12

❧

December 1940
Monday, 9th

> Last night was very bad indeed. Began soon af-
> ter 5:30 pm. . . . I had to run from my place to the
> Sanctuary as the barrage was working up. It never
> ceased until 2:30 am. Many bombs came down . . .
> some in our district. On enquiry today I find it was
> around the Sion Convent, Chepstow Villas and
> Dawson Place . . . people buried.
> —*Vere Hodgson,* Few Eggs and No Oranges:
> The Diaries of Vere Hodgson, 1940–1945

"FIRST TIME I'VE EVER had a bloke faint on me," Gemma
said, her mobile connection sounding a bit scratchy in Melody's ear.

"Was he faking it, do you think?" Melody asked. She
was still in Gemma's office, where she had been combing Internet and newspaper files for more information on Dominic
Scott.

"No, I don't think so. He was really out for a couple
of minutes, eyes rolled up in his head. Then he was diso-
riented when he came round. But I still wouldn't rule him
out as a suspect. It might have been pure fright at the idea
that we thought he was connected, or who knows, maybe he
smacked her with the car and then convinced himself she
wasn't hurt. I've seen stranger things."

Melody flipped through her notes. "That's a bit complicated, boss, as he's another one that doesn't drive, and has
no car. He had his license revoked for drink driving, and
the records show the Mercedes registered in his name was
sold. Did you get anything else out of him when he came
round?"

"No." Gemma sighed. "He seemed genuinely devas-
tated. And his mum went into protective mode, so we said
we'd take a statement when he was feeling a bit better."

"When he's had time to get his story straight, more likely.
But if he'd said anything useful in those circumstances,"
Melody added, "she'd have the lawyers on you like flies.

"Ellen Miller-Scott has a history of undertaking litiga-
tion with anyone who crosses her, including her ex-husband,
Dominic's father, Stephen. Apparently the marriage only
lasted a couple of years. By the time she'd finished with Steve
Scott, he was willing to give up all custody of Dominic and
disappear without a penny. The last trace I could find of him,
he was living in Canada, running an art gallery in some little
village in Quebec."

"She must have been very persua—" Gemma cut out for
a moment. When Melody could hear her again, she was saying, ". . . before we interview Dom Scott again, we need to
check out his story. He says Kristin left him at the Gate, and
that he stayed until closing.

"Melody, Duncan's asked Cullen to go along. Would you
mind meeting him there? You've got Dom's photo, and besides, I'd like your take on the interview." She added, with
some hesitation, "I wouldn't ask, but I've got to get to hospital . . . and Duncan's got to get home to the kids . . ."

"Of course," said Melody quickly, but she was torn between being flattered that Gemma wanted her opinion and
annoyed at having to share the task with Doug Cullen. Looking at her watch, she saw that it was after seven. "I suppose
I should go along now?"

"Cullen's on his way from the Yard."

Maybe she would beat him there, thought Melody, if
she got her skates on. But before Gemma could disconnect,
Melody said, "Listen, boss, about your mum . . . I—" Then

she found that anything she had meant to say seemed trivial and useless, and she stuttered to a halt.

But there was a smile in Gemma's voice as she answered, "Yeah. Thanks."

By the time Gemma reached St. Barts, visiting hours were over and she had to bully the charge nurse into letting her into the ward, pleading she'd been delayed by urgent police business—which she supposed was true enough. The plus side to her tardiness was that her sister and father had gone, and her mum was awake, alert, and glad of the company.

"Hullo, love," said Vi as Gemma kissed her on the cheek. "How are you?"

"I should be asking you that." Feeling contrite, Gemma pulled a chair close to the bed. "I'm sorry, Mum. But there's this case . . ."

Vi smiled affectionately. "There always is."

"Never mind. Tell me about your day. I haven't talked to Cyn since this morning. Did you have more tests?"

"Oh, it's all a load of nonsense." Vi sounded exasperated, more like her usual self. "But the doctor's very bossy, and he says I have to start these treatments tomorrow."

So quickly? Gemma felt a lurch of fear. "Chemotherapy?" she asked, trying to keep her tone matter-of-fact.

"They say it's not so bad now," Vi said with determined cheerfulness. "And I'd much rather hear about your day than talk about mine. Tell me about your case."

So Gemma did, settling more comfortably in her chair and starting from the beginning, with Erika's request that Gemma look into the reappearance of her missing brooch, and ending with their interview that evening with Dominic Scott.

By the time she finished, her mum's eyes had drifted closed, and she was silent for so long that Gemma thought she had fallen asleep. She was reaching for her handbag when her mother said softly, "It must have been hard for your friend Erika, during the war. You can't imagine what it was like, during the bombing. You never knew if you were going to get through the night. But we were family, all the neighbors, and everyone looked out after everyone else. If you had no one . . ."

Gemma sat back in surprise. Her mum never talked about the war.

"Of course, it was easier for children," Vi went on, her eyes still closed. "Children adapt. We forgot, after a bit, that we had ever known anything different." She opened her eyes and smiled at Gemma. "Little savages, weren't we? Got up in the mornings and ran to see what had been hit the night before. And we got used to people disappearing from our lives.

"Children are such odd creatures, like sweets, hard on the outside and soft on the inside. It was only later that the memories would creep up on us."

"I never knew." Gemma took her mother's hand, stroking her thumb over the soft skin between her mum's thumb and finger. The tissue felt thin, fragile.

"Oh, I never meant you to. Don't know why I'm going on about it now. Except . . . I was thinking about Kit today." Vi met Gemma's gaze. "He'll be worried about me."

"Yes," Gemma admitted. "He is."

Her mother gripped her hand. "It's hard for you, isn't it—to tell Kit that you love him."

"I—" Gemma stared at her mum, blindsided. "I—I don't want—I never want him to feel I'm trying—"

"Kit won't think you're trying to take his mother's place," Vi said with unexpected fierceness. "You've gone past that now. He loves you, and he needs to know that *you* are not going away."

It wasn't until Melody stood on the pavement outside the nightclub at Notting Hill Gate that she thought about her clothes. The street was in shadow as the setting sun dipped behind the buildings to the west. The amplifiers in the club pumped music up the stairs, pushing it out into the street in throbbing waves of sound, and the handful of girls that slipped into the doorway as Melody watched looked like butterflies in their jeans and gaudy tops.

Melody glanced down at her suit, charcoal that day, with the skirt showing an entire daring inch of thigh. Her legs were bare, at least—it had been too warm for tights—and were worth showing off a bit, but she was going to look as out of place as a polar bear at the equator. This was an occasion when her protective coloring would put her at a disadvantage, and she found that bothered her more than she expected.

"Oh, bugger," she muttered, and slipped off her jacket. She pulled out her shirttail and unbuttoned the second button on her white shirt, then the third, then ran a hand through her dark hair, mussing her usual tidy style.

Grimacing at her own foolishness, she added, aloud, "Fat lot of good that will do."

"Have you started talking to yourself?" said a voice behind her.

She jumped, swearing, and turned to find Doug Cullen watching her with a grin. "I was just—never mind," she said. "You shouldn't sneak up on people."

"And you shouldn't do a strip in public if you don't want people watching."

Melody flushed, furious with him and with herself. "It's warm, and warmer down there."

"You were going to steal a march on me, weren't you?" said Cullen, giving her a considering eye.

"And you weren't?" she challenged.

"I couldn't," he answered mildly. "You have Dominic Scott's photo."

Somehow this made her more aggravated, not less. Gritting her teeth, she said, "Yes. So let's get it over with," and charged towards the stairs.

But she found immediately that it was a steep, straight flight, and not made for plunging down in heels. Forced to slow down and step carefully, she felt Doug Cullen's eyes on her back and it made her as awkward as the schoolgirl she had once been.

But as she reached the floor of the club, the pulse of the music and the liquid blue light subsumed all other perception. Even though it was still early, the floor was crowded. Melody found she had to twist and sidle to make her way through the crush of bodies.

Managing to squeeze into a space at the bar before Cullen, Melody smiled at the barmaid, a pretty girl with Scandinavian-fair hair woven into a thick plait. Melody watched her making a cocktail, graceful as a dancer as she mixed, shook, and poured.

When she'd served the pink concoction to the waiting customer, she turned to Melody. "What can I get you?" Her accent was as English as Melody's own.

"We just want a word, if you don't mind." Melody held up her warrant card and the two photos she had pulled from her bag. "I'm DC Talbot." She nodded at Cullen, who had maneuvered into a space beside her. "Sergeant Cullen."

The girl looked slightly wary, but after checking that no one was waiting to be served at her end of the bar, said, "Okay. Shoot. I'm Eva, by the way."

"Were you working Monday night?"

Eva frowned, thinking, then nodded. "Yeah. I was on. Not my usual, but I was filling in for Jake."

Melody handed over the photos. "Did you see either of these people that night?" She wondered how the girl could remember anyone in the constant onslaught of faces at the bar, but to her surprise Eva nodded again and tapped the photos.

"Yeah. I've seen them before. But that night they didn't seem to be getting on. He was waiting for her, and she was stroppy from the minute she came in. Said she didn't want a drink, then when he ordered for her anyway, she practically downed it in one go."

"Then what happened?" asked Doug, interrupting the flow of the girl's narrative and irritating Melody. But Eva gave him an assessing look and smiled.

"I got busy. Next thing I saw, she was leaving, and he looked royally pissed off."

"Did he follow her?" Melody kept her tone as casual as was possible at a half shout.

Eva shook her head. "No. Had another drink. But he was

broody, and didn't talk to me when I served him. Didn't tip me, either. Pretty boy," she added, with another smile at Cullen. "But I've seen him with some dodgy blokes."

"Anyone you know?"

"No. Just didn't look the sort you'd want to meet in a dark alley, if you know what I mean."

"Did you see what time he left?" asked Cullen, raising his voice against a new influx of customers.

"No. We get really busy just after the pubs close, and I don't remember seeing him after that." She glanced at the raucous crowd shoving up to the bar. "Look, sorry—" She handed the photos back.

"Thanks," said Melody. "You've been great. One more thing—where did they sit?"

"Front corner." Eva gestured towards the banquette tucked up against the street side, and glancing at the photos of the couple she had never met, Melody had a moment's vision of Dominic Scott and Kristin Cahill hunched over the table, arguing, their faces tense. Had it been about more than Dominic standing Kristin up on Saturday night?

Bringing her back to the present, Eva gave her a smile even more brilliant than the one she'd given Cullen, then said, "Why are you asking, by the way?"

Melody found she didn't want to be the one to bring a shadow on this bright girl. "Oh, just routine. Ta. Have a good night."

Melody raised a hand in salute, ignoring Cullen's frown, and led the way back through the crowd and up the stairs to the street.

It was a lovely evening. The setting sun had turned the buttermilk clouds in the sky behind the Coronet Theatre to a brilliant gold, and it looked as though cherubs might bounce down from them at any moment, blowing trumpets.

As they stood side by side on the pavement, for a wild instant Melody considered asking him if he wanted to get a meal and a glass of wine at the Pizza Express up the road.

But before she could speak, Cullen said, "It's iffy, then." He stared out at the traffic rushing past as the light changed at Pembridge Road. "The witness report puts Kristin's accident at not long after pub closing. Could Dominic have followed her, knowing her pattern, then run her down?"

"If that were the case, where did he get the car?" argued Melody, her goodwill dissipating. "I don't imagine Dominic Scott grew up learning how to hot-wire joy rides on the street. And if his mum took his Mercedes away when he lost his license, I don't imagine she gave him free access to her car for a night on the town." She shrugged. "I don't know. Somehow this doesn't feel like a lover's quarrel."

"And you're the expert?"

Melody turned to look at him. Even though she sensed he didn't like her, she was surprised by the meanness of the dig.

Retaliating, she said, "She fancied you, the girl at the bar, don't you think?"

Cullen flushed. "You're taking the piss."

"And what if I am?" She gave him a mocking smile and slung her jacket over her shoulder as she turned away. "Don't you have a warrant to run down?"

Cullen watched Melody Talbot walk away. What was it about the woman that got up his nose so?

For one thing, she seemed to assume that she had the right to lead an interview, even though he was the ranking officer and it was officially his and Kincaid's case.

She had an assurance he envied, and then there was this sense he had that she could see through him, knew all his little insecurities as well as she did her case notes—and that made him want to lash out at her. It was stupid, he knew, and if he kept it up, it would get back to Kincaid and might jeopardize his job. If he had a political bone in his body, he was going to have to be civil to her.

But that didn't mean he couldn't come up with other ways to show her up.

He began to walk aimlessly towards Holland Park, even though he knew he should get the District and Circle train from Notting Hill Gate back to Victoria and the Yard.

He thought back to their interview at Harrowby's that morning, and to the slightly shifty Amir Khan and the matter of the brooch. What if Kristin Cahill's death had nothing to do with her row with her boyfriend, and everything to do with the Goldshtein brooch? Kincaid had told him that Kristin's associate, Giles Oliver, had said that Khan had raked Kristin over the coals the day Gemma had inquired about the brooch, and that Khan had seemed to have it in for Kristin in general.

What if Kristin had known something about Amir Khan, or about the brooch, that had made it worthwhile to shut her up?

Cullen had a friend in Fraud, a chap who had been one of his classmates in the academy. Charles Lessing, like Cullen, had been saddled with the disadvantage in police work of a public school education, and that background had formed a bond between them.

He would give Charles a ring at home and see if Amir Khan had come across the sights of SO6.

That decision made, he looked round, saw that he had come even with the Pizza Express, and realized that he was starving. A pizza and a glass of house red would be just the ticket while he made his phone call and waited for the Harrowby's warrant to process.

"I'll have the Chateaubriand. And the best Côtes du Rhône on the list." Harry closed the French House menu with a snap. The waiter, who had served Harry many a soup du jour and glass of plonk, raised an eyebrow.

"Mr. Pevensey—"

"It's quite all right." Harry gave him his most magnanimous smile. "And I'll be having a pudding as well."

"If you say so, Mr. Pevensey." The waiter, still looking skeptical, went to place the order, and Harry sat back in his chair, surveying the tiny first-floor dining room with a proprietary air.

The French House was an actor's pub, and Harry had been coming here as long as he had been in the business. The staff had always welcomed him, even when he could afford no more than one cheap glass of wine, and tonight he meant to treat them royally. After dinner, he would go down to the bar and order another bottle of wine, perhaps even drinks all round. And if, at the end of the evening, he was too tipsy to stagger his way from Dean Street back up to Hanway Street, he'd bloody well take a cab.

Today he had stood up for himself, for the first time in his life. His fortunes were going to change, and in anticipation of his newly liberated state, he'd taken out the money put by for next month's rent to finance his little celebration.

The waiter brought his bottle of wine and ceremoniously uncorked it. Harry took the obligatory taster's sip, then nodded, and watched the ruby liquid spill into the glass. Of all the words he could think of for red—vermillion, scarlet, ruby, garnet, claret, burgundy—at least two were related to wine and two to gems, which seemed a particularly appropriate combination.

Harry had always loved the color of red wine, and had wondered if the quality affected its richness and depth. Tonight, as he held his glass to the light, he had no doubt that he had been right.

Swirling the wine in the glass, he drank a silent toast to himself. He deserved this, and more, for all the years he had settled for second best and let himself be treated like a lapdog at the beck and call of his betters.

And they owed him, the Millers. It was a debt he'd been waiting a long time to call in. Of course, even though he'd had a very interesting chat that afternoon with a friend in the antiques trade who had told him the brooch might fetch well over the reserve, he supposed he could be generous and give Dom a percentage. After all, he didn't bear the boy any malice, and wouldn't want to see him come to serious harm from the heavies with whom he'd got himself involved.

It wouldn't hurt Dom Scott to sweat a bit, however—perhaps he'd learn the error of his ways—and besides, Harry thought it a good idea to see what the brooch actually fetched before deciding on the extent of his generosity.

He settled back in his chair, sipping his wine and enjoying the ambience of the little restaurant, with its crisp white tablecloths and the large front windows open to the fine May evening. There was no music, and no mobile phones were allowed, so that the cadence of conversation rose and fell in its own musical counterpoint. This was the way life should be lived. A pretty woman dining alone across the restaurant kept glancing away when Harry caught her eye, but her lips curved in the little smile that meant she was enjoying the attention. Perhaps, thought Harry, he had not lost all his charm, and a little flirtation would be the perfect final act to his evening.

By the time his main course arrived, he had made considerable inroads on the bottle of Côtes du Rhône, and the woman across the room had given him an enticing glance across the top of her glass.

"Another one, Mr. Pevensey?" the waiter asked.

"Yes," said Harry, with his blood singing. "I believe I will."

*As the CID room emptied in the late afternoon, the air cooled and Gavin began to feel he could breathe again. He had come back from the museum and sent out a request for the previous week's newspapers. Although he thought it most logical that the paper from which David Rosenthal had torn the cutting had been Saturday's, he thought it prudent to widen his search.*

*Now the piles of newspapers teetering on his desk threatened to bury him. He had separated the broadsheets from the tabloids, on the assumption that something that had interested David Rosenthal would have been in a more reputable paper. But even the task of sorting through every page of the* Times, *the* Telegraph, *the* Guardian, *and the* Evening Standard *proved daunting, as he had no idea what might have caught David Rosenthal's eye. A mention of Nazi war trials or criminals? Mistreatment of Jewish refugees? A hint that terrorist organizations might be operating in London? A mysterious death or murder?*

*Sighing, he had put the* Times *aside and begun on the* Guardian *when his superintendent's secretary appeared at his desk.*

*"You're working late, Gladys," he said, pushing the hair from his brow with grimy fingers.*

*Gladys was a well-padded girl, with a propensity for flowered prints and tightly crimped hair, but was good natured enough to rub along with the guv'nor, no mean accomplishment. Now she gave him a concerned look. "His Highness wants to see you, in his office."*

*"What now?" Gavin looked down at his newsprint-blackened hands and his loosened collar and tie.*

*"Bee under his bonnet about something. I'd go soonest, if I were you. I'm off." She favored him with a toothy smile. "Cheerio. Hope you're not for the block."*

*"Thanks, Gladys," Gavin muttered under his breath. He slipped into his jacket, but took the time to stop in the lav and wash his hands, pull up his tie, and comb his hair. There was no point in facing his guv'nor at more of a disadvantage than necessary. The super was a man of moods and best approached with discretion on a good day.*

*Francis Tyrell was an Irish Catholic who wore his ambition on one shoulder and a chip on the other, so that one's reception depended on which side one faced. Gavin knocked at the open door, and when Tyrell looked up at him with a scowl, Gavin's heart sank.*

*"Sir. Gladys said you wanted to see me."*

*Tyrell nodded towards the chair, a hard-seated, slat-backed affair that always made Gavin think he might be tied up for an execution. Occupants of the chair were not meant to be comfortable, nor were they made any more so by the superintendent's looming bulk and florid face. Tyrell's still-thick hair was of a color that many a new officer had learned at his peril was not under any circumstances to be called ginger.*

*"This case you're working on," Tyrell said without preamble. "This business of the murdered Jew."*

*The pejorative use of the word* Jew *raised Gavin's hackles immediately. Tyrell was known for his prejudices, but this sounded ominously political.*

*"David Rosenthal," Gavin corrected. "A husband, a teacher, and a scholar. Brutally stabbed as he sat in Cheyne Gardens—"*

"*I know the facts of the case, man,*" Tyrell said impatiently. "*And I know that those facts are all you've got. You're wasting your time, Hoxley, and the department's resources. The man was robbed and killed. No suspects. End of story.*"

Gavin stared at him, shocked. Then he said, "*I don't believe for a minute that this was an ordinary robbery. David Rosenthal's possessions were removed to hide his identity—*"

"*And you have what proof of this?*" Tyrell's face was turning an unbecoming shade of puce, a clear danger signal.

"*I have a number of leads, sir—*"

"*You have a desk full of moldy newspapers, and about as much hope of finding anything as a blind man looking for a tit. Drop it, Gavin.*"

"*But, sir, I have reason to believe that Rosenthal saw something in the newspaper the day he died, something that sent him to Chelsea. And I think that either he met someone or he was waiting for someone—*"

"*I don't give a fig what you think. You don't have a shred of evidence, and that's the end of it.*"

"*But—*"

"*Inspector, unless you want to lose your job, you'll leave this alone.*"

Gavin made an effort to stop an angry retort. This was beyond a reprimand, and certainly beyond issues of CID manpower.

Superintendent Tyrell shifted in his chair and looked, for the first time, uncomfortable. "*You're a good copper, Hoxley. Don't make a balls-up of this. This is coming straight from the top. I can't ignore it, and you'd be a fool to.*"

"*The top?*" Gavin still wasn't quite believing what he was hearing.

"*Whitehall, man. So save us all a load of grief. Go home, and forget you ever heard of David Rosenthal.*"

The gig had finished a little before midnight. They'd played in a public hall in Guildford, and Andy Monahan thought for the hundredth time that they were going to have to take a stand, the three of them, and tell Tam, their agent, not to take any more bookings in places like that.

The room had been filled with teenagers intent on snogging; drinking anything they could get their hands on; or smoking, inhaling, or ingesting likewise. There had been a few kids, up towards the front, who had actually listened to the music, but at the end of the evening he always felt they might as well have been playing for sheep.

Tam called these bread-and-butter bookings, but in Andy's opinion they didn't generate enough income to be worth the time and disappointment. And it was time they might have spent playing in a club where someone who mattered might have heard them.

They'd had to load up their own equipment, of course, then cross their fingers as usual and hope that George's van made it back to London in one piece. As Andy hadn't been driving, he'd drunk his share of the bottle of vodka going round in the back, but rather than making him mellow, by the time they reached Oxford Street, he was more pissed off than he'd been when they left Guildford.

George slowed at Hanway Street and pulled into the curb. "Close enough, mate?" he asked. "Don't want to try to get the van round that corner." Hanway Street made a sharp right into Hanway Place, where Andy lived in a housing-authority flat, and if anyone had parked illegally, the van would have to be backed out into Oxford Street, no mean feat even for the entirely sober.

"Yeah, thanks." Andy climbed out, cradling his Stratocaster in its case. His amps he would leave in the van, as they had another gig tomorrow night—or tonight, he reminded himself, glancing at his watch, which showed it had just gone two.

Nick, who had drunk more than his fair share of the vodka, leaned out the window and intoned with great seriousness. "Chill, Andrew. You've got to chill, man."

Andy's frustration flared like a lit fuse. "Fuck you, man," he shouted back, and aimed a vicious kick at the side of George's van. But George was already pulling away, and the attempted blow only made him lose his balance. "Fucking morons," he muttered, teetering for a moment, then righting himself, holding the Strat case to his chest as if it were a child.

Maybe it was time he started looking for another band, one that really wanted to make music. And maybe he'd drunk a bit more than he'd thought, he decided as he trod carefully up the narrow street. Had to watch where you put your feet, people were always leaving bloody rubbish on the pavement. He'd stepped over a paper McDonald's bag, a broken beer bottle, and what smelled suspiciously like a puddle of urine, when he saw what looked like a large plastic bin liner lying in the middle of the street, just after the bend. A bin liner with things spilling out, even worse. But it was an odd shape, with what looked like arms and legs, except the angles were wrong.

Andy slowed, squinting, wishing he wasn't too vain to wear his glasses to a gig. Reaching the bundle, he pushed at it with his toe and met a slightly yielding resistance, and then the shape resolved into a human form, a man in a dark suit, lying in the street. Drunk, Andy thought fuzzily, but no one could lie like that, even if they'd passed out, legless. And the face—the face was turned away from him, but he could see that its shape was wrong, too, as if it had been mashed by a giant hand. Worse still, even distorted, it was a face Andy recognized.

Dear God. Andy backed up until his heels hit the curb, sat down with a graceless thud, and vomited right down the front of his Stratocaster case.

# 13

❧

*On numerous occasions during the 1930s—even after Kristallnacht—British diplomatic observers concluded that anti-Jewish violence had passed its peak.*

—Louise London, Whitehall
and the Jews, 1933–1948

GEMMA HAD SAT AT the hospital bedside until long after Vi drifted off, watching her mother's face, made unfamiliar by repose. When had she ever watched her mother sleep, seen the tiny tics that signaled dreams, wondered what her mum was dreaming?

What did she know of her mother's memories or desires, of her life outside of the daily routine of husband, children, and work? Had her mum imagined a different life for herself, adventures that had never come to pass, a husband or lover who expected more than familiarity and tea on the table?

Even now, lying in bed watching the splash of early morning sun on the opposite wall and enjoying the warmth of the cocker spaniel sprawled across her feet, she felt unsettled in a way that was deeper than worry over cancer and treatments, although that was bad enough.

Last night she had sensed a resignation that frightened her. What if her mum didn't want to fight this thing? Could she, who had always seemed indomitable, leave them so easily? Would she slip away, leaving Gemma to discover she had never really known her at all? And someday would her own children feel the same way about her?

She could hear the boys' voices floating up from downstairs, a medley of the usual morning laughter and complaint. They had been asleep by the time she'd got home last night, and this morning Duncan had been up early, whispering that she should have a lie-in, that he would get the boys ready for school.

But suddenly she wanted to be up, wanted to be in the midst of the clamor, wanted to spend the time she'd missed with the children the past few days. She threw back the covers and jumped out of bed, saying, "Sorry, boy," as she gave Geordie an apologetic pat. Grabbing a dressing gown, she padded barefoot down the stairs, the dog following.

She found the boys in the kitchen, dressed in their school uniforms, eating toast, and Kincaid slipping into his jacket.

"I've got to go," he said, kissing her on the cheek. "I'll take Toby. Come on, sport," he added. "Last bite, and get your satchel."

"No, wait," said Gemma. "He can be late. You go on."

"You're sure?"

"Positive." She brushed a stray dog hair from his jacket and waved him off. "Go."

"I'll ring you."

When the door had closed behind him, she turned to the boys. "What's your first class, Kit?"

"History," he mumbled through toast and jam, making a face.

"Any papers due, or quizzes?"

"No. Just old Toady lecturing." He gave an exaggerated snore.

"Old Toady?"

"Mr. Tobias," Kit corrected, rolling his eyes. "Why would anyone want to know about the War of the Roses? Dead boring, if you ask me."

"I'm sure I don't know, but I suppose it wouldn't hurt you to miss a lecture." When Kit stared at her in surprise, she grinned back. "I have a plan."

*  *  *

Cullen paused at the door to Kincaid's office. His boss sat at his desk, head bent over a disordered fan of papers. His hair stood on end and the knot on his tie was pulled loose, unusual evidence of frustration so early in the day. Maybe, thought Cullen, he could improve things.

"Name and address, guv," he said, entering.

Looking up, Kincaid rubbed at his eyes. "What?"

Cullen had got the warrant first thing that morning, and had been at Harrowby's door when the salesroom opened. Mrs. March had shown him to Khan's office, and Amir Khan had offered him a seat before perusing the paperwork.

Although as immaculately turned out as he had been the previous day, Khan's handsome face looked a bit hollow, as if he was tired, and he was warily polite. Cullen, who had gone in hyped for a protest, found himself a bit disappointed.

"It's all in order," he said when Khan started through the warrant for the third time.

"I'm sure it is, Sergeant Cullen. But it's my nature to be thorough, and I have to protect the interests of our customers. Do you mind if I make a copy for our records?"

"Be my guest," Cullen said, thinking he wished the man would bloody get on with it.

Khan stood and ran the warrant through the copier on top of a file cabinet with what seemed to Cullen agonizing slowness. Then he handed the paper back and opened one of the files, taking out a card. Returning to his desk, he transcribed the information from the card onto a sheet of notepaper and handed it across.

Cullen squinted at his unexpectedly illegible handwriting. "Harry Pevensey? And that's Hanway Place?"

"Yes," said Khan, sounding slightly irritated.

"And you met this Harry Pevensey?"

"Of course." The irritation seemed to be quickly turning to annoyance. "He said he was an actor, although I suspect not a terribly successful one."

"Did you think he came by the brooch legitimately?" Cullen asked, dogged.

"Sergeant Cullen. As I've said before, if we made sure that every client who brought in an item to sell had come by it legitimately, we'd have little business. People tell us what they want to tell us, and we check that information as far as we are able. In a case like this, the item speaks for itself, and it didn't really matter if Mr. Pevensey said he'd found it in a rubbish bin."

"He didn't—"

"A figure of speech, Sergeant. Now, if you don't mind, I have work to do. You can ask Mr. Pevensey yourself."

Smarting at the dismissal, Cullen had taken the information Khan had provided, but numerous attempts at ringing the phone number had not even got a response from an answering machine.

Now he said, "The seller of the brooch, guv. A Mr. Harry Pevensey of Hanway Place, London. No joy with the phone number, so I thought we should go along."

Kincaid glanced at his watch. "This is his home address you've got? Won't he be at work?"

"It's the only address he gave Harrowby's. But he did tell Mr. Khan that he was an actor, so perhaps we can find him at home this time of day." Cullen gestured at Kincaid's unfinished paperwork. "Anything interesting?"

"House to house, accident report, complete postmortem, forensics report on Kristin Cahill's room, and the records from her mobile phone carrier, which confirm that she had multiple calls to and from Dominic Scott, and that she had regular calls from Giles Oliver. Maybe she and Oliver were more friendly than Oliver admitted.

"As for the house to house, no one saw or heard anything, except for the witness who went to the scene and called 999." He leaned back in his chair, ticking things off on his fingers. "Cause of death, bleeding from severe internal injuries, consistent with being hit midbody by a car traveling at high speed. No trace evidence from the car found on her clothing or body, however.

"Otherwise, Kristin was a normal, healthy young woman. No sign of pregnancy or nonaccident-related injuries. No signs of recent sexual activity or assault. No drugs, and blood alcohol below the legal limit."

"And the CCTV?" Cullen asked.

"The footage shows a dark SUV. Possibly a Land Rover. But the plates are either obscured or missing."

"Definite premeditation, then," said Cullen. "But no one so far had a link with the car?"

"Not unless it's your Mr. Pevensey, and I think we should give him a try before we have a word with Giles Oliver." Kincaid pulled up the knot on his tie and smoothed his hair with his fingers, a maneuver that was only marginally successful. "How did you get on last night, by the way? Gemma said you went with Melody to check out the Gate."

"Dom Scott's story checks out to a point. The barmaid said Kristin met him there. They argued. She had a drink and then left. The barmaid, Eva, thinks he stayed until pub closing, but wouldn't swear to it. She—Eva—also said she'd seen Dom with Kristin before, but she'd also seen him with what she described as some 'dodgy' characters. If she knows more, she wasn't sharing."

"Eva?" Kincaid grinned at him, raising an eyebrow. "Fancied you, did she?"

"I'll give you a note excusing your tardiness," Gemma told Kit. "And if you think you can eat a bit more breakfast, we'll go to Otto's. I'll just go get changed."

Toby had jumped up and down, making the dogs bark, but Kit had stopped her as she turned away. "Gemma, this isn't about Gran, is it?"

"No," she assured him. "I just want to spend some time with you. But I will tell you about my visit with her last night."

They took the car, so that Gemma could drop Kit and then Toby off at school afterwards, but Kit wished they might have walked. After yesterday's heat, the day had cooled to crispness again, the sun was shining in a clear blue sky, and the brightly colored houses in Lansdowne Road looked freshly washed.

When they reached the café in Elgin Crescent, Otto greeted Gemma with a hug and kisses on both cheeks. "Gemma! I thought you were too busy for your old friends."

"Busier than I should be," she agreed. "But I'm taking a bit of time off this morning, and letting the boys play truant." The café was still half full, and Otto, tea towel tucked into his apron, bald head gleaming with perspiration, seemed to be managing on his own.

"Where's Wesley?" Kit asked as they took a table by the window.

"At one of his university classes. He will be in after lunch. And you, Kit, we are honored to see you two days in a row, and yesterday with your lady friend. Now, what can I get for you?"

Gemma gave Kit a curious look, but waited until they had ordered bacon and eggs before she said, "You were here yesterday, Kit?"

He felt himself color, felt stupid because of it, and blushed harder. "It wasn't a *girl*. I was with Erika. She wanted to go for a walk. So we stopped and had coffee, and a cake that Otto had made. Erika said it reminded her of things she used to eat in Germany."

"Was she all right about—" Gemma glanced at Toby, who was half out of his chair, picking at something on the underside of the table. "With what happened yesterday," she amended, capturing Toby's wrists in one hand. "Stop that, lovey."

"But somebody's left chewing gum, Mummy," he protested.

"Yes, and that was very naughty. They should know better, and you should know better than to touch it." She scooped him off the chair and gave him a pat on the behind. "Now be a good boy and ask Otto if you can wash your hands."

When she looked at Kit again, he frowned. "I don't know," he said. "We— She told me— I didn't know what to say."

"What did Erika tell you, Kit?" Gemma asked, with that look that meant you had her full attention and she wouldn't let it go.

Kit straightened his cutlery. "I'd asked her about her father. About why her father didn't get out of Germany—I know I probably shouldn't have."

He waited for censure, but Gemma frowned and said, "Why didn't her father get out?"

"He—" Kit fought a sudden and ridiculous urge to blink back tears. "He waited, because he didn't want to draw attention to Erika and her husband getting away. But by then it was too late." He swallowed, glad to have got through that bit without a quaver.

"Oh, no." Gemma looked stricken. "No wonder the brooch her father made means so much to her."

"But that's not the worst thing." Kit was determined now to tell her all of it before Toby came back. "Her husband was killed. Murdered."

"What?"

He glanced at Gemma, then back at the alignment of his knife. Erika had told him while they were sitting here, having coffee, and she had said it in a matter-of-fact way that he envied. Would he ever be able to tell someone his mum had been murdered without choking up and making a fool of himself? He was careful at school, often pretending that Gemma and Duncan were both his parents, and that they had always lived together. No one thought much these days about a mum having a different name.

Hearing Toby talking to Otto in the kitchen, Kit said quietly, "Someone stabbed Erika's husband—his name was David—in a park near the Albert Bridge. No one was ever charged, and Erika said"—Kit made an effort to remember her words exactly—"she said she didn't know if she could bear another unresolved death." He had understood, because he couldn't imagine how he would feel if he didn't know who had killed his mum.

"When?" asked Gemma. "Did she say when this happened?"

Kit shrugged. "A long time ago. After the war. But I don't see what that can possibly have to do with the girl who was killed yesterday."

Having tried Harry Pevensey's phone again from the office with no luck, Kincaid and Cullen had taken a car and driven to the address Khan had given Cullen.

The first sign of trouble was the police roadblock across the bottom end of Hanway Street.

"Bugger. Wonder what's going on," Kincaid said, but he had a bad feeling. Finding the police in attendance when one arrived to interview a possible suspect in a crime was usually not a good omen.

Parking on Oxford Street itself was completely impossible, although he had known Cullen to risk the lives and limbs of pedestrians by pulling the car up on the pavement. "Let's try the other end, off Tottenham Court," he added hurriedly.

From behind the wheel, Cullen gave him a look that said he didn't appreciate backseat drivers, but said merely, "Right, guv."

When Cullen rounded the corner into Tottenham Court Road and pulled into the other end of Hanway Street, Kincaid saw immediately that the junction of Hanway Street and Hanway Place was blocked as well, and on the other side of the barricade he saw the ominous blue flashing of police lights.

Pulling up on the double yellows in front of the flamenco club on the corner, Cullen said, "Unfortunate coincidence?"

"Don't believe in them."

Kincaid got out of the car and, ducking round the barricade, forestalled the uniformed constable's advance with a flash of his warrant card.

"Oh, sorry, sir." The constable, who didn't look long out of the academy, relaxed and looked a bit sheepish. "Should have realized," he said, nodding at the car and the POLICE notice Cullen had propped in the windscreen.

"What's happened here?" asked Kincaid, uninterested in apologies. Cullen had followed and stood silently beside him.

"You've not been called in?"

"No, but I suspect I will be," Kincaid said through gritted teeth. He could see an accident investigation team working farther along Hanway Place.

"Bloke got himself run down in the middle of the night,"

said the constable. "Bit hard to step out in front of a car along here," he added, with a puzzled shake of his head. "But could be he had a bit much to drink. Nasty business, though. Car didn't just knock him down, but ran right over him. Neighbor came along and found him, sicked up all over himself, so I heard."

"Loquacious bastard," Cullen muttered under his breath.

"The victim. Do you have an ID?" asked Kincaid, wishing a plague on all newly hatched constables.

The young man frowned, his spotty forehead wrinkling with effort. "Something poncey sounding. Pevensey," he said after great deliberation, putting the accent on the middle syllable. "Harry Pevensey."

*Gavin knew there was something different about the flat as soon as he unlocked the door. After his interview with the super, he had collected the assortment of newspapers from his desk, and then, having no further excuse to tarry, had gone home.*

*He stood in the hall, listening, hearing nothing but the faint ticking of the clock in the sitting room. The clock had been a wedding gift from his in-laws, a carved Bavarian piece with little male and female figures that toddled out on the hour, and he hated it.*

*"Linda?" he called out tentatively, but his own voice sounded unnaturally loud and echoed back to him. The flat, he realized, was dark as well as quiet. Linda was frugal in saving on the electricity, but usually she left a small lamp burning, even if she was out.*

*He set his bundle of newspapers on the shelf in the hall and walked slowly towards the sitting room, chiding himself when he realized he was tiptoeing. It was his house, for God's sake—what reason had he to be afraid?*

*But when he reached the sitting room, he found it dark as well, and when he switched on the lamp, it took him a moment to work out what was wrong.*

*The children's photos were missing from the side table. As was Linda's basket of darning, and the stack of women's magazines in the rack beside the sofa. Nor were there any children's shoes or scattered schoolbooks.*

*The clock, however, remained, and it struck the hour, making him jump. The little painted husband and wife trundled out in their ritual parade, and it seemed to Gavin that they were mocking him.*

*"Linda?" he called again. "Susie? Stuart?" But this time he didn't really expect an answer.*

*He found the note in the kitchen, beside a slab of cheese and the heel end of a loaf of bread left on a plate.*

*She said she had taken the children to her mother's. She didn't say if she meant for a visit or for good, but when he went into the bedroom, he found her clothes missing from the cupboard and the dressing table empty of hairbrush and cosmetics. The bed was neatly covered with the candlewick spread, and the faint scent of Linda's perfume lingered, like a ghost of all the things his marriage might have been.*

*Gavin sat down on the bed, the springs creaking beneath his weight, and wondered how long it had been since they had had to be careful not to wake the children. He closed his eyes against a sudden vertigo. Had she really left him?*

*He wavered between relief and terror, then laughed aloud, hearing the edge of hysteria and not caring.*

*His wife and children were gone, his job at risk. What had he left to lose?*

"Bloody hell," Cullen heard Kincaid mutter. Then Kincaid snapped at the constable. "Who's in charge here?"

The PC looked at him blankly.

"Your SIO, man. Senior investigating officer. Don't they teach you anything these days?"

"Sir, they just told me not to let anyone through the barricade." He gestured at the accident investigators. "I don't think CID's been called in. An accident—"

"It wasn't an accident. And I'll be taking over this case. Now go tell the lads this is a crime scene while I get things organized." He was already pulling out his phone as the constable gave him a harried-rabbit look and sprinted for the investigators.

"You're sure?" asked Cullen, before Kincaid could dial.

"Of course I'm bloody sure." Kincaid turned on him, and Cullen realized he was in a blazing fury. He didn't blame the constable for hightailing it out of range. "Someone is a step ahead of us, and this poor bastard—Harry Pevensey— is dead because of it. I don't intend to let this happen again, and heads are going to roll for no one having had the sense to call in CID before now. We should have seen the body in situ. The pathologist should have seen the body. And I want the uniform who interviewed the neighbor who found him."

He punched in numbers as if the phone were complicit in the cock-up.

As Cullen listened to his boss working his way up the food chain, first at the local station, then at the Yard, with increasing ire, he was glad not to be on the receiving end. Kincaid usually managed through diplomacy, and Cullen guessed that some of his uncharacteristic burst of anger was directed towards himself.

But how could they have prevented this chap's death when they hadn't known who he was until that morning? If Kincaid thought they could have talked the information out of Amir Khan without a warrant, he was overestimating their powers of persuasion.

Could Khan, who had known the warrant was imminent, have decided to silence Harry Pevensey? Cullen's friend in Fraud had not got back to him—he would give him another call at the first opportunity.

Now he studied the accident scene, and when Kincaid had ended his calls, said, "Guv, how the hell did someone manage to run this bloke over here? It's a bottleneck, and difficult enough to get a car round the bend at a crawl."

Kincaid followed his gaze, frowning. "They didn't come round the bend. See that?" He pointed to a refurbished block of flats that faced Hanway Place's sharp right-hand jog. "They could have reversed into that little alcove, and waited. That way they had a straight shot down this section of the street."

"Still," argued Cullen, "they wouldn't have been able to get up much speed."

"Enough to knock him down," Kincaid said grimly. "And if it was the same car that hit Kristin, it was an SUV, and it might have been possible to reverse over him."

"Ugh. Risky as hell."

"So was Kristin Cahill's murder, which was one reason I thought it might not have been premeditated. But perhaps getting away with that one made him cocky."

"Whoever it was knew Kristin Cahill's patterns, and this bloke's—Pevensey," Cullen speculated.

"Or made a damned good guess," Kincaid said. "While we're waiting for uniform to get here with the witness's name and statement, let's see if the accident lads confirm our theory. And then we need to get into Harry Pevensey's flat."

"Good God, the guy was an old maid," said Cullen, surveying Harry Pevensey's flat from the door. "This stuff looks like something out of my gran's."

They had not waited for uniform to bring them a key from the victim's effects, but had got the flat number and rung a mobile locksmith.

The flat, in a housing-authority block that had seen better days, was little more than a bedsit, one room, with a small kitchen alcove and a doorway leading to what he assumed was the bath. The furnishings, like the building, were well worn, but what Kincaid saw was quality, carefully, perhaps even desperately, preserved.

The bed was neatly made, the kitchen tidy. One wall held a collection of signed photographs of actors Kincaid vaguely recognized, while on the other a false mantel framed an electric fire. Propped on the mantel were postcards and invitations, some yellowing with age. A small painted secretary looked like the only possible receptacle for papers.

"He liked his gin," said Cullen, who had gone straight for the rubbish bin in the kitchen. "Cheap stuff, for the most part."

Kincaid had gone to examine the little gallery more closely. Several of the obviously dated photos showed a handsome, dark-haired man with more well-known stage actors, and were signed, "To Harry."

Cullen had moved on from the kitchen and was riffling through the bills tucked into one of the secretary's compartments. "Electricity overdue. Overdue account with a local off-license—that's no surprise—and it looks like he owed his"—he held the paper up and squinted at it—"his tailor. This guy had a tailor?" He gave a dismissive glance round the flat. "Money could have been better spent, if you ask—"

"Who the hell are you?" The raised voice came from the door, which they had left off the latch.

Turning, Kincaid saw a young man in a T-shirt emblazoned with GOT SLIDE? and ragged jeans, staring at them belligerently. His bleached-blond hair stood up as if he'd just got out of bed, and his eyes were dark-shadowed in an oval and somewhat androgynous face.

"The police," Kincaid said easily. "Who are you?"

"Oh, Christ." The young man sagged against the door-jamb, as if punctured. "You know, then? Harry's dead."

"You were Harry's friend?" Kincaid asked, thinking it unlikely, but he'd seen stranger alliances.

"I'm his neighbor. Andy Monahan."

"You found him?" said Kincaid, remembering the name the local station had given him.

"Christ," said Andy Monahan again, blanching so that the dark smudges under his eyes were more pronounced.

Kincaid crossed the room in a swift stride and, taking Monahan firmly by the arm, guided him to a chair. "Here, sit." To Cullen he added, "Get him some water." It was a distraction, but often a successful one, and he didn't want anyone sicking up in Pevensey's flat.

Monahan took the glass Cullen brought and drank it steadily down, then leaned back and closed his eyes for a moment. "Sorry. It's just that I think I'll see that—see him—for the rest of my life."

"Why don't you tell us what happened," Kincaid suggested, perching on the arm of the other chair. "Start at the beginning. Were you and Harry friends?"

"Not exactly. But he was all right. He'd feed my cat for me when I was away on a gig. He liked to talk, when he was into the gin, about the times he'd acted with Hugh Laurie, and Nigel Havers, and oh, he even said he'd done a play once with Emma Thompson and Ken Branagh. It was probably bollocks, but I didn't mind."

"Harry was an actor?"

"Yeah. But not a very lucky one, obviously." Monahan gestured round the flat. "I mean, I'm one to talk, but he was like, old. Fifties. I'm just starting out."

"You're a musician?" Kincaid asked.

"Guitarist. Been playing since I was twelve. Band's called Snogging Maggie, but it's not, honestly, as good as it could be."

*Snogging Maggie*? Kincaid thought. He didn't even want to go there. A closer look had made him revise his estimate of Andy Monahan's age. He might be in his late twenties—it was the blond hair and the prettiness that made him seem younger. And he suspected that it was shock that had prompted the confessional state.

"So tell us about last night."

Andy gripped the frayed knees of his jeans. "We had a gig in Guildford. Total shit. By the time we got back to town, it must have been going on two. The guys dropped me off at the top of the street—you can't get the van through if there's anyone parked.

"We were drinking a bit. Nick and me. Not George, who was driving," he assured them, as if he thought they would run his friend in. "So I was a bit pissed, you know, and when I saw—I thought it was some old bit of rubbish—I thought he was—I pushed at him with my toe—" Andy covered his face with his hands, rubbing at his cheekbones to ease what Kincaid suspected was the ache of tears. "Puked all over my fricking Strat case, didn't I?" he said through his fingers. "Jesus Christ. Harry."

"You called the police?"

"Dropped my mobile in the gutter, in God knows what. Couldn't punch the fricking keys." He dropped his hands and looked up at Kincaid. "I couldn't watch. When they put him in the bag. I thought that was only on the telly."

Kincaid glanced at Cullen, saw that he was listening alertly. It was do-or-die time. "Andy, did Harry ever say anything to you about antiques?"

"Antiques? You mean like this stuff?" Andy gestured at the furnishings.

"No. Like jewelry. Did he say anything to you about an antique brooch?"

Andy looked from Kincaid to Cullen. "What the fuck is a brooch?"

Kincaid had to suppress a smile. "A pin. This one was diamond. Art Deco. Made in Germany just before the war."

"Where the hell would Harry get something like that?" said Andy, his voice rising in incredulity.

"That's what we were wondering. Have—"

"Wait a minute." Wariness returned to Andy Monahan's face. "You said you were cops, right? But you're in plainclothes. You're detectives, aren't you? Why are you asking about a traffic accident?"

The accident investigators had given Kincaid an initial confirmation on his guess that the car had pulled out from the bay at the jog in the street. It looked from the tire marks, the officer in charge had added, as if the car had gone up on the curb in order to hit Harry Pevensey before he reached his door. "Because," Kincaid said, "we think someone deliberately ran Harry down, and we want you to help us find out who did it."

"You're saying someone wanted to kill Harry?" Andy's face hardened, and he suddenly looked his age. "You couldn't find a more harmless sod than Harry. Vain, maybe, but there was no meanness in it. What do you want to know?"

"If Harry didn't say anything to you about the brooch, did anything else happen lately that was unusual?"

"Harry didn't exactly lead the most exciting life. He was usually *resting,* as he liked to call it, but the last few weeks he'd had a part in a play. Some community theater. He said it was a load of pretentious bollocks, but he got a check. I can't— Wait." Andy frowned. "Yesterday morning. We both liked a lie-in, Harry and me, because we work late. But yesterday morning some git comes pounding on Harry's door. I got up and looked out—thought the fucking building was on fire. But Harry got up and let him in, and a few minutes later I heard them shouting, then the door slammed."

"I've seen him round once or twice before, this bloke. Not Harry's usual—he goes for blond actress wannabes, for the most part, with fake tits." Andy shrugged. "What they see in him, I don't know."

"Did you hear what they were arguing about, Harry and the bloke who came yesterday?" asked Cullen.

"No. Sorry."

"What did he look like, then, this bloke?"

"Young. Dark hair, dark eyes. The kind of looks that girls start heavy breathing over. And dripping with it." When Kincaid raised an eyebrow, Andy elaborated. "Money. Clothes. Shoes. Haircut. Probably fucking manicure to boot. But—" He stopped, eyeing them with caution.

"But what?" Kincaid asked.

"Look. I'm in a band. I know shit when I see it, and this guy was into something, big-time."

"Drugs?" asked Cullen.

Andy gave him a quelling look. "No. Sweeties. What do you think?"

"Any idea what Harry's connection with him was?" put in Kincaid.

"No. I didn't ask. Harry didn't tell. We didn't talk about personal stuff, Harry and me."

"Andy." Cullen was quivering like a bloodhound. With studied casualness he pulled a photo from his inside pocket and handed it across. "Have you ever seen this man?"

Andy Monahan gazed at the photo, then looked from Cullen to Kincaid, as wide-eyed as if they'd just pulled a rabbit from a hat. "Bloody hell," he said. "That's the pretty boy. Who is he, then?"

"His name," Cullen said, glancing at Kincaid with ill-concealed satisfaction, "is Dominic Scott."

# 14

❧

*But [Tim] Llewellyn's main point, to which he re-
turned several times, was that Sotheby's was not a
police force. "We have a right to protect the anonymity of our clients. We avoid breaking the laws
in the countries where we operate. Our clients seek
anonymity for a variety of reasons, but it is not our
job to police our clients."*
     —*Peter Watson,* Sotheby's: Inside Story

GEMMA'S FIRST IMPULSE, when she had dropped the boys
at their respective schools, was to confront Erika about her
husband's murder.

But then, Gemma considered a little more calmly,
maybe Erika had not thought it relevant, and perhaps David
Rosenthal's death had no connection at all with Kristin Cahill's.

But Gemma wouldn't know until she had the facts, and
so decided she should start with the case itself, and talk to
Erika when she knew enough to ask useful questions.

Kit had said that David Rosenthal had been murdered in
a garden near the Albert Bridge. It would have been Chelsea's patch, then. So for the second time that week, Gemma
found herself heading for Lucan Place, and an interview
with Detective Inspector Kerry Boatman.

"Dominic Scott knew Harry Pevensey *and* Kristin Cahill.
And it was Kristin who took the brooch in for sale," Cullen

said as they got back into the car, sounding exultant. "And he had rows with both of them on the days they were murdered. That puts him square in the frame, alibi or no alibi, if you ask me."

Kincaid didn't like it when things seemed too pat, nor could he dismiss alibis so easily. And it didn't tell them where Harry had got the brooch, or why Amir Khan had had a row with Kristin, or why he had been so reluctant at first to cooperate with the police.

"Let's talk to Dom Scott again before we start jumping to conclusions. Does he have a job, do you think, or will we find him at home?"

"Melody said something about him being on the board of his grandfather's company," Cullen said a bit grudgingly.

"Having met him, I can't quite see him turning up for work on the dot every day in some City office. And Andy Monahan said he was sure Dom Scott was using drugs. That fits in with what the barmaid told you about his dodgy friends, but how does that fit in with Harry Pevensey, who liked his gin? And what on earth brought the two of them together?"

Kristin Cahill, and now Harry Pevensey, dead on his watch, two people perhaps not blameless, but certainly not deserving of ruthless and brutal murder. He would find out who had done this, but not by jumping the gun. When he got there, he would make sure it would stick.

Dominic Scott answered the door. This morning, however, he wore a slightly less ratty version of jeans and T-shirt than Andy Monahan, and looked infinitely more exhausted. He stared at them, recognition of Kincaid only slowly dawning in his eyes.

"You came about Kristin," he said. "Is there—have you—"

"No, we haven't any news about Kristin. We wanted to talk to you about something else. Can we come in?" Kincaid sensed Cullen's impatience, but he didn't want a repeat of yesterday's rather bizarre fainting spell, and he meant to take on Dom Scott at his own pace.

"Oh, right." Dom Scott held the door for them, then hesitated in the hall. "We can talk upstairs," he said, with a grimace at his mother's living room. "Not exactly my idea of comfort, the barrage of great art in the arctic space." He turned instead towards the stairs, and they followed, Kincaid looking round with interest.

In the stairwell, Ellen Scott-Miller had abandoned the snowy expanse and gone for a dark, cool green, against which small landscape oils glowed like little jewels.

They climbed all the way to the top floor, Dom Scott taking a surprisingly quick lead considering the lassitude with which he'd greeted them.

A door stood ajar on the top landing, and when Dom pushed it wide, Kincaid saw that it was not a room, but a flat with a small kitchen and separate bedroom and, he assumed, a bath.

There was no evidence of Dom's mother's hand in the decorating. The furniture seemed to be odds and ends collected from other parts of the house; the gray walls displayed framed posters featuring current bands and comedy acts, a few from the Edinburgh festival.

Clothes were strewn across sofa and floor, the coffee table was littered with glasses and mugs, and the room had a slightly unwashed aroma.

"Didn't seem much point in tidying," said Dom, with a shrug of apology, but he swept the sofa clean and tossed the bundle of clothing in the direction of the bedroom. He motioned them to the sofa and sat on the edge of a scuffed leather Morris chair, seemingly unaware of the crushed suit jacket beneath him. "So what did you want to talk about?" he asked, and Kincaid saw that his eyes were more focused than the previous day.

"Harry Pevensey."

"Harry?" Dom looked at them blankly, but his hands twitched. "What about him?"

"How do you know Harry, Dom?"

"He's just a bloke I met in a bar." Dom's fingers moved to his T-shirt, began to pick at the fabric. "What does Harry have to do with anything?"

"Why did you go to see Harry yesterday?" Kincaid asked, his voice still casual.

"What? But I— How could you—" Visibly rattled now, Dom clutched at his shirt with one hand and rubbed at his nose with the other.

"What do you know about a diamond brooch that Harry Pevensey put up for auction through your girlfriend, Kristin Cahill?"

"I don't—"

"Oh, come on, Dom." Kincaid leaned forward, holding Dom's gaze, and said quietly, "I don't believe you. Were you Harry Pevensey's connection with Kristin?"

Dom let go of his shirt and seemed to make an effort to pull himself together. "So what if I was? Look, I told you. I met Harry one night in a bar, the French House, in Soho, when I went with some friends. It's an actors' bar. Harry liked to hang out there. We talked, and sometimes I'd pop in when I was in the West End. It was . . . comfortable . . . you know. Not like most of the places I go. And no one knew me.

"Harry was always hard up. I'd buy him a drink, but he never asked anything of me." There was a plaintive sort of innocence in the words, as if Dom Scott didn't have many interactions with people who didn't want something from him.

"Until a couple of weeks ago," Dom went on, his voice going flat. "He rang me. He said he had this brooch. He said he'd found it in an estate sale, but he thought it might be really valuable. So I introduced him to Kristin. I thought that if it was true, it might be a good thing for her, too, to bring in something.

"But then the police came round asking questions about it, and Kristin got into trouble with her boss. So yesterday I went round to ask Harry to take it out of the sale. I told him that the bloody thing was jeopardizing Kristin's job, and that was never part of the agreement. But he said he wouldn't do it, and I couldn't change his mind, so I left.

"And then—then you came, and said Kristin was dead." He sagged into the chair, his eyes dull again.

Kincaid didn't mean to let him off so easily. "Dom," he said sharply. "Did Kristin tell you why Mr. Khan was angry about the brooch?"

He frowned, as if thinking were an effort. "She said there was some woman claiming it was stolen from her during the war. It was that part that pissed him off. Mr. Khan said they would take items of unknown provenance, but they didn't want the kind of investigation that would ensue from claims that might involve war looting. Like it was Kristin's fault."

"And that's why you had a row with Harry?"

"That's what Harry told you? I wouldn't exactly call it a row, but Harry likes his bit of drama— What?" He had caught some telltale flicker in their faces. "What aren't you telling me?"

"Harry's dead, Dom," answered Kincaid. "Just like Kristin. Where were you last night between midnight and two?"

Kerry Boatman greeted Gemma with a warm smile as she ushered her into her office. "I didn't expect to see you back so soon. Is it the Cahill case?"

"It's actually not about that at all," admitted Gemma, taking a seat. "Or only in a very odd and roundabout way. My friend who claims the brooch Kristin Cahill put into the sale at Harrowby's . . . well, I've just learned from another source that her husband was murdered here in Chelsea, after the war. I don't see any obvious connection, but I thought I should know more before I spoke to my friend. Don't want to put my foot in it." She smiled, feeling an idiot. "I wondered if I might look through your files. His name was David Rosenthal."

"And the year?"

"I don't exactly know. Say within ten years after the war?"

Boatman raised both brows and peered at Gemma over the tops of the reading glasses she'd perched on her nose. "Good God, Inspector, have you any idea of the state of our records?"

"Well, if they're anything like ours . . ." Gemma looked

down at the pretty skirt and top she'd put on that morning, and shrugged.

Boatman grinned. "You'll find them in the basement. Enjoy."

"So what did you think?" Kincaid asked Cullen when they were back in the car.

Cullen gave a snort of disgust. "Total bollocks."

Dom had not repeated his dramatic faint, but he had gone white as a Victorian damsel and said he refused to believe Harry was dead. When Kincaid had told him that the police didn't usually lie about things like that, Dom had just shaken his head like an obstinate child.

"I'm afraid it's true, and I am sorry," Kincaid had said. "And we still need to know where you were last night."

"I was here. What would I be doing, with Kristin dead?"

"Did you drive your mother's car?"

Dom looked as horrified as when they'd told him Harry was dead. "Are you out of your mind? And even if I were that daft, her car's been in the garage for two weeks, waiting on a part from Germany."

Cullen had got the name of the garage. Now he said, "Want me to check out the car, guv?"

"Yes, and see if you can find any mobile records for Harry Pevensey. There was no mobile phone on his body and we didn't see one in the flat." To Kincaid's astonishment, the phone in Pevensey's flat had been rotary dial. No wonder Cullen hadn't reached an answering machine.

"What about Amir Khan?" asked Cullen. "I talked to my mate in Fraud. He said the salesroom has skirted the law a number of times, falsifying imports, documentation, and so on. What if Khan knew more about the brooch than he let on? Could he have recognized it as stolen and allowed it in the sale anyway? I could have sworn he looked worried this morning."

"I'm not sure Erika ever reported it as stolen." Kincaid glanced at his watch. "I need to check with Gemma, and before we tackle Mr. Khan again, I'd like to know a little more about Harry Pevensey. I think I'd like to check out the bar where Dom Scott said they met, the French House."

By the time Gemma found David Rosenthal's case file, her back hurt, her fingers were grimy, and the smell of old dust seemed permanently embedded in her nostrils.

"Why the hell couldn't the Met pay some low-grade clerk to sit in the dungeon all day and transfer the bloody things to computer?" she'd groused when she first began searching the boxed files.

But when she had taken the box to the table, sat down in the utilitarian chair provided, and finally held David Rosenthal's file in her hands, she changed her mind. Slowly she shuffled through the pages. Typed reports, with the occasional uncorrected error. Handwritten notes by the senior detective in charge of the case, an inspector named Gavin Hoxley. It all felt suddenly, undeniably, real.

David Rosenthal, she read, had been found lying on the ground beside a bench in Cheyne Gardens, on a Saturday night in May 1952. He had apparently been robbed of all his belongings, so that he had not been identified until his wife reported him missing.

His wife. *Erika*. Good God.

He had been stabbed multiple times with a double-edged blade, the reports went on, and was thought by the pathologist to have died instantly. There had been no defensive wounds.

He had lived in Notting Hill, and the address was the same as Erika's house in Arundel Gardens. He had worked in North Hampstead, and had spent any free time at the British Museum. There was no known reason for him to have been in Chelsea on that Saturday evening.

And then Gemma came to the photos. This—this had been Erika's *husband*. Even in monochrome, the crime scene photos were brutal, the blood on his shirt front starkly black against the white of the fabric and his blanched face. But even in death she could see that David Rosenthal had been striking, handsome in a fine-boned, careworn sort of way.

Why had she never seen a photo of him in Erika's flat? Not even a wedding portrait. And Gemma, doing a quick calculation, guessed that Erika had been only in her thirties when her husband had been killed. Why had she never remarried? Had David Rosenthal been the great love of her life, never to be replaced?

And why had she, Gemma, never thought to ask?

Pushing back her chair, Gemma separated Gavin Hoxley's notes from the other papers. He had made jottings to himself, just as she kept running commentary in her own notebooks, and his handwriting was well formed, with a bold downstroke. It made her think he had been a careful man, but determined, perhaps even obstinate, and she smiled at her amateur analysis.

She had just begun to read when her phone beeped, telling her she had a text message waiting, and she realized that she had been without a signal until she moved her chair. Her first thought was that she had missed some news about her mum, but the message was from Kincaid, asking if she could meet him at an address in Dean Street.

Kincaid leaned against the lamppost in front of the French House, looking up at the cheerful blue awnings above the bar. The windows of the upstairs dining room were thrown wide to let in the air, but the French flags flying over the first floor gave only a desultory flutter in the warm air.

He had taken off his jacket, and glanced with some dismay at the crush of customers spilling from the doorway of the bar and into the street. If it was warm outside, it would be warmer still within, and any thoughts he'd had of a cool drink and something to eat while they chatted with the staff were probably doomed to logistical failure.

Still, he was not, like Cullen, on his way back to a stuffy office in the Yard to subpoena phone records. The thought made him grin. Cullen had wanted to be in on this interview, and hadn't hesitated to protest.

But Cullen was good at detail—as Kincaid had reminded him—and ferreting out facts was an important part of a sergeant's job.

And the rebellion augured well for future promotion, but in the meantime Cullen had a ways to go in developing patience, and in Kincaid's opinion, empathy. He was quick to judge, and lacked Gemma's intuitive desire to understand what made people tick.

But then Kincaid knew that he would probably always, and perhaps unfairly, use Gemma as a benchmark for a partner's performance, and he realized how readily he had jumped on an excuse to pull Gemma in on this case. Perhaps he couldn't blame Cullen for being touchy.

As if he had conjured her, he glanced down Dean Street and saw Gemma walking towards him. The sun glinted off her copper hair, and even in a skirt, she moved with the long, swingy stride that always made his heart lift. She saw him and smiled, and he suddenly felt distinctly unprofessional.

When she reached him, he leaned over and brushed his lips against her cheek, then pulled away, studying her. "You've got a mucky streak across your forehead," he said, rubbing at it with his thumb. "What have you been doing, excavating a tomb?"

"Nearer than you'd think," said Gemma. Pushing his hand away, she fished in her bag for a tissue and wiped at the smudge. "Did I get it?"

"All better. Now, what were you doing at Lucan Place?"

"Digging through file crates in the basement. I'll tell you later. What are we doing *here*? I could do with some lunch." She gestured at the pub.

"You should be so lucky." He told her what they had learned from the Harrowby's warrant, and that they had then discovered that the seller of the brooch had been killed the night before. "His neighbor, the poor bloke who found the body, identified Dom Scott from Cullen's photo. Said he visited the victim yesterday, and that they had a row. When we asked Dom, he said he wanted Pevensey to take the brooch out of the sale, as it was causing Kristin trouble, and Pevensey refused."

"So Dominic Scott knew the guy who put the brooch up for sale, this Pevensey, as well as Kristin?" Gemma frowned.

"But what has that to do with this place? If we're not having lunch," she added, and he grinned.

"You're fixated on food. Dom Scott says that this is where he met Pevensey, that they were only casual bar acquaintances, and that when Pevensey told him he had jewelry to sell, he put him on to Kristin as a favor to them both. He seemed quite shocked to hear that Pevensey was dead."

"He was quite shocked to hear that Kristin was dead, too," said Gemma. "Either he's a very good actor or he's having very bad luck."

"All a bit much of a coincidence for my liking," Kincaid agreed. "I thought we should see if any of the staff here knows either of them."

"Along with lunch and a drink?" Gemma asked, with a determination that would have done Cullen proud.

Their hopes of sustenance were quickly dashed. The late-lunch crowd was thinning by the time they muscled their way to the bar, but the bartender still looked harried. When queried, he said briskly, "We don't do food. You'll have to go upstairs for that. And we only do beer by the half. Now, what can I get you?"

"Information, actually." Kincaid took out his identification. Even though he had spoken quietly, he had the sudden sense of attention in the room. There was no music, and he had noticed the other patrons glancing at them as they crossed the room. The bar was small, with a clubby feel, and for the most part the clientele seemed to lean towards the flamboyant side of eccentric.

The bartender slotted a wineglass into the rack with a clink and eyed them warily. "What sort of information?"

"I see you have Breton cider," Kincaid said, waiting for the murmur of voices to rise again. He didn't want the barman influenced by an audience. Catching Gemma's affirmative nod, he added, "Give us two bottles, why don't you?" although inwardly he winced at the price. This one was definitely going on the Yard's tab.

When the barman had filled their glasses and Kincaid

didn't feel quite so many eyes boring into his back, he said, "Do you know a bloke by the name of Harry Pevensey?" He'd taken one of the smaller photos on Pevensey's wall out of its frame and now showed it to the barman.

"Harry?" The barman broke into an unexpected grin. "That's Harry, all right," he said, handing the photo back. "What's our Harry supposed to have done? Held up a director for a part?" He wiped and slotted another glass. "Of course I know Harry. I've been here for donkey's years, and Harry's been coming in longer than that. He's a harmless sod."

Kincaid sipped his cider, then centered his glass on the beer mat, suddenly reluctant to impart bad news to someone who had obviously liked Harry Pevensey. "Unfortunately, it's not what Harry's done, but what someone has done to him. He was killed last night, in front of his flat."

The bartender stared at him, all the good-natured teasing wiped from his face. "You're taking the piss."

"No. I'm sorry."

"But that's not possible," he protested. "He was here, until closing, and he was in rare form."

"Rare form?" asked Gemma. "In a good humor, was he?"

"I don't think I've ever seen Harry so full of himself." The bartender frowned. "Jubilant, I suppose I'd call it. And flush. Had a proper dinner in the restaurant, *and* bought rounds for everyone in here." Thoughtfully, he added, "But he was a bit secretive about it. Said his ship had come in, that sort of thing. We all thought he'd got a part in some big production, although it didn't seem very likely. Harry was . . . well, Harry was all right, but it just wasn't going to happen, know what I mean?"

Kincaid thought of Harry's flat, of the photos on the wall, the yellowing invitations, and nodded. "Did Harry have any special friends here?"

"Special? Not really. He knew all the regulars, and vice versa, but I doubt he ever saw anyone outside the bar. He was chatting up some woman last night, but she left not long after he came down to the bar, so I suppose he didn't quite have the pull." His brow creased as he added, "Harry was a bit of a loner, really. I don't think anything ever quite lived up to the good old days—or at least what he imagined were the good old days."

" 'The good old days'?" Gemma repeated, leaning forward with such interest that the bartender reached up and smoothed what was left of his hair.

"The seventies. Harry ran with a posh crowd then, at least according to him. Partied with the Stones, invited to all the best clubs in the West End and Chelsea." He shook his head. "No one ever quite believed him, but maybe it was true. He was quite a looker in his day, or so he was always happy to tell you. And I wasn't too bad, myself," he added, with a smile at Gemma.

"The seventies? Really?" said Gemma, as if that were the Dark Ages, and the bartender sighed, deflated.

"Told you I'd been here for yonks."

"What about this bloke?" Kincaid asked, taking Dom Scott's photo from his pocket and handing it across the bar. "You recognize him?"

The bartender wiped his fingers on his apron, then took the photo, holding it at arm's length in the classic posture of middle-aged nearsightedness. "This guy? Yeah, I've seen him in here with Harry a few times. I remember him particularly because I had to tell him to turn off his mobile—we don't allow them in here."

"So the two of them met here?"

"If by that you mean making an acquaintance, no, I don't think so. The first time this guy came in, oh, say a month ago, he and Harry were huddled in the corner, and Harry looked none too pleased. If you want my opinion, I'd say they knew each other very well."

# 15

❧

> *... class pervaded almost everything that took place at Sotheby's. If people came from the right background they would start as porters, to introduce them to the objects, or maybe, if they were women, they would be put at reception, where they were felt to be more presentable. But this was only for a short time, after which they would be promoted on a fast track directly to the specialist departments, as cataloguers, prior to becoming junior experts.*
> *—Peter Watson,* Sotheby's: Inside Story

**THEY SETTLED FOR SANDWICHES** and tea from a snack bar, but Gemma managed to grab one of the two plastic tables on the pavement, and so they sat in the sun as they ate and watched the crowd flow by. It always seemed to Gemma that on warm spring days like this she could feel an extra surge of energy pulsing through the city. The colors seemed brighter, more intense, the sounds sharper. And all around them, light-starved Londoners bared as much skin as they could manage, regardless of the consequences.

She looked across at Kincaid, who had not only removed his jacket but stuffed his tie in his pocket and rolled up his shirtsleeves. The bridge of his nose was beginning to go pink, and Gemma was glad she'd learned the trick of using face cream with sunscreen—otherwise she'd be freckled, as well as the color of a lobster, if she sat out in this glorious heat much longer.

When they were down to pushing crumbs round on their plates, she said, "So where are we, then?"

He frowned and swirled the dregs in his teacup. "If the bartender is right, Dom Scott lied about having met Harry by chance at the French House."

"Maybe the bartender didn't see the first meeting."

"Even so, the unhappy, huddled-in-the-corner conversation he described argues for more than a brief—or casual—acquaintance, wouldn't you say?"

"Could they have been lovers, Harry and Dom?" Gemma countered.

"Not according to Harry's neighbor, who said Harry liked girls." Kincaid shrugged. "But then again, Andy the wannabe rock star may not be the most reliable source. Maybe he and Harry were better friends than he admitted. It could be Harry liked anyone who paid him attention, but I can't see what would have been in it for Dom."

"The bartender said Harry claimed to have had connections with a fast crowd in the seventies. That probably meant drugs—maybe Harry still dabbled," Gemma suggested.

"Could Harry have been supplying Dom with drugs?" Kincaid asked, then shook his head. "But if that were the case, from the looks of his flat, it was a poor living. And that doesn't explain what Harry was celebrating last night, or where he got the funds, or what he was doing with Erika's brooch—" His mobile rang, and with a glance at the caller ID, he mouthed, "Cullen," as he answered.

She watched him as he said, "Right. Right. Okay, meet you there," feeling a small stab of jealousy. Ridiculous, really, when the severing of the partnership had been her choice, not his, and she should consider that she had the best of both worlds now. But sometimes it seemed that the almost instantaneous communion they'd felt when they worked a case together got lost in the domestic shuffle, and that it had been easier to share their disparate personal lives when they'd worked together than the other way round.

Oh, well, she'd made her bed, as her dad would say, and she doubted she'd won any points with Doug Cullen by sticking her nose in this case.

"Woolgathering?" said Kincaid, and she realized he'd disconnected.

"Knitting with it." She smiled. "What did the fair Doug have to say?"

"Harry Pevensey had no mobile phone account with a provider—not even a pay as you go. And Ellen Miller-Scott's Mercedes is in the garage, and has been for more than a week. So dead end on both those fronts."

"So what's next?" Gemma asked.

"I think we'll pay another call on Mr. Khan at Harrowby's. These two deaths, Kristin's and Harry Pevensey's, have to be connected, and the two points of contact are Dom Scott and the brooch. Dom seems to be a nonstarter as far as the car goes, so I want to talk to Amir Khan again. We know he had an argument with Kristin the day she died, but it's only an assumption that it was about the brooch. And we've assumed that it was Giles who was jealous when Dom Scott sent her roses at work, but what if it was Khan?"

"She was a very pretty girl, and it certainly wouldn't be the first time a woman has fallen for her good-looking boss." Gemma gave him a sly look.

"Or vice versa. And I'll take that as a compliment. Do you want to come to Harrowby's with us?"

Considering, Gemma shook her head. "Thanks, but no. I think I'll go back to Lucan Place for a bit."

"You never told me what you were doing there."

"No." A little reluctantly, Gemma said, "I discovered that Erika's husband was murdered, and I feel an idiot for not having known."

"Erika never told you?" Kincaid looked as surprised as Gemma had felt.

"I'd no idea. It happened in 1952. So far I don't see any possible connection with the brooch or our murders, but I haven't finished reading the case file. So I think I'll go back to Lucan Place for a bit before I go to see Mum, and leave you and Doug to the charms of the handsome Mr. Khan."

Standing, she leaned over and touched her cheek to his, feeling sun-warmed skin and the slight friction of beginning stubble. "I'll see you tonight."

\* \* \*

Mrs. March greeted Kincaid and Cullen with a smile of pleasure, as if they'd become old friends. It was a part of her job, making the regular clients feel welcome, and it came naturally to her. "It's Mr. Kincaid, isn't it? Is there any news . . ." Then her face fell, as the thought of the reason for their presence overcame her instinctual response.

"No. But we wondered if we might have a word with Mr. Khan." A quick glance into the main arena of the salesroom revealed an auction in progress, and as Kincaid focused on the large overhead television, he saw that it was jewelry being sold. The seats were full, and the bidding seemed to be quite brisk.

"Is this the Art Deco jewelry?" In his concentration on Kristin Cahill's death, he hadn't realized the sale was coming up so soon.

"Yes, but if it's the Goldshtein brooch you're concerned about, Mr. Khan removed it from the sale this morning. After *you* came," she added, with a disapproving glance at Doug, as if he were personally responsible for upsetting their routine. "Mr. Khan felt that since the house had been forced to compromise the seller's privacy, he couldn't in good conscience offer the item without checking with the seller, and I understand that he was not able to get in touch."

No, not unless he had the ability to commune with ghosts, Kincaid thought, but he quelled any comment. He wanted to be the one to tell Khan that Harry Pevensey was dead. That was the only way he could attempt to gauge Khan's reaction. "Could you tell Mr. Khan we'd like to see him?" he asked.

"Oh, but you can't." Mrs. March again gave Cullen an accusing look. "He left at lunchtime. Said he wasn't feeling well, although I really can't imagine that. Mr. Khan is never ill."

"How very coincidental," Cullen muttered, but Kincaid smiled and said, "Do you have a home address for him?"

Mrs. March drew herself up, all her earlier bonhomie gone. "I can't give you that. Not without speaking to one of the directors."

"Then I suggest you make a phone call, Mrs. March. You

can tell your director that we *will* get the address—it's just a matter of how much inconvenience it causes the firm."

"It's most irregular." Mrs. March gave an offended sniff, but began thumbing through a phone list. Kincaid didn't like bullying her, but he suspected that delaying tactics had already cost one life.

A dazzle of color caught his eye from the television screen in the main room. Focusing, he saw that the piece was a bracelet, a wide band set in a glittering chevron pattern made up of red, green, and blue stones, all appearing seductively larger than life. Such baubles had inspired envy and greed at the very least, he thought. What would people have been willing to do for the diamond brooch Gemma had described?

"And in the meantime," he added, "I'd very much like to see the Goldshtein brooch."

It was Giles Oliver who led them back to Khan's office. He was less red faced and puffy eyed than when Kincaid and Gemma had seen him at his flat the previous day, but not much more attractive. Mrs. March had fetched him from one of the phone stations on the auction floor, and he looked none too pleased.

"I see you felt well enough to come back to work," said Kincaid as the auctioneer's voice faded behind them.

"Can't afford to lose my job." Oliver unlocked the office with a key from a key ring Mrs. March had given him. "It's not as if I can take off whenever I bloody well please."

"Like Mr. Khan."

Oliver gave Kincaid a resentful glance. "And he locked the office, so that every time I need a document, I have to get the key. Damn nuisance, and for what? Daft, if you ask me."

"Do you not usually keep it locked?"

"No. But usually he or I or Kris—" He stopped, looking stricken, clutching the keys in his fist. "Christ. I just can't— I keep thinking she'll walk in the room, or that I hear her voice."

"I expect it will get easier." Kincaid's sympathy was genuine, and Oliver's posture relaxed a little.

"I don't know. I'm not sure I can stay on here, after what's happened. And it was bad enough without Khan going round like a simmering volcano after you served that warrant this morning." He nodded at Cullen, who looked as if he'd just received a compliment.

Kincaid sat on the edge of a desk and crossed his ankles, deliberately inviting Oliver's confidence, while Cullen leaned against a file cabinet, doing his best to look unobtrusive. "He was upset, then?" Kincaid asked.

"Maybe I should have said 'gliding round like a glacier,'" said Oliver. "He was icy, the way he gets when he's about to give someone a royal bollocking."

"Like the one he gave Kristin the day she was killed?"

"Yeah. Well, I suppose . . ." Giles Oliver fiddled with the keys, looking suddenly uncomfortable. Did he know more about that argument than he had admitted?

"You said Mr. Khan always had it in for Kristin. Had it grown worse lately?"

An instant's calculation flickered in Oliver's eyes, then he shrugged and said, "Look, I've never been one to get anyone into trouble . . . but he *had* been harder on her the last few weeks."

Kincaid waited, but Oliver was looking uncertain now. The kid knew something he wanted to give up, but apparently wasn't prepared to do it easily. Did he feel guilty, Kincaid wondered, or did he just enjoy the drama? Either way, he was willing to play along. "You were Kristin's closest friend here, weren't you?"

"Yeah, you could say that. I mean she talked to the girls, but not the way she talked to me."

"So she confided in you. Did she tell you what was going on with Mr. Khan? Was there something between them?"

"Kristin and him?" Oliver looked shocked. "No way. She couldn't stand him. Especially after—" He paused again, pushing out his lower lip.

"Come on, Giles," Kincaid said, knowing he wouldn't stop now. "After what?"

The keys jingled in Oliver's hand as he said in a rush, "She caught him. Khan. Copying papers. I don't know what they were, but Kristin did, and she wouldn't tell me. Khan was furious with her, and after that he'd use any excuse to tear into her. She thought he was trying to get her fired."

It was after five by the time Gemma emerged from the police station, blinking like a mole forced out of its burrow in daylight. She was tired and grimy, and her head hurt from squinting at papers in inadequate light. Slowly, she walked up Lucan Place towards the Brompton Road, musing over what she had learned.

Gavin Hoxley had been a good copper. He had followed every lead meticulously, and had documented his results with a thoroughness that Gemma respected. But his every avenue had led to a dead end, and as she read she had begun to feel his frustration as if it were her own.

If Hoxley's perceptions had been accurate, David Rosenthal had been an enigma, a withdrawn and reclusive man who shared little of his thoughts and feelings with his colleagues and acquaintances. Had he, Gemma wondered, shared anything with his wife?

And had he, as Hoxley had begun to suspect, been involved in some way with Jewish vengeance? Gemma could not imagine that Erika would have countenanced such behavior under any circumstances. Was that why she had never spoken about her husband or his murder?

There had been things moving in the shadows, of that she felt sure. Hoxley had merely hinted at the blocking of inquiries, but she was used to official jargon and could read between the lines.

Then, just when she had begun to think that Hoxley was making progress, the notes had stopped. She'd searched the file pages once, then again, then a third time. There was simply nothing else. David Rosenthal's murder had not been solved, nor had the case been declared officially cold. Had Rosenthal's murder been shelved because he was Jewish and therefore the crime had been considered insignificant? Or had it been just the opposite? Either implication made her equally uneasy.

She would like to have asked Kerry Boatman to trace

records, and to pull Gavin Hoxley's personnel file for her, but Boatman was gone for the day, and there was no one on evening rota at the station with access to the information she wanted.

Having reached the South Ken underground station, Gemma hesitated, torn between going in one direction for Notting Hill and the other for St. Paul's.

There was, of course, the one obvious source of information about David Rosenthal's death—Erika. But she felt unsure of herself now, as if the sands of their relationship had shifted, and she wanted to know more before she asked questions that could be more painful than she had imagined.

And besides, if she didn't get to hospital, she'd have missed official visiting hours again, and would have hell to pay with the charge nurse.

St. Paul's it was, then, and a visit to her mum in St. Barts. But as she edged herself into the mass of people descending the stairs to the South Ken platform, she pulled out her mobile and rang Melody Talbot.

The brooch was beautiful, Kincaid had to admit. Giles Oliver had taken it from the small safe and placed it on a black velvet board with such care that it might have been made of eggshells rather than the hardest substance on earth.

Kincaid had admired the design and the artistry of the piece—it had undoubtedly been made by a master craftsman—and the diamonds were quite literally brilliant. Real diamonds of that size, and displayed in such a way, were unlikely to be mistaken for their cheap imitations.

But in spite of its beauty, the Goldshtein brooch left him cold. Diamonds did not fascinate him—in his mind they carried the reek of corporate corruption and of the spilled blood of innocents—but most of all, he did not understand the desire for possession.

Cullen, apparently, was no more taken than he, having merely glanced at the piece, murmured something appreciative, then fidgeted, ready to get onto the scent.

"Thanks very much," Kincaid had told Giles Oliver, and

was amused to see that Oliver seemed disappointed by their lack of reaction.

But as they passed back through the salesroom, stopping to retrieve Amir Khan's personal information from a grudging Mrs. March, Kincaid had seen that all the seats in the auction were still full and that the clerks handling the phone and online bids were busy as well. There were many people, obviously, who did not share his sentiments.

As they reached the doors, Kincaid stood aside for a dapper elderly man who was leaving as well.

"Any success?" Kincaid asked.

"Oh, I only come to look," the man answered in an accent that still bore a trace of French. Smiling, he added, "But that is enough." He lifted his catalog to them in salute, and Kincaid felt suddenly a bit more optimistic about the motivation of his fellow man.

Amir Khan lived in a terraced house on the Clapham side of Wandsworth Common. It was, Kincaid knew, pricey enough real estate, as was anything near central London, but it was not what he had expected. This was suburban London, an area where the Victorian red-brown brick terraces had back gardens and were mostly occupied by families, while he had imagined the debonair Khan in a Thames-side loft conversion with a panoramic view.

It was late enough in the afternoon that cars lined both sides of the street, and they had to circle round several times before Cullen managed to maneuver the car into a space in the ASDA car park at the top of the hill. They walked back, listening to the sounds of televisions and children's voices drifting from the occasional open window. But most of these families, Kincaid thought, would be like his own, with children in after-school care and both parents working.

Khan's house was midterrace, and undistinguished except for the ornate black-and-white-tiled path that led through neatly trimmed privet hedges to the front door. There was only the one bell, which meant that Khan owned the entire house, not a flat, and that piqued Kincaid's curiosity.

Amir Khan answered the door himself. He still wore

suit trousers, but his collar was open and his shirtsleeves rolled up. His perfectly barbered dark hair was tousled, and in one arm he held a chubby, red-faced infant. "What took you so long?" he said.

There was such a thing as being too dependable, thought Melody, when the first thing your boss said on finding you at the office after five o'clock was "Oh, I knew you'd still be there."

She was, of course, finishing up paperwork that Gemma would normally have been doing herself, and she felt the tiniest twinge of resentment. Not that Gemma could help her mother being ill, but Melody felt unsettled and would like to have been out doing something other than tackling Gemma's latest request, which meant ringing up newspaper morgues trying to track down copies of every paper printed on the day David Rosenthal had died in May 1952.

She sighed as she pulled out her phone list. As much as she liked working with Gemma, maybe she should put in a request for a transfer to an MIT—a Murder Investigation Team at Scotland Yard. As much as she hated to admit it, she was beginning to envy Doug Cullen his job.

For a moment, Melody let the idea take hold, then shook her head. If this job was risky, that one would be akin to running blindfolded into oncoming traffic. It was definitely out of bounds, and if she knew what was good for her, she wouldn't kick at the traces.

"I take it you were expecting us?" Kincaid asked as Khan motioned them inside.

"I'd have been an idiot not to. And I couldn't talk at work, although my taking the afternoon off will probably fuel the gossip mill for a month." Khan's Oxbridge accent had softened round the edges, and his tone lacked the animosity Kincaid had heard when they'd met in the salesroom. Khan's expression was still tense, however. "Let's not stand about having a convention on the doorstep." Shifting the baby on his hip, he called up the stairs, "Soph!"

There was the sound of quick footsteps, and a woman

came round the landing carrying another child, this one a sleepy-eyed toddler with her thumb in her mouth. "Just now changed," she said, and gave them a cheerful smile.

She was fair-skinned, with a pleasant face and a mass of brown hair that curled in corkscrews. "Hullo. I'm Sophie. And this," she said, jiggling the child on her hip, who promptly hid her face against her mother's breast, "is Isabella, and that," she said, nodding at the baby, "is Adrianna, as Ka probably hasn't bothered to tell you. You must be the police."

"Ka?" Kincaid repeated, certain he had missed a page, but not quite sure which one.

"Sorry," said Sophie Khan. "Silly university nickname. He hates it when I call him that in public, but then this isn't exactly public, is it?"

"Can you take the baby, Soph?" Khan asked, sounding only mildly exasperated.

"Why don't you put her in her high chair in the kitchen? Then you can go out into the garden for a bit of peace and quiet, and I'll bring you something to drink."

They followed Khan and his wife through a sitting room that at a casual glance had more the ambience of IKEA than antiques, and then through a kitchen, where Khan stopped to ease the baby into a chair that latched on to a sturdy tile-topped table.

French doors led out to a flagged patio overlooking a long, narrow garden with neat borders and grass still the emerald of spring. A red-and-blue plastic swing set took center stage on the lawn.

"Dreadful, isn't it?" said Khan as he sank into a chair in the shade. "I've a kit for a proper one in the storage shed. I just haven't had the time to build it. Maybe when this is all over . . ."

"What exactly are you talking about, Mr. Khan?" asked Kincaid, now completely at a loss.

Khan stared back at him, looking equally befuddled. "Are you saying they didn't tell you?"

"Who didn't tell me what?"

"Jesus bloody Christ." Khan closed his eyes and wiped a

hand across a forehead already damp from the heat. "Don't you people ever communicate with one another? SO6. Fraud. Whatever the hell they're calling themselves these days."

"I talked to Fraud," said Cullen, sounding defensive. "They said they didn't have anything definitive on Harrowby's."

"Not yet, they don't." Khan leaned forward, hands clasped on his knees. "Look, I'm really sorry about what happened to Kristin Cahill. She was a nice girl, and I tried my best to get her out of it.

"But do not, do not"—he chopped a hand in the air for emphasis—"come stomping in with big boots and screw up what I've been working on for the last three years. I don't know what you've stumbled into, but it has no bearing on what's going on at Harrowby's."

"What do you mean, what's going on at Harrowby's?" asked Cullen. "And what do you mean, you tried to get Kristin Cahill out of it?"

But it had clicked for Kincaid. "You tried to get Kristin to quit, didn't you? Giles Oliver said she saw you copying papers."

"So she told the little weasel. Damn." Khan looked pained. "And he thought he'd finger me before I fingered him. Tosser."

The door opened and Sophie Khan came out with glasses on a tray. "Orangina," she said, placing the tray on a small table. "Not elegant, but there it is. That's the last of the ice, I'm afraid. We've rather gone through it today."

She gave Khan a questioning look, but when he merely said, "Thanks, Soph," and took his glass, she went back into the house, giving them a nice retreating view of jeans and her colorful batiked cotton top.

"You've known each other a long time, I take it," Kincaid said, after a grateful sip of his own drink.

"Since university. Oxford. We were at Balliol together. I read art history, and Sophie literature, for all the good it does her now." His fond grin transformed his lean face.

Khan was, Kincaid decided, perhaps only in his midthirties. His poise, his clothes, and the veneer of arrogance he had worn so well at the salesroom had made him seem older.

He said, "I think, Mr. Khan, that you had better start at the beginning."

"Ah, well." Khan's smile vanished. "I never thought it would come to this. I specialized in Eastern art and meant to teach. But there were no suitable openings after uni, and the job at Harrowby's came up. I thought it sounded glamorous, wet behind the ears as I was.

"I came up from the floor, like Kristin and Giles Oliver, and I soon found out that it wasn't glamorous at all. But by the time I really began to see all the cracks in the porcelain, Soph and I were married and had bought a house. So I had commitments, and couldn't afford to jump ship, but the higher I climbed, the more rotten things got."

"What sort of rot are we talking about?" Kincaid asked.

Khan waved a hand. "You name it. Dealing in stolen or illegally exported antiquities. Falsifying import documents. Forging provenance. Collusion in the setting of the reserve. Phantom bidding. That, by the way, is Giles Oliver's little specialty, when he works the phones."

"Is it, now?" Kincaid asked thoughtfully, reconsidering his opinion of Oliver. "And this dirty dealing—it goes all the way up?"

"To the top. And between international branches of the firm."

"Why doesn't Fraud step in?" asked Cullen, sounding incensed.

"Because they can't prove anything. And even if they managed to bring a charge against the firm—and believe me, a collector who has paid an obscene amount of money for an antiquity that he thinks might have been illegally exported is *not* going to admit it, much less complain to the police—the relevant documents would disappear in a heartbeat."

"The documents that Kristin saw you copying—what were they?" asked Cullen.

"Memos from one of the directors to the heads of several departments, very clearly setting out a scheme for the smuggling of listed Italian objects."

"Did Kristin know what they were?"

"God, no. That would have been disastrous. She just saw me copying things in the director's office when I had no reason to be there. I thought if I was hard enough on her, she'd leave."

"It seems to me that you—"

Kincaid cut Cullen off. "You still haven't said exactly what you were doing." He wasn't ready to antagonize Khan, not until they had the whole story. "Or why Fraud should have told us about it."

"No." Khan sat back in his chair and looked out at the garden. One of the little bucket swings moved very slightly in the breeze. "I wish now I'd never had the mind to be so bloody noble. It was before Soph got pregnant with Izzy, and I hadn't so much to lose.

"It ate at me, to see what I'd loved so tarnished, but I didn't know what I could do. Then one night I ran into a friend from university, an investigative journalist. We got to talking, and after a few too many bottles of wine, I told him everything. He lit up like a bloody Christmas tree. He said that if I was patient, I could collect enough evidence to mount a damning exposé. And that we could sell it. Not only to a publisher, but he had a contact at ITV that might be interested in doing a program."

"And the police?"

"My friend met with SO6, told them what we were planning. They said they'd keep a watching brief, whatever that means. I've never spoken directly to anyone, for fear that it would compromise my position. But I assumed that someone would have told you, or at least asked you to tread carefully. I suppose they took our request to keep it quiet a bit too literally."

Khan smiled, this time with no humor. "I didn't know the meaning of *patient*. Or what it would be like to lead a double life. I suppose I had juvenile fantasies of being a spy." He shook his head, and in the shadows the planes of his face looked hollow.

"Sweating. Lying. Sneaking. I'd always put on a bit of a facade, as it impressed the punters, but this went much deeper. I began to bring that other man home, and Soph was getting fed up. I was getting fed up. But we—my friend and I—had finally come up with a concrete scheme for nailing them, a trail of documents that led all the way through the chain. But my position is getting more precarious every day, and you can see why I couldn't appear to be cooperating with the police.

"I want out." Khan sliced his hand through the air, a figurative cut. "I've had a teaching offer from the University of London, but first I have to finish what I started."

"I can see you wouldn't want to lose out on the money, after all you've done," said Cullen.

Khan gave him an unfriendly glance. "Money would be welcome, especially now that Sophie isn't working. But so far I've not seen a penny, nor do I have any guarantee that I will. It's just that I'd like all my effort to count for something.

"It's a bloody racket," he went on, shaking his head in disgust. "Buy something from a barrow boy at a market, mark it up twenty, fifty, a hundred times, and call it a priceless antique. It's bollocks."

"You're not saying it's all worthless?" said Cullen, sounding as if he'd been told there was no Father Christmas.

"No, of course not. But you have to know what you're doing, and you should never trust an auction house—at least not ours. Kristin liked to sneer a bit at her mum's little antiques shop, but from what Kristin said, her mum is an honest trader and makes an honest living at it."

"And the Goldshtein brooch?"

"Oh, that's real enough. The hallmark and the work are unmistakable," Khan answered with a shrug. "Although I never thought to see an authentic Goldshtein that had not been cataloged. But these things do happen, even if not as often as the salesrooms and the telly auction shows would like you to think. But my guess, with a piece like that, would be that someone had it tucked away. I doubt it's been floating about unidentified on the market for years."

"And you had no previous connection with the seller, Harry Pevensey?" Kincaid asked.

"No. Although I didn't buy the story about the car boot

sale—Pevensey just didn't seem the type to go digging about in car park stalls—but you can't exactly call a client a liar if you want to keep the business."

"And Kristin? Do you know what her connection was with Pevensey?"

"She didn't say, and I didn't ask, although I thought it was an unlikely liaison. Kristin was a bit of a social climber, and Pevensey was obviously not going anywhere but down, no matter what sort of profit he might have made on the brooch." Khan frowned. "You'll have talked to him, now that you have the warrant? What did he say?"

"We didn't have the chance to ask," Kincaid answered levelly. "Someone ran Harry Pevensey down last night, just like Kristin. He's dead."

"Dead?" Khan stared at them blankly, then his face hardened and he stood. "You bastards. You came here, to my home, accepting my hospitality, and all the while you meant to trick me into making some kind of admission? You think *I* killed that poor sod?" There was nothing icy about his rage now, and Kincaid saw him glance at the open kitchen window and make an obvious effort to lower his voice. "Have you put me in the frame for Kristin, too?"

"Mr. Khan." Kincaid stood, but more slowly. "You must realize, from what you yourself have told us, that you had a great deal to lose if Kristin Cahill reported your undercover activities to the directors of your firm. And if she had some connection with Harry Pevensey, he might have been able to compromise you as well." He lifted his jacket from the back of the lawn chair, feeling suddenly weary. He would find no enjoyment in bursting the bubble of this man's family life, and if Khan were genuine, he admired what he had set out to accomplish.

"But Kristin Cahill and Harry Pevensey died very nasty deaths," he went on, "and if what you've told us is true, you should certainly know that the job sometimes requires doing things one doesn't personally like.

"We'll need to talk to your wife, and your journalist colleague, and we'll need to check over your house and your car."

Khan met his eyes for a long moment, then nodded. "You can do whatever you like. But if I were you, I'd spend my time looking for the person who really killed Kristin Cahill. She was young and a bit shallow—like most of us at that age—and she didn't deserve what happened to her."

*If Gavin had stopped to wonder why he hadn't rung first, he would have had to admit that he was afraid she would turn him away. He had walked from the empty flat in Tedworth Square, up Sydney Street and Onslow Street, then through Knightsbridge and across the park by the Broad Walk. He was sweating and his feet ached, but he hadn't been able to bear the thought of the tube or a bus in this heat. And choosing a destination, rather than letting his body do it for him, was, again, more of an admission than he was willing to make.*

*He had walked a beat as a constable, and the rhythm of his stride seemed somehow to connect him with that phantom Gavin who had walked the bombed-out streets after the war and seen potential in the destruction. When had he lost that gift?*

*When he reached Notting Hill Gate, he wavered, and at the last moment delayed again, taking the fork into Pembridge Road and turning down Portobello. He loved walking down the twisty hill as evening came on. The shops were closed, the street quiet, and the colors of the buildings always seemed most intense when the light was fading. It made him think of villages he had seen in France during the war, as if a small piece of a foreign country had been set down in the midst of staid London like the wrong piece in a puzzle.*

*But when he reached Westbourne Grove he turned left, without more debate, and from the open windows of the flats above the shops came the sound of voices in languages he didn't recognize, and the odors of strange foods cooking.*

*The assault of the unfamiliar on his senses seemed to galvanize him, and a wave of giddy recklessness carried him into Kensington Park Road and round the corner into Arundel Gardens. Finding the address, he rang Erika Rosenthal's bell with an only slightly trembling heart.*

*But Erika answered the door as naturally as if she had been expecting him. "Inspector. Please come in."*

*He shivered slightly as he followed her into the flat—the air had cooled suddenly as the darkness came on. But she saw it and said, "Here. Please sit down. I think there might be some sherry, if you'd like."*

*Taking the chair she had indicated, he looked round the lamp-lit room, exhaling in relief as a dread he only now acknowledged eased away. This room, this flat, felt as if it were Erika's alone, and he sensed no hovering shade of David Rosenthal.*

*An open book and an empty teacup sat on a table beside the other chair, and beside it, a basket of sewing. A worn rug that had once been of good quality covered most of the bare floorboards, glass-fronted cases on either side of the fireplace held books, and the mantel top held a collection of colorful and eccentrically carved wooden animals. He knew instinctively that they were Erika's.*

*"From Bavaria," she said, having come back into the room and seen his gaze. "My mother brought them to me when I was a child. One of the few things I managed to save when I went back to Berlin after the war, as they weren't considered of any value by the Nazis or the looters."*

*"And that?" he asked, nodding at the small grand piano that took up most of the remainder of the sitting room.*

*Erika handed him a small crystal glass, and as he took it he felt ham-fisted, clumsy. But the sherry was dry and gold and, when he sipped it, tasted like distilled sunlight.*

*"The piano?" She sat in the chair beside the open book, crossing her ankles beneath the bell made by the skirt of her pale blue shirtwaist dress. "I worked the neighborhood watch during the war. When a house was bombed, we tried to find relatives to take any undamaged possessions. Sometimes the owners had been killed, or sometimes families had left London and we had no way to contact them. The piano was the only thing left standing in a house on Ladbroke*

*Road. No one wanted it, and so some of the men made a sort of pallet with wheels and rolled it here for me.*

*"We became very ingenious at making things to do what we needed—cobbling together, I think you would call it, although I can't imagine why."*

*"Something to do with shoes," said Gavin. "Do you play?" he added, not distracted from the piano.*

*She smiled. "My mother made me take lessons as a child. But I was always better at listening than playing."* She took a small sip of her sherry, not, he thought, out of abstention, but because she wanted to savor it. Erika was a person who savored things . . . a book, a sip of wine, an abandoned piano, the faded colors in a rug. How had she lived in compromise with David Rosenthal, whom Gavin had come to believe had occupied only the blind tunnel of obsession?

"I can't imagine your husband here," he said, astounded by his rudeness even as he spoke his thoughts aloud.

"Oh, but he wasn't here very much," Erika answered, with no hint of offense. "He was working or he was at the Reading Room, and often he did other things that he did not choose to share with me."

"You didn't mind?"

"It would have made no difference whether I minded or not." She set her glass on the table, the crystal making the faintest chink against the wood, and met his eyes directly. "Inspector Hoxley, what have you come to tell me?"

"It's Gavin," he said, knowing he had introduced himself to her when they first met, and feeling a fool.

"Gavin. Yes, I know." She regarded him with the same gravity that had so fascinated him during that first interview.

The words came out in a rush. "I've been warned off the case. Told I'd lose my job if I didn't leave it alone." He lifted his glass, saw to his surprise that he had finished the sherry, and to his further astonishment, added, "And my wife left me."

"Because of this? Because of David?" For the first time that night he heard distress in her voice.

"No. Or if so, it was just the last little piece."

She nodded slowly. "I know about last little pieces. They are the ones that cause the edifice to topple."

He had stopped noticing her accent until she said a word like *edifice*, and then it made him want to smile. "Yes."

Erika rose and took his glass. "I will find us something else to drink. Tea, if all else fails. I became very English, during the war."

Finding he couldn't sit, Gavin followed her into the kitchen. Had she meant her husband, when she said she knew about last little pieces? Had her marriage failed before her husband's death?

She stood with her back to him, reaching up into the cupboard for cups and saucers. Gavin felt a return of the light-headedness that had brought him to her door, although surely it couldn't be the sherry.

Erika paused with the cups in midair, as if she sensed his nearness. Then she very carefully lowered the china to the worktop and rested her hands on its edge. She stood so still that she might have been waiting for a clock to tick or the world to turn on its axis.

He cupped his hands round her shoulders and felt the heat from her skin through the thin cotton of her dress. A quiver ran through her body, but she neither turned nor pulled away. "Erika," he whispered, "I shouldn't—your husband—this is wrong—"

In answer, she placed her hands on his and slipped them down until they covered her breasts, and he gasped with a desire so intense it left him shaking.

She said, "My husband never touched me after the night we left Berlin." Then she turned in his arms and tilted her head until she could meet his eyes. "And this—this is whatever we make it, my love."

# 16

❦

*Even though the Allies were fighting a war against
Nazi Germany, whose anti-Semitism was a central
plank of its public policy, anti-Semitism did not suddenly disappear from Britain during the war, but
persisted and even increased.*
—*Pamela Shatzkes,* Holocaust and Rescue:
Impotent or Indifferent? Anglo-Jewry, 1938–1945

SHADOW HAD FALLEN IN the courtyard at St. Barts by the
time Gemma reached the main gates. She ducked inside and
pulled her mobile from her bag, checking for messages now
that she was out of the bright afternoon sun and could actually see the display. Nothing yet from Kincaid, and nothing from her sister. Closing the phone, she glanced up and
caught sight of her father emerging from the temporary corridor that led round to the back of the complex.

She had seen him before he saw her, and in that instant took in his slumped shoulders and bleak expression.
"Dad," she called out, and hurried towards him. "Is Mum all
right?" Glancing at her watch, she added, "I haven't missed
visiting—" The words died on her lips. At the sound of her
voice, he had looked up, his face hardening, his chin coming
up with the familiar bulldog pugnaciousness.

"You've missed seeing her, if that worries you at all,"
he said as he came up to her. "She's sleeping. It was a bad
day, but then you'll know that, won't you? With all the time

you've been taking from work to spend with your mum."

"Dad—I was—I am—but—"

"You have something better to do with your time? Is that what you're telling me?"

"No, Dad, of course not. But someone was killed last night—"

"And that's more important than your mother dying?"

Gemma stared at him, feeling as if she'd been punched. "What are you talking about? Mum's not dying. They've said it's treatable—"

"That's doctor talk for when they don't want to tell you the truth. She's bad. I've never seen her like this."

To Gemma's horror, she saw that he was close to tears. "Dad, she's going to be all right." She reached out, touched his arm, but he shook her off.

"Don't you dare talk down to me," he spat at her. "You've no right, missy, and this is one time when you don't know best."

All his criticism, all his disapproval, suddenly seemed more than she could bear. A red wave of fury exploded behind her eyes. "And don't *you* talk to me like that," she shouted back at him. "What have I ever done to deserve being treated like that?"

Vaguely, she was aware of other people moving past them, of whispered comments, but she was past caring. "I've made something of myself, something that should make you proud. I'm responsible. I've got a good career. A beautiful child. A good relationship. Why can't you for once give me a lit—"

"So that's the way it is, is it?" Having got a rise out of her, he had gone cold. "If your life is so perfect, why don't you marry him and give your mum some peace of mind while you can?"

"I still don't like him," said Cullen when he and Kincaid were at last back in the car. "He's very convincing, but he was just as convincing as an arrogant shit at Harrowby's. So how can you be sure which one is the act?"

They had called in a search team for the Khans' house,

and a tow for their dark blue Volvo SUV, which turned out to be registered to Sophie Khan. "Ka never drives it, unless we go out together in the evenings or on weekends," she had told them.

When asked to confirm her husband's whereabouts on the two nights in question, she had said that of course he was home in bed, and what sort of idiot did they take her for if they thought she wouldn't have noticed him leaving to go run someone down?

She'd had one child on her hip and the other wrapped round her leg, and had looked fierce enough to rip their entrails out if they threatened her family.

Khan had gone quiet and distant, and Kincaid couldn't read behind the mask. Having told them quite civilly, once he'd calmed down, that they were wasting his time and theirs, Khan had added that any documents he had copied from Harrowby's he had passed on to his journalist colleague, and that he would not give his friend permission to release them.

"And if you think I'm a hard case," he'd added with a faint smile, "you haven't met Jon. You'll not get a scrap of paper from him with anything less than a subpoena."

"Should we tackle the journalist?" Cullen asked now with what sounded like relish.

Kincaid considered, then said, "Not until we've had another word with the slippery Giles Oliver."

Gemma watched her father walk away, her anger ebbing as quickly as it had come. She wondered if she would ever learn not to bite, not to try for the last word, because it was inevitably a losing battle. All she had done was prove that he still had the capacity to hurt her, and to make her doubt herself.

But what he had said—was he right about her mum? She turned and started down the long tunnel of the makeshift corridor, her heart pounding as if she'd just run a sprint. When she reached her mother's ward, she stood at the desk, swallowing against the dryness in her mouth as she waited for the charge nurse to be free.

It was the same Pakistani man she had spoken to the first

night her mum had come in, and he smiled in recognition as he handed off a chart to another nurse and turned to her.

"You can go in," he said. "She's resting, but—"

"Is she worse?" Gemma asked. "My dad said she was"— she couldn't bring herself to say the word—"that she was having a bad day."

"Oh, I wouldn't go that far." The nurse shook his head. "She's just tired from the chemo, and the antinausea medication makes her a bit sleepy. She's doing just fine. You go in and see for yourself." He waved her off, turning to someone else, and she had no choice but to follow his command, even though her heart was still skipping erratically.

The curtains were drawn round her mum's bed. Gemma took a breath, then parted them and slipped quietly into the chair by the bedside. Her mum was sleeping, just as the nurse had said, and her breathing was easy and regular.

Relief flooded through Gemma and she closed her eyes against the sudden welling of tears.

Her dad had meant to hurt her. He had always been sharp with her, and critical, and she had assumed it was because she was the eldest and he expected more. But this— she hadn't seen this. When had her father's feelings towards her changed into something more than impatience?

Sensing a change in her mum's breathing, she looked up and found her mum awake and watching her.

"I'm so sorry, Mummy," she whispered. "I didn't mean to wake you."

"I'm just glad to see you, love." Vi lifted a hand towards Gemma's wet cheek, but the IV line hampered her and she let it fall back to the bed. "You've not been crying, have you?"

"No, I—" Gemma wiped the back of her hand across her cheeks and blurted out, "Mum, why does Dad hate me?"

"Hate you? Don't be silly, love," Vi said, with a hint of her usual briskness. But even that seemed to tire her, and she sank back into her pillows, adding more quietly, "Of course your dad doesn't hate you. Whatever gave you that idea?" She searched Gemma's face and sighed. "Don't pay him any mind. He's worried, and he's taking it out on you."

"But why me? I always wanted him to be proud of me." She thought of Hugh Kincaid, Duncan's father, and of how surprised she had been when he'd treated her immediately with liking and respect.

"Oh, your dad is proud of you, in his way. But he's more frightened by you."

Gemma frowned, not understanding. "Frightened? Why?"

"Because . . ." Vi seemed to search for words. "Because he sees you, and what you've accomplished, as making a mockery of who he is and what he's done with his life."

"But I haven't—Cyn always stands up to him, and he doesn't—"

"But your sister has stayed safely in her pigeonhole," said Vi. "She's no threat to him."

Gemma sat back, trying to get her mind round a different view of the man who had always seemed to her so certain of himself that he measured everyone else's aspirations by his own.

"But what can I do?" she asked, bewildered.

"Nothing, lovey." Vi sighed. "Nothing but go on being yourself. But you might try"—her mother smiled—"as hard as it is, you might try being a bit more patient with him."

"Doesn't look too flash to me," said Cullen, looking at Giles Oliver's building with a grimace of distaste.

"I wouldn't be too sure," Kincaid replied. His curiosity roused by what Khan had told them, he was eager for another look at the inside of Oliver's flat.

They had struggled to park in Fulham, as they had in Wandsworth, and had at last settled for a spot in the Waitrose car park near Fulham Broadway, walking the few streets to the flat. Kincaid thought Cullen looked hot and irritable, just the thing for a good interview. And likely to be more irritable yet, he thought as they opened the building door and the smell of nicely warmed cat urine met them like a noxious cloud.

"What the—" Cullen gulped. "No wonder there's no security. No burglar worth his salt would come in here."

"That's not why Oliver doesn't need security," Kincaid said as they mounted the stairs, and he managed not to jump when the first bark shook the walls of the top landing.

Cullen, however, stopped dead in his tracks, and Kincaid grinned. "He's harmless, really. You'll be best friends before you know it."

Looking not the least bit reassured, Cullen stepped behind him. The dog's barks rose in pitch as Kincaid rapped on the door. "Giles, it's Duncan Kincaid."

After a moment there came the same sound of scuffling and swearing he and Gemma had heard before, and Giles Oliver opened the door. He'd managed to get the mastiff into a sitting position behind him, but on seeing Kincaid the dog charged forward, tail wagging like a metronome gone berserk.

Kincaid gave Cullen points for having held his ground. "Hullo, Mo," he said as the dog sniffed him thoroughly and drooled on his trouser leg. "We'd like a word, Giles."

"Again?" Giles Oliver sounded aggrieved. He'd changed from work clothes into jeans and a T-shirt that revealed the bulge of his belly and did nothing to improve his appearance. "I don't know what else I can tell you, and I was busy—"

"What happened to all your concern about Kristin?" Kincaid said, moving the dog forward so that Cullen could get in the door. The flat was hot, even with the windows open, and Oliver's limp hair was plastered to his forehead. "I thought you wanted to help."

"I didn't mean— Of course, I want to help. I was just—" A tub of ice cream sat on the coffee table, and having thoroughly examined Kincaid and a rigid Cullen, the dog wandered over and plunged his nose in. "Mo, damn it." Oliver grabbed the dog by his collar and dragged him off.

"I expect you can scrape off the top layer," Kincaid said sympathetically. "No harm done. But I'd get it back in the freezer if I were you."

Oliver gave him a dirty look but retrieved the tub and took it into the kitchen, sliding it lidless into the small freezer. The tub had left a wet ring on the polished wood finish of the table.

Kincaid took a seat, uninvited, and Mo came to him and laid his massive head across his lap, this time leaving a trail of slobbery ice cream. A trip to the dry cleaners was definitely in the offing.

Cullen had stayed by the door, looking like he might bolt any second. Oliver came back into the sitting room, wiping his hands on his jeans. Scratching the dog behind his ears, Kincaid smiled at him. "Now that we're off to a good start, Giles, why don't you tell us about the phantom bidding?"

Oliver's eyes widened and he swayed, as if he couldn't quite manage his body without the dog as a prop. "I have no idea what you're talking about," he managed to croak.

"Oh, yes, you do," Kincaid said. "That's where you make an agreement with the auctioneer to invent bids before a sale starts. It keeps the bids going up, creates a bit of excitement, and both the seller and the house make more money. The only person who loses out is the buyer, but then they should know what they're getting into, shouldn't they?"

"I don't know what—"

"I imagine it works particularly well when you're handling a phone line, as those bidders on the floor have no way of knowing whether the phone-in bid is genuine. Clever, isn't it? And not even illegal," Kincaid added cheerfully.

Oliver had flushed an unbecoming red that made his spots stand out. "If Khan told you that, it's a lie. He'd say anything to make me look bad."

"What if Khan didn't tell us that? Is it still a lie? And why should Khan have some sort of personal vendetta against you, Giles? Have you been spreading rumors about him?"

"I— You're deliberately trying to confuse me. And I don't see what any of this has to do with Kristin." He shot a distracted glance at Cullen, who had relaxed enough to come all the way into the room and was examining Oliver's audio equipment with interest.

"Well," Kincaid said, stroking the top of the dog's head. Mo groaned and rested more of his weight against Kincaid's knee. "It's not just about Kristin anymore," Kincaid continued, ignoring the damp patch spreading towards his crotch. "The man who gave Kristin the Goldshtein brooch to sell was killed last night. Did she tell you his name? A sort of quid pro quo for your bragging to her about your profits on your bidding scheme? And if she told you about *him,* maybe it occurred to you that she might have told him about *you.*"

"You are totally fucking mad." Giles Oliver licked his lips as if they had suddenly gone dry.

Kincaid knew he was spinning it, but if it was getting Oliver rattled he wasn't going to stop. "Or maybe you thought she'd told Harry Pevensey that you were harassing her, spying on her, and that put you square in the frame for her murder—"

"Holy shit." Cullen was peering at one of the two speakers flanking Oliver's audio setup. He jabbed a finger at the speaker. "Do you know how much one of these things costs? These are B and W's. Five thousand pounds apiece. Five thousand pounds for just one of these, and you've got two. You could buy a bloody car for what these things are worth."

Kincaid wasn't sure if he sounded more outraged or envious. "B and W's?" he asked.

"Bowers and Wilkins. Based in Worthing. They make the best high-end loudspeakers this side of the Atlantic."

Oliver backed up a step, as if looking for a bolt-hole. "No, man, you don't understand." He shook his head. "I got them secondhand. I never paid that much for them."

"Yeah, right." Cullen rolled his eyes. "I get the catalogs. These are new."

Cullen, a secret audiophile? Kincaid logged the fact for future reference, then said, "My, my, Doug. You have big aspirations on a policeman's salary." He turned to Oliver. "And, Giles, when you add in the rest of this equipment, I suspect you seem to have even bigger ones for someone making a salesclerk's wages. That must be some fiddle you've got going, if you can afford equipment like that. Maybe there's a bit more to it than the odd percentage on a phantom bid. Did Kristin find out you had your finger in more than one pie?"

"You have no business questioning how I spend my money." Oliver drew himself up, but Kincaid could see that he was shaking. "I have an allowance from my parents, if you must know. And none of this has anything to do with Kristin. She never came here. She never saw any of this."

Thoughtfully, Kincaid said, "That brings us very nicely back to where we started, doesn't it, Giles? Rejection. Jealousy. Kristin turned you down flat that night, and not very nicely, either, according to her mum."

"Just because you don't have a driving license doesn't mean you can't drive," chimed in Cullen. "And with all this equipment, I'd be willing to bet that hot-wiring a car is not beyond your skills. One was stolen just a few streets from here the night Kristin Cahill was killed. It was found abandoned the next day—the police assumed it was joyriders. But maybe you took it, Giles, and left it after you ran Kristin down."

"I never hurt Kristin," protested Giles, sounding near tears. "I loved her."

"That's obsession, Giles. Not love," Kincaid said. "She didn't even like you." The dog lifted his head at the change in his voice, then settled back down with a grunt. "Did you get Harry Pevensey's name from the files?" Kincaid went on. "Did you think he was Kristin's secret lover? The one who sent her the roses?"

"I'd never heard of him until you said his name a few minutes ago." Oliver looked round wildly, as if help might appear out of thin air, but even his dog had abandoned him. "I'm not talking to you anymore. I don't care what you say."

Kincaid sighed and, slipping the dog's head from his knee, stood. "Then I think we'd better take you into the Yard. We'll see if your prints match any of those found on the stolen car."

"But— You can't." Oliver sounded more shocked than belligerent. "What about Mo?"

"Surely you have a friend or a neighbor who could look after your dog."

"No. There's no one. There's this daft woman with cats downstairs, but she can't stand him. I don't know anyone else."

"Your parents?"

"They're in Hampshire."

Kincaid glanced at his watch. "Too late for the RSPCA. I suppose we'll have to have him impounded."

"No!"

"They won't put him down for twenty-four hours," Kincaid said, disliking himself for the deliberate cruelty, but willing to use it. "Doug, ring the animal warden—"

"No, wait." Oliver looked as though he might imitate Dominic Scott and faint on them. "I'll tell you everything."

*They made love the first time with the ferocity of starvation, abandoning clothes in an awkward stumble to the bedroom, desperate to touch skin to skin.*

*The second time they had been tender, gentle in discovery, laughing a little at the wonder of it.*

*And much later, once more, with a lazy, sated pleasure that turned suddenly to urgency, leaving them gasping and shaken.*

*And in between, they had talked. He told her about his childhood in Chelsea, about his fascination with the ever-present river and his love of the Albert Bridge, about life in London before the war. She told him about a Berlin that had seemed to her enchanted in those years before the war, about her writing, and about continuing her studies, a secret she had not shared with anyone, even David.*

*Easily, they traded favorite foods, and books, and music, and places they had seen. And all the while they navigated around the boulders beneath the surface of the stream— David, and David's death, and Gavin's wife and children, as if by doing so they could make a world that contained nothing but the two of them, and they said nothing, nothing at all, about the morrow.*

*Erika knew now that the way she and Gavin had come together was the way it was meant to be between two people, and that for David sex with her had been little more than a duty. Her husband had been her first lover, and she had thought herself somehow lacking, or her desires unnatural.*

*And the other—the other didn't bear thinking of, especially not here, not now.*

*Gavin had left her at dawn, even though she'd begged*

him to stay. *"I don't want your neighbors talking,"* he said, and she'd reluctantly let him ease his warm body from hers.

When he'd dressed, he'd bent to kiss her once more, whispering, *"This is too fine a thing to spoil,"* and when she'd heard the latch of the door click behind him and his footsteps fade away in the quiet street, she had hugged her joy to herself like a pearl, and fallen instantly into a dreamless sleep.

# 17

<br>

*April 1945*
*Thursday, 5th*

> *No more bombs for more than a week. No one knows*
> *what it means to us to go to bed in peace, and not*
> *take leave of all our possessions, and wonder if we*
> *shall wake up in pieces, or with the roof collapsing*
> *on our heads, unless they have lived with it.*
> —*Vere Hodgson,* Few Eggs and No Oranges:
> The Diaries of Vere Hodgson, 1940–1945

<br>

"**YOU'RE RIGHT. I WAS** jealous," admitted Giles. "But I can't drive. I failed my bloody test three times before I came up to London, and there's really not much point here." He sat in the chair with the curved wood arms, and the dog went to him and collapsed at his feet with a sigh.

"So is that your excuse for running Kristin down?" asked Cullen. "Bad driving?"

"Don't be stupid. I'm telling you that I wasn't driving. But I knew where Kristin lived. We'd talked about it—about how she wanted to get out from under her parents—and it wasn't that far from here.

"So that night, I wanted to see who she was meeting. I didn't think I could hang about outside the Gate without her noticing, but I thought if I waited for her to come home, I'd see who dropped her off, and there are plenty of places along the King's Road where you can fade into the shadows."

"And you knew this because you'd done it before?" Kincaid asked.

Oliver scowled at him. "What do you think I am? Some sort of pervert? No, I hadn't waited for her at night before, but I knew where her building was. I mean, if you go down the King's Road, you can't help but notice." When Kincaid merely raised an eyebrow, he swallowed and went on. "But it was a stupid thing to do. It was getting cold, and I'd walked up and down enough that I thought people would start to notice me. There was a woman out with her dog who looked at me like—well, never mind. So I'd just about decided to go home when I saw her."

"You saw Kristin?"

"Walking down the King's Road, like she'd come from the bus stop. I wasn't close. I'd started walking west, but I'd turned to look back. The light turned at Edith Grove, and then, just as she stepped out into the street—" Giles slid from the chair to the floor, ducking his head and wrapping his arms round the dog.

"Giles," Kincaid prompted, and Oliver lifted his head. "What happened then?"

Giles swallowed hard. "A car pulled away from the curb in front of her building. And it just—it just—it sped up, instead of stopping at the light. And it just—hit her. She—Kristin—bounced, like she wasn't even human, and hit the street. The car just kept going."

Making an effort to keep the disbelief from his voice, Kincaid said, "Giles, what did you do?"

"I was—I was going to—but a man came out of one of the flats. And then I—I couldn't—"

Cullen had no such compunction. "You mean you just left her? You just left her lying there?"

"I wasn't— She had help." Giles looked up, his face tear-streaked. "I couldn't—there was nothing I could do. So I went home. And then I waited to hear. There was no one I could call. I didn't know where they'd taken her. So I had to—I had to go in to work, knowing—"

"You little tosser," said Cullen, not disguising his disgust. "How could you? How could you just go off and leave her?"

"I thought she'd be all right," Giles shot back. "And then I'd have to explain what I was doing there. And she—she would think—she would never—"

"Understand," Kincaid finished for him. If it was true, Giles Oliver had been an idiot and a coward, but he was also a witness—at this point their only witness. "The car, Giles. What was it?"

Giles shook his head. "I don't know. I'm not very good with cars."

"You don't know?" Cullen's voice rose in outrage, and the dog lifted his head.

"Okay, let's go back a bit," said Kincaid, attempting to ratchet the tension down. "You said you walked back and forth for a bit. Did you see the car before it pulled away from the curb?"

"I—I don't remember."

"Think, man."

Giles screwed up his face in concentration. "I was on the opposite side of the street. There were cars parked all along. I didn't notice. I'm sorry."

"Let's go at it a different way, then. You're accustomed to looking at things. You saw the car pull out from the curb. You must have had some impression, even if you didn't recognize the make. Was it light colored or dark?"

"Dark," Giles said without hesitation.

"Okay, good. Large or small?"

"It was big. And sort of square."

"A coupe?" Kincaid asked, deliberately leading.

Giles frowned. "No. I remember the back end looked big. It was an SUV, I think. A country sort of car. A Land Rover, maybe."

"Anyone home?" Gemma called out as she let herself in the front door. The dogs came running to her, sniffing her legs and jumping up in excitement as if she'd been gone a week rather than most of the day.

She hadn't stayed long at the hospital. Her mum had been obviously exhausted, and Gemma felt she was doing more harm than good by keeping her from resting.

And she felt guilty for having let her temper get the better of her with her dad, and even worse for having inflicted an emotional outburst on her mother. That was the last thing her mum had needed.

"In here" came Kit's answer from the kitchen. The house was warm from the day's heat and smelled tantalizingly of baking dough and spices. Pizza.

Giving Geordie's ears a last fondle, she followed her nose. Kit stood at the fridge, examining the contents as if he were looking for buried treasure.

"Where is everyone?" Gemma asked.

"I thought we had more milk," Kit said, then shut the fridge door and turned to her. "Wes had to go. Toby's watching a cartoon in the study. I said he could, if he finished his lessons. Duncan rang and said he'd been held up—he tried to ring you but your phone was off."

"Oh, damn." Gemma realized she'd switched her phone off at the hospital and had forgotten to switch it on again. "Did he say why?"

"Just that he'd ring you later. Do you want some pizza?" Kit asked. "It's Pizza Express from the freezer."

"Oh, Kit." This seemed to be Gemma's day for feeling contrite. She had left the children to fend for themselves, and had been so caught up in her own worries that she hadn't even thought to check in. "I *am* sorry. We expect you to do too much, and you never complain." Impulsively, she went to him and slipped an arm round his shoulders in a hug.

He ducked his head in a way that reminded her of Toby, but smiled. "It's okay," he assured her. "Really. I don't mind."

She let go before he reached complete embarrassment overload, but couldn't resist ruffling his hair.

"Get off," he said, bouncing away from her with a grin. "Toby and I were going to take the dogs for a walk before it got dark. Do you want to come?"

Gemma hesitated, then shook her head. "Um, no, but

thanks. I'll think I'll stay here and have a bit of your pizza."

While Kit got the dogs' leads, she fetched Toby from the study, switching off some American cop show on the telly while giving him a hug and as much of a cuddle as he'd allow.

"I was watching that." Her son pulled away from her with a scowl, a sure sign of a five-year-old's temper tantrum brewing.

"You're a bit stroppy today, sport," she said, using Duncan's nickname for him.

"I'm not stroppy," Toby protested. "Whatever it is."

Gemma pretended to think hard. "Obstreperous."

"You're silly, Mummy," said Toby, not mollified. "I'm not that, either." He punched at her with his fist, but she caught him by both wrists.

"Enough of that." And enough of things he shouldn't be watching on the telly, she added to herself. She'd have to speak to Kit about it, as Toby was obviously changing the channel when Kit left the room, but she hated to nag Kit when he made such an effort. It was a case once more of giving Kit more responsibility than he should have to bear, not to mention her falling down on her parenting.

Swinging Toby round, she tickled him until he squealed, then marched him from the room. "You go with Kit to walk the dogs, and when you get back we'll have a special treat. A game."

"Can we play Giant Snakes and Ladders?"

Gemma cursed herself. That was Toby's latest favorite, and required more energy than a marathon, especially when you added barking dogs and a cat interested in anything spread out on the floor. "Of course," she said, hoping that dinner would revive her a bit.

But when the boys and dogs had gone out in a flurry of motion, she decided she wasn't hungry after all, and instead poured herself a glass of white wine from the fridge, popped a CD in the kitchen player, sank into a chair and kicked off her shoes.

Closing her eyes, she tried to shut out the replay of her row with her dad and her worry over her mum. She wiggled her toes and held the wine in her mouth before she swallowed, tasting all the flavors.

After a moment, the music began to do its work. She'd put on Barb Jungr, one of her favorite singers, but it wasn't Jungr's smoky voice that caught her attention now, but the sweet, spare notes of the piano accompaniment.

God, how long had it been since she'd played the piano? She'd canceled lesson after lesson, and without that discipline, had practiced less and less. How had she let something she loved so much slip away from her?

But with the job, and Duncan, and the boys, and the dogs—as if to remind her of his presence, Sid chose that moment to pad into the kitchen and jump up on the table—and the cat, Gemma amended, she seemed to have little time for herself.

And yet, even with more in her life than she could manage well, she still felt the sting of loss, and cataloging the practical difficulties they'd have faced in caring for another child made not a whit of difference.

Pure selfishness, she told herself firmly. And she had been selfish enough lately.

With that reminder, she exchanged her glass for her mobile and rang Erika's number. It was past time she checked on Erika rather than sending Kit as an emissary, and she had questions she needed to ask.

But Erika's number rang on unanswered. Gemma drank a bit more wine, then dialed again, but there was still no reply, not even the answer phone. Although Gemma knew Erika was careless in remembering to switch the machine on, she felt frustrated by her inability to leave a message, and a little uneasy.

She was wondering how she might convince her very independent friend that she should get a mobile phone when her own phone rang. She jumped, sloshing her wine, and answered a little breathlessly.

It was not Erika, however, but Melody Talbot.

"Boss," said Melody, "before you ask, yes, I'm still at the office, but I really am going home.

"But there was something a bit odd. I was looking through

those newspapers you asked me to collect for you. Did you know that Erika Rosenthal had a piece in the *Guardian* the day David Rosenthal was killed?"

*Erika moved through the day as if held to the earth by the slenderest of tethers.*

*She rose at her usual time, even though she'd been given a temporary bereavement leave from her job in the administrative offices at Whiteleys department store. Finding she was ravenous, she'd made tea, with two pieces of toast and two soft-boiled eggs, an unheard-of indulgence with rationing still in effect, but she felt reckless with hunger. If she had nothing to eat the rest of the week she couldn't bring herself to care.*

*Carrying her plate and cup out into the garden, she sat on the stone wall in the one spot penetrated by the morning sun. In spite of her hunger, she ate slowly, savoring every taste and texture as if it were for the first time—the buttery richness of the egg yolk, the crunchiness of the toast, the earthy astringency of the tea.*

*And she, who had lived in her own mind for so long, found that she wanted to share every thought, every impression, every instant of experience with Gavin. He would understand. He would know what she meant, what she felt, almost before she knew herself, and the perfection of it made her eyes fill with the tears she had not cried for her husband.*

*David. She knew that somewhere within her she carried a kernel of grief for the man she had lived with for almost fifteen years, and that most of all she would mourn what might have existed between them, and for the long, barren waste of their marriage.*

*But now she felt distanced, as if a stranger had lived that life, or as if it were a distant memory, something seen from the wrong end of a telescope. David had been lost to her long ago, and she knew now that grief had been woven into the very fabric of her life.*

*As she did the washing-up and went about her daily routine, she wondered if a time would come when she would feel guilt for having taken another man so precipitously into her bed. But she couldn't imagine that her union with Gavin Hoxley could ever seem an act of disloyalty, and she didn't want to think of consequences, or of the obstacles that stood between them.*

*Not now. Not yet. Nothing could take this moment, this hour, this day, from her. She had been waiting for it her whole life.*

Gemma had survived Giant Snakes and Ladders, had put Toby to bed, had had a bath herself, had said good night to Kit, who was reading in his room, and Kincaid still had not rung. She tried calling him, but his phone went straight to voice mail, and she didn't leave a message. Something must have happened, and he would let her know when he could.

Nor had she had any success reaching Erika, although she kept trying until she felt it was too late to call. She told herself she was being paranoid, that Erika had every right to go out of an evening, or to leave the phone unanswered if it suited her. But no amount of rationalizing quieted the little tickle of worry.

Had Erika's story in the *Guardian* had some bearing on David Rosenthal's death? But Melody had told her that it was an opinion piece, something about the shifting role of women in the postwar workplace, which sounded so like Erika that it made Gemma smile. She couldn't imagine it had been more than coincidence. But, she couldn't stop reminding herself, the two other people who'd had a connection with Erika's brooch were dead.

In pajamas and dressing gown, Gemma went downstairs and idled restlessly at the piano, trying to pick out a tune that teased at her memory, but her fingers seemed disconnected from her brain. Giving up after a few discordant notes, she wandered into the kitchen and contemplated the wine still in the fridge, but it had lost its appeal.

Instead, she filled a mug with milk and popped it in the microwave, then took the steaming drink to the table. She wanted to think more clearly, not less.

Geordie and Tess had stayed upstairs with Kit, but Sid,

who seemed to be her shadow today, had followed her. He jumped up on the table and wrapped his tail round his paws, regarding her with unblinking green eyes, and for once Gemma didn't shoo him off. Instead, she scratched him under the chin until his eyes narrowed to slits and he began to purr. "You know everything, don't you, boy?" she said softly, and at the sound of her voice, the cat blinked and curled his tail a bit tighter, as if containing his contentment.

As Gemma began to relax, her mind drifted randomly through the things that were worrying her. Her mum . . . her dad . . . Kristin Cahill . . . the poor man she hadn't met, Harry Pevensey . . . Erika . . . and Gavin Hoxley. She kept coming back to Gavin Hoxley. It was odd, but a day spent reading Hoxley's notes had made her feel she knew him, and she had liked him. It seemed to her that he had cared about David Rosenthal in a personal way, as she often cared about her own cases. And he had been too good a detective to have just dropped an unsolved case, so what had happened?

She could ask Erika, of course. Erika would have known Hoxley—it was obvious from his notes that he had interviewed her. But then, Erika had never told her that David Rosenthal had been murdered. Why?

Gemma circled round to Gavin Hoxley again, and she realized she had made a decision. She would ask Erika about her husband's death, but first she would go back to Lucan Place and find out why Hoxley had dropped David Rosenthal's case.

*As the day slid into evening, Erika found herself staring more and more often at the telephone, as if she could will it to ring, or holding her breath as she listened for the sound of footsteps in the paved yard outside her door.*

*Gavin hadn't said he would ring, after all, or that he would come back to her as soon as he was able, but that he would do so had seemed as natural to her as breathing.*

*She did chores already done once. She made herself eat a little something, a habit from the war, when one never knew when one might get another meal, but her appetite of the morning had gone. She switched on lamps, brushed her* dark hair until it crackled, and smoothed her hands down the skirt of her best dress.

By nightfall, doubt had come creeping in. Had she been a complete fool? Had she only imagined that what had happened between them was special? She was, after all, inexperienced in these things, and probably more naive than she had realized.

Had she fallen for the oldest chestnut in the world, that of the married man who claimed to be unhappy with his wife? She had been wrong, so wrong, about David. Had she been wrong about Gavin as well?

But as the hours passed, and she played over and over the things they had said, and done, and shared, she knew in her heart that it had been real, and that knowledge chilled her to the bone.

# 18

❧

*Certainly, hostility towards Jews contributed to the lassitude with which Foreign Office officials generally responded to proposals for humanitarian aid to Jews. . . . After the war, and notwithstanding the revelation of the full horrors of Nazi crimes against them, Jews were still perceived as undesirable immigrants.*

—*Louise London,* Whitehall
and the Jews, 1933–1948

GEMMA HAD JUST DRIFTED off to sleep when Kincaid climbed into bed beside her. When he spooned his body against hers, she could feel the chill even through the fabric of her pajamas. "Where have you been?" she said groggily. "And why are you so cold?"

"The weather's changed. And I just had Cullen drop me at Holland Park Road, as it was late."

"You saved him five minutes' drive so you could freeze walking down the hill? Are you daft?" But she pushed back the covers and shrugged out of her pajama top and bottoms, tossing them onto the floor, then slid back into bed and fitted her body to his, skin to skin.

"Oh, that's better." He wrapped his arms round her, adding, "Shove over, you two," to Geordie and Sid, who were occupying too much real estate on the foot of the bed.

"Now, spill," she commanded, snuggling a little more firmly.

While their body temperatures equalized, he told her about his interview with Amir Khan, and then with Giles Oliver. "We had to take him in to print him and get an official statement, but I'd promised I'd get him back tonight so that he could look after the dog. Otherwise, I'd have had to bring Mo home with me."

"God forbid. We'd have had Armageddon. And you are a complete pushover for that big beast," she added sternly, but she couldn't stop a smile. "So, do you think he did it?"

Kincaid sighed, and his breath tickled her ear. "Oliver? I can just imagine he might have hit Kristin, out of spite, if he'd had the means to hand. But I think it highly unlikely he had the bollocks to steal a car and plan to run her down, and I really can't come up with a plausible reason why he would kill Harry Pevensey."

"And I think they must have been killed by the same person."

"And Khan?"

"Again, he had motive to kill Kristin, and a stronger one than Giles, if she'd discovered what he was doing and threatened to give him away. But why would he have thought Kristin would tell Harry Pevensey?"

"Still, he does have an SUV. Do you think Giles could have mistaken a Volvo for a Land Rover? I mean, even I know the difference."

"You have the advantage of Giles Oliver in more ways than one, love," he said, with a breath of laughter that stirred her hair again. He ran a hand over the curve of her hip and cupped her breast as he added thoughtfully, "But we should know more tomorrow, when we get a report on Khan's car. And we'll see if there's any trace evidence, or Giles Oliver's prints, on the car that was stolen."

"Was that an SUV?"

"Yes, but a Toyota. And the CCTV does indicate that the car was a Land Rover—although the film only shows it accelerating into the intersection. It doesn't prove that was the car that hit her."

"That's splitting hairs," said Gemma drowsily. "So either Giles was there as a witness, or he stole a different car, a Land Rover that hasn't been reported missing. And in that case, why would he say he saw a Land Rover?" She tilted her head so that his lips found the hollow of her neck. "I'm turned in circles now."

"So you are." He laughed and trailed his fingers down her belly. "Now, tell me about Erika."

But by that time, Gemma had lost all interest in conversation.

Gemma woke to find that Kincaid had been right. The day was gun-metal gray, with a sharp little wind that snaked round corners and bit. She dressed in trousers and pullover and the long buff-colored suede jacket that she'd thought put away for the season. When Kincaid had left for the Yard and the children were off to school, and she had checked in with the hospital, she walked up past her own police station and took the tube to South Kensington.

The journey to Lucan Place had come to feel familiar, and the duty sergeant greeted her with a smile of recognition. She asked to see Inspector Boatman, and within a few minutes was shown into Kerry Boatman's office.

"Gemma," said Boatman, sitting back in her chair and pulling off glasses that had already left a mark on the bridge of her nose. "Did you find what you were looking for yesterday?"

"Yes and no." Gemma explained that part of David Rosenthal's case file seemed to be missing. "The detective in charge of the case was very thorough. I can't imagine that he'd have given up on the investigation so quickly."

Boatman frowned and rubbed at her nose. "I don't know where else you might look. If part of the file got put in with something else, it would be like looking for the proverbial pin in a haystack. Makes me shudder just to think of it."

"What about the detective's personnel file?" Gemma asked. "His name was Gavin Hoxley."

"Never heard of him. Long before my time, I'm afraid. But I can certainly have someone pull the record, if you like." She glanced at her watch. "I have a meeting in the super's office, but you're welcome to make yourself at home, and I'll have the file brought in to you."

Gemma thanked her, appreciating the courtesy.

She didn't have to wait long before a uniformed constable brought her a dog-eared folder. Gemma blew at the film of dust on its surface, then opened it carefully.

The pages inside had been typed on cheap paper with a manual typewriter, and the print was smudged and smeared from handling. She took in the vital statistics. Gavin Hoxley had been a Londoner, she saw, born in this very borough, and he had seen service in the war before joining the Metropolitan Police, where he had risen quickly in the ranks.

She thumbed through the annual reviews, skimming the familiar police jargon. Then her breath caught in her throat and she stared at the page before her. She reread it once, twice more, then she slowly set the folder aside and pulled her mobile phone from her bag.

*It was the early hours of the morning before Erika slept, and then she dreamed, not of Gavin or of David, but of her father, in fleeting glimpses that left her aching with loss. She woke with a little sob of longing, then lay in the faint gray predawn light, watching the hands of her bedside clock tick the minutes until it was time to rise.*

*She forced herself to eat a few bites of toast—it wouldn't do to faint—then she bathed and dressed with more than usual care. Her dress was the same she had worn yesterday, her best pale blue poplin, but to it she added white gloves, and a little hat she had bought in the spring sale at Whiteleys, an eon ago, when it had seemed that such things mattered.*

*And all the while she heard her mother's voice, whenever they had dressed to go out when she was a child, telling her that they were Jews, and so must never allow people to think the less of them.*

*Sometime in the long hours of the night, she had realized she knew nothing of Gavin except that he worked from the Chelsea Police Station, and so when she was ready she got out her London A–Z and found the station, in Lucan Place, near the Victoria and Albert.*

*And then she walked, because although she knew she must go, she wished she could put off arriving forever.*

*She crossed Hyde Park by the Broad Walk. The trees were in full leaf, the grass an impossible green. The air felt mild as a caress against her skin, and it seemed to her that even nature had betrayed her. The pinching of her best shoes against heel and toe became an anchor, a bright pinpoint of pain that kept her moving, one step after another.*

*The bustle of Knightsbridge came as a relief after the almost unbearable beauty of the park, and then she had reached Cromwell Road. Her steps slowed further. In front of the Natural History Museum, she stopped, her nerve deserting her. But the thought of going home, and waiting, was worse than going on, and so she walked slowly past the South Kensington tube station and crossed the Brompton Road, and then she had reached Lucan Place and there was no turning back.*

*Erika straightened her spine and entered the reception area of the station. The officer at the little window glanced up, his attention sharpening as he looked her over.*

*"Can I help you, miss?"*

*"It's Mrs.," said Erika. "Mrs. David Rosenthal. And I'd like to speak to the officer in charge of my husband's murder."*

*She saw the flicker in his face, the change she had never seen in Gavin's when he realized she was a Jew. "Just have a seat," he told her. "Someone will be with you." And then he didn't meet her eyes again.*

*After a few moments, a young woman opened the door leading to the interior of the station and said, "Mrs. Rosenthal? If you'll follow me?" She was plump and overly made up, with crimped hair, and she didn't meet Erika's eyes, either.*

*The certainty that Erika had been courting settled in her chest like a fist. She followed the woman through the door and up a worn flight of steps. Uniformed officers passed them, but they were faceless, like ghosts. The woman stopped at a door with a frosted glass pane in the upper half, gave a quick knock, then ushered Erika in and backed out, closing the door behind her.*

*Erika found herself facing a large, florid ginger-haired man who rose ponderously from his chair.*

*"Mrs. Rosenthal, is it? Do sit down." His brief smile showed yellowed teeth, and there was no warmth in it. Erika sat obediently in the hard chair he indicated, but did not trust herself to speak.*

*"I'm Superintendent Tyrell," he said, taking his own chair again, as if standing had been an inconvenience. "You said you wanted to see Inspector Hoxley. Is there something I can help you with?"*

*Erika swallowed and found her voice. "No, I—Inspector Hoxley said he'd learned something about my husband's murder. And then he didn't—I thought perhaps there was news. If I could just—"*

*"I think Inspector Hoxley must have been mistaken, I'm sorry to say, Mrs. Rosenthal." He didn't sound sorry at all. "And Inspector Hoxley won't be able to help you."*

*"But I—"*

*"There's been an accident. Inspector Hoxley's body was found washed up on the bank of the Thames this morning." Tyrell shook his large head and gave a little tut-tut of disapproval. "Very unfortunate. Of course, it won't go on his record, but it looks very much as if Hoxley took his own life."*

When Kincaid walked into his office, he found Cullen sitting at his computer, scowling. "Maybe I don't want my desk, after all," he said, by way of good morning.

Glancing up, Cullen included him in the frown. "I doubt you do. And you look happier than anyone has a right to be."

Kincaid merely raised an eyebrow. "No joy, I take it."

"None. Bloody eff-all. No trace on Khan's Volvo. Nothing in the house. His journalist friend confirms his story, and refused to let us see any of the paperwork without a warrant, which I'm processing now." He shrugged. "Not that I think we'll come up with anything. Khan's far too careful."

"Well, he would have to be, if he's done what he said." Kincaid gave Cullen a *move it* nod, then sat at his desk while Cullen took the straight-backed visitor's chair. "What about Giles Oliver?"

"No match on the prints. No trace on the stolen car. Do you think we can at least charge him on the phantom bidding scam?"

"He didn't actually admit it," Kincaid reminded him. "And even if he had, we'd have a tough time proving anything. If it makes you feel any better," he added, "I think that if Giles Oliver can't resist easy money, he'll screw up in a big way eventually. But it won't be our problem. So." Kincaid stretched his legs out, in order to think more comfortably. "If Oliver and Khan look like nonstarters, where does that leave us?"

"We know—or at least we think we know—that Harry Pevensey gave Kristin Cahill the brooch to sell. So far that's the only connection we've found between the two victims—"

"Except for Dominic Scott," put in Kincaid, frowning. "Dom Scott's relationship with Kristin may have been pretty straightforward—rich bloke meets pretty girl in bar and decides to slum it. But if we assume the bartender at the French House is reliable, Dom didn't tell us the truth about how he knew Harry Pevensey. So there's something we've missed there, but I still can't see Dominic Scott as a killer, no matter the motive. And none of this explains where Harry Pevensey got the brooch, unless he really did pick it up at an estate sale, as Khan suggested."

Cullen shrugged. "If Amir Khan is such a good actor—and I'm still not entirely convinced—maybe Dominic Scott isn't the useless twit *he* seems. Could he have stolen it? He does have access to homes of the rich and famous, I'd assume."

"You sound like a telly series," Kincaid said, grinning. "But you could be right. Say Dom Scott has a nasty drug habit and desperately needs money to pay off his suppliers. He realizes he has a ready-made opportunity in having a girlfriend who works for an auction house. So he steals the brooch, perhaps from some friend of the family, then recruits

Harry, however they may be connected, to put the piece up for sale, because he wouldn't want his name associated with stolen goods—"

"But Kristin would have known, because he would have had to introduce her to Harry. And then when the brooch's provenance was called into question by Gemma, he tried to make sure he wouldn't be linked to the brooch, by killing them."

"Still doesn't solve the problem of the car. But, like Oliver, he could have stolen one or borrowed one." Kincaid ran a hand through his hair, a nervous habit when thinking that he had never been quite able to conquer.

"And," he went on, "if we start assuming that Scott is *not* a complete twit and could have planned a theft and two premeditated and risky murders, we have to wonder if he really did meet Kristin by chance."

"Time to put him on the hot plate again?" asked Cullen.

"I think—" Kincaid's mobile rang, and when he saw that it was Gemma, he answered.

Before he could speak, she said, "Duncan, we need to talk."

"We're just going to have another word with Dom Scott in Cheyne Walk. Meet us there, why don't you?"

*"No." Erika stared at the superintendent, who seemed to be receding to a great distance. "I don't—" Her voice came out a whisper. She tried again. "I don't believe it. He can't be dead." If she didn't believe, it wouldn't be true. "I just spoke with him. Two days ago. He said he had a—a lead. And he was going to follow—"*

*"Mrs. Rosenthal, he was doing his job," Superintendent Tyrell said with a great show of patience. "That doesn't mean that all was well. In confidence," he added, lowering his voice, "there were domestic . . . difficulties. And the war. He served, you know, and for some men, it only takes a small thing to tip the balance—"*

*A rush of anger filled the void within her. "I do not believe for one minute that Gavin Hoxley was the sort of man who would commit suicide." She stood so that she could look down at Tyrell. "There must be some other explanation."*

*Tyrell laced his fingers across his paunch and looked at her with a sudden speculation that made her feel unclean. "Mrs. Rosenthal. You do realize that if it ever were to come out that Gavin Hoxley had crossed the line with a witness, it would ruin his reputation. I'm sure you wouldn't want that. Nor would you want to cause more grief to his family. His wife and children have suffered enough as it is, don't you think?" He fixed her with pale blue eyes that made her think of the dead fish on the market stall.*

*It was blackmail, no matter how politely it was couched. And she was helpless against it. Gavin was lost to her. Even in death she could not touch him, could not help him.*

*Everything that had mattered to her was slipping away, dissolving like mist when she clutched at it. Erika made a last desperate effort. "But my husband—what about my husband's murder?"*

*Tyrell smiled. "Someone else will look into it, Mrs. Rosenthal. I promise you."*

Gemma hailed a cab and within minutes was standing on the Embankment across from Cheyne Walk. She stared out at the river, framed between the Albert and Battersea bridges. The day was still overcast, and the water looked dull and impenetrable.

The report on Gavin Hoxley's death said his body had washed ashore farther downstream, near Chelsea Bridge. That didn't mean that was where it had gone in, however, but there would have been no way of calculating tide and current unless one knew *when* he had gone in.

She looked east. According to his personnel file, Hoxley had lived in Tedworth Square, near the top of the Royal Hospital Gardens. Had he, as the report inferred, simply walked down Tite Street and jumped in the river? The report said there had been no marks on his body to suggest an altercation, and that the balance of his mind may have been disturbed due to domestic problems. No postmortem had been ordered.

It seemed to Gemma a very cavalier judgment, even for a time when procedures may not have been as stringent—and if that was the case, Gavin Hoxley had been an anomaly. If his work on David Rosenthal's murder had been anything to go by, she couldn't have done a better job herself.

She watched a number 11 bus trundle down the Embankment, and suddenly felt a weird sense of displacement, as if time had rippled. Gavin Hoxley had surely stood here, watching the buses go past, admiring the delicate tracery of the Albert Bridge, puzzling over a crime he couldn't solve. In the hours spent reading his notes, she'd come to feel she knew him, and now she experienced a sharp and personal sense of loss.

Silly, Gemma told herself. Gavin Hoxley had been dead for more than fifty years. But somehow that made no difference.

And because Gavin Hoxley had died, she thought, David Rosenthal's murder investigation had been shelved. Or . . . had it perhaps been the other way round?

Hearing a shout, Gemma turned and saw Kincaid and Doug Cullen getting out of a car in Cheyne Walk. She waved, then walked back to the crossing and waited for the light.

When she reached them, she said, "Anything new?"

"More a lack of anything new," Kincaid answered. "We keep coming back to the fact that Dom Scott and the brooch are the only two links between the victims. We thought maybe Dom stole the brooch and used Harry to sell it so he wouldn't be connected. Then when Erika came forward he had to cover his tracks."

"So you're just stirring it?"

"Basically, yeah." He shrugged. "What was it you wanted to talk about?"

Gemma hesitated, looking up at the house. "It's complicated. I'll tell you after." She mounted the steps and pushed the bell.

The door flew open before Gemma's finger left the buzzer.

Ellen Miller-Scott stared out at them. Gone was the salon polish they had seen before. Her blond hair was disheveled, her face bare of makeup and tear-streaked. "But I just called," she said on a sob. "How did you— You've got to help me— He— I can't—"

"Where?" Kincaid barked at her. "Show us."

She turned and started up the stairs, stumbling and grabbing the banister for support. As soon as Kincaid saw where she was going, he shot past her, and Gemma followed, taking the steps two at a time, leaving Cullen to help the woman.

But Kincaid came to a dead stop at the door of Dominic Scott's apartment, and Gemma almost cannoned into his back.

"Oh, Christ," he said, stepping slowly into the room, and without his body as a shield, Gemma saw what he had seen.

Dominic Scott hung from the beam in his sitting-room ceiling. A rope made of neckties was knotted round his neck, and a chair lay on its side beneath him. He wore jeans and a dress shirt, unbuttoned, and his feet were bare. His handsome face was purple, suffused with congestion, and his open eyes had the opaque flatness that belonged only to the dead.

There was a terrible smell, and urine dripped from inside the leg of his jeans onto the carpet.

"Can't you do something?" wailed Ellen Miller-Scott, and Gemma realized that she had come in behind them, and that Cullen was trying to restrain her and dial his mobile at the same time. Gemma put her arm round the woman so that Doug could release her.

Dominic's mother turned to her, pleading, "Can't you get him down? Please? I tried, but I couldn't—"

Gemma met Kincaid's eyes and tightened her hold. "Mrs. Miller-Scott. Ellen. I'm sorry, but I'm very much afraid it's too late."

# 19

❧

> *Oranges in Notting Hill today.*
> —*Vere Hodgson*, Few Eggs and No Oranges:
> The Diaries of Vere Hodgson, 1940–1945

WHILE GEMMA RESTRAINED Ellen Miller-Scott, Kincaid took Cullen aside and asked him to ring for the pathologist and SOCOs.

"Right, guv," said Cullen. Then he added in a whisper that carried, nodding in the direction of Dom Scott's body, "But how likely is it that someone did that to him?"

Kincaid gave him a quelling glance and shook his head, but Gemma knew what he was thinking. It wouldn't be the first time they'd seen it happen, someone strangled, then strung up to make it look like a suicide.

Ellen Miller-Scott pulled away from Gemma. "What do you mean, a crime scene? You can't think—Dom—" She looked at her son's body and took a heaving breath.

"Mrs. Miller-Scott, let's get you downstairs." Ellen Miller-Scott was definitely not going to fail a hearing test, Kincaid thought. "Doug, will you wait for reinforcements?"

Gemma didn't think Cullen looked terribly thrilled at the prospect, but he nodded and pulled out his phone.

But it wasn't until the ambulance team had arrived,

shaken their heads and said, "Not our job, guv'nor," that Gemma and Kincaid managed to get a protesting Ellen Miller-Scott downstairs and into her white sitting room.

The bold splashes of color in the paintings on the white walls seemed garish and somehow indecent after what they had seen upstairs. "I don't want to leave him," Ellen said again, looking back towards the stairs.

Gemma guided her to a spot on the sofa, deliberately positioning her so that the front hall was out of her view, while Kincaid pulled up an occasional chair so he could look at her directly.

"Mrs. Miller-Scott—Ellen—I know your son was upset over Kristin Cahill's death," he said. "But was there anything else troubling him?"

Ellen Miller-Scott rubbed hard at the fingers of her left hand with her right, as if she might peel the skin off. Shock and distress had left her looking her age, and Gemma could see the imperfections in her skin that makeup had covered on their first meeting.

"He— There were men, wanting money," Ellen said. "Dom had had some problems with drugs since, oh, since school. Prescription stuff, mostly. You know, he injured his knee at football, and then it was difficult for him to stop the pills. I'm sure it happens all the time." Even now, it sounded as if it were hard for her to admit. "And I—I didn't like people threatening him, but this time I decided that it had to stop, that he would never get better if I helped him. But I never thought— What if—" Her face contorted in a sob, and turned, looking again at the doorway.

It seemed to Gemma that the human need to keep watch over the dead was beyond reason—rooted in the knowledge that once the loved ones left your sight, they were lost to you forever. She couldn't imagine how she would feel if it were Kit or Toby.

Just as quickly as that thought flickered across her mind, she tried to shut it out—you couldn't do the job if you saw your own family in every victim. But because she had known Dom Scott, she was more vulnerable. Her mind strayed to her own mum. How hard must it be for her mother, who worried about her, not to tell her so? And now that their roles were reversed, could she do as well?

Kincaid's gentle voice drew Gemma's attention back to Ellen. "You can't think that your decision had any bearing on your son's actions," he said. "You did what any parent might have done."

"But— What if—" Ellen went back to rubbing at her fingers, her eyes blank.

"What about this morning, Ellen?" asked Gemma. "Did you talk to Dom this morning?"

Ellen gave Gemma a startled glance, as if she'd forgotten her presence, although Gemma sat near enough to touch. "I— We had a row," she said, haltingly. "There was a company meeting and he didn't want—Dom was always—I told him to get ready whether he wanted to go or not, that he couldn't spend the rest of his life moping over that girl."

Gemma saw Kincaid's eyes widen, but Ellen didn't seem to realize she'd said anything offensive.

"I took a shower," she said, "thinking he'd cool off, be reasonable about it, but when I went back upstairs— He was— I couldn't—" She put a hand over her mouth, then wailed, "Oh, dear God. I can't believe it. He can't be dead— Dom—"

"You did the right thing, ringing for help," Kincaid assured her hurriedly, and Gemma hoped Cullen had called for a family liaison officer. They couldn't leave her on her own when she was this distraught. "Ellen," Kincaid went on. "I know this is difficult, but we need to ask you some things. You said Dominic was upset about Kristin Cahill's death. Did he talk to you about Harry Pevensey?"

"Who?" Ellen looked bewildered.

"Harry Pevensey. The man who was killed yesterday. Did Dom not tell you?"

"I don't understand. Who was he?" She looked utterly bewildered. "What do you mean, he was killed?"

"Someone ran him down. Just like Kristin Cahill," said Gemma.

"But— What does that have to do with Dom?"

Kincaid leaned forward. "That's what we were hoping you could tell us. Harry Pevensey put a brooch up for sale at Harrowby's through Kristin Cahill. And it was Dom who introduced them."

"A brooch?" Ellen Miller-Scott fastened on the word. "Dom wouldn't—Dom didn't know what a brooch was. He had no interest in art, or collecting"—her gaze strayed to the paintings—"or any of the things our family—my father—had worked so hard to achieve. The business—" She shook her head. "Dom just couldn't seem to learn the simplest things. My father—I'm glad he didn't live to see *this*—"

Gemma stared at her, reminding herself that people who were in shock often said things they didn't mean, but that didn't stop her feeling a wave of revulsion for the woman sitting beside her.

"So Dom never spoke to you about Har—" Kincaid had begun, when the sound of voices came from the front door.

Doug Cullen came in, saying, "Guv, the pathologist is here. It's Dr. Ling. She's gone straight up. And family liaison's here as well."

Gemma found herself more ready than usual to leave the bereaved in the competent hands of the family liaison officer. This one, who followed Cullen into the room, was a good-looking man about Gemma's age with curly dark hair.

As Gemma stood, he gave her a quick smile, then focused on Ellen. "Mrs. Miller-Scott? I'm Mark Lombardi. I'm very sorry for your loss." He glanced at Kincaid, said, "Sir?" and at Kincaid's nod of assent, took Gemma's place. "Mrs. Miller-Scott, can I get you anything? A cup of tea?"

"But I—" Ellen protested. "My son. What are they doing?"

As Lombardi said, "Why don't we go into the kitchen, and I'll explain everything to you," Kincaid motioned Gemma into the hallway.

"Looks like she's in good hands." He nodded towards Lombardi. "And I suspect she does better with men. Let's go see what Kate has to say."

"I— You go on." Gemma didn't usually willingly leave

Kincaid at the mercy of Kate Ling's flirtatious banter, but she suddenly found she was not eager to see Dominic Scott's body again.

"Are you all right?" Kincaid asked, his brow creasing in instant concern, a habit held over from the days of her precarious pregnancy.

"I'm fine, really," she reassured him. "Just need a breath of air. Tell Kate I'll say hello when she comes down."

The crime scene techs arrived right on Kate's heels, and Gemma let them in as she let herself out. She stood for a moment on the steps, imagining the routine going on inside. The sun had come out, but the wind was still cold, and she shivered. Pulling her jacket a bit tighter, she crossed the road again, and when she reached the Embankment, looked down at the sun sparking off the broad curve of the river.

How, she wondered, could a mother care more for her dead father's opinion than for her son, whose pathetically grotesque body still hung suspended from a beam in her house?

Kate Ling stood in the door of Dominic Scott's apartment, white coveralls slung over her arm like a party wrap. "Duncan," she said as she turned to him. "You've made my day."

"Not my call, I promise. But I'm glad it's you." He was, too, as she was a good friend, and never hard on the eyes. She was perfectly turned out, as always, in tight buff trousers and a crisp white shirt, and her dark, shining hair swung straight as broom bristles round her delicate face.

Kate nodded at the room as the techs came in and started to work. "Looks to me like something just got up this poor bugger's nose."

Kincaid had yet to see Kate Ling ruffled by death—she saved her compassion for the living, and had been tactfully kind to them both when Gemma had lost the baby. "I daresay," he answered. "This poor bugger is connected to two homicides."

"You think he was the perpetrator?" Kate asked, her words punctuated by the repeated flash of the camera.

"It would explain this." But even as he said it, Kincaid wasn't sure that he believed it. It had taken ruthlessness as well as a capacity for risk to murder Kristin Cahill and Harry Pevensey, and he wasn't sure either of those things squared with the taking of one's own life, whether out of despair, fear, or guilt.

"Have enough, Joe?" Kate asked the photographer.

"Couple more, Doc." The photographer shot a few more angles, then gave her a nod of assent. "All yours, then."

"Okay, let's get him down," Kate called out to the mortuary attendants who had come in with her, and slipped on her coverall.

They were already suited, and had brought a folding ladder—they looked, Kincaid thought, like painters. And like painters, they efficiently spread a cloth on the floor, and went to work.

It was a job Kincaid did not envy. One climbed up on the ladder, and while Kate and the other attendant lifted Dom Scott's body enough to take the tension off the makeshift rope, he untied it from the beam. Then Kate and her partner gently eased the body down onto the cloth.

"Nice-looking lad," she said, studying the congested face. "And nice taste in ties." She touched the silk with a gloved fingertip. "Hermès. One of these would set you back a month's wages."

Kincaid raised an inquiring eyebrow, wondering at her sartorial knowledge, as well as what she considered his month's wages, but she merely quirked a corner of her mouth. He knew nothing of her personal life, except that she was not married, or at least if she was, she wore no ring.

Looking back at the ties, Kincaid wondered if their use had been a last bit of rebellion aimed on Dom Scott's part towards his mother—she had told her son to get dressed whether he liked it or not, as if he were a recalcitrant child, and he had made the ultimate refusal.

"He struggled," said Kate, lifting Dom's hands and examining the fingertips. "They usually do when they strangle themselves rather than breaking the neck. See, there's some bruising and torn nails, and here"—she touched the silk at his throat—"there are some little tears in the fabric."

Kincaid made an involuntary grimace and Kate shot him a quick look. "Had you met him, then, before this?"

"Yes. We'd interviewed him a couple of times."

"Always makes it harder," she said. "Fortunately, I seldom have that problem. At least there doesn't seem to have been any autoerotica involved. He kept his trousers on. But I've certainly seen more determined suicides." She looked up. "That wasn't a very good knot. Or a very big drop. And the neckties were resourceful enough, but if he'd really been determined, he'd have used a length of flex, something like a lamp cord, maybe. If you want my very professional opinion, I'd say it took him a good few minutes to die."

"His mother was here. He might have had a half-formed hope that she would find him."

"Well, speculating's your job," said Kate. "Let's see what I can tell you for certain." She pushed back the cuffs of the unbuttoned sleeves of his shirt, then turned his wrists over. "Ah. Look at this." She traced the faint white lines on the pale, smooth skin on the underside of Dom's wrists. "More on the left than on the right. Was he right-handed?"

Kincaid thought back, recalling Dom lifting a hand to pick at his shirt, or to push the hair from his forehead. "I think so. Hesitation scars?"

"Yes. And let's see what else." She pushed the left sleeve up above the elbow. The inside of Dom Scott's arm bore a trail of purple marks, some faded to scars, some fresh bruises, the punctures still visible. "And on the right, too," Kate said, pushing back the other sleeve. "I won't be surprised if we find tracks on the thighs as well, and any other place he could find to stick a needle." She looked up at Kincaid, all humor gone, her face implacable. "This boyo needed help in a big way."

*Gavin Hoxley was buried the next day in Brompton Cemetery, with full police honors. Erika had found the notice in* the Times, and in doing so had learned for the first time his date of birth, the names of the parents who had predeceased him, and the names of his wife and children. His death had, of course, been reported as an accident, and she recalled with bitter irony his superintendent telling her that the department took care of its own.

The preponderance of mourners, however, allowed Erika to stand back from the crowd, unnoticed. The fine May weather continued unabated, and Gavin Hoxley's widow—Linda, she was called—wore black linen, and a hat that Erika would have admired when she'd worked in the millinery department at Whiteleys, early in the war. The children, a boy and a girl, looked stodgy and dull, as if they had failed to inherit their father's looks as well as the spark that had set him apart.

At any other time, Erika would have scolded herself for the unkind thought, but on this day she did not care. She watched the grieving widow, supported on either side by an older couple who must be her parents, throw a clod of earth on the coffin, and Erika felt not even a stirring of pity.

For Linda Hoxley would recover, would marry again, would perhaps even have more children.

For a moment, as Erika watched Gavin's children follow their mother's example, she felt a wild flare of hope—perhaps she was carrying Gavin's child. But the thought faded as quickly as it had come. She had been too damaged by the things that had happened to her. The doctors had told her so in her first weeks in England, and although she had never been given a chance to test their diagnosis, she'd not doubted the truth of it.

And tomorrow she had her own husband to bury. The police had released David's body, and she had made arrangements for a service and a burial plot in the Jewish cemetery in Willesden. But tomorrow she would feel no less out of place than she did here, watching a Christian funeral for a man she had loved for a day.

Her father had not been an observant Jew. He had felt that being perceived as "too Jewish" would damage his prospects—and yet his degree of Jewishness had mattered not one jot in the end.

And David—David had felt that his God had betrayed him, had betrayed them all—what rational god, after all, would allow six million Jews to die? And David had been a rational man.

Erika watched as the service drew to a close and the mourners straggled away. She saw the large, ginger-haired Francis Tyrell glance at her, picking her out among the headstones where she stood, but after a moment's hesitation, he turned and followed his fellow officers.

And when they were all gone, the sextons went about the business of returning the earth they had removed. Erika lowered herself to the grass and began to pull the spring weeds from the grave of a child whose name had been half rubbed from the headstone by weather and time.

The sun beat down on her head. Her vision blurred, and her fingernails grew caked with crumbly dark soil. Dust to dust. Ashes to ashes. She knew the Anglican litany; she had buried enough friends during the war.

After a while, she looked up and saw that even the sextons had finished. Slowly, she stood, brushing her green-stained hands against her skirt, and walked across the rough grass.

There was no headstone, of course, only the raised mound of the grave, which would settle with time as the grass and nettles grew over it. Erika knelt, but could not bring herself to touch. It would bring her no closer.

What would she do now? David was gone, and the past with him. Whatever he had done, or tried to do, she knew it was not within her power to achieve justice for him, if Gavin had failed.

And Gavin was gone. There her mind stopped. She could not contemplate the why, or how, or what might have been. She could think only of how she would go on, who she might become. What had she left within the husk of her heart?

Reason, she told herself. Logic. The intelligence to look after herself, to make a mark in the world. And those things would have to be enough.

* * *

Gemma was waiting when Kincaid and Cullen came out of Dominic Scott's house. "Kate's not finished, then?" she asked.

"Not quite," Kincaid told her. He looked tired, she thought, as if the last half hour spent with Dominic Scott's body had drained him. "His mother said he had a problem with prescription drugs. Well, it was a bit more than that. It looks like we guessed right. He was a raging junkie, and had been for a good while. And he was self-harming, at the least."

"Cutting?" When Kincaid nodded, she said, "Do you think his mother knew?"

He sighed. "I don't know. I can't gauge her. And parents have an enormous capacity for self-deception."

"Why does it matter whether she knew or not?" asked Cullen. "It puts him squarely in the frame, and so does his suicide. He needed money to pay off his suppliers. He nicked the diamond brooch, then got his girlfriend to put it up for sale through Pevensey. Then, when you came round saying Erika had claimed it, he got the wind up. Didn't want his name connected, so killed the girlfriend, then Pevensey, then topped himself because he felt guilty."

"First off," Gemma said sharply, "she wasn't the *girlfriend*. Her name was Kristin. And it doesn't tell us where he got the brooch, where he got the car, or what Harry Pevensey had to do with it. Or why Dom would think he couldn't bluff it out—we still have no more than circumstantial evidence that he was even connected."

"Maybe he just didn't want his mum to find out," Cullen shot back.

Kincaid shook his head. "No. There's something we're missing. We—"

"David Rosenthal's murder," said Gemma, and they both stared at her. "I've been thinking. Erika's husband was killed a stone's throw from here. In Cheyne Gardens." She pointed east, towards the Albert Bridge. "His murder was never solved."

"A long stone, that," Cullen said skeptically, but Gemma cut him off.

"No, listen. The detective who was investigating the case died—accidental drowning, possibly suicide, according to the report—and David Rosenthal's murder was never officially closed."

"But that was more than fifty years ago," put in Kincaid. "How can that have any bearing on this?"

"I don't—" Gemma's phone rang. She gave Kincaid an apologetic glance as she pulled it from her bag. When she saw that it was Melody, she answered. "Melody, can I ring you back? There's been—"

"Boss," Melody interrupted, "you know that issue of the *Guardian*? I thought I'd have another look. And I found something odd."

Gemma listened, and when Melody had finished, said, "Can you send it to me? Right. Thanks. I'll ring you back."

She disconnected and looked at Kincaid and Cullen. "I think I just might be able to tell you."

# 20

❧

*We all underestimate the power of human beings to
endure.*
    —*William L. Shirer,* Berlin Diary: The Journal
      of a Foreign Correspondent, 1934–1941

THE PHOTO ON GEMMA'S phone was black and white, obviously reproduced from old newsprint, but it was still possible
to see that the man in the picture bore a strong resemblance
to Ellen Miller-Scott.

"It's Joss Miller," Gemma told Kincaid and Cullen as
she passed the phone across. "Accepting some sort of award
for his philanthropic contributions to an art museum."

"Ellen Miller-Scott's father?" said Cullen. "But I don't
see what an old photo—"

"Wait." Gemma grabbed her phone back and tapped the
screen. "It's not just an old photo. This picture ran in the
*Guardian* on the day David Rosenthal died. Don't you see?
If David Rosenthal was looking through the newspaper for
Erika's article, he could have seen this."

"So he saw—or *might* have seen," Cullen emphasized,
"this photo. What difference—"

"David Rosenthal never came to Chelsea. According to
the detective who investigated his murder, Rosenthal had a
very fixed routine. He taught at a Jewish school in North
Hampstead. He lived in Notting Hill. And any free time he
had, he spent in the Reading Room at the British Museum,
working on a book about which he was very secretive.

"And yet he was found dead here, in Cheyne Gardens, just down the way, with his throat cut and his manuscript missing."

"The Millers lived here in 1952?" Kincaid asked, beginning to look interested.

"Since the forties. Melody said Joss Miller prospered after the war. He bought this house, and a country place as well."

"So you're thinking Rosenthal came across Miller's picture in the paper that day, and that's why he came here, to Chelsea. To see Joss Miller?" He looked up at the town house, frowning. "But what was the connection between them? And why was Rosenthal murdered?"

"Are you thinking Miller did it?" Cullen asked, with a skeptical expression that would have done Kincaid justice.

"Why isn't it possible?" The more Cullen argued, the more certain Gemma became. "The detective—Hoxley— came across rumors that David Rosenthal might have been involved with some questionable people. There were offshoots of Jewish terrorist organizations operating in London after the war, as well as in Europe."

"Vengeance groups?" asked Kincaid.

Gemma nodded. "According to Hoxley's notes, there were those who felt that the war crime tribunals had not even skimmed the surface. And a man who worked alongside Rosenthal at the British Museum said he thought Rosenthal was working on some sort of exposé."

"You're not suggesting that Miller was a war criminal?" Cullen laughed in disbelief. "He was English, for God's sake."

"I don't know," said Gemma. "Maybe Gavin Hoxley was just paranoid, but I got the impression from his notes that he felt our government was somehow complicit. And it seems an unlikely coincidence that Hoxley should die so conveniently with David Rosenthal's murder unsolved."

"But even so," argued Cullen, "it still doesn't add up. You're saying that if Miller was a war criminal, that the powers that be would have let Rosenthal kill him. But it was

Rosenthal who ended up dead. And what does any of that have to do with Kristin Cahill and Harry Pevensey?"

"I don't know," Gemma repeated, frustrated. "But there's something here we're not seeing, and I just can't quite—"

"We can start by asking Ellen Miller-Scott if her father knew David Rosenthal," Kincaid suggested.

"No," Gemma said slowly, as she thought it through. "I've got to talk to Erika first. And I'm worried about her." She turned, gazing at the redbrick town house, thinking of what they had found inside. "Dominic Scott is the third person connected with the Goldshtein brooch to have died. And I kept trying to ring Erika all last evening. She didn't answer."

Gemma stopped by Notting Hill Station, to pick up a proper print from Melody and to borrow a car from the pool. She didn't want to take the time to walk to Arundel Gardens, nor to walk home for her own car. Melody had offered to come with her, but she'd refused again.

"I'll ring you," she said. "If— Well, I'll ring you."

She parked with unexpected ease, just across from Erika's house, and when she glanced at her watch she saw with surprise that she had missed lunch. But she felt hollow with anxiety rather than hunger. And she had not yet made it to hospital. At the thought of her mother, the knot in her stomach tightened even further.

Reaching Erika's door, she rang the bell. Her heart gave a little skip. She waited a moment, then rang again, punching at the button, then trying the door, but it was firmly locked. Why had she never thought to ask Erika for a key in case of an emergency?

The shade was pulled down in the bedroom that faced on the little yard, so she could see nothing inside. She had taken out her mobile to ring Melody for reinforcements when the door swung open and Erika looked out at her.

"Gemma, my dear, whatever is the matter?"

Gemma's knees went wobbly with relief. "Are *you* all right?" she asked in a rush.

"Of course," said Erika, looking bemused. "I was out in the garden. And you look as if you're about to collapse on my doorstep from heatstroke. Come in."

"But where were you last night?" Gemma asked as she followed her into the house. "I rang and rang."

Erika led her into the kitchen. "Sit, and I'll get you some water." When she had handed Gemma a glass filled from the tap, she said, "I was out at a university dinner. For some reason they saw fit to trot me out for an award, but I have to admit I enjoyed being made much of. But why should you have worried?"

"Erika, last night . . . how did you get home from your dinner?"

Erika looked more puzzled than ever. "I took a taxi. The cabbie fussed over me as if I were doddering and waited until I got in my door. Why should it matter?"

"But before you got in, did you see anything unusual?"

"No, I can't recall—" Erika's eyes widened in surprise. "Wait. There *was* a car idling a few doors down, but I didn't think anything of it—"

"What sort of car?"

"Oh, one of those big square ones. Like a Land Rover."

Gemma felt as if all her muscles had turned to jelly. "Thank God for that cabbie."

"Gemma, what on earth is this about?" Then the penny dropped, and Erika looked frightened. "Does this have something to do with that poor girl?"

"It might do," said Gemma. "I think I'd better start from the beginning." She reconsidered, and said, "Or better yet, I need you to start from the beginning." She sipped at her water, warm as a bath straight from the tap. "Erika, why did you never tell me that your husband was murdered?"

"David?"

"Unless you were married more than once," Gemma answered a little tartly, and realized she felt hurt by Erika's silence.

Sinking into the chair across from Gemma, Erika said, "It never occurred to me. It was so long ago, and I thought that part of my life long buried—why should I have burdened you? And why should it matter to anyone now?"

"Would your husband have read the *Guardian* the day he was killed?"

"My article." Erika closed her eyes. "Yes. David would have bought the paper. It was my first published piece, and David was dutiful, if not deeply interested. But I still don't understand."

Gemma pulled the print Melody had made her from her bag and handed it across the table.

"Oh, dear God." Erika stared at the page. "Where did you— How did you—"

"It was in the *Guardian,* on that very same day. In the society page."

"But this—" She looked at the photo again and pushed it away, as if it were contaminated. "That's Joseph Mueller. Why does it say his name is something else?" She had gone pale as the white lilies in the vase on the kitchen table. "I never thought to see that face again."

"Who was he, Erika? How did you know him?"

"He was German," Erika insisted, her voice shaking. "What is he doing in an English newspaper, with an English name?"

"He *is* English," Gemma assured her. "His name was Joss Miller. He was a financier, and an art collector, and he just died two years ago."

Erika stared at her, her face contorted, then turned her head and spat. "That is lies, all lies. This man was a German, and a trafficker in human lives. He took money from Jews, promising to get them safely out of Germany. And if we had no communication with others he said he had helped escape, we assumed it was because they didn't dare write to us. But now I wonder if anyone whose money he took ever came out of Germany."

"But you did," said Gemma, frowning.

"Only by the grace of God and the kindness of a German farmer. I went back, after the war, but I couldn't find the farm. Perhaps it was destroyed. Perhaps my memory was faulty. I never knew the family's name, but I fear they cannot have gone unpunished."

"Punished for what? I don't understand."

"No. You could not." Erika seemed to shrink into her chair. "But I suppose I must tell you, because it has to do with the brooch, and if my silence is in some way responsible for that girl's death—"

Gemma bit her lip. She had never had the chance to tell Erika about Harry Pevensey, but now was not the time. "Please," she said, leaning forward and touching Erika's hand. "What happened?"

Erika gripped Gemma's hand, then let hers fall to her lap. Her eyes lost focus. After a moment she began to speak, so softly that Gemma had to strain to hear.

"I told Kit, just a little. About how my father's work was patronized by the wealthy Germans, and how he did not believe that we would be touched by the madness being spouted by the Nazis. But by 1938, it became evident even to my father that things were out of control, that there was no surety of safety for any Jew. And I had married David.

"David had been a lecturer at the university, in philosophy—we Germans had always been great believers in philosophy, much good it did us—and after the Nazis banned Jews from faculty positions in all the German universities, David tutored students privately. Many Jewish professors did—it was a way round the restrictions."

Gemma thought of the difference in ages between Erika and her husband. "You were David's student?"

"Yes." Erika gave a ghost of a smile. "The age-old story. Naive young girl falls in love with wise older man. And David was a radical, who spoke out against Hitler's regime, and that recklessness made him all the more appealing. As for him, I think he was flattered by my attention, and he saw himself as furthering my political and intellectual education. I don't think he was ever in love with me, but of course I didn't know that then.

"But David's outspokenness made my father even more concerned for our safety, and he made arrangements to get us out of the country. It would cost, we were told, but there was a man who would take us out through the Netherlands and from there into England. My father said we should go first, and that he would follow when he knew we were safe.

"There was another couple, older, friends of my father's, who would go with us. They vouched for this man, Mueller"—Erika did not glance at the photo—"and they paid him handsomely, as did my father.

"When we parted, my father gave me the diamond brooch, the last thing he had made, to keep secretly. Not even David knew of it."

Now she looked up and met Gemma's eyes. "He was a big, handsome man, this Mueller, with a Berliner accent. He said he had many connections. He had a small van, with the markings of a carpet firm, and he had papers showing that he and his helper were salesmen. We rode in the back, with instructions to cover ourselves with the carpets if we were stopped.

"The first night we stopped at a traveler's hotel. We were allowed out only to relieve ourselves in the darkest part of the night, and once back in the van we were given a little black bread. David and the other man, Saul, began to complain, but when they saw Mueller's face, they stopped."

Gemma had to still the impulse to stand and move about. She didn't dare even to drink from the glass of water, for fear of halting Erika's story.

"The next night," Erika went on, "we stopped at a farm very near the Dutch border. As I said, I was never sure of the exact location. Once it was dark, we were taken out of the van and led into the barn. We thought we would be fed and allowed to sleep in the straw. But that was not the case." Erika paused, clasping her hands together, and Gemma held her breath, fighting a wave of nausea.

When Erika continued, her voice was a thread of sound. "Mueller had a gun. His helper held the gun on the others while Mueller raped me. Then Mueller held the gun. Then they did the same with Sarah. When Saul tried to stop them, Mueller shot him. When they were finished with Sarah, he shot her."

Gemma swallowed. The smell of the lilies was sickly

sweet, overpowering. She realized she had tears running down her cheeks, but Erika's eyes were dry. "And David?" Gemma managed to croak.

"David did nothing," Erika said without intonation. "Mueller found the brooch when they stripped me. To this day, I don't know why they didn't shoot us then. Perhaps they weren't finished with me. Perhaps they enjoyed humiliating David. Or perhaps, having found the brooch, they thought they might somehow get more money from my father if they kept us alive.

"They tied us up, on the floor of the barn, beside Saul's and Sarah's bodies. I suppose they went into the farmhouse to drink. We heard laughter and shouting."

She took a little gulping breath. "David didn't speak to me. Not a word, all that night. Just before dawn, the farmer came out and untied us. He gave us some money and told us in which direction to run, towards the border. I have always been afraid that he and his family must have died for his kindness.

"We ran, stumbling in the dark, hiding at any sound, and by daylight we found we were in Holland. Some people fed us and helped us get to a Jewish aid organization. From there we came to London. We were penniless, and I was . . . injured." She met Gemma's eyes, then looked away. "I had started to bleed after they raped me, and it only got worse. By the time we reached London, I had lost my baby. A girl. I was very ill. For a time they thought I might not live. And the doctors told me I would have no more children."

"Erika," Gemma managed to whisper, "why did you never tell me?"

"I thought—I thought it would only add to your pain. And I—I had never spoken of it to anyone. Not even—" She shook her head. "And we—David and I—he could never bear to touch me afterwards. Perhaps he felt I was defiled. But I think it was also that he felt he had failed me, failed himself, failed utterly as a man.

"He became a shell, a ghost of a man. Until he began to write his book and to speak with strangers in whispers. I never knew what he was writing, or who these people were. I suppose I was a coward myself, because I did not ask. It was only when Gavin told me what he suspected that I began to guess what David had been doing."

Of course Erika would have known Gavin, Gemma realized. He had interviewed her. She started to ask, but Erika began to speak again. "Perhaps David felt retribution would somehow absolve him. But if, on that day, he saw a photo of Joseph Mueller in an English newspaper—Mueller was here, in London?"

"In Chelsea. He lived not far from Cheyne Gardens."

"Chelsea? My God." Erika was trembling. She pressed her clasped hands to her lips, then dropped them again as she said, "I would never have thought to glance at the society page—such things had no interest for me. But David—David always read whatever newspaper he bought from front page to back. It was a compulsion. If he had seen that photo, he would have found where this man—"

"Miller."

Erika nodded. "Miller. Where Miller lived. But if David went to his house, how did he . . ."

Gemma finished it for her. "End up in Cheyne Gardens? Maybe Miller arranged to meet him there. To talk."

"Yes." Erika nodded. "David still expected people to talk, to be rational, even after everything that had happened."

"But Miller would never have allowed David to connect him with his past. It's said his money came from construction after the war, but he had to have started with something—"

"The profit from theft, and murder. Mueller, Miller," Erika said slowly. "His family must have been Germans who Anglicized their name. That would explain his fluency with the language, his knowledge of the countryside, how easy it was for him to go back to the German version of his name, to pretend to *be* German."

"If David found him, he would have had much to lose. And . . . he enjoyed violence."

"So he arranged to meet David, planning to kill him." Gemma felt certain of it now. "But was taking the manuscript just a bonus?"

Erika sighed. "David might have believed he could threaten him with it. How could he have been such a fool?"

"And instead, Miller took it and stripped David of any identification. But then you reported David missing, and identified his body. Miller hadn't counted on that. So he tried to have the investigation stopped."

"Gavin said the order came from the top," said Erika. "And if . . . Miller . . . had found out that Gavin had made the connection with the newspaper—"

"Gavin." Gemma looked at her friend with a sudden knowledge that wrenched her heart.

Erika met her eyes, but there was no need for her to speak.

"I read his notes," Gemma said after a moment. "He was a good man, and a good police officer. And I thought it very odd that he died just after he was told to leave off looking into David's murder."

"His superintendent said it was suicide, but I never believed it."

"If Gavin had shown you that day's paper—"

"I would have known who had killed David, and why," said Erika.

"If Miller heard from some of his pals that Gavin had connected David with vengeance groups, he might have thought it too close for comfort, even before Gavin made the connection with the newspaper photo," Gemma mused. "And if making a few discreet suggestions that David's death wasn't worth pursuing didn't do the trick —"

"Francis Tyrell, the superintendent, didn't seem to care for Jews. Perhaps Miller knew that it wouldn't take much urging to convince him."

"But Tyrell didn't convince Gavin Hoxley, so Miller arranged a meeting with him, an anonymous tip, perhaps—"

"Gavin," said Erika, her eyes bright with tears for the first time. "Gavin was a strong man. But he would not have known what he was facing. And if he'd thought he might learn something about David's murder, he wouldn't have rung me until he was certain. But he never had that chance."

# 21

❧

*At last the secret is out, as it always must come in the end...*
        —W. H. Auden, "Twelve Songs"

**"BUT WHAT ABOUT** the brooch?" asked Erika. "I still don't understand why that poor girl was killed. Or why the brooch was never sold in all those years."

"I'm afraid it's a bit more complicated than that." Gemma stood, and discovered that all her muscles had cramped, as if she'd been tied in knots for hours. "I'm going to make us some tea. And something to eat. Are there any biscuits?" She needed time to process what she'd learned, and she wasn't eager to tell Erika the things she hadn't yet been told.

"I made braune Zuckerplätzchen. Brown-sugar cookies. For Kit and Toby."

Gemma looked up from filling the kettle in surprise. Had she ever heard Erika speak German?

"I found myself wanting to remember things," Erika explained. "I hadn't had them since I was a child. They're in the tin."

The red-and-green tin, incongruously Christmassy, sat next to the cooker. Gemma put the comfortingly lumpy biscuits on a plate and got out cups and saucers. Erika, who usually quickly took charge in her own kitchen, sat and watched her without protest.

She looked exhausted, and yet it seemed to Gemma that

some of the strain had gone from her face. And Gemma thought, as she often did, how beautiful Erika was, still, and wondered what she had been like when she had known Gavin Hoxley.

"Erika," she said, realizing something she had never consciously noticed as she popped tea bags into the pot and filled it from the kettle, "why don't you have any photos of yourself?" She didn't ask why there were none of David, not now.

"I brought nothing out of Germany." Erika gave a little shrug. "Not that it would have mattered, as things happened. And then, I don't know. David never touched a camera, and I—" She frowned. "I think there is one, taken not long after the war, by a neighbor. It's in the top drawer in the secretary."

Leaving the tea to steep, Gemma went into the sitting room and opened the top drawer of the little writing desk. Among the bills and pencils, she found a few loose photographs. Some were obviously more recent, taken in color, and were of Erika at various university functions. But there were a few in black and white at the bottom of the drawer, and these Gemma removed and took through into the kitchen.

They appeared to have been taken on the same day, and she recognized the communal garden behind Erika's house. The trees were in full leaf, and groups of people she didn't recognize smiled into the camera. The women wore sundresses and cotton blouses, the men had opened their collars and rolled up their sleeves.

"It was a victory party," Erika said. "That August. For those of us who had made it through."

And then Gemma found the photo. Erika must have been only a few years younger than Gemma, but she looked slight as a girl. Her dark hair was loose, and her deep brown eyes looked into the camera with the gravity that Gemma had come to know so well. She was astonishingly lovely.

Erika took the photo from her, gazing at it. "I remember her as if she were someone I knew once." She put the photo aside and took the teacup Gemma offered her. "Now," she said, "what is it you don't want to tell me?"

* * *

Elated by her success in finding the photo of Joss Miller in the same edition of the paper that had contained Erika Rosenthal's article, Melody was more than a little disappointed when Gemma wouldn't take her along to talk to Dr. Rosenthal.

But she knew Gemma always made an effort to include her when possible, and she had to trust Gemma's judgment on this one. She was nervous, though, as Gemma had said she might call for backup, and Melody knew little more than that Dominic Scott had apparently committed suicide, and that Joss Miller might have had some connection with David Rosenthal.

The minutes ticked by and Gemma didn't ring. Melody ate a cheese-and-pickle sandwich at her desk and drank a nasty cup of vending machine tea that tasted like pond sludge. She sorted through incoming reports, initialing the things that didn't need Gemma's perusal, then, checking the time again, she realized her access to the *Guardian*'s digital archives had not yet expired.

Turning back to the computer, she put in an advanced search for articles or clippings concerning Joss Miller from the war onwards. She found articles on investment mergers and art acquisitions, and a few photos similar to the one in the May 1952 edition. Her attention had begun to waver when she saw the notice of a wedding in June 1953 between Josiah Miller and the Honorable Lady Amanda Bentley.

So Miller had married a minor but well-funded title—if her memory served her, the Bentleys had been in the biscuit trade. But by that time, Joss Miller had probably been more interested in the title than in the money.

Alert again, Melody kept on with her search. Ellen Ann Miller had been born in 1955, according to the birth notices. And in 1960, the Honorable Amanda had quietly passed away, according to the obit, "after an illness."

"No fuss, no muss," Melody said aloud. Apparently Amanda Bentley had served her purpose, for Josiah Miller did not remarry, although there were occasional reports of society liaisons.

In the early seventies, photos of Ellen Ann Miller began to appear at society parties. Melody whistled through her teeth. Even in her late teens, Ellen Miller had been stunning. Not beautiful, exactly, but she had possessed a feline, predatory sexiness that practically oozed off the page.

And then, in 1978, Ellen Miller smiled out of a photo captioned *High Time at the Roxy,* and beside her name was that of the handsome, dark-haired young man with his arm round her shoulders. Harry Pevensey.

"This other man, killed like the girl," Erika said when Gemma had finished. "And Joseph Mueller's grandson hanged himself? Dear God, there has to be an end to it."

"So what if Joseph Mueller kept the brooch because he was afraid it might be identified, or perhaps just because he liked keeping reminders of his cruelty," Gemma mused aloud. "And when Dom was desperate for money, and his mother wouldn't help him, Dom took it and had it put up for sale." Had he found it by chance? she wondered.

"Then, when I told Kristin that you had made a claim on the brooch, she told Dom, and he panicked."

"Even if he didn't know how it had come into his family," agreed Erika, "he couldn't afford to be associated with it."

"The barmaid at the club where Dom met Kristin said they argued that night," she went on. "If he told her she had to take the brooch out of the sale, that he had to have it back, and she told him she couldn't—or wouldn't—then he must have been desperate. But I still don't see where he got a car in time to get back to Chelsea and wait for her to get home."

"And the other man, this Harry—"

"Pevensey. A washed-up actor. Dom used him to cover his connection with the transaction. He was protecting himself from the first—"

"And then you think this young man, who could kill so ruthlessly, took his own life out of guilt?" Erika shook her head. "That I find difficult to believe. The suicide is an act of a different type of character entirely."

"Perhaps not guilt, but desperation—if he meant to run

you down last night, and failed——" Gemma shuddered, not only at the thought of how close Erika had been to peril, but because by sending Kit to check on Erika she might have put him in danger, too.

Erika set her cup in its saucer with a clink. "I think you're wrong, Gemma. If he failed last night, why not try again? And how would he have known that my recognition of the brooch would damn *his* family? Even if the sale had been traced back to him, why not claim he picked it up at an auction or an antiques stall?"

Gemma stared at her, trying to fit all that they had learned into a cohesive whole. "Unless Joss Miller kept David's manuscript,"—she said slowly, "and in it David revealed everything——"

"You think this young man would have put the brooch up for auction knowing its history—knowing how his grandfather had come by it?" Erika raised her delicate eyebrows in disbelief.

Gemma thought of Dominic Scott as they had first met him, white and sweating, collapsing at the news of Kristin Cahill's death.

They knew now that he had been a junkie, strung out and ill—was it conceivable that he had taken an object that he knew tainted his family, then planned and carried out two murders, and attempted a third?

Dom Scott, who had been so bullied by his mother that he had hated to go into her sitting room, with its reminders of his grandfather's success?

Dom Scott, whose grieving mother had compared him to his grandfather, even as his body hung cooling upstairs, and found fault?

"Oh, no," Gemma breathed. "We got it wrong. We got it all wrong."

"Bingo." Cullen came into Kincaid's office looking jubilant. "I've got the bastard. I found a Land Rover still registered under Joss Miller's name. And, in the property tax rolls, I found a lockup garage in Chelsea Square, also in Joss Miller's name. That's where Dom Scott will have kept the car.

I've put in a request for a warrant to search the garage. We need to get any trace evidence from that Land Rover before his mum twigs and cleans it. You know she won't want her son to go down as a murderer."

Kincaid pushed back the reports he'd been poring over and sat back in his chair, frowning. "Another car. And a lockup. Of course." He shook his head. "But even assuming we found trace evidence on the car, we still couldn't put him in the driver's seat at the scene of the accident." He straightened the papers, thinking. "Not that proving him guilty would do anything other than tidy up our case results. We can't prosecute a dead man."

"No," said Cullen. "But it won't be prosecution that will worry Dom Scott's mother. Just the rumor of her family's involvement would be enough to send her into a tizzy. You know she—"

"Reputation." Kincaid sat up so quickly the chair rocked. "Nothing matters more to Ellen Miller-Scott than reputation. What if Gemma was right? What if Erika Rosenthal's husband had some proof that Joss Miller was involved in war crimes?"

"David Rosenthal has been dead for years," Cullen argued. "Whatever he knew obviously died with him."

"But what if it didn't?" Kincaid glanced at his watch. It was long past time for Gemma to have checked in. The formless anxiety that had plagued him ever since they found Dom Scott's body suddenly coalesced into a hard knot of worry, and he reached for his phone.

"Where are you?" Kincaid said sharply in Gemma's ear. "You've been ages—"

"I'm still at Erika's. I'm sorry, my signal's iffy—"

"We found the Land Rover, still registered to Joss Miller. And a lockup garage in Chelsea Square, about a seven-minute walk from the house. But I don't think Dom—"

"I know." Gemma stepped out into the garden, where her mobile reception was better. "It was Ellen."

She told him all she'd learned from Erika, then added, "What if Dom came across the brooch and chanced selling it, because he was desperate and had nowhere else to turn? He probably had no idea of its history or of its true value until he showed it to Kristin."

"But Ellen would have known," Kincaid continued. "Either because she'd seen David Rosenthal's manuscript or—"

"Or because her father told her." Gemma's voice was flat with disgust. Could Joss Miller possibly have bragged to his daughter about rape and murder?

"Deathbed confession, maybe," Kincaid said more charitably, but then he hadn't heard Erika describe what Joss Miller had done. "But if Ellen learned the history of the brooch, no matter how or when she came by the knowledge, she would have known that if the piece were publicly connected with her family, it could prove disastrous.

"She would have been livid when she found it missing." Gemma imagined Ellen going to her father's desk or safe— surely the Millers had a safe—perhaps to get a piece of her own to wear, and realizing the brooch was missing. "Oh, God, she'd have ripped poor Dom to shreds. And she would have told him he had to get it back, at all costs."

"So then Dom sent Kristin flowers," Kincaid continued, "and got her to agree to meet him that night at the Gate. But Kristin told him she couldn't take the brooch out of the sale—"

Gemma thought of the girl she had met. "My guess is that she was fed up with him. And she wanted the money from the commission. That four percent of the sale price would have meant something to her, if not to Dom. And she would have told him that we'd been there, saying someone had claimed the brooch, that it had been stolen during the war. That would've put the wind up Dom completely. But then . . . how did Ellen—" Gemma hesitated, still not quite sure she could put it together.

"I think," said Kincaid, "I think that Dom rang his mother, after Kristin left him at the Gate that night. We'll have to ask Eva, the barmaid, if she remembers him using his mobile. And Ellen . . ." Kincaid paused, and Gemma knew he was running his free hand through his hair until it stood on end, the way he did when he was working something out.

"Maybe at first she just meant to talk some sense into Kristin," she said. "Ellen's Mercedes was in for repairs, so she might have had the Land Rover out for a small errand, then parked near the house rather than in the lockup—"

Kincaid picked it up. "But the car had no plates—from the records I'd guess it's an old mud car from their country place—and that might have occurred to her while she was sitting in front of Kristin's building, waiting for Kristin to come home. And Dom's news about Erika coming forward would have raised the stakes enormously. It meant not possible ruin, but certain ruin. She must have realized that if Erika came forward, it wasn't just reputation, but the possibility that the Millers and their business assets could have faced a lawsuit. There are enough precedents. There have been both individuals and corporations sued for profiting from atrocities committed against Jews during the war."

"And then she saw Kristin walking down from the bus stop, alone." Gemma watched the leaves of Erika's fig tree move in the breeze. "And she knew Kristin would have to cross the road—"

"And Ellen would have guessed that she could risk the CCTV, because the car had no plates, and the camera would never get a clear view of the driver's face." Kincaid paused, and when he went on, his voice held a hint of awe. "What a risk she took. But she couldn't stop there. She still had to try to get the brooch removed from the sale. So the next morning, she sent Dom to see Harry Pevensey. That was the row Harry's neighbor heard. But Harry refused as well—even a percentage of the reserve on the brooch would have been a godsend to him—"

"And Dom had no proof of ownership, not without doing the very thing he was trying to avoid." Gemma couldn't help but feel pity for Dominic Scott. "And then when he went home to tell his mum Harry wouldn't cooperate, we were there to tell him Kristin was dead, murdered. No wonder he fainted on us. He must have realized his mother had killed her."

Kincaid finished the thought for her. "And then, because Dom had failed in his mission, that night Ellen killed Harry, too."

Gemma felt ill, not only for the vicious deaths of Kristin Cahill and Harry Pevensey, but for the brutal choice Ellen Miller had forced on her son. "And Dom—Dom had to decide whether to inform on the mother who had bullied him his entire life, in the process ruining his family's—and more important, his grandfather's—name—"

"Or let his mother get away with murdering two innocent people. No wonder the sad bugger decided it was easier to top himself."

"Or three people," said Gemma. She looked through the conservatory window at Erika, still sitting in the kitchen, and told him that Erika had seen a car waiting in her street last night, its lights dark, and that she had described it as looking like a Land Rover. "If her cabdriver hadn't waited until she got in her door—" Only then did the enormity of what might have happened really hit her.

"Bloody hell!" Kincaid swore so viciously that Gemma jumped. "Of course. Erika. Erika is the last, and the most vital, link. You were right to have been worried about her. Listen—" He stopped and Gemma heard Cullen's voice in the background, and Kincaid responding with "No, hang on to the warrant. We're not going to search the garage yet. We don't want to tip Ellen Miller-Scott off. I have a much better idea."

"I will not let you put another young woman's life in jeopardy." Erika crossed her arms, looking as stubborn as Gemma had ever seen her.

Gemma sat once more in the chair opposite and studied her friend across the small kitchen table. Although when Kincaid had explained to her what he meant to do, she'd agreed reluctantly, she knew that he was right. Now she just had to convince Erika.

"I know you don't want to do that," she said earnestly, meeting Erika's gaze. "But you don't want to see Ellen Miller-Scott get away with two murders, not to mention

what she did to her son. And we can't place her at the wheel
of that car at the time of the collisions, any more than we
could have placed Dominic."

"But if you find evidence on the car—"

"It doesn't matter. Any good lawyer would make mince-
meat of it, and Ellen will have the best. All she has to do
is say her son was driving, and that he took his own life
because he felt guilty over what he'd done. She could even
say Dom was drink-driving and both deaths were tragic ac-
cidents, and we couldn't prove otherwise. But"—she leaned
forward, pushing her empty teacup and plate aside—"we believe she's going to give us the perfect opportunity to prove
intent to commit murder.

"I think she waited for you to come home last night. I
suspect she rang first to see if you were in—we'll check your
caller ID—and when you didn't answer, she took her opportunity, and if not for your cabbie, she might have succeeded.
We'll need to be prepared for her to ring you again," Gemma
added, "because if you are at home, she'll need some ruse to
get you out of the house."

"But her son is dead! How could this woman go on
with—"

"I don't believe for one moment that Dom's suicide will
stop her from trying again. Ellen doesn't know how much
we know, so as far as she's concerned, if she silences you,
she removes the threat to her way of life and preserves her
father's legacy."

Erika gazed out into the garden, and the slight movement of air from the open window moved a feather of white
hair against her cheek. She sighed. "Gemma, I'm not disa-
greeing with any of that. No one wants to see this woman
caught more than I. But I want to do it myself. I don't believe
that a decoy will convince her, and it's my right to take the
risk. If I hadn't kept silent all these years—"

"Her father would have killed you the way he killed
David," Gemma said brutally. "Joss Miller must have been
sure David hadn't told you what he'd learned, and decided
that killing you after he'd murdered David might cause un-
necessary interest. But now you have a chance to close the

books, and you need to let us do our job. And our job is to protect you as much as it is to catch a killer."

There was a long moment, in which Gemma heard the neighbors who rented the flat upstairs from Erika scraping furniture across the floor. And then, in the following silence, a faint thread of music, the theme of an afternoon show on the telly.

"All right," Erika agreed at last. "But I don't like it. And I still don't believe anyone can play me convincingly."

Gemma smiled, her relief making her flippant. "If I didn't know you better, I'd say you were a bit full of yourself. Give us a bit of cred—"

The door buzzer sounded, making them both start. When Erika started to rise, Gemma motioned her back with a hand. "No," she said softly. "Let me get it." She grabbed her phone, her heart thumping, and went quietly towards the front of the flat. They had assumed Ellen Miller-Scott would stick with the tried and true, keeping her hands clean, but assumptions were just that. They had no assurance that she wouldn't try to attack Erika in her flat in broad daylight.

But before she could peek out the bedroom window, she heard Melody's voice calling out, "Boss, are you okay in there?"

"Melody!" Gemma unlatched the door and urged Melody inside. "What are you doing here?"

"Your mobile's not picking up. I was worried about you."

"Damn," said Gemma, wondering if she'd missed other calls. Her signal had been patchy when she talked to Duncan.

"And I had something to show you," Melody went on. She pulled a sheet of paper from her bag, and Gemma recognized it as another copy made from the *Guardian* archives.

Gemma took the page and moved farther into the hall, where she could hold the picture under the wall sconce, and stared at it, trying to take in what she saw.

"Ellen Miller-Scott and Harry Pevensey knew each other? She said she'd never heard of him."

"I'd guess it was more a case of knowing in the biblical sense than a casual acquaintance," said Melody. "I did some more research. Six months after this photo was taken, Ellen Miller married Stephen Scott, who was tall, blond, and blue eyed. It was a society wedding, and they made a very handsome couple. The next year, Ellen and Stephen's son, Dominic, was born a bit prematurely.

"I looked up some background on Harry Pevensey as well. His mother was Indian, from Calcutta. Even though she apparently came from a well-connected family, I doubt that would have cut any ice with Ellen Miller's father."

"So when Ellen got pregnant, he found a more suitable candidate?" Gemma looked back at the photo, saw in the young man's smiling face the dark good looks of Dom Scott. She handed the pages back to Melody and wiped her fingers against her trousers, as if she could erase the imprint of Dom's face from her mind. There was no way Ellen Miller-Scott could not have known whose child she had borne.

"Boss—"

"That was the one connection we couldn't make, between Harry and Dom." Gemma swallowed. "Ellen Miller-Scott killed her son's father."

# 22

*It is not merely of some importance but is of fundamental importance that justice should not only be seen to be done, but should manifestly and undoubtedly be seen to be done.*
Lord Hewart, Rex v. Sussex Justices, *9 Nov. 1923*
*(King's Bench Reports, 1924, Vol. I, p. 259)*

THE DECOY ARRIVED WELL before dark. Her name was Wendy Chen, and she was a detective sergeant with whom Gemma had worked when at the Yard. Not only was she as slight in stature as Erika, but Gemma had remembered that she had a flair for amateur dramatics.

Now, with a white wig and some of Erika's clothes, they would have to hope that in the dark she would pass for Erika.

Melody had left to liaise with Kincaid and Cullen, and Gemma couldn't blame her for wanting to be in on the action. But even though there was now another police officer in the flat, Gemma had no intention of leaving Erika alone until this was over.

She had rung Wesley Howard and asked him to take the boys to his mum's for the evening—Kit would object to being assigned a minder, but she didn't feel comfortable leaving them on their own. She had no way of knowing if Ellen Miller-Scott had realized she had a personal connection with Erika, but she was taking no more chances with her family's safety.

And she had rung the hospital and spoken to the charge nurse, who told her that her mum was resting comfortably and had started instructing the aides in how to care for the patient in the next bed—a sign, Gemma thought, that her mum was feeling at least a bit perkier.

When she tried to check in with Cyn, her sister's phone went straight to voice mail, and her dad answered neither flat nor bakery. Like Harry Pevensey, her father refused to carry a mobile phone, and his stubbornness irritated Gemma no end. Hanging up, she came in from the garden feeling worried and aggravated in equal parts.

As Gemma didn't want anyone to go out, just in case Ellen was watching the flat, they made do with a supper of salads and meats that Erika had on hand from the deli. Neither Gemma nor Erika, however, had much appetite.

As dusk fell, Wendy put on a pair of Erika's trousers and one of the long, colorful jackets Erika favored, then fitted the wig and pulled the thick white hair up into a twist.

At Gemma's insistence, Erika had drunk her usual before-dinner glass of dry sherry, and now her cheeks were flushed pink against her pale skin. "That's not right," she said, and made Wendy sit at her dressing table while she redid the wig, but after two attempts she dropped the brush in frustration. "It's like a man trying to tie a necktie on someone else. My muscle memory isn't cooperating. And that awful wig doesn't look a thing like my hair," she added, her nose wrinkled in distaste.

"Let's try movement, then," suggested Wendy, leading her into the sitting room. "That's the most important thing. Walk across the room for me."

When Erika complied, Gemma saw that she was holding her spine stiffly upright, and moving more slowly than usual. "No, just relax," said Gemma. "Talk to me while you walk. Pretend you're going to the shops."

"That woman will never fall for this," Erika muttered as she took another few turns around the room. "She doesn't make mistakes."

"Let me try." Wendy demonstrated, holding her shoulders forward just a bit, changing the angle of her head, and adding a very slight halt to her step. The transformation was amazing.

"I don't look like that," protested Erika, incensed.

"Oh, but you do," said Gemma, laughing. "That's very good. It would fool me, at least from a distance."

"The eye sees what it expects to see," explained Wendy. "Miller-Scott had a chance to watch you last night, Erika, and maybe other times as well, so she'll have a visual imprint. That's all it takes for most people to make a quick identification if you give them the right cues."

Gemma sobered instantly at the idea that Ellen Miller-Scott might have watched Erika more than once, and nerves began to get the best of her. The time seemed to pass like treacle dripping from a jar, and she had to stop herself checking the clock every other minute. "You'll be all right, won't you?" she whispered to Wendy when Erika had gone into the kitchen. "If she believes you're Erika, she won't hesitate to run you down."

"I was a gymnast," Wendy assured her. "I can drop and roll like a champ."

When it grew so dark that Gemma could see her reflection in the garden window, she drew the shade. It would have to be soon, or Ellen wouldn't believe she could lure Erika out.

Kincaid had rung to tell her they had the unmarked cars in position, two at the bottom of Arundel Gardens—one either side of the Kensington Park Road T-junction, and two at the top end—either side of Ladbroke Grove. They believed Ellen would come down the curve of Landsdowne Road and cross Ladbroke Grove. Her car had been facing down the street when Erika had seen it the previous evening, and that route would give her the best visibility as well as the best chance to get up speed.

But how, Gemma wondered, did Ellen intend to get Erika out of the house and into the street? She couldn't drive the car up on the pavement, as she had with Harry Pevensey—the cars parked either side of Arundel Gardens would block her access.

"Erika—" The burr of the phone made them all start, even though they'd been prepared.

They looked at one another, then Gemma nodded. "Easy now," she whispered to Erika. "And whatever she says, agree."

"Hello?" Erika clicked the phone on, sounding only a little breathless, as if she'd had to cross the room to answer. "Yes. Yes, it is," she said, then listened intently, and Gemma heard the faint sound of a woman's voice issuing from the handset. "You do?" Erika sounded a little befuddled, and Gemma thought Wendy Chen wasn't the only one with a flair for drama. "But that's— Well, it's rather late, but— Are you sure you won't— Yes, I see." She nodded, as if the caller could see her. "Yes, all right. Five minutes, then. Across the street. Thank you," she added, then disconnected.

"Of all the bloody nerve," she said, turning to Gemma and sounding not the least bit confused. "She said she worked at Harrowby's and knew something about my brooch, but that if anyone knew she'd spoken with me, she'd get into trouble. She said she'd be waiting in a red Fiat across the street."

"Is there a red Fiat?" Gemma asked Wendy.

"Yes. She's scouted."

The knowledge that Ellen Miller-Scott had been spying on Erika made Gemma feel cold. Had she seen the unmarked cars? "I'll ring Duncan. Wendy, countdown."

"I'll just make sure my hair's on straight," said Wendy, showing her first sign of tension. "We want to be certain she's in position before I go out."

Stepping into the conservatory in order to get the best reception on her mobile, Gemma called Kincaid. "She's on her way," she said when he answered. "She said five minutes, and we're down one. She told Erika she'd be waiting in a red Fiat across the street."

"Right. Tell Sergeant Chen to be careful, but she has to give her a chance to make the attempt."

"She knows," said Gemma, but he had already rung off. She looked at her watch. Two minutes.

Hurrying into the sitting room, she found Wendy emerging from the loo, patting her hair and straightening her long jacket. "Feel like I'm going for a bloody audition," she said.

"They'll be right behind you." She glanced at her watch once more. "Showtime." Then the absence hit her.

"Wendy, where's Erika?"

"She went into the bed—"

The front door latch snicked.

"Shit." Gemma felt the blood draining from her face as she met Wendy's eyes. "She's done a bunk—"

"I'll get her," said Wendy, starting for the door.

"No." Gemma grabbed her sleeve. "We can't let Ellen see two Erikas. Stay inside."

Then she dashed for the door. If she could pull Erika back, maybe they'd still have enough on Ellen to prove intent.

But when Gemma emerged from the flat, she saw Erika just stepping in between the two cars parked in front of the building. And then Erika was in the street, and a dark shape came hurtling down the chute of Arundel Gardens, straight for her.

Gemma leaped for the pavement, shouting, as the world erupted into a barrage of sound and motion. Erika seemed to bounce back from the Land Rover's front fender, disappearing between the parked vehicles, just as two cars came screeching round from either side of Kensington Park Road, blocking both lanes of traffic.

The Land Rover braked hard, skidding. As the driver threw the car into reverse and looked back, Gemma saw her face clearly. Ellen. They had been right.

But two more cars roared round from Ladbroke Grove and pulled up behind the Land Rover. Ellen Miller-Scott was boxed in.

As Gemma ran down the steps towards Erika, the front doors on the parallel lead cars flew open and four uniformed and armored officers jumped out, shouting, "Armed police!" guns drawn as they crouched behind the shields of their doors.

Reaching Erika, Gemma knelt, mouth dry with fear for her friend, but Erika was already pulling herself up.

"Are you—"

"I'm all right. Just bruised. I—"

The far-side doors of the rear car sprang open. Cullen emerged from the front, then Melody from the back. They were wearing body armor over their street clothes, and they advanced on the passenger door of the Land Rover, guns drawn.

Then, just as Kincaid jumped from the rear car's driver's seat, Gemma saw Ellen's blond head disappear from view.

"Gun!" Cullen shouted. "She's got a gun!"

Kincaid and Melody froze. Cullen, his eyes not wavering from Ellen Miller-Scott, yelled, "Put your hands up! Let me see your hands!"

Time seemed to stop between one breath and the next, and Gemma heard the blood pounding in her ears. Then she jerked into action, throwing her arms round Erika, pulling her down and shielding her with her own body, her heart contracting with terror.

Then Ellen Miller-Scott's blond head reappeared above the seat, slowly, and Doug was shouting, "Open your door! Let me see your hands! Do it now!"

The driver's door of the Land Rover swung open and Cullen screamed, "Take her! Take her!" to Kincaid.

Kincaid sprinted to the car, and then Ellen Miller-Scott was tumbling out, her wrists pinned in Kincaid's hand. He spun her round against the car, hard, and patted her down.

Diving into the passenger side, Cullen emerged holding a small, neat gun. "Bloody bitch!" he said, raising it in the air, and Gemma knew he was feeling the adrenaline dump. "She had a fucking gun! She was fucking going to shoot me!"

Ellen Miller-Scott turned her head to look back at Kincaid. "You've nothing against me." Even restrained against the Land Rover, her voice was a level drawing-room drawl. "I was defending myself against harassment. My lawyer will be in touch with your commissioner before you can draw breath."

Struggling out of Gemma's loosened grasp, Erika stood and limped towards Ellen Miller-Scott. Her hair had come free from its twist, falling in a mass of white about her shoulders, and when she raised a pointing finger, she looked like a Fury unleashed.

"That was your father's gun," she said coldly, clearly. "And you are your father's daughter. I will see you rot in hell."

# 23

*And I'm not saying love will make you happy—
above all, I'm not saying that. If anything I tend to
believe that it will make you unhappy; either immediately unhappy, as you are impaled by incom-
patibility; or unhappy later, when the woodworm
has quietly been gnawing away for years and the
bishop's throne collapses. But you can believe this
and still insist that love is our only hope.*
      Julian Barnes, A History of the
      World in 10½ Chapters

ON FRIDAY MORNING, Gemma arrived at the hospital as
soon as visitors were allowed on the ward. For the first time,
she managed to catch the consultant as he made his rounds.

"I want you to tell me the truth," she'd said, taking him
aside. "How bad is it?"

The doctor considered her, as if checking for signs of
hysteria, then shrugged. He looked tired, and his skin had
the slight gray tinge of someone who slept little and worked
too many hours.

"Leukemia is very serious, of course," he told her. "But
your mother seems to be responding to treatment. It's early
days yet, and there are other options if the chemotherapy
isn't successful."

With that Gemma had to be content for the moment. She
waited for her mother to come back from her treatment, then

sat with her while she dozed. When Vi woke, Gemma told her a bit about Erika and what had happened the night before, leaving out any mention of how close they had come to disaster. She wasn't ready to think about that quite yet.

"Will you get a conviction?" asked Vi.

"It's early days yet," Gemma told her, echoing the doctor. "We've a lot of evidence to sift through."

"And you want to be there, in the middle of it. Go," Vi scolded. "I don't need you to sit here reading silly magazines to me." She flapped a copy of *Hello!* at Gemma as if she were shooing a fly.

"But I want to be with—"

"Gemma, you're no better at twiddling your thumbs than I am. And I'm not going anywhere. I've stuffing in me yet."

Gemma laughed. "So you do. Okay, you've convinced me." She stood. "The nurse says I can bring Kit for a visit tomorrow. And Toby's making you a card at school today."

Patting her hair, Vi said, "I'd better have Cyn make me presentable, if I'm going to have handsome young men visiting."

But as Gemma bent to kiss her mother's cheek, Vi clasped her hand and held it. "Gemma, it's your dad I worry about. Promise me you'll look after him."

"Mum." Gemma shook her head. "Don't say things like that. You're going to get—"

"I know I am," her mum assured her. "It's just—he's got the bakery to run on his own, and with the worry on top of that— And he misses you, Gem, but he won't tell you. I shouldn't say this," she added, lowering her voice, "but you always were his favorite, and that just makes it all the harder for him."

"I'll go see him," Gemma said. "Tomorrow. I promise."

Ellen Miller-Scott had done exactly what they expected, but not even the most high-powered of solicitors had been able to engineer an immediate release for a woman who had attempted a hit-and-run in front of police officers.

When Gemma arrived at the Yard, Ellen was still "helping the police with their inquiries," which meant that she was sitting in an interview room with Kincaid and Cullen, backed by her solicitor, coolly refusing to answer any questions.

Rather than join this frustrating and unproductive party, Gemma had Melody escort Erika into the Yard, where Gemma took her detailed statement herself.

"Was I right about the gun?" Erika asked. "I had seen it in my dreams for more than fifty years."

"It is a Walther PPK," Gemma told her. "And it dates from the early thirties, when they were very popular in Germany with both police and civilian shooters. And it certainly is not legally registered to Ellen Miller-Scott, nor to her father, so I would say it's a pretty good bet he brought it back from Germany."

"But you can't prove it."

"No," Gemma said, gently. "I wish we could. But we have a warrant to search the Cheyne Walk house this afternoon. We may find other things."

"Do you think he kept it—David's book—all these years?"

"If he did," Gemma said, "will you read it?"

Erika paled, but after a moment said, "Yes. I suppose I must. I owe that much to David. And to the others."

They found the pages, tucked into a brown pasteboard file, in the safe in Joss Miller's office. David Rosenthal's name was at the top, and every margin of the thin onionskin paper was covered with tiny black script—it looked as if David had feared he would never find room to put down everything he had to tell.

In places on the top page, the ink was smeared by small brown teardrops—the unmistakable splatter of blood. Gemma could only guess that David Rosenthal had been holding his manuscript in his hands when Joseph Mueller stabbed him.

Gemma and Kincaid found other pieces of jewelry in the safe as well, although none as exquisite as Jakob Goldshtein's diamond brooch. When Dominic Scott had needed money, he had gone for the prize.

Unfortunately, it seemed that Ellen Miller-Scott had been more careful than her father. There was nothing in the house that obviously tied her to the killing of Kristin Cahill or Harry Pevensey. But as the SOCOs began their minute examination, Cullen rang to say that the lab had found blood and tissue matches from both victims on the front of the Land Rover, and that the steering wheel bore only Ellen Miller-Scott's prints.

"She can say she wiped the wheel after Dom drove the car, to protect him," said Gemma.

"She could," Kincaid agreed. "And she probably will. But that doesn't mean anyone will believe her. Let's leave them to it," he added, nodding at the techs.

As they let themselves out into the cool evening, Gemma took a last look back at the house. "Could she have saved him, do you think?"

"Dom?" Kincaid shrugged and shook his head. "I doubt we'll ever know for certain. But my guess is that she might have seen Dom's death as the solution to a very big problem. A necessary sacrifice."

Dusk had fallen while they were inside, and the lights had come on along the river. Instead of going to the car, Gemma took Kincaid's hand and they walked across the road.

They stood on the Embankment in silence, between the Battersea Bridge to the west and the Albert Bridge to the east, gazing at the river making its slow muddy way towards the North Sea.

All the victims, past and present, thought Gemma—David, Gavin, Kristin, Harry, and poor Dominic—were a drop in the ocean compared to the millions of lives taken by those like Joss Miller and his daughter, but that made their loss no less significant, nor the things they had cared about any less important.

The wind that blew off the river felt more like March than May. Gemma shivered, and Kincaid put his arm round her shoulders. She leaned against him, looking away from the sunset, and said, "Erika told me that Gavin Hoxley loved the lights on the Albert Bridge."

* * *

Doug Cullen found himself leaving the main entrance of the Yard at the same time as Melody Talbot. "Back to Notting Hill, then?" he asked, as casually as he could manage.

"Yeah. Seems a bit dull, though, after yesterday." She smiled at him, satisfaction still bright in her eyes, and he wondered how he could ever have thought her not pretty.

"As ditchwater," he agreed, trying for an air of insouciance he didn't feel.

The truth was that he had been scared shitless. All the firearms training in the world hadn't prepared him for the adrenaline rush of jumping out of a car and aiming the bloody gun at a real person. Then, when he'd seen the weapon in Ellen Miller-Scott's hand, his guts had turned to water.

But Melody—Melody had been practically bouncing with excitement, her face shining, and yet she had held her gun on Ellen Miller-Scott with the steadiness of a rock.

"You were good last night," he told her, and when Melody gave him a surprised glance, he wondered if he had sounded grudging.

But she smiled again and said, "So were you. A regular cowboy."

He shrugged, as if he did things like that every day, and an awkward silence fell between them.

But before he could think of what else to say, Melody broke it. "We should maybe sort of celebrate or something. Want to get a drink?"

Doug stared at her—the efficient and sarcastic Melody Talbot was asking him out? Trying to stutter an acceptance, he said, "I—"

But then he thought of Maura Bell, and of the last time he had made a fool of himself, imagining that a woman fancied him.

He wasn't going to risk that humiliation again, not any time soon, and not with someone who could rip him to shreds if it suited her. "I, uh—I have to be somewhere," he amended. "Some other time?"

He saw an unexpected flash of disappointment in her face, quickly concealed, but before he could figure out how to take back his refusal, she said evenly, "Right." This time her smile was brittle. "See you, then," she added, tossing the words back at him as she turned and walked away.

"What will you do about the brooch?" asked Gemma. It was late on Saturday morning, and she was in Erika's sitting room, drinking the strong and bitter—and, Erika had added fiercely, not decaffeinated—coffee that Erika had made them.

Early that morning, Gemma had taken Kit to see her mother, and then they'd ridden the tube to Leyton High Road. Her father, caught unawares in the midst of serving a customer, had looked ridiculously pleased to see them. Kit volunteered to stay and help out, with touching enthusiasm, and before Gemma left she had taken her dad aside.

"We'll get through this," she said. "I'm taking some time off work. I can help out in the mornings for a bit, and maybe Kit can come in after school. And Mum's going to be okay."

As her father's face worked with emotion, she saw how perilously close he had come to collapse.

It wasn't in his nature to accept with grace, but he nodded, then turned away, patting at his eyes with his apron, and Gemma vowed to do better by them both. If he couldn't move towards her, she would have to move towards him.

"The brooch?" repeated Erika thoughtfully. "I went to Harrowby's first thing this morning. Your nice Mr. Khan showed it to me. Very charming fellow."

Gemma waited, wondering if she would ever see the charming side of Amir Khan, and after a moment, Erika went on, "It is a beautiful thing, even more so than I remembered. And Mr. Khan gave me the number of Harry Pevensey's cousin, his next of kin. When I rang her, she offered it to me, as a gift. She said she thought it should go to its rightful owner. It was very generous of her."

"Then you—"

"Yes, I told her I would take it, but not to keep. There's too much pain attached to it. That's not what my father intended when he made it."

"But it's worth—"

"Nothing. Or everything," said Erika. "I'm going to give it to the Victoria and Albert. The museum has a fine jewelry collection, and my father would have been proud to see it there."

"I would like my father to be proud of me." The confession caught Gemma unawares. "He told me that I was hurting my mother by not marrying Duncan."

"Well." Erika sipped at her coffee without wincing. "I am not a psychologist, but it may be that your father is projecting his own wishes onto your mother, perhaps in part because he cannot fully admit them.

"But you shouldn't let your decisions be influenced by what will make your father or your mother happy, but rather by what will make you and Duncan happy."

Gemma twisted her cup in her hands. "But I'm . . . afraid." There, she had said it. "Why isn't Duncan afraid? There are so many things that could go wrong. I don't want to—"

"You cannot stand still. And Duncan knows all about fear. He lost Kit's mother. He almost lost you. And he lost the baby that was his as well as yours. I suspect that is when he made the leap that you are afraid to make. And what, after all, have you to lose?"

"Myself," Gemma said softly. "I don't want to be like my mum. I don't want to orbit around someone else's sun."

"Are you sure it's not the other way round with your parents? That it's your father who orbits your mother?" asked Erika. "And besides," she added with emphasis, "you are not your mother, and Duncan is certainly not your father."

"But what if . . ." Gemma forced herself to admit the thing that terrified her most. "What happened the other night . . . It was Doug in the line of fire, but it could have been Duncan . . . What if I lost *him*?"

"Then," said Erika, "you have to consider the alternative to taking the risk. And that is many long nights of lonely suppers and cold beds. And teetering on the fence doesn't protect you from pain; it merely gives you more to regret."

Gemma slid round on the piano bench just a little, running her fingers lightly over the keys. There was a chime of sound, so faint she thought she might have imagined it, but it seemed to reverberate through her body.

Without looking at Erika, she said, "I got a call today. From Duncan's cousin Jack's wife. My friend Winnie, the Anglican priest. She's pregnant."

"Ah. How do you feel about that?"

"I'm not sure. Happy. Sad. Jealous. Confused."

"Yes." Erika nodded. "I expect so. Have you told Duncan?"

"Not yet. I was in the City, visiting my mum."

"Then you should go and tell him now. It's cause for celebration."

"I should, shouldn't I?" Gemma felt a sudden, unexpected fizz of exhilaration, like champagne bubbles in her blood, and almost laughed aloud. Winnie was *pregnant*.

She stood and went to Erika, dropping down on one knee so that she could look up into her face. For an instant, she saw the young woman Gavin Hoxley had loved, and who had taken the leap of loving him back, regardless of the consequences. "Will you be all right?"

"I'm not sure I know what all right is." Erika smiled, and the twinkle was back in her dark eyes. "But I think I will ask my friend Henri to dinner."

Gemma walked down Arundel Gardens, feeling the slight spring as her heels connected with the pavement. The sun shone in a blue and perfectly cloudless sky, and the air seemed to have texture to it, so that she almost felt as if she were swimming in its crystal clarity.

When she reached Portobello Road she bought flowers from the corner stall, two dozen red tulips, imagining, as she watched the vendor wrap them, the bright splash of color they would make against the white wall of the sitting room when she put them on the bookcase. Then, a bit farther along, she chose strawberries and asparagus, taking her time, as if finding the perfect specimens was the most important thing in the world. The street was crowded, the shoppers brought out in force by the beautiful day, but for once she didn't mind the jostling, and the colors of people's clothing and stall awnings seemed unnaturally bright.

With the flowers cradled under one arm, she swung the carrier bag from the fruit and veg stall in the other hand, making her way farther down the road, glancing desultorily into shop windows. She thought she might buy shoes, or an inexpensive bracelet under the Westway, something entirely frivolous, entirely out of character.

But just before the Westway, her eye was caught by a print on a photographer's stall. She bought it without deliberation, handing over a note with a smile, then walked away, examining her find. The house she thought she recognized as one nearby, but its cream brickwork and the French blue of a bay window on the first floor served merely as a backdrop for the graceful curved limbs of an apple tree that filled the frame, bursting with white blossom.

It was an ordinary scene, simple and uncomplicated, full of promise.

Duncan met her in the hall, taking her bags and the paper cone of flowers. "I'd have bought them for you," he said.

"I know." She followed him into the kitchen. "But I wanted to buy them myself. Kit stayed with Dad at the bakery. Where are Toby and the dogs?"

"I've fed Toby lunch and sent them outside again. They're like dervishes in the house today. Spring fever. Shall I get a vase, or do you want—" He stopped, looking puzzled. "What is it? Did I miss a spot shaving? Egg on my face?"

Gemma found that her hands were trembling. She took a breath, hoping her voice wouldn't squeak. "No. It's just . . . I was wondering . . . I was wondering if we might invite Winnie and Jack up for a weekend. Sometime this summer. And Hazel. And your family, of course."

He frowned. "What—"

"I was wondering if Winnie could, you know, officiate. In a parish that wasn't her patch. At a . . . wedding."

"A wedding?" He stared at her, the tulips tilting dangerously in his grasp, forgotten. In his eyes she saw a flare of delight, and herself reflected, infinitely, like an image in a hall of mirrors.

"A wedding. If you wanted . . . That is . . ."

"I think," he said slowly, setting the flowers on the table, "that something of the sort could be arranged."

**Turn the page for a sneak peek
at the next thrilling
Gemma James/Duncan Kincaid mystery
NECESSARY AS BLOOD
Coming Fall 2009
in hardcover from William Morrow**

Once the haunt of Jack the Ripper, London's East End is a vibrant mix of history and the avant garde, a place where elegant Georgian town houses exist side-by-side with colorful street markets and the hippest clubs. But here race and cultures still clash, and the trendy galleries and glamorous nightlife of Whitechapel disguise a violent and seedy underside, where unthinkable crimes bring terror to the innocent. A young mother has gone missing, and only Scotland Yard's Superintendent Duncan Kincaid and his partner, Gemma James, can stop a vicious killer and protect the child whose fate hangs in the balance.

*Umbra Sumas—"We are shadows."*
*—Inscription on the sundial of the*
*Huguenot church, now the Jamme*
*Mosjid Mosque, on Brick Lane*

THAT SUNDAY BEGAN LIKE any ordinary Sunday, except that Naz, Sandra's husband, had gone in to work for a few hours at his law office, an unusual breach of family time for him.

Having pushed aside her initial irritation, Sandra had decided to use the time for one of her own projects, and after breakfast and chores, she and Charlotte had gone up to her studio on the top floor of the house.

After two hours work, Sandra stepped back, frowning, from the swatches of fabric she had pinned to the muslin stretched over the work frame in her studio. The carefully shaped pieces of materials overlapped, forming a kaleidoscope of images, so that at first the whole seemed abstract, but on closer inspection, shapes appeared: streets, buildings, people, birds, animals, flowers—all representing in some way the history and culture of Sandra's particular part of London, the East End, in and around Brick Lane.

Sandra's love affair with fabrics had begun as a child, with the acquisition of a tattered quilt from a market stall on Brick Lane. She and her gran had pored over it, marveling at the intricacy of the pattern, wondering which bits had come from an Auntie Mary's best pinney, which from a little girl's Sunday dress, which from an Uncle George's cast-off pajamas.

That passion had survived art college and the pressure to join the vogue for shock-art. She had learned to draw and to paint, and gradually she'd translated those skills into what she still thought of as painting with fabric. But unlike paint, fabric was tactile and three-dimensional, and the work fascinated her as much now as it did when she had haltingly composed her very first piece.

Today, however, something wasn't quite right. The piece wasn't generating the emotional impact she wanted, and she couldn't quite work out why. She moved a color here, a shape there, stepped back for a different perspective and frowned again. The dark brick of Georgian town houses formed a frame for a cascade of color—it might have been Fournier Street, or Fashion Street, with the women parading in their gowns, intricately worked iron cages held high in their hands. The wire cages held, however, not birds, but women and children's faces, dark to light, a few framed by the hijab.

Late morning sun poured through the great windows in the loft—a blessing for the warmth in mid-winter if not in mid-May—but it was the clarity of the light that had drawn her to the place, and even when the work wasn't going well, it still had the power to hold her transfixed.

She and Naz had bought the Fournier Street house ten years ago, when they were first married, disregarding rising, damp, crumbling plaster and minimal plumbing, because Sandra had seen the potential of the studio space. And it had been cheap, then, affordable on Naz's solicitor's earnings while Sandra was still in art school. They had worked hard, making many of the repairs themselves, to create their vision of a home, not realizing that in a few years time they would be sitting on a property gold mine.

For the town houses on Fournier Street were Georgian, built by the French Huguenot silk weavers who had come to London's Spitalfields to escape persecution in Catholic France. The weavers had done well for themselves for a time their looms clicking in their spacious lofts, the women congregating on the front stoops in their lustrous taffeta gowns, while their canaries sang in the cages the women carried as marks of status.

But the importation of cheap calico from India had threatened the weavers' livelihood, and the invention of the mechanized loom had sounded its death knell. New waves of immigrants had followed the Huguenots—the Jews, the Irish, the Bangladeshis, the Somalis—but none had prospered as the Huguenots had done, and the houses had sunk into a long, slow decay.

Until now. The city was moving eastward, encroaching on Spitalfields, bringing a new wave of immigrants, but these were yuppies with fat pocketbooks who were snapping up the houses and warehouses of the old East End, pushing the lower income residents out as they came in. For the present bled into the past, and the past into the present, always, and to Sandra it seemed particularly so in the East End, where the years accumulated in layers like the fabrics on her board.

Sandra sighed and rubbed her fingers over the scrap of peacock-blue taffeta she held in her hand, contemplating its position in the overall design of her collage. It was inevitable, she supposed, change, and she had friends now on both sides of the economic divide—and if anything she owed her ability to make her living doing what she loved to those on the upper end of the scale.

She glanced at the pile of fabric scraps under the loft casement. Charlotte lay nestled among the silks and voiles, drawn to the pool of sunlight like a cat. She had settled there when she tired of a long and one-sided conversation with her favorite stuffed elephant—Charlotte, like her mother before her, would have nothing to do with dolls.

Graceful as a cat, too, her little daughter, even asleep with her thumb in her mouth, thought Sandra. At almost three, Charlotte had held on to her thumb-sucking a bit too long, but Sandra found herself reluctant to deprive her precocious child of a last vestige of infant comfort.

Her frustration with the collage-in-progress momentarily forgotten, Sandra grabbed a sketchbook and pencil from her worktable. Quickly, she blocked out the spill of fabric, the small French panes of the casement, the curve of Charlotte's small body in dungarees and tee-shirt, the delicate and slightly snub-nosed face framed by the mass of toffee-colored curls.

The sketch cried out for color and Sandra exchanged her #2 for a handful of colored pencils pulled from a chipped Silver Jubilee mug—a flea market treasure kept for its accidental misspelling of the Duke of Edinburgh's name.

Red for the dungarees, pink for the tee-shirt, bright blues and greens for the puddled silks, warm brown for the polished floorboards.

Absently, she went back to the silks, her hand attempting to reproduce the half-formed memory of an intricate silk pattern she had seen. It had been sari silk, like those spilled on her floor, but an unusual pattern—tiny birds handwoven into the apple-green fabric. She'd asked the girl who wore it where it had come from, and the child had said her mother had given it to her. But when Sandra had asked if her mother had bought it here, in London, the girl had gone mute and looked frightened, as if she'd spoken out of bounds. And the next time Sandra visited, she had been gone.

Sandra frowned, and Charlotte stirred, as if unconsciously responding. Afraid she would lose her opportunity to capture the tableau, Sandra reached for her camera and snapped. She checked the image, nodding as she saw Charlotte's sleeping face captured, timeless now.

Timeless, like the faces in the cages in her collage . . . A sudden inspiration made her glance at the collage. What if . . . What if she used photo-transfer for the faces of the women and girls rather than fabric and paint? She could use the faces of women and children she knew, if they would agree.

Charlotte stirred and opened her eyes, smiling sleepily. A good-natured child, Charlotte was seldom cross, unless tired or hungry, a blessing Sandra was sure she had not bestowed on her own mum. Setting down her camera, she knelt and lifted her daughter. "Nice nap, sweetie?" she asked a

Charlotte twined her arms round her neck for a hug. Charlotte's hair was damp from sun and sleep and her pale caramel skin still held a faint scent of baby muskiness, but she didn't give her mother much chance to nuzzle.

Squirming from Sandra's arms, she went to the worktable. "Duck pencils, Mummy," she said, eyeing the empty mug. "I want to draw, too."

Sandra considered, glancing at the clock, at the sun-brightened windows, and once again at the half-finished collage on the worktable. She knew from experience that she'd reached the point where staring at the board wouldn't provide a solution, and besides, she wanted to try out her photo idea. A break was in order.

It was not quite noon—Charlotte had been up early and Sandra had let her fall asleep before her usual nap time. They'd agreed to meet Naz for lunch at two—that is, if he could drag himself away from the office. She gave a sharp shake of her head at the thought. He and Lou had both been working much too hard on an upcoming case, and Naz was showing uncharacteristic signs of strain. Family Sundays had always been a priority for them, especially since Charlotte's birth, as they both were determined to give her the secure childhood neither of them had experienced.

Naz had been orphaned, his Christian parents murdered in Pakistan by the swell of fundamentalist Muslim violence in the early nineties. Sent to London in the care of an aunt and uncle who felt themselves burdened by the charge, he had grown up adjusting to the loss of both family and culture.

And Sandra, well, her family didn't bear thinking about.

But as for her husband, no Bangladeshi restaurant owner's troubles with the law were worth damaging what they had so carefully built. She would have to have a word with Naz. In the meantime, it was a perfect May day, and there was still time to go to Columbia Road.

"I have a better idea," she told Charlotte, putting the pencils firmly back in the cup. "Let's go see Uncle Roy."

* * *

Sandra held Charlotte's hand as they made their way up Brick Lane through the bustle of Sunday market. Fall-off-the-lorry day, Naz always called the Sunday market, with a hint of disapproval. He was right, of course. Half the things hawked by the traders had either fallen off a lorry or been smuggled across the Channel in the back of one. But Sandra loved it—loved the tatty chaos of it, the vendors with their makeshift trestle tables selling everything from French wine to cases of oranges (no doubt rotten at the bottom) to old car batteries.

When they passed the Old Truman Brewery, Charlotte tugged at her hand. "Roots, Mummy," she said, pointing into Ely Yard. In the car park behind the brewery, an old Route-master bus had been turned into a vegan restaurant called Rootmaster. Charlotte didn't understand the pun but loved to eat in its top deck. The bus rocked with the wind and with the waitress's tread on the curving stairs, and Charlotte would shriek with joy at every sway.

"Not now, sweetie." Sandra clasped her hand more firmly. "We'll meet Daddy there in a bit. And when we get to Columbia Road, I'll buy you a cupcake for after."

She waved at her friends in the vintage clothing shop where she often bought things to use in her collages but re-sisted the temptation to go in. The window gave back a dis-torted reflection of her mop of blond hair, and of Charlotte's, a few shades darker but just as curly.

It was only as they neared the railway line that Sandra slowed, then stopped. When Charlotte tugged at her hand again, she scooped her up and propped her on her hip. In one of the recessed brick arches near the old railway bridge, an anonymous artist had pasted a black and white photo image of a young woman. She was nude, shown from the pelvis up, her torso almost as slender as a boy's. The surrounding brick arch suggested an icon, and the subject gazed out at the viewer with such a serene grace that Sandra had mentally dubbed her "the Madonna of Brick Lane."

But she was fading, the Madonna, the paper wrinkling, the edges beginning to peel and curl. Soon she would disappear, in the way of street art, to be replaced by another artist's vision.

The inspiration she'd had in the studio suddenly crystallized. She would use photo transfers, yes, but fade them . . . They would vanish as had the women and girls held captive in so many ways over the years. Vanish like the girl with the sari—

Oh, no, surely not . . . Sandra tightened her grip on Charlotte. She'd heard the stories, of course, but not connected them with anyone she knew. It was impossible. Unthinkable. And yet . . .

She must be mad, she told herself, shaking her head. But now that the idea had taken hold, it grew, blossoming in all its permutations into something monstrous.

Charlotte squirmed. "Mummy, you're hurting me."

"Sorry, sweetheart." Sandra relaxed her grip and kissed the top of Charlotte's curls.

"I want to go. I want to see Daddy," said Charlotte, kicking her trainer-clad toes against Sandra's leg.

"We'll see Daddy. But—" Sandra glanced once more at the Madonna, then turned away, keeping Charlotte on her hip, hurrying now. The suspicion might be mad, but she would have to prove herself wrong. With her free hand she felt in her bag, making sure she had brought her camera. She had an excuse for a visit—she'd ask to take a photo for the collage. It wasn't far. She'd just need to leave Charlotte with Roy for a bit.

She crossed Bethnal Green Road, then made her way through the quiet, council estate-lined streets of Bethnal Green. Her hip began to ache from Charlotte's weight.

As she neared Columbia Road, she began to pass pedestrians going the other way. Some carried bunches of cut flowers, some potted plants, some even pulled wagons filled with shrubs or small palm trees.

She heard the market before she saw it, the noise coming in staccato bursts. At first it sounded like a foreign language, then, as they grew nearer, the words resolved themselves into English, bawled in a cockney sing-song patter. "Nice buncha daisies a five-a. Get yer tulips now, three bunches a tenn-a."

Turning a corner, she passed by the pocket park and plunged into the bottom end of Columbia Road Market. Every Sunday morning at the break of dawn, the flower vendors set up their stalls here, hawking everything from flats of bedding flowers to small trees. It was only as an adult that Sandra had come to know the market from an outsider, as she had worked her way through school and art college here, helping Roy Blakely at his stall.

Sandra hugged Charlotte closer and pushed through the crowd, ducking away from the tendrils of a stall's climbing roses that threatened to catch in her hair. Roy stood beneath his green-and-white striped awning, tucking a folded note into the purse he wore at his waist. When he saw Sandra and Charlotte, he winked. "Come for the best of the lot, have we?"

The vendors would sell everything before they closed down, and Roy would only let Sandra pay a pittance for the leavings on the stall. Her loft was full of potted plants, her small garden riotous, and most weeks she took home bunches of cut flowers for the house, but not today.

"Cupcakes," said Charlotte seriously, eyeing Treacle, the shop near Roy's stall. "Lemon."

"Not just yet." Sandra let her slide to the ground. "Roy, can I ask a favor? I've something—I've an errand. Would you mind watching Charlotte for just a bit? It won't be long—we're supposed to meet Naz at two." She glanced at her watch, feeling the pressure of time.

Charlotte jumped over a flat of pansies and wrapped herself around Roy's knees. "Can I sell flowers, Uncle Roy?"

"That you can, love." Roy stooped to give her a hug. "Go on then," he added to Sandra. "I can manage, now the punters have thinned."

Sandra hesitated just for a moment, tempted by the comforting familiarity of the market. It would be easy to slip on an apron and give Roy a hand. But she'd made up her mind, and now she must see it through.

Bending, she gave Charlotte a kiss. "Right. Thanks, Roy. I'll owe you."

Sandra glanced at her watch. It was five minutes past one. Waving to Charlotte, she turned away. When she reached the corner, a sudden impulse made her glance back, but the crowd had obscured her daughter as seamlessly as a closing zipper.